TALES OF THE CONCHARTY HILLS

STEPHEN P. GRAY

ISBN-10: 1502327422
ISBN-13: 978-1502327420

DEDICATION

This book is dedicated to a variety of people I have had the privilege of knowing and sharing life with. The persons in particular to be recognized are the Beshara sisters – Marguerite Beshara, Madeline Beshara and Mrs. Toni Beshara-Haney. These women were inspirations for characters in this book. All three were members of the Beshara clan of Haskell, Oklahoma, who had a life affirming touch on whoever they met. The book is also dedicated to my two lifelong friends, Reverend Kent Shirley and Joe Avanzinni, who were also inspirations for two of the characters in the book. These two friends have spent their lives unobtrusively influencing countless others wherever they have gone. This book is also dedicated to Joyce Cartwright and Louise Hammond who befriended and loved all those around them and formed the basis for the character of Aunt Louise in the book. This book is also dedicated to Joe White, who was the inspiration for Uncle Raymond.

Special thanks to Sally Lambert, who tirelessly typed this book and encouraged me through prayers and tears to finish the book. Thanks to my old friend Ginger Farthing who edited revision after revision with unflagging zeal, together with Craig Hoster. Many thanks to my wife and daughters who patiently put up with my writing and rewriting this story. A great thanks to my mentor Dr. Dan McCaghern who said in every person was at least one good book that needed to be written and gave me the push to put pen to paper. Finally, thanks be to God who put this story on my heart and gave me the privilege to write this story to be a blessing to others.

CONTENTS

ACKNOWLEDGMENTS

1) The Prayer of the Confederate Soldier
2) Edgar Lee Masters, Spoon River Anthology, Lucinda Matlock

TALES OF THE CONCHARTY HILLS

PART I – NEW BEGINNINGS

CHAPTER 1

OKLAHOMA

"Please observe the non-smoking sign and please put your trays and seat back in their upright position. Buckle your seatbelt; we will be landing in Tulsa in twenty minutes."

I looked out the window. Everything below me looked green interspersed with cattle, ponds, creeks, rivers, and lakes. That was a pleasant surprise! I had a bleak vision of Dust Bowl from reading John Steinbach's *The Grapes of Wrath* in my junior year in high school. But appearances can be deceiving from several thousand feet up. I was going to Oklahoma to live with Great Uncle Raymond and Great Aunt Louise Hammond at their ranch outside a town called Haskell, Oklahoma.

Where in the sam hill was Haskell, Oklahoma? It was a far cry from Barrington Heights, the wealthy north side suburb of Chicago where I grew up. Heck, there were probably more people who lived on my block than in the town of Haskell. I was being sent to live with my Mom's Aunt and Uncle my senior year in high school. I was leaving St. Cyngen Episcopal

Academy for the Haskell Public High School. Dad thought it best especially after Mom's car accident that left her comatose.

Dad was a Professor of Medicine at Northwestern University in the field of Psychiatry. He was also a M.D. That meant he was never home because he was either teaching, monitoring young doctors, or seeing hospital patients. "Taking care of everyone else's problems but your own family's" as my Mom used to say. Dr. William Franklin Robertson, M.D., Professor at Northwestern University Medical School, Past President of the Southern Psychiatric Association, author, lecturer, friend of U.S. Senators, mayors of numerous suburbs, and my Dad; only I never saw him or talked to him.

If Dad wanted to talk to you, "your ass was grass" as my oldest brother Frank used to say. Frank was my hero, that unique blend of consummate diplomat, clown and favored oldest son who uniquely knew how to humor Dad; and at times Dad needed a lot of humoring.

It was my Dad's lack of humor at my latest misadventure after my Mom's car accident that resulted in my exile to the cul de sac of America-Oklahoma. This was a place you could get in but not out, as my brother Frank would say. Frank was in North Dakota working for our uncle's engineering company when I pulled my latest faux pas. It was a bad idea to hook a chain on the front doors of two houses facing each other along Avery Drive. The driver of the car that hit that chain at 1:00 a.m. not only damaged his front grill and knocked out a light, but also took out the doors of the houses the chain was hooked up to. Unfortunately, one of the houses we arbitrarily chose to prank belonged to a Trustee of Northwestern University and the other to a board member of St. Cyngen's Episcopal Academy; wrong people to pull such a prank on! Great fun, but my buddies and I ultimately got caught. One of them shared our diabolical deed with his girlfriend. She then told her friends who spread it all over school.

The Dean of Women, Miss Goldheison, got wind of this and we all were called in the office of the Dean of Men, Frank Ward, tennis coach and a former Marine. Confrontation with him was like being turned over to the Gestapo for questioning. He had us all confessing within 15 minutes. St. Cyngen was an old school and did not tolerate pranks like mine. One buddy was graduating but three of us were brought up for expulsion from St. Cygnen Episcopal Academy. My two buddies' families cured the expulsion dilemma with a hefty donation to the school. Money always seemed to cure all sorts of mischief that rich kids would create for themselves. My father, however, did not believe in throwing money to bail out delinquent kids, especially his own, based on my older siblings' track record. He, in his blunt style, met with Headmaster Marley prior to my being brought up for expulsion and informed him that he was pulling me out of St. Cyngen after the end of my junior year. Dad made it into a win-win situation. The school did not have to cause a publicity issue by expelling a student from a premier family and Dad did not have to bear the shame of a disgraced son expelled from school. I was in complete shock at my removal from St. Cyngen. I just could not believe it, but Dad reminded me that denial was not a river in Egypt!

Dad was born in 1913 and he spent his college years in the throes of the Great Depression busting his butt, as he often lectured us. "I didn't have a dime to buy a coke," he frequently reminded us kids. There were four of us Robertson kids. My brother Frank partied and drank his way through two semesters at the University of Illinois. He had pledged the Lambda Chi Alpha Fraternity and had become a beer connoisseur. As a result of his extracurricular activities, he managed a 1.8 GPA his freshman year.

Dad refused to finance such academic irresponsibility and pulled him out of college. He put my brother's bags on the front porch, saying you're off the tit and on your own!

Frank went to work for our Uncle Ed Smith at Smith Engineering. Now his one year of beer drinking resulted in seven years of tromping around God forsaken corners of America, running survey crews. Frank was getting an education in life as Mom used to tell us.

My other brother John William went to a small school in Indiana called DePauw University; pledged Phi Kappa Psi and discovered, like many collegians of his time, the medicinal properties of a substance with a Latin name of Cannabis. He also became a devotee of Carlos Castaneda and his writings. He was now at the University of the Americas in Mexico City and experimenting with the medicinal purposes of peyote to follow his folk hero Mr. Castaneda on his own journey to Ixalton.

My sister Susannah Theresa had a ne'er do well boyfriend and gold digger, as Dad said, Jacob Lawrence. He had demonstrated in the 1968 riots at the Democratic Convention and Sue went along for the kicks. These kicks cost my Dad over $5,000 in legal fees and court costs as she was arrested for disorderly conduct! This caused exceeding embarrassment for my Mom in her country club circles. After her freshman year in college in 1969, my sister ran off with Jacob to find herself and live on a hippie commune in New Mexico.

That was the last straw for my Mom. She really began drinking hard after that event. It was after one night of drinking at a dinner party that spring of 1970 when she had her accident. Mom had gone to the party alone and wrecked her car. It left her comatose and me without a parent. The prognosis was not good for her. It was shortly after her accident that the Avery Avenue prank occurred. My fate was sealed.

Dad was not going to be extorted to make a donation to keep his "sorry excuse for a son" in that snob school. "My blankity blank kids don't appreciate a damn thing I do. They wreck my cars, shame our family, and spend all my money. They are just out of control brats." It was true that I was out of control but I hardly thought I was a brat! However, I didn't try to medicate my pain with alcohol or dope like many of my school chums. Mom's alcoholism alienated me from drinking and Dad's war stories of teenagers who cooked their minds on drugs scared the hell out of me. Plus, I had seen the war stories he spoke of in the form of some of my spookier classmates.

I dealt with my pain by pushing myself athletically and academically. I was an All-State swimmer from my freshman year through my junior year. I made All-American in my junior year at some A.A.U. swim events. I carried a 3.4 GPA in honor courses. A lot of my success was due to Coach Tony DeLagarza. He was our swim coach and a former Marine. But more importantly, he was like a father to me. He was also my trigonometry teacher. It was tough to disappoint him in the pool or in the classroom. It was hardest to tell him I was leaving St Cyngen's Academy after my junior year. But, hopefully, I told him, it was only for the first semester of my senior year so I would be back to anchor the 400 medley relay for State. The truth was I didn't want to go to Oklahoma at all nor did Coach DeLagarza want to lose me. He told me that he wanted his only All-American swimmer anchoring the team for State next year. Coach DeLagarza assured me that he would deal with both my dad and Headmaster Marley when the time came.

Funny, it was not hard to tell my girlfriend Ann Burns that I was leaving even though we had a thing for each other since we were kindergartners. We had agreed that we would redefine our relationship from boyfriend/girlfriend to just friends as we were going to be so far apart. There was a going away party for me, hosted by my teammates on the swim team. They bought me a cowboy hat and cowboy boots for my great "Oklahoma" adventure. My best friend on the team, Mitch O'Nalley, even bought me a book for speaking and understanding the "Okie" dialect of English. One friend bought me a record of Bob Wills and the Texas Playboys from a live performance at Cain's Ballroom in Tulsa, Oklahoma. Good grief! I didn't know they danced in Oklahoma, much less had ballrooms.

My reverie over the past four months events was disrupted when I heard the landing gear of the jet as it touched down on the tarmac. We taxied to the gate. "Ladies and gentlemen, thank you for flying TWA Flight 289 from Chicago to Tulsa. Time now is 12:45 p.m. The temperature in Tulsa is 96 degrees. This flight will continue on to Dallas for those passengers continuing on with us." Now my adventure was to begin. I was in Oklahoma.

CHAPTER 2

<u>AUNT LOUISE AND UNCLE RAYMOND</u>

As the door of the jet opened, a sudden blast of hot air entered the cabin. As the passengers prepared to deplane, the cabin became hot and stuffy. "Gawd," I thought. "Am I in Oklahoma or the Amazon?" I felt like I was walking down into a blast furnace. So this was Oklahoma in July. I walked down the stairway and across the tarmac to the entrance of TWA Gate Number 37. The sun was beating down on us as we walked across the tarmac. I could feel the sweat oozing from my pores. The line of deplaning passengers walked into the terminal. What a relief to be out of the sun baking heat and in an air-conditioned terminal. The terminal was full of people. I had been introduced to Great Uncle Raymond and Aunt Louise when I was thirteen, when they came to visit my mother in Chicago. I had an old Christmas card picture of them and had no idea if they would recognize me. As we walked through the gate, people were milling about, greeting and hugging one another. There were some soldiers in the crowd and joyful family members surrounding them at their safe return from wherever they had been stationed.

Suddenly, a man and woman came up to me. It was a somewhat older version of Uncle Raymond and Aunt Louise than the picture that I had. He was tanned with close-cropped graying black hair like a Marine. I remember mom talking in hushed tones to my Aunt Esther, dad's sister-in-law, that Great Aunt Louise had married an "Indian." Uncle Raymond had tanned dark skin, dark hair and eyes, but he looked like no Indian I had ever seen in the movies. He looked more like some of the Southern Italian boys from the Little Italy section of Chicago. Aunt Louise had graying blond hair with hazel green eyes. She reminded me of Mom a lot. The Hammonds had had one son, my Mom's first cousin. His name was Gerald Hammond and he had grown up on the ranch in Haskell. Upon graduating from high school, he had become a Marine like his father had done in World War II. The only difference was he was posted to a Southeast Asian peace keeping mission in a former French colony called Vietnam. Unlike his father who survived the South Pacific Theater, Gerald was killed in action in late 1966. It was a grievous loss to Uncle Raymond and Aunt Louise.

Mom had even persuaded Dad to provide them free clinical psychiatric therapy at Northwestern University when they came for a visit the summer in 1967, to help them deal with their grief. Something good must have come of those sessions because Mom used to talk about how much better the Hammonds were after that. Aunt Louise wrote Dad a letter thanking him profusely with the offer if our family ever needed anything at all, to just call them and they would be there.

Well, I bet Dad never dreamed he would take them up on that offer and ask them to care of me! Uncle Raymond gave me a firm handshake and said in a deep southern drawl, "Howdy Phillip, welcome to Oklahoma." Aunt Louise gave me a wonderful smile and hug and said how glad she was to have me here. I must say that made me feel more relaxed and at ease with these "alien" surroundings and accents. We walked down the terminal to the baggage claim. Aunt Louise was a gracious conversationalist. Uncle Raymond was more reserved. But there was a boyish twinkle in those dark eyes that belied how Mom once described him, "a 19-year old Marine recruit held hostage in a 60-something body." He walked with an easy air and self-confidence that spoke of an athletic authority. Dad had told me that Uncle Raymond was an all-around athlete and had been a boxer in the Marine Corps. He had joined the Marines during the depression to feed himself and had married his high school sweetheart who was three years younger.

After World War II, he came back to Oklahoma and earned his teaching certificate on the GI Bill while Aunt Louise worked. He had graduated from Northeastern University at Tahlequah with a teaching certificate and coached football at Haskell, Oklahoma, from 1949 to 1970. He worked his ranch on the side and had retired from teaching and coaching after his son's death. He had been frugal and acquired more land to run his cattle upon. Between the cattle and some producing oil and gas leases, Dad said Uncle Raymond and Aunt Louise were doing okay, so it would be no problem for them to take me in despite my protests about being exiled to "poor" distant relatives at the end of the earth. "Haskell is not the end of the earth, Phillip," Dad said. "But you can see it from there," he added with a wry grin. I think my father was enjoying my launching from Chicago a little too much to my liking. No kid likes the feeling of a parent's relief at a child's expulsion from the nest.

Uncle Raymond retrieved both my bags from the baggage claim. He carried them out to the car like they were grocery sacks. If he was trying to alpha dog me and impress me that he was strong, well, it was sort of working. Uncle Raymond was probably 5'10" and 165 lbs. I was now 6 feet and approaching 170 lbs. But not even I could have carried those two suitcases like Uncle Raymond did.

We got into a 1968 white Chevrolet 4-door Impala. Thank God, it had air conditioning. It was so bloody hot my dress shirt was soaked under my armpits and I could feel sweat running down my neck. I had worn brand new khaki slacks because our housekeeper Mrs. Agnes Kotlarski had insisted I dress nicely for the trip to make a good impression on my relatives. Now I wished I had worn an old Polo shirt, Madras shorts, and Serapis.

Uncle Raymond and Aunt Louise wanted to show me the "big city" skyline of Tulsa. As we drove through downtown Tulsa he described all sorts of quaint historical trivia about the downtown buildings. He then turned to me and asked what I thought.

"Sort of looks like Chicago after a nuclear blast," I blurted out unthinking. I heard Aunt Louise snuffle a snicker but Uncle Raymond turned back around. I couldn't see his furrowed brow nor did I have any idea what he was thinking. But it was a long quiet drive to Haskell after that. God, were there no freeways worth spit in this town? It seemed to take forever to get to where we were going. At one point we crossed the mighty Arkansas River to a town called Bixby. The river looked more like a sliver of muddy water running through a mile wide sand box. If that was the largest river in Oklahoma, no wonder they called this the Dust Bowl.

I had a pleasant surprise as we drove south of Bixby down U. S. Highway 64. All of a sudden there were these huge hills. "Those are the Concharty Mountains. The Creek Indians believed there was something magical about those hills," Uncle Raymond said. I was impressed. The so-called mountains were actually large hills that rose close to 500 feet above the surrounding countryside. Furthermore, they were heavily timbered. Wait a minute, I thought. Trees don't grow in Oklahoma. This is the "Dust Bowl!" What gives, I thought.

"Lots of history in these hills. Back in the 18th Century the Spaniards prospected for gold. Then in the 19th Century a lot of outlaw gangs hid out in these mountains before statehood," Uncle Raymond said. "Especially the Belle Starr Gang. This was a notorious haunt of thieves." I wondered what son of a buck called himself "Belle."

"There was a guy named Belle Starr who had a gang?" I asked.

"Not a guy but a gal," Uncle Raymond replied, "Oklahoma has always been progressive when it came to women. We even elected a woman to Congress in 1920, the year women got the right to vote, Miss Alice Robertson." I chuckled to myself. My feminist hippie sister Sue would have approved that a woman was in a male leadership role. Well, maybe, Oklahoma was not as bleak, boring or as backward as my friends and I had thought it to be. Boy was I ever to discover just how true that was.

"We are coming into town," Uncle Raymond said. A water tower loomed ahead with the name "Haskell" in bold letters.

"You thirsty?" Aunt Louise asked.

"Yes, I am," I replied.

"Raymond, pull into the Tastee Freeze and get me a limeade. You want one too, Phillip?"

I nodded. I looked out the window and saw a pretty dark haired girl serving as a carhop. "That is Miriam Abboud. She will be in your class this year. She is one of the best kids in this town," Aunt Louise said. Little did I know I was to meet a girl who would not only open wide the heart of this big city Chicago snob who was so out of his element in Haskell, but also make me see the world with a whole new set of eyes.

CHAPTER 3

MIRIAM AND JOE

"Uncle Raymond, is there a bathroom here?"

"Yes, Phillip, around the back there." I got out of the car and walked to the men's restroom. I passed the young woman named Miriam. She had a pretty smile and nice demeanor. Her hair was jet black that framed an attractive face with emerald green eyes. Her skin tone was a light olive. She would have turned heads at St. Cyngen Academy for sure.

Miriam came up to the car and took Aunt Louise's order for two small limeades and an ice tea for Uncle Raymond. "Was that your nephew, Mrs. Hammond? I heard Aunt Marguerite talking at the flower shop last week that he was coming to school this fall."

"Yes, he is, Miriam," replied Aunt Louise.

"Well, you didn't tell me he was so tall and good looking."

"He gets his good looks from my side of the family," Aunt Louise said. "He reminds me of my father Will Knight."

"Well, handsome is as handsome does," Uncle Raymond quipped.

Aunt Louise ignored that statement and went on to say, "We need your help to acquaint Phillip with the kids at the high school, Miriam. Is that okay?" asked Aunt Louise.

"Sure is," said Miriam. "That is one job I will enjoy for sure."

"I am sure he will too," Uncle Raymond said with a grin.

I came back to the car as Miriam brought the drinks. "Miriam, this is our nephew Phillip," said Aunt Louise. I smiled and extended my hand.

14

"Hi, I am Phillip. Nice to meet you, Miriam."

"Nice to meet you, Phillip. Your Aunt Louise says you will be in school with us this fall. I can show you around sometime, if you would like."

"That would be great, Miriam," I replied. I noticed what pretty green eyes she had. A guy could lose himself in those eyes.

"Well, I had better get back to work," Miriam responded, smiling. "Look forward to talking to you later, Phillip. Good to see you, Mr. and Mrs. Hammond." Miriam returned to her job duties, and I followed her with my eyes. This was noticed by Uncle Raymond, watching me in his rearview mirror.

Uncle Raymond put the car in reverse and we pulled out of the Tastee Freeze. We then drove out of town and headed to Uncle Raymond's ranch. It was at the base of the Concharty Mountains, northwest of town. We pulled up to their house. It was a nice one-story ranch style home. There was a large white barn to the west of the house and a separate metal building with two garage doors. Uncle Raymond had a black truck parked next to the barn. There was also a white truck parked there. He said that truck belonged to Joe Corsinni, his hired hand. You could see a large hill they called the Concharty Mountain from their picture window. It was a pleasant place. As we drove up, I saw a ranch hand at the barn. "That is Joe Corsinni," Uncle Raymond said. "He is up here three days a week and helps me work the cattle. Let's unpack your bags, Phillip; and then we will come on out and meet Joe. But you had better change first."

Uncle Raymond helped me carry my bags to my room. There was a large den with a fireplace as we entered. The wooden floors had a slight creak to them as I followed Uncle Raymond. Uncle Raymond motioned me down a hall to a spare bedroom. Aunt Louise had put a wooden letter "P" on my door. I smiled. She really was glad to have me here. Uncle Raymond said,

"Put on some blue jeans, Phillip. If you have a T-shirt, put that on, too. What size are your feet?"

"About 10-1/2 D," I said.

"That was about the size of Gerald's feet. I still have some of his old boots you could wear. You change out of your slacks and I will see if I can find them for you." As I changed, it really hit me that I was in Oklahoma, a place as foreign to me as China. This big city kid felt as out of place as a Cub's fan in Yankee Stadium.

I did not realize at the time what a gesture of goodwill Uncle Raymond made by offering his late son's boots to me. I changed clothes and met Uncle Raymond in the kitchen in my stocking feet. He had a pair of old cowboy boots he gave me to try on. I slipped them on and it was a good fit. "Fine," said Uncle Raymond. "Let's go meet Joe. Before the sun sets, there is some more work to do in one pasture and Joe can show you what to do. You both will be working together the rest of this summer," Uncle Raymond explained that Joe worked three days a week on the ranch and the rest of the time worked at his father's hardware and feed store, C & C Hardware & Feed Store.

We went outside to meet Joe. He was leading a horse by the halter to the barn. Joe was 18 years old and an upcoming senior at Haskell High School. He played football, basketball and baseball. He was six feet, four inches and weighed 220 pounds. His dark brown hair was bleached blond from working outdoors on Uncle Raymond's ranch. He had an impressive pair of hammers and Uncle Raymond said he had a great arm for football. He was going to be the QB. He had a deep tan that accentuated his steel gray eyes. I felt like a wimp compared to Joe's physical stature.

"Joe, come here, son, I want you to meet my nephew, Phillip Robertson." Joe tied up the horse and walked over to introduce himself, "Howdy, Phillip, I am Joe Corsinni."

"Hi, Joe, good to meet you." This guy had huge hands that gripped my hand with a leathery grip. He had a killer smile that framed a handsome face.

Joe was saddling a horse for me. He called him the "Paint." Apparently it had been my late cousin Gerald's horse. Uncle Raymond said the horse was a "Choctaw" pony from the Kiamichi Mountains in southeast Oklahoma. "They make the best cow ponies," Uncle Raymond had said. Well, they were not the most impressive horses for size and had thicker foreheads than I had seen at the equestrian stable up in Chicago, where I took riding lessons. But they had stamina which is what Uncle Raymond said was needed in a working horse for a ranch. Joe had another horse saddled already. We both mounted our steeds and Joe said he would show me the lower pasture. Joe's legs could almost wrap around the horse's midsection and we both looked supersized for the horses we were riding. But the horses had a gentle gait about them I found surprising. The sun was hot in the late afternoon but at times there were breezes and we were shaded by trees a lot. Nevertheless, I could feel the sun burning my neck and arms. Thankfully, Uncle Raymond had given me a cap that shaded my face and head.

We rode along the fence line and Joe explained to me why we had to check the fence. "Fences go down all the time," Joe said. "An old tree limb breaks off the tree and falls on a fence; old fence posts rot out and the barbed wire strands come loose; sometimes a car hits a fence along the section line road and knocks it down. A lot of times livestock will knock the fencing loose. You always have to monitor the fence and do a 'fence survey' once a week as Coach Hammond calls it." Funny, I never thought of Uncle Raymond as "Coach Hammond." Joe explained to me that Uncle Raymond had coached Peewee baseball in the summer leagues for nearly 20 years. "I grew up with Coach

Hammond from the time I could pitch a ball till I was nearly 16."

"Uncle Raymond says you have an incredible arm as a quarterback," I remarked. Joe didn't really respond. He was not the sort of guy who was real outgoing and readily accepted compliments, especially from the nephew of his lifelong coach and summer employer. You could almost describe him as shy. How ironic, I thought. Here was a guy with the body of a Greek god, crowned by a tanned handsome face. He should have been the most out-going, confident, self-assured guy; yet he was reserved and humble. What an interesting contrast to the guys I had known with good looks and athletic prowess at St. Cyngens Preparatory Academy. Their self-conceit and arrogance were only exceeded by their parents' bank accounts and income.

The sun was getting low in the western sky and the shadows lengthened. At one point, I heard a bell tolling that wafted over the pasture and through the trees. "What in the world is that from, Joe?"

"That is the 6:00 Vespers bell at the Concharty Hills Monastery."

"There is a monastery around here?"

"Yeah, just over that ridge beyond the tree line."

"How long has it been here?" I asked.

"It was started after World War II," said Joe.

"Wow," is all I could say.

"Your Uncle Raymond's ranch abuts the monastery lands. Sometimes you will see the monks working their livestock in a pasture over yonder."

"Do you talk to them?" I asked and almost immediately realized that was a dumb question based on Joe's non-verbal cues.

"Nah," said Joe. "They have taken a vow of silence when it comes to strangers as they work in the field. So it's best to honor their vow and not disturb them, or that's what my Dad says anyway."

"Amazing," I said. "So are these monks a bunch of old geezers?"

A twinkle came into Joe's eyes. "You might be a bit surprised," he said. I wasn't sure what he meant, but I sensed there was a deeper story to the twinkle in Joe's eyes.

We finished the fence survey of the lower pastures and headed back to the barn. The shadows were really getting longer now and a nice breeze was picking up. The wind rustling through the trees was almost soothing but for the cicadas. The cicadas' chorus was almost deafening at times. It seemed to me I would hear more from the cicadas than conversation from Joe Corsinni. I smiled to myself. So this was going to be my co-worker this summer! Well, between the heat, the dust, the sweat, the cicadas, and Joe's stoicism, it seemed like it was going to be a really long dull summer! Mercifully, I was to learn differently, though.

As we rode up to the barn, Aunt Louise came out of the house on the back porch. "You boys hungry?"

Joe became animated all of a sudden and said, "Yes, Ma'am. We will put the horses up first, though." I nodded in agreement. We took our horses to the barn and took their bridles and saddles off.

"Go on," Joe said and pushed the two horses out of the barn into the pasture. Uncle Raymond had already put some feed out for the pair of horses. They sauntered over to the feed trough and began greedily eating the oats there. Uncle Raymond came around the barn and said, "You boys wash up over at the barn's sink and come on in for dinner." The barn had a couple of big sinks and Joe immediately grabbed the lava soap and was washing his arms and hands. I reached over for a bar of soap just in time for him to hoist an ice-cold splash of water in my face.

"Spring well water, Phillip," he said with a grin. If I had not been so hot, dusty and sunburned, I would have been tempted to clock him. But the truth was the splash of cold well water felt great.

I smiled and said, "You just wait, Mr. Corsinni. Pay backs are hell."

He laughed and threw me a towel to dry off. "Come on, supper's waiting! You never keep a lady like Mrs. Hammond waiting, especially if she made her fried chicken and gravy and green beans." We jogged to the back porch of the house, removed our boots, and came inside in our bare stocking feet.

The aroma of fried chicken filled the room, "You boys sit down and I will fix you a plate," Aunt Louise said. Aunt Louise served us up a plate filled with fried chicken, mashed potatoes and gravy, and green beans cooked in fresh tomatoes. She squeezed fresh lemons over the chicken and it made for a tangy but delicious plate of chicken. Uncle Raymond came in the room and joined us.

"Phillip, I just got off the phone with your Dad. He wants you to call him later tonight. But I told him you were fitting in fine and had already started wearing your own cowboy boots. Don't have the Oklahoma drawl down, but we are workin' on that," said Uncle Raymond, and he winked at Aunt Louise. She smiled with great satisfaction. You could tell Aunt Louise was the queen of her kitchen and her domain was good food, warm hospitality, and friendly conversation. No wonder a quiet reserved jock like Joe had an almost mystical transformation of personality at the thought of supper in Aunt Louise's kitchen. It made me realize where Mom got her warm hospitality. This discovery also reminded me of the pain at the loss of Mom. I tried not to think about that as I listened to Uncle Raymond talk to Joe. Coach Hammond peppered Joe with questions about this upcoming crop of high school football players. Joe fired back his responses as to his prognosis of the various players. I could see I was certainly out of my league with the old bull and the young rock jock as I listened to their football talk. All I had been athletically was a sprinter for the 60-yard free style and 400 IM medley in swimming. What did I know about Haskell football? Seems like destiny was going to school me, that was for sure.

We finished dinner with a serving of hot coffee and homemade lemon meringue pie. Boy was I stuffed. If I had eaten like this at home in Chicago, I would have been built like a linebacker for the Chicago Bears. As our dinner conversation ended, Joe took his leave and told Uncle Raymond he would be back Monday morning at 7:30 A. M. Tomorrow was Sunday and we were going to the First Baptist Church of Haskell. "Baptist, one step above Neanderthal," I had once heard my Dad joke.

"Not noted for intellectualism or broad mindedness," Mom had once remarked. Now, that was interesting in that she herself came from a Southern Baptist background. My parents had joined an Episcopal church with a traditional liturgy. "High church" was what Mom called it. I called it boring. Oh, well!

"Uncle Raymond, may I call my Dad now?" I asked.

"Sure, Phillip, use the phone in the den. Louise and I will clean up the dishes."

I went to the den and called my Dad collect. Before I left Chicago, he had given me a stern lecture not to make any calls to Chicago that weren't collect. That meant I am only calling him as my buddies would probably not accept the expense of a collect call from Oklahoma.

"Collect call from Phillip Robertson. Will you accept the charges, Sir," I heard the operator ask.

"Yes, I will," Dad answered. Whereupon, we had a brief chat about my flight, the day's activities, how things were back home, and how Mom was. Dad, being anything but an extrovert much less a phone conversationalist, satisfied himself by my answers that his youngest son was in good hands. He could now focus on other issues besetting our family. The conversation lasted maybe ten minutes; Dad said he would call sometime in the next week or so. We said goodbye. In a way I felt utterly alone in this strange setting called Oklahoma after I hung up the phone.

I walked back into the kitchen and Uncle Raymond and Aunt Louise were drying the dishes and putting them back in the cabinet. There was something remarkably different about these two. He was a man's man and she was a lady, but they really got a kick out of each other's company. Now that was different from what I had seen between older married couples up to now. Mainly, it was a tolerant co-existence at best and a divorce at worst, like a lot of my teammates on the swim team. It seemed like a month didn't go by my sophomore and Junior years that a classmate's parents were splitting up. I had never observed an older couple who genuinely enjoyed each other's company and displayed warm affections like two teenagers. This was one for the books. What would my brother Frank say about this!

We went into the den and talked for an hour or so about my family up in Chicago. Around 9 o'clock Uncle Raymond drew the conversation to a close. "Phillip, church is at 10 o'clock, so we will get you up around 8:30 A. M. You can wear slacks and a Polo shirt. We don't wear ties and coats in the summertime. It is too hot and we figure the good Lord wouldn't mind if we dressed for the weather," Uncle Raymond remarked with a twinkle in his eye. "See you in the morning, Phillip." And with that he turned off the lights in the den and walked to his bedroom. Aunt Louise finished up and followed him. As for me, I went to the bathroom and showered off the day's dust and sweat. As a swimmer all those years in a pool made me feel unclean to go to bed sweaty and unwashed. I was tired and hot. The sun and heat had taken it out of me despite the good meal of Aunt Louise; and we really had not done that much physical labor – yet. Although I felt like a big city outsider, Uncle Raymond and Aunt Louise had gone out of their way to make me feel special here. Somehow I fell asleep with that warm feeling of welcome permeating my being. I would sleep well tonight.

CHAPTER 4

SUNDAY CHURCH

The next morning I heard Uncle Raymond stirring around, but it was still dark outside. I picked up my wristwatch and bleakly focused on the dial. It was 5:30 a.m.! Jeeze .... What sort of person wakes up at 5:30 a.m.? I heard the door close and could discern Uncle Raymond's footfall on the gravel driveway as he walked to the barn. I rolled over and buried my head in the pillow. He said 8:30 was wake-up time and, by golly, I am taking him up on that. I went back to sleep.

Later I heard Aunt Louise's knock on the door at 8:30. "Good morning, Phillip. Breakfast is almost ready. See you in the kitchen." I rolled out of bed and yawned. I was blurry eyed, sunburned on my neck and arms, and my inner thighs ached from "saddle sores." The thing about riding horses was that you rediscover muscles you forgot you had, especially if you had not been working with horses in a while.

I stiffly walked around my room and pulled on an old Polo shirt and some shorts. I slipped on my Serapis and opened the door and walked down to the kitchen. The aroma of fresh bacon, toast and fried eggs filled the room. "Wow!" I blurted out. "Something smells awesome." Aunt Louise smiled and asked me have a seat at the kitchen table. "Aunt Louise, have you always been such an incredible cook?" I asked as she set a plate full of bacon, toast, fried eggs and fried potatoes (southern style) on my plate.

Aunt Louise smiled and replied, "Well, I do enjoy working in a kitchen and feeding my men folk," she chuckled. Little did I know she had won several Muskogee County Fair competitions for her pies and jams. I was to learn that later.

Uncle Raymond came in dusty and a little sweaty. "Honey, I will wash up and be back in 15 minutes."

"Not a problem, Raymond; Phillip and I will keep each other company." Aunt Louise then began regaling me with tales of our family. I was to hear stories and learn family lore I had never been told before.

"Aunt Louise, may I ask you a personal question?" I asked.

"Ask away, Phillip, we are family here."

"Is it true Uncle Raymond is an Indian?"

She chuckled and replied, "Well, only one-eighth Indian, seven-eighths something else."

"Wow, which tribe?" I asked.

"Tribes, you mean," Uncle Raymond said as he entered the kitchen. "I have tribal heritage from both the Choctaws and the Cherokees."

"We are part Indian too, Phillip. As a matter of fact, we are more Indian than your Uncle Raymond," Aunt Louise said.

"What?" I asked in astonishment. "How is that possible? You have blond hair and green eyes. Even Mom was a blond even though she had hazel eyes. But I am blond haired and blue eyed."

Uncle Raymond chuckled, "Lots of blond haired and blue eyed Choctaws, Chickasaws, Cherokees and Creeks, Phillip." I stared, gaping at the thought.

"My grandmother was a full blood Cherokee, Phillip. She married a white man back in Georgia before the Civil War. They lived up in the Appalachian Mountains in Northwest Georgia and no one bothered them. So, you see I am a one-fourth Cherokee, Your mother is a one-eighth, and you are a one-sixteenth. The same equation as Uncle Raymond."

"But..." I stammered. "I don't look it."

"Don't you?" Aunt Louise mused. "Haven't you ever wondered about your Mother's high cheek bones, slanted eyes, and nose? You have the same features.

Very Cherokee... albeit mixed blood Cherokee," Aunt Louise smiled.

"But Louise doesn't have a tribal membership card, but I do for the Choctaws one-sixteenth. When you add the Cherokee, I am a one-eighth," added Uncle Raymond.

I was stunned. All the stuff I had grown up with treated the Indians not as noble savages but as enemies to the advancement of American civilization. Whenever I had played cowboys and Indians as a boy, we had always gunned down the "savages" for the safety of the woman folk on the wagon train. I had no idea that I was one of the savages I was so eager to gun down in my playtime as a boy. That was a pipe load to swallow, I thought.

"You need to get ready for church, Phillip. It is 9:10 now. You have 20 minutes to clean up and get dressed," Uncle Raymond said. He rubbed my chin that had that slight stubble between boy and man that most guys had at the age of 17 and winked at me. "I have an extra razor if you need it," he added. I followed him to his bathroom and got the extra razor and shaving cream.

I got shaved and dressed. I put on some navy blue slacks and a yellow Polo shirt. This accented my sunburn from yesterday, but it was a nice effect.

"You look very handsome, Phillip," Aunt Louise remarked, approvingly. We got in the car and drove to the First Baptist Church. Boy, was I in for a surprise.

It was a yellow brick building that had already been added onto over the years. There were a lot of cars in the parking lot as we arrived at 9:45. Uncle Raymond dropped us off at the porte cochere and I walked Aunt Louise into the church. Immediately, people came up to talk to Aunt Louise and I glad handed more people that morning before church than I had ever done running for a class office in the eighth grade.

"Good to meet you, Phillip."

"Fine looking young man, Louise."

"Is this that tall Swede of a nephew I have heard about."

"Where are you from, boy? You a Yankee?"

Finally, Uncle Raymond came in and rescued me from all the fawning and cross-examination of curious friends.

We walked into the sanctuary and sat down. The service was not at all what I expected. The church service was more down home with little or no High-Church liturgy. That was a change. I didn't recognize the hymns we sang nor had I heard the offertory song. It was more contemporary with three women singing in a trio. Actually, they sang very well. The song "It Only Takes a Spark" was totally foreign to me. But it was pleasant to listen to these ladies sing. The Pastor then began his sermon. But he preached as if he were having a conversation with you. The sermon focused on if we as believers really trusted God and he illustrated this story with rides on airplanes. Now, this spoke to me, just having flown in yesterday. In effect, if we trusted our lives to an airline pilot to safely deliver us from point A to point B, how much more should we trust our life's problems to the Lord, the creator of the universe. Never heard that before! More importantly to this teenager, he was done in 30 minutes. The sermon was not "boring" as I had expected, and the entire service lasted maybe an hour. We emerged from the sanctuary right after 11:30 a.m.

"We can still beat the Pentecostals to the Holland House for lunch," I heard some of the parishioners say.

I saw a group of teenagers who appeared to be around my age milling around after church. One guy in particular stood out and it was readily apparent that he was the center of attention of the other kids. He appeared to be joking around and teasing the other kids, especially the girls. As we were walking towards the car, I overheard some of the conversations. Based on the comments I overheard the girls saying, it would seem that this guy was pretty full of himself. But the girls at St. Cyngen Academy could have said the same about me, so I did not take it to heart. Aunt Louise motioned for the guy to come over and introduce himself, "Kent James, come over here, please!"

Uncle Raymond quietly said to me on the side, "that is one of the finest running backs and wide receivers we have ever had," Uncle Raymond said. "Only problem is that he knows it and sometimes thinks a little too highly of himself. But he is a work in progress" with that Uncle Raymond winked at me.

"Kent, this is my nephew Phillip Robertson. He will be at the senior high with you this semester," Aunt Louise told this guy as he came over. He sized me up pretty quickly and ascertained I was an athlete of some sort.

Immediately, he said, "Hey, great to meet you, Phillip," and extended a large muscular leathery grip. "You going out for the Haskell haymaker's football squad? We could use a big guy like you." He said this as he turned to Uncle Raymond as if to inquire if I were a new recruit. However, football was never my paradigm of sports. Football was as foreign to me as Haskell, Oklahoma, was to Chicago, Illinois. Moreover, Dad said my knees and ankles were more important than the vainglory of female adulation for a high school football jock.

Kent James was over 6 feet tall with an athletic build, weighing nearly 180 lbs. He had a shock of long thick brown hair and hazel eyes. He had a handsome face that was well tanned. This was complimented by his welcoming smile that was downright disarming. Before I could answer, Uncle Raymond interjected, "Your daddy letting you have a mop for a head of hair?"

"Dad said I could let it grow out just for the summer, Coach. I will get it cut in time for two a day workouts in August," Kent said, sort of sheepishly.

Even though Uncle Raymond was coaching no longer, what he said was "gospel" to the young jocks at Haskell High School. He had only retired two years ago, but his reputation and history cast a long shadow. You didn't want to cross Coach Hammond or earn his disfavor.

"Good deal, son. I may even go to Jack's Barber Shop to make sure you are clear around the ears, " Uncle Raymond half teased.

"Yes, sir, Coach," Kent earnestly responded. Interesting to watch Uncle Raymond alpha dog this guy. I had never seen him go after Joe Corsinni like this, but Kent seemed cockier and more full of himself, I thought. All of that military training and service as a Marine Drill Sergeant had taught Uncle Raymond a trick or two to take a cocky young jock down. I would have to remember that in living with Uncle Raymond. I sure didn't want to curry his disfavor either.

"So you and Joe are working together this summer?" Kent turned back to me. "Yeah, we are," I answered.

"Cool," Kent said. "Mind if I join you guys this Monday?"

"You hard up for sunburn, dirt, ticks, chiggers, blisters, and horsefly bites?" Uncle Raymond teased.

"Nah," Kent said, turning to Uncle Raymond, smiling. "But I have some free time tomorrow and if you could use an extra hand, Coach, I would like to help. Caywood Homes in Muskogee doesn't need me for the rest of the summer so I am looking for odd jobs."

Unbeknown to me, the guys on the football team held it to be a special honor to occasionally help out Coach Hammond at his ranch. This was especially the case for Kent since his best friend Joe Corsinni worked for Coach Hammond. It was a bonus when Aunt Louise got word of him coming over on Monday morning and began planning the menu for breakfast, lunch and dinner for the three of us boys. Kent was no fool and knew he would be fed well for his help. Plus, he got to hang with his buddy Joe and talk football strategy with Coach Hammond. It was readily apparent to me that the people in this community really trusted and loved my aunt and uncle. You would never have any jocks from St. Cyngen Academy offer to work anywhere for a day just for a good meal and to hang out with a 60 year old former coach.

We got back to the ranch and had left over chicken from the day before for lunch. Cold chicken on a hot afternoon actually tasted pretty good. I washed it down with some of Aunt Louise's homemade lemonade. Life didn't get much better than that! I asked Uncle Raymond if I could saddle the Paint and ride the fence of the upper pasture. I wanted to go exploring and as I had nothing else to do, I might as well make myself useful. Uncle Raymond said that was fine but to wait till after 3:00. He wanted me to let the food sit on my stomach and the shadow lengthen on the east side of the mountain.

I went back to my room to read for a bit and write letters; I had brought a reading list of books for my Senior Honors English class. When I returned in the spring semester to St. Cyngen's Academy, I wanted to keep up with the class. I also wrote Ann Burns about my trip down here. Even though we were no longer a "couple," I was missing Ann. In some ways she was a link back home to Chicago. I jotted a short note to Agnes Kotlarski as she would want to know if I made the proper impression on my relatives.

I changed into my jeans and t-shirt at three. Only this time I got my suntan lotion and rubbed it on my arms, face and neck. I was not getting burned again like I did yesterday. I then went to the barn and got a bucket of oats to entice the Paint. He came over to me and let me put the bridle on him. I then led him to a hitching post by the barn and tied him to it, leaving him with a bucket of oats. I went in and grabbed the blanket and saddle. In a short while I was tightening the cinch and ready to ride.

"That boy has the mark and attitude of a good horseman, Louise," Uncle Raymond said as he watched me from the kitchen window.

"He does sit well in the saddle, Raymond," Louise responded.

"His dad told me he had seven years of horsemanship and English riding at Millerwood Stables up north in Chicago. So he knows a thing or two about handling a horse," Raymond said as he drank some coffee and watched me ride off. "I like that boy, Louise. There's something about him I just like."

"I know," Louise added. "I think so, too. In some ways he reminds me of Gerald, but in other ways he is like a lost pup just looking for direction. Only he doesn't know it yet," Aunt Louise added.

"Joe Corsinni said he was a quick study on riding the fences and herding cattle and complimented him. And you know Corsinnis are not known for giving out compliments," Uncle Raymond added, turning from the window to Aunt Louise.

"Do you think he will go out for the football squad, Raymond? He has only been competitive swimming most of his athletic career." Louise said.

"Well, he is bigger than most of the guys on the squad with the exception of Joe and Kent. He seems to be able to handle the heat, which is a lot of football in August and September. The issue is his eye-hand coordination and how fast he is."

"You think his dad would object?" Louise inquired.

"No, I already asked him that. One semester of 2A football in Oklahoma shouldn't adversely affect Phillip's swimming career. Besides, they want him back at St. Cyngen's Academy to anchor their swim team. That boy was not only All State for three years but was also an All American this year in the 400 IM.

In spite of the ruckus he caused, they will want him back all right. We just need to not only provide him with your good home cooking, Louise, but feed his heart and soul, too. There is a hunger in that boy I can't put my finger on. But his father told me he lived and breathed whatever his swim coach asked him to do. As a former coach, that tells me volumes about him."

"Hmmm, gives me something to pray about for sure," Louise said as she pondered Raymond's comments.

"But his dad did say that of all his kids, Phillip was a winner," Raymond added. "He kept up his grades and didn't do drugs or drink, but that prank and his dad's reaction to it were not good." Raymond swirled his coffee as he stared into the cup. "But, all is not lost for Phillip," he smiled. "You just keep on feeding him and he will be as big as Joe Corsinni," Raymond teased.

"Raymond Hammond," Louise's eyes narrowed. "There are some things you will never be forgiven for." At that she laughed.

CHAPTER 5

THE LADY AND THE ABBOT

I rode out through the corral to the lower pasture and then took a trail Joe told me about that led to the upper pasture. The trail was shaded by trees and it was almost pleasant. It was close to the fence so I could check the fence as I rode up to the middle pasture. By now it was drawing nigh to 4:00 p.m. in the afternoon. I came upon a clearing and there was a spring fed pond that Uncle Raymond had built. The water was somewhat clear because it had rocky ledges around the pond's edges and a rocky bottom. The Paint strained for a drink as we walked to the edge of the pond and I let him have one. I slid off the Paint and looked around. We were at the middle pasture. Further up the trail from here was the upper pasture. It was harder to follow the fence on horseback from here because of the rocky terrain. Joe had warned me not to do that alone, or at least not without dogs. He was going to bring his two labs named Zeke and Jake to accompany us on Monday.

"Too many copperheads and rattlesnakes in the really rocky areas where the fence runs," Joe had said. I had followed the fence up to now and eyed it as it sloped up to the higher elevation. But I recognized my limitations and heeded Joe's warning. I had no desire to get snake bit this far out. But I did want to see the upper pasture. Joe said it really had a pretty view of everything below it. Then I heard a bell tolling. I looked at my watch. It was 4:00 p.m. What was that for, I wondered? I got back on the Paint and headed up a trail away from the fence to the upper pasture. It was a steep trail but the trip was well worth it. The view of Haskell and the river valley was beautiful. I just sat in the saddle, transfixed by the view. No one would believe me if I told them what Oklahoma really looked like.

It was then that I heard voices and I turned around and saw a group of men in black robes walking at a brisk pace along the trail on the other side of the fence. "Oh, my God," I thought. "These are some of the monks." Only these guys were not old geezers. A lot of them looked my age or a little older. And they didn't look like a bunch of geeks but rather looked like a bunch of Marine recruits doing physical training. And there were nearly 30 of them in black robes. I waved and they nodded but said nothing to me. That was one for the books. These guys looked like a bunch of virile jocks, not cloistered monks. I was dumb struck. So that was why Joe had a twinkle in his eye when he said I might be surprised.

The longer I was here at the ranch of the Hammonds, the more I realized that there was a much bigger world than the cloistered upper class ghetto of Barrington Heights, Illinois, I grew up in. It was almost too much to take in. First off, this Oklahoma was not a desert; Baptist didn't appear Neanderthal and now a bunch of jocks have taken vows of poverty, chastity and silence at a Catholic monastery. "Toto, you are definitely not in Kansas," I thought to myself.

If that were not bewildering enough, I then saw an older man and woman walking along the path the monks had just trodden. The man had a shaved head but was wearing a straw hat and was dressed in a monk's garb. The woman was dressed in Sunday clothes but did have tennis shoes on. They both appeared to be somewhat older than Uncle Raymond and Aunt Louise.

I nodded and waved and smiled at them. "Hello, there," said the woman. "You talk," I said stunned.

"Of course I talk," the woman chuckled. "Come over here and introduce yourself," she said.

I rode the Paint over to the fence line, slid off of him and said, "I am Phillip Robertson. Raymond and Louise Hammond are my great aunt and uncle."

"Oh, you're that Hammond relative Miriam told me about. I am Marguerite Fugali, Miriam Abboud's aunt."

"And I am Anton Delaurier, the Abbot of the Concharty Mountain Monastery," the man said with a decided French accent.

"Enchante, Monsieur, I said." My three years of French then came in handy and we carried on a brief conversation in French. "Your French is not bad, Phillip. Was your teacher from Burgundy? There is something about your pronunciation that sounds Burgundian."

"Yes, he was," I stammered in amazement.

"It is a pleasure to meet you and converse in my native language. I do not often get the chance to do that here in Oklahoma," he smiled.

"Nor do I," I answered. We chatted for a bit more and then the Abbot asked, "Would you like to have dinner at the monastery sometime, Phillip? You would be welcome as my guest."

Marguerite smiled and said, "You had better accept because I for one know for a fact the Abbot does not take no for an answer." Her dark eyes danced as she spoke.

"Ahh...Ms. Marguerite, do not give all my bad habits away," the Abbot teased.

"It would be a pleasure, Abbot Delaurier," I said. "Just let me know when and where."

"Certainly, Phillip, I will do that. It was nice visiting with you, but I must get Ms. Marguerite back to the monastery before our time of visitation runs out. There are some lovely hiking trails with incredible views on the monastery grounds and you are welcome to traverse them at your leisure," the Abbot said.

"Merci beau coup," I replied. And they returned to their afternoon walk and talk, which I was to later learn, was often part of Abbot Delaurier and Miss Marguerite Fugali's regimen.   This part of the Concharty Mountain was on the east side and the afternoon shadows shaded most of the monastery lands where the monks, the Abbot, and Miss Marguerite were walking.   Plus you had afternoon breezes such that walks here even in July, during this time of day, were almost pleasant even in 90-degree weather.

Two days ago I had left the tony suburb of Barrington Heights, not far from the shores of Lake Michigan and ended up in a place I had never dreamed of. Only this small town of Haskell was not as dumpy, backward or uncivilized as this Chicago snob had initially thought it to be. Nevertheless, I still missed Chicago and felt like an outsider – albeit a very welcomed one!

CHAPTER 6

<u>MORNING RITUAL</u>

I was awakened early the next morning when I heard Uncle Raymond stirring around. It was still pitch black outside. "Gawd," I thought, "don't these people sleep?" It was 5:30 A.M., as I blurrily scanned my wristwatch in the dark. I rolled over to go back to sleep when I heard the kitchen door open and close. I could make out Uncle Raymond's footfall on the gravel as he walked to the barn. I tried to go back to sleep but sort of felt guilty by staying in bed. I wrestled with my guilt for 30 minutes and finally gave up. I got up and began getting dressed. I went to the bathroom to wash my face, shave and brush my teeth. When I came out, Aunt Louise was heading into the kitchen.

"You're up early. Phillip," she remarked.

"I couldn't sleep, Aunt Louise, when I heard Uncle Raymond up." I poured myself a cup of coffee that Uncle Raymond had obviously made earlier and drank it. I put the cup down and said, "Well, maybe I had better go to the barn and see what help Uncle Raymond needs."

Aunt Louise nodded approvingly and said, "I'll have breakfast ready at 7:30 when Joe and Kent arrive."

I headed out to the barn to see what help Uncle Raymond would need. "Good grief," I thought, "What does that son of a buck do this early in the barn." I soon had my answer. On a working ranch there are always chores to be done. Fences need checking and fixing; the barn always needs work; stalls need raking out; livestock needs to be attended to; any oil and gas wells need to be checked on to ensure there was no salt water pollution or contamination of the creek water the livestock would drink; hay and feed to put out....The list was endless. This morning Uncle Raymond was administering some antibiotic shots to some sick mama cows. Uncle Raymond raised Herefords.

"Uncle Raymond, I thought you might need some help," I said. He turned around, smiling, and nodded his agreement. He then explained what we need to do. I went out to a special corral where he had segregated three of the pregnant heifers who appeared ill.

Trying to secure the mama heifers' cooperation to administer a shot at 6:15 in the morning was fraught with challenges if not downright peril! But we got the shots done and I felt like I had accomplished something for Uncle Raymond. It was odd in a way, but I was starting to sense why the football jocks liked this man and were drawn to spend time with him by doing odd jobs at the ranch. He knew how to explain a difficult job in simple terms such that it was easy to do. Plus he instilled a sense of confidence in you. Uncle Raymond was as tough as they come, but there was a tender side to him that was winsome to boys who were growing into men. "No wonder he was such a good coach," I thought to myself. When he put his hand on your shoulder and told you, "Good job," you felt really special. Moreover, I was to discover you hungered for his approval and wanted to do more for him. He had an ability to empower you to grow into your manhood that made him likeable to be around.

"Strength in control," was what Uncle Raymond told me later was what he hoped to instill in young men with a genuine concern for your fellow man. Coach DeLagarza was sort of like that too, but not nearly as warmhearted as Uncle Raymond or concerned for others. Coach DeLagarza taught us it was a dog-eat-dog world out there in the big city and to always keep our guard up. I never got that from Uncle Raymond. He had the small town belief to help your neighbors and give them the benefit of doubt. Uncle

Raymond was to tell me that if you looked for the best in young men as a coach, you could often bring out the best in them. I was not sure Coach DeLagarza really understood the strength in control philosophy of Uncle Raymond, which Uncle Raymond blended with a warm southern hospitality. However, I could tell that Uncle Raymond's persona was beginning to cast a spell on me, and I enjoyed it!

I looked up to see Joe Corsinni and Kent James pull up to the barn in Joe's white truck. One black lab and one chocolate lab were in the bed of the truck anxiously pacing and barking. Joe got out of the truck and whistled between his teeth.

"Zeke, Jake, sit down." The dogs whimpered and sat down in the truck bed. Kent James got out of the truck cab and said,

"Dang, Joe, I wish you could train my little brother and sister like that." Kent had jeans on and a t-shirt. His mop of hair was somewhat tucked beneath an OSU football cap; nevertheless a ducktail was sticking out in the back and hair was protruding along the sides.

"Good morning, Kent and Joe," I said as I came walking out of the barn with Uncle Raymond.

"You still need a haircut, boy, even with that cap on," Uncle Raymond teased. You could see Kent wince slightly and Joe said, "See. I told you coach would notice. That's a dollar you owe me. You should have let Miss Toni cut your hair when we were at Miriam's house last night."

My ears perked up at the name of Miriam. "What did you guys do last night?" I asked.

"Oh, we hung out at the Fugali house and talked to Mr. and Mrs. Abboud, Miriam and Ms. Fugali," Kent said.

"All night long?" I asked.

"Nah," Joe said. "We were only there for two hours. But they always have good coffee and the best baklava, mamoul (a Lebanese cookie), and peach cobbler." So, these two jocks explored the world gastronomically, I thought. Throw in a pretty green eyed, raven-haired beauty and you had a bird's nest made on the ground. I chuckled to myself.

"You hungry dogs," I teased as we walked into the kitchen. Sure enough, Aunt Louise had a full feast of flapjacks, Canadian bacon, freshly sliced "Porter" peaches and a new pot of hot coffee. Where did this lady get the time and energy to throw things together so quickly. She fixed meals effortlessly and with a zest I had never seen before. Meals back in Chicago were either take out or Agnes Kotlarski affairs. Agnes was a good cook but her years as a Polish refugee in WWII left her with an almost Eyor quality of personality. The food was good but you paid the price with double helpings of Agnes' dour outlook on life as she served you dinner.

Aunt Louise was the complete opposite. I was to learn later she often was the short order cook for the Haskell Haymakers football squad – breakfast, lunch or dinner. She just never knew who Uncle Raymond or her late son Gerald might invite over for a meal. If she had ever appeared on the TV program "What's My Line," her theme would have been "Guess Who's Coming to Dinner." She embraced this role and I was to learn her refrigerator and freezer were a hungry jock's dream. Name your meat of choice and she could cook it, albeit southern style! That meant fried – be it chicken, steak, fish, venison, turkey or whatever else she bought at the supermarket or Uncle Raymond shot during hunting season for various game.

We three guys finished breakfast and left Aunt Louise and Uncle Raymond to enjoy their morning regimen of coffee as they discussed the day's activities and chores.

"So, Raymond, you think Phillip will get along with Kent and Joe," Aunt Louise asked.

Uncle Raymond put his cup of coffee down, "I hope so, Louise. Joe seems to get along with Phillip really well. I think Kent will too. If Joe likes a guy, most likely Kent will too. But what a threesome you have. One shy reserved athlete; one chock full of himself extrovert; and then you have Phillip, a big city rich kid, who has found himself with some backwoods relations," Uncle Raymond chuckled.

"Speak for yourself, cowboy," Aunt Louise shot back. "I may be a small town girl, but I am not backwoods....Well, not until I married you." She laughed and Uncle Raymond came over and kissed her on the cheek.

"Well, this backwoods cowboy better get to work today, Mrs. Hammond," and Uncle Raymond headed out of the house to check on things.

CHAPTER 7

JOE AND KENT

The three of us guys headed to the barn for the ritual of catching the horses and saddling them. Joe's dogs whimpered and he told them to sit and stay in the pickup bed. It was amazing. I had heard of bee charmers and horse whisperers but these two dogs lived for Joe's approval. The guy can't talk to people real well, I thought, but he does speak canine pretty good!

We headed out to the lower pasture to herd the cattle to the upper pasture. Joe whistled for Zeke and Jake and they come bounding out of the truck following us, barking and tails wagging. Kent then told me that he had spent the night at the Corsinnis after they left Miriam Abboud's parent's house. They explained to me that it was actually Miss Marguerite Fugali's home and that Miriam's family lived there with her. "They are a Lebanese family. That means extended family and meals all the time," Joe told me. I also learned that the Corsinnis and the Fugalis had been family friends for nearly 70 years. At one point they were some of the few Catholic families in a sea of Protestants in Haskell.

Being such a minority had brought them together in business. The C & C Hardware store in downtown Haskell had once been a joint venture of Joe's grandfather and Miriam Abboud's grandfather Emile Fugali, affectionately known by his nickname Papa C. Why the "C Joe or Kent were not absolutely sure of and Joe thought he took the letter "C" from the Concharty Hills. In any event that is how C & C Hardware was started and named. The "C" was for Papa C and the other was for a young northern Italian immigrant named Josef Corsinni. That was Joe's grandfather. After Papa C had died in 1949, the Corsinnis bought out the Fugali's family interest but kept the name.

We began herding about 30 Hereford cattle. Joe issued whistles through his teeth and the labs chased the stray cattle in the direction we were headed.

"And I only thought labs were bird dogs," I joked.

"No, they are that too when I take them hunting," Joe said.

Slowly we made our way up to the middle pasture with the cattle. It took nearly two hours. We dismounted our horses and tied them to a tree. Joe called the dogs over. We then began checking the fence in the steep rocky area with the dogs going ahead of us, barking and chasing an occasional squirrel or bird.

"No chance of snakes today, Joe?" I asked.

"I wouldn't say that," Kent said.

"But not likely with the dogs," Joe replied. We hiked to the upper pasture following the fence. It was a steep climb and rough going at times. But we made it to the top. By then, all three of us were sweating profusely. No issue with the fence today, I thought. We walked over to the trail I had taken the day before on the Paint and began walking down. By now it was close to 11:30 in the morning and the summer heat was intense. The dogs went running down the trail, barking, to where the horses were tethered. We got back to the middle pasture and Kent walked over to the spring fed pond. He took his cap off and then his shirt. He was barrel-chested and just beginning to show signs of hair on his chest. What he did next surprised me. He took his boots and socks off, then his jeans and undershorts, and then dove into the pond stark naked.

"Come on, Corsinni." I turned around just in time to see Joe's bare ass plunge into the pond. I was to learn later that this was often a time-honored ritual of the jocks who worked on Uncle Raymond's ranch. Instead of coffee breaks, the guys had skinny dipping breaks to beat the heat.

"Hey, come on city boy," Kent said. "You afraid of the water," he teased.

"Wrong thing to say to a swimmer, cowboy," I thought. I stripped and slowly waded into the water. The pond water was great. It was just slightly warm on top, but was really cold about three feet down. I swam out to the deeper part of the pond and started splashing Joe and Kent. They swam after me into the deeper part of the pond. When they attempted to attack me, I maneuvered under water to pull them under. I grabbed Kent's legs first and pulled him down before he could get a breath. I let him go and then grabbed Joe's legs and pulled him under. Kent came up, sputtering and whined, "Dude, you got water up my nose. Not cool."

"Tough guy," I teased and splashed water at Kent.

"You're mine, city boy," Kent said and then he lunged at me but was blocked by Joe who grabbed Kent to wrestle him. Joe and Kent were laughing now as they were locked in a no win contest of the "tough guy." We alternated on who was ganging up on who. We were quite a sight; the three of us thrashing around with each other, naked in that spring fed pond. At times the dogs joined in the throng as we roughhoused.

Little did I know that higher up on the monastery lands Miss Marguerite Fugali was walking one of those paths Abbot Delaurier had told me about that had a beautiful view. The Abbot was with her. They both had a stunning view, all right!

"Look at those young rascals," Marguerite chuckled.

"The glory of a young man is his strength," Abbot Delaurier smiled quoting Proverbs 20:29, "It makes me miss my youth, Miss Marguerite." They continued walking along the path but it took them away from the spectacle of three naked jocks trying to prove who was toughest of them all in the water.

"You know, Marguerite, the monastery owes your family so much for the gift of this land and we deeply appreciate that," the Abbot commented.

"I owe the church so much for what they did for the family when Mama died in 1928. I was only 17 years old and had eleven younger brothers and sisters to watch after. Father McNearney stepped in and rallied some of the church folk in Muskogee to help Papa make it through those first few years of being a widower. I don't know what we would have done without that help. Papa told me he wanted the church to have this land when he died. It had a pretty special meaning to him, given the history he had with it." The Abbot and Marguerite continued walking.

"How did your father get to Oklahoma, Miss Marguerite?" the Abbot asked.

"Papa was 17 years old when he left Lebanon to come here. His family had been massacred by the Turks when they attacked his village in the Chouf Mountains. He was taken in by some cousins in another village who gave him shelter. He survived the massacre because he was tending his family's flock of sheep high up in a mountain pasture. He sold his family land and livestock to immigrate to America. His father had a cousin who had emigrated from the village years before and moved to a town called Wagoner in Indian Territory. Papa wrote him and the cousin invited him over. Papa got to St. Louis and then walked nearly 400 miles from St. Louis to Wagoner, Indian Territory, by following the railroad tracks. It took him only a month to walk here."

"Why didn't he take the train?" the Abbot asked.

"Papa was tight. All along the way from New York to St. Louis people were trying to cheat him because he was an immigrant. There were always some sons of bitches trying to swindle a foreigner simply because he didn't speak English well. They thought he was an easy pigeon," Marguerite answered. "In St. Louis, the railroad ticket taker tried to charge him a fee on top of his ticket and wouldn't let him board the train without it. So Papa went to the ticket agent and cashed in his ticket. All he had was a small bedroll, a small bag with his tender box, a knife, a gun, and the money he sewed into the clothes he wore. He figured out which way led to Indian Territory and started walking."

"How did he survive?" the Abbot asked.

"Well, Papa was tough. You can't herd sheep in the mountains of Lebanon unless you have a lot of grit. He was used to herding and hiking up to ten miles a day through the mountains so a flatland hike was not much to him, even if it was nearly 400 miles," Marguerite chuckled. "He figured he could hike ten miles a day along the railroad track. He survived by buying cheese along the way in the various towns and hunting game as Papa had brought a gun with him and was a pretty good shot. He could clean a squirrel or rabbit in no time at all. At night he would build a small campfire and curl up in his blanket and go to sleep. Many nights he would cry himself to sleep. He was lonely, in a foreign land, didn't speak the language well, and had no family. It was tough. But he remembered his Mama's prayers she taught him as a boy and he often said the Rosary at night. It gave him a lot of comfort."

"Indeed, yes," the Abbot said in reflection. "The Desert Fathers often believed being alone in a foreign place was the best lessons for growing in faith with God."

"Well, Papa was a stranger in a strange land and his faith sustained him in those early years."

"So how did he end up here in Haskell?" the Abbot asked.

"Well, Papa's cousin had a lively trade in Wagoner. In those days Wagoner was a thriving town. Papa's cousin did not want to hit the road to serve the various farms and villages out this way so he gave this territory to Papa – for a price. There weren't many customers at first so Papa had to slowly build his customer base and trust with the people. Papa said it was a strange place back then when it was Indian Territory. There were white settlers, Creek Indians, and Creek Freedmen. He had to learn Creek Indian as well as English. Plus he had to earn the trust of the white settlers, Creek Indians, and the Creek Freedmen. His cousin failed to inform him there was an outlaw gang that hid out in these parts that robbed many a stranger and unwary traveler. That was another reason his cousin was willing to part with this trade area and sell it to Papa."

"Didn't your Papa run into this gang of Belle Starr outlaws up here, somewhere on the Concharty Hills?"

"Yes, he did."

"I heard the story from Friar Lawrence, but would like to hear it from you."

"Papa was 19. He had been here for two years. He still lived at times with his cousin's family in Wagoner when he came back from making his rounds to the farms and villages around here. He was traveling his trade route from farm to farm, village to village in this part of Indian Territory. Often he would sleep in a family's barn on his routes. One night he was going to sleep in an old abandoned barn at the base of the Concharty Hills on his way to Haskell. Only it was already occupied by some young bucks. They had a campfire going and were cooking dinner. They invited him to stay and even fed him a meal. They offered him some moonshine but he wouldn't take it. He just said he was too tired and turned in. Those men stayed up by the outside fire when Papa went into the abandoned barn. But he didn't go to sleep. He knew better. He had an uneasy feeling about these men. They got drunk and started talking with each other about robbing him later in the morning. However, they passed out from the moonshine but Papa was stone cold sober. He had spent the night in that barn before and knew the barn had a hole in the back. Papa crawled through that hole and escaped from the Belle Starr Gang. He walked all night to the town of Haskell and just collapsed from exhaustion at a customer's place of business. The customer was Josef Corsinni. He let him rest in the back of his store after Papa told him the story. Mr. Corsinni and Papa became close friends and lifelong partners when Papa moved his base of operations from Wagoner to Haskell.

"Years later Papa bought the land up here and used to take us kids to the ruins of that old barn. Mama would pack a picnic lunch and we would take a wagon ride up here. He would tell us tales of the Concharty Mountain and his life as an iterant peddler throughout the region. He had many stories from his life on the road. He loved this country and the outdoors. He used to hunt all sorts of game up here for our family's dinner table. A month didn't go by that Mama was cooking game. This included deer, wild turkey, rabbits and squirrel. He and Josef Corsinni once even shot a mountain lion up here somewhere."

"Mon dieu!" remarked the Abbot. "I have heard that there are occasional mountain lions in these parts. But fortunately we have not encountered one yet on the monastery land."

"Well, we best be getting back, Abbot. Thank you for walking with me down memory lane as it were," Marguerite chuckled. The two headed down the trail back to the monastery.

CHAPTER 8

A NEW FOOTBALL RECRUIT

The problem with spontaneous skinny-dipping is that you never have a towel to dry off with! That didn't stop Kent and Joe, however. They took their t-shirts and used them as a towel to dry off. I dried off too, taking their cues using my shirt as a towel. I thoroughly dried myself off. I had experienced the chafing you get from wet undershorts and knew it would be doubly bad on horseback. Kent told me not to worry about that, "We will be almost dried out by the time we get back to Mrs. Hammond's kitchen." I hoped he was right or it was going to be a long afternoon!

We mounted our horses and Joe whistled to Zeke and Jake to follow us. We began working the cattle again. Joe stopped and whistled to his dogs to sit. They came to a standstill whimpering. We could hear a cow bellowing. "Sounds like one of Coach Hammond's heifers is calving," Joe said. "Stay here guys till I motion you over." He rode over to a stand of trees where the noise was coming from. Joe slid off his horse and quietly crept over to a thicket of trees to spy things out. We got off our horses and held their reins.

Kent turned to me and asked, "So, Phillip, tell me about yourself."

"Well, what do you want to know," I responded.

"All I know is that you're Coach Hammond's nephew from Chicago. I thought you were just a big city kid. But working with you this morning I can tell you know a thing or two about horses. And you're sure not afraid of standing your ground, even when two naked guys attack you!" he said with a grin.

"Well, as I recall, you got attacked by two guys ala no clothes more than I did," I replied.

Kent punched me in the shoulder and said, "Phillip, you're all right. I can see why Coach and Mrs. Hammond like you and why Joe says you are okay!" He then explained that the Hammonds and his family had been praying for me for weeks before I had arrived. Apparently, his parents and the Hammond were in a weekly prayer group from church. He knew about me before I even dreamed of his existence, and with that it seemed I had Kent James's good housekeeping seal of approval for friendship.

"Okay, city boy, tell me about yourself."

Kent's comment about Uncle Raymond, Aunt Louise and Joe totally caught me off guard. If Kent had wanted to capture my affection as a buddy, he had just hit a bull's eye. I felt like an outsider but Kent had a warmth about him that made him draw me out. I was drawn to Joe but when I found out Joe liked me too as a friend, my big city caution was diminished. I had been trained to be very guarded about my feelings and sharing who I was. But to hear that Aunt Louise and Uncle Raymond deeply cared for me and had been praying with Kent's family for me completely disarmed me. I threw down my defenses, and then gave Kent a Reader's Digest Abridged version of my life. This included school, my athletic career as a swimmer, my broken family, and my Avery Drive misadventure that resulted in my exile to Oklahoma.

Kent whistled, "Dude, a comatose mom! Now that would be tough." He got quiet for a bit, looking at the ground, and then added, "Your prank on Avery Drive would get you time at Big Mac Penitentiary around here," Kent said, trying to lighten things up.

"What sort of school was it you went to? Never heard of a prep school before much less one called St. Slim Jims," Kent mused. "Sounds like a highfalutin blue blood academy for rich kids. Think I will start calling you Phillip F. Austin Robertson. You need a blue blood name to match your pedigree." Kent laughed and I did too. Kent may have had a high opinion of his athletic ability and good looks, but there was a genuineness about him when it came to his friends. His warmth totally surprised me and I welcomed his friendship. I was to learn that he truly cared about those in his sphere of influence, sometimes more than others realized. This big city kid was not used to a stranger welcoming you like a long lost cousin and it was disconcerting to me at first. My northern reserve was at odds with this southern openness.

Joe whistled at us and motioned us to join him. We got there just in time to see a brand new calf lying on the ground as the mama cow licked the calf. The afterbirth was nearby. It was a sight this Chicago boy had never seen before.

"Ugh," I said.

Joe looked around at me and grinned. "Yeah, it takes some getting used to," Joe said. "I am concerned that there might be some coyotes or packs of wild dogs around."

"What?" I said.

"Yeah, the coyotes are always a problem when the heifers have their calves. But they tend to hunt alone. The packs of wild dogs are more dangerous and they hunt like wolves," Kent added.

"Packs of wild dogs?" I questioned in amazement.

Kent turned to me and explained, "Yeah, lots of city folk dump their unwanted cats and dogs out this way. If they survive, they turn feral with no fear of man like a coyote or wolf. That makes them doubly dangerous."

"Wow," I said. As I looked back at the new calf he had got up on his wobbly legs and was nursing.

"She and her calf should be okay," Joe said. "But we had better leave the other cows up in the middle pasture for now. There is safety in numbers for these cattle. Mama needs to rest a bit before she rejoins the herd and the baby needs his strength from mama's milk before we move them to another pasture."

We got back on our horses and rode back down to the house. By now the heat had totally dried our hair and I could feel my body starting to sweat again. We tied the horses to a hitching post by the barn next to a water trough and walked over to the house. Aunt Louise had a lunch prepared on the back porch for us. BLT sandwiches, sliced carrots and celery, and fresh sun tea with mint. It was southern style, which meant it was sweet tea. She had fresh sliced Porter peaches, which she had refrigerated so they were cold. Aunt Louise knew how to coordinate her menu with the weather. When it was blazing hot, better to feed her men something light; that meant fruit, vegetables, sandwiches and homemade tea. It really hit the spot.

The three of us joked around and Aunt Louise joined in our conversation from time to time. She was an astute observer of human nature and knew her boundaries with these teenage jocks.

"Besides," she later was to remark, "God gave us two eyes, two ears and one mouth and the Good Lord intended us to use them in that proportion." She was watching our interaction and gauging how well I was fitting in. "So far so good. My prayers are being answered" she thought. She had been concerned that Kent James may have been a bit territorial over his friendship with Joe. But Kent was not threatened by me and accepted me as if I had been a kid he had grown up with in Coach Hammond's Pee Wee baseball team. Moreover, after I shared with him, I felt strongly drawn to him as a friend. But I felt the same attraction to Joe. He seemed to accept me and like me also. However, feeling so close to two strangers was unsettling to my big city caution and was almost upsetting to me. "Things like this just don't happen," my mind kept telling me. However, being alone in such a strange place made me more open to new people as friends; and I appreciated these guys and wanted their friendship!

"You can tell if Joe likes you," Uncle Raymond told me early on, "Not so much by what he says but how much he smiles when he teases you." Joe really didn't talk much but when he teased you he had a million dollar smile that spoke of friendship. He had the perfect combination of stoic masculinity with a boyish tenderness.

We finished lunch and went back to the barn for the horses. We continued working the cattle in the middle pasture and checked on the heifer with her new calf. She was with the other cattle now and the calf was by her side. We worked another pasture where Uncle Raymond had some pumping units and other cattle. We checked the pumping units to make sure there was no pollution or leakage around the units and surveyed the cattle to make sure they were healthy.

"No sick cows in this bunch," Kent said. Joe grunted his concurrence.

We finished up our chores and headed back to the barn. We tied the horse bridles up to the hitching posts. We took the saddles and bridles off the horses and then brushed them down. The horses really seemed to enjoy this. We turned them loose and they trotted out to the lower pasture where Joe had put some feed out for them.

We washed up at the barn sink and this time I hit Joe with a face full of cold well water.

"Pay backs are hell, Corsinni!" I said with a laugh. Kent joined in and the three of us were horsing around, throwing water on each other. All three of us were soon soaking wet.

"You trying to make a Baptist out of this Catholic boy, Kent?" Joe teased. Aunt Louise called us into dinner and we raced each other to the kitchen door laughing. Kent and Joe were blocking and body slamming each other as we ran. We took our boots off and came into the kitchen, panting and sweating and joking.

"Joe, if you ran like that, we would have beat Wetumka last season," Kent teased.

"And if you had blocked like you just did as we ran to the house, I wouldn't have been sacked when we played Eufaula!" Joe retorted. You could tell these two guys really liked each other in spite of their teasing. It meant a lot to me as a big city stranger to be included in their circle of friendship. This was a far cry from the relational dynamics I had experienced on the swim team and water polo teams at St. Cyngen's Prep Academy. Too often it was every man for himself. You had to constantly keep your guard up as many of the guys were only out for themselves and their own advancement. Guys were always jockeying for positions, whether academically or athletically. They had been "home" schooled very well in this regard by their parents many of whom were high-ranking ruthless corporate executives. Hence, my big city caution and reserve!

Aunt Louise had prepared fried pork chops, mashed potatoes, gravy, green beans and hot biscuits. Uncle Raymond joined us in the kitchen and the football jock talk began. Halfway into dinner, four pairs of eyes were boring into me after Kent asked me, "Will you go out for the Haskell Haymakers football squad? Then turning to Uncle Raymond, Kent added, "Coach, we wrestled around today and based on his toughness, I think Phillip would be a good defensive end."

What was I supposed to say? I really liked these guys and enjoyed their comradery in the strange and wonderful place called Oklahoma. I didn't know much about how to play the game and told Kent that.

"That's okay, Phillip! Kent and I can teach you with Coach's help," Joe chimed in. Uncle Raymond was looking at me, bemused. He and Aunt Louise were smiling. There was a moment of silence that was broken when Aunt Louise said,

"You could do it, Phillip," Aunt Louise said.

I was cornered and outflanked. I might have demurred to Kent's request, but couldn't say no to both Aunt Louise and Joe when they ganged up on me. Any objections died in my throat. I had only known Uncle Raymond and Aunt Louise for three days but I had fallen for the spell they had cast. Moreover, I enjoyed hanging out with Joe and Kent. Good food, honest laughter, hard work, warm conversation, and a sense of belonging had captured my heart and soul. I would march around the world if they had asked me to!

"All right, I will do it," I said. Uncle Raymond looked at Joe and Kent and all three were smiling.

"You will be a great addition to the team, Phillip. We need a good defensive end. And I will help you with an exercise regimen to get you in shape and can explain to you the role of defensive end," Uncle Raymond said. He leaned across the table and shook my hand and welcomed me to the team.

Joe and Kent slapped me on the shoulder and then Kent said, "Coach, can we take Phillip out with us tonight? We will have him back by 11:00." Uncle Raymond said that was fine. We finished dinner and then helped with the dishes in the kitchen with Aunt Louise.

"You ready to go?" Kent asked.

"Not until I clean up," I said. "I am not going into town smelling like I have been dancing with horses and cows all day. First impressions are lasting impressions! Let me shower off and change and I will be ready to go with you guys."

"Okay, but don't keep us waiting long, Cinderella," Kent teased. Kent, Joe and Uncle Raymond went to the den and continued their jock talk with the prospect of a new defensive end and game strategy.

I went back to my room, grabbed a change of clothes and hit the shower to clean up. I was out in less than five minutes. I dressed in a Polo shirt and shorts and my favorite pair of Serapis (a Mexican sandal) my brother John had brought back for me from Mexico City. I walked down the hall to the den and Kent whistled at me. "Well, don't you look pretty," he teased.

"I'm ready to go guys," I said.

"Have a good time, Phillip," said Aunt Louise from the kitchen. And with that the three amigos headed out for a night on the town in Haskell, Oklahoma.

Aunt Louise sat down in a chair in the den by Uncle Raymond and sipped on her sweet tea. "Well, it certainly has been a whirlwind these last three days, Raymond. You have a new ranch hand who catches on quickly; Kent and Joe have a new buddy; and the Haskell Haymakers have a new defensive end. My, my, my! Who would have thought the Good Lord could fit things together so well. My prayers are answered."

"Yeah, mine too!" said Raymond. "I don't know how quick he is on the field, but anyone would be better for the team than what they have! Joe has taken a shine to Phillip; and Kent appears to like him, too. Phillip couldn't have found two better young men to befriend him at Haskell High School. He will fit in all right. He may even expand their horizons, too, with his experience in Chicago. As for the new ranch hand, that boy is not afraid to work. He was really helpful this morning inoculating the sick heifers. I think I am going to enjoy having him around and teaching him a thing or two about playing football," Raymond smiled as he stretched back in his Lazy Boy recliner.

CHAPTER 9

THE CORSINNI'S AND THE JAMES'

We drove first to Joe's house so he could clean up. I got to meet Mr. and Mrs. Bill Corsinni. Mr. Corsinni was a gray-haired version of Joe. The Corsinnis were very nice but somewhat reserved. Kent loosened them up with his teasing and humor while Joe ran upstairs to shower and change. Kent had a unique ability to put people at ease in awkward situations and he carried the bulk of the conversation. Joe's little brother Jimmy and sister Lucy came in to talk to us also. Joe's brother was three years younger but was already six feet tall and had Joe's coloring. Joe told him I was going out for the team and Jimmy warmed up to this big city stranger. He was going out for the squad too and let me know he would be working with me on the team. Seems like little brother wanted to be one of the guys! Lucy, the baby sister was ten and had blue eyes and blond hair. She was sweet and outgoing unlike her reserved eldest brother. Amazing to meet full-blooded Italians in Haskell, Oklahoma, with blond hair and blue eyes, I thought. Joe came downstairs in jeans and a button-up short sleeve western shirt.

We took our leave and went to Kent's house. Kent introduced me to his parents and left Joe and me with them while he cleaned up. Kent's dad was a dentist with offices in Haskell and Muskogee. He and his wife chose to live in Haskell. His wife was a Spanish teacher at Haskell High School. Mrs. James made a point of telling me that Kent's little brother and sister were not home but with some friends this evening; otherwise, they would have been here to introduce themselves. Dr. and Mrs. James reminded me of Uncle Raymond and Aunt Louise with their friendly conversation and warm hospitality. They seemed genuinely interested in who I was. And I received a thorough inquiry from Mrs. James about myself and my family. "Geeze, were all Southerners so curious and ingratiating?" I wondered. Up in Chicago, people may be polite to strangers, but they wouldn't necessarily welcome a stranger as a long lost relative or pepper him with a myriad of personal questions at the first meeting. That was very disconcerting at first to my Chicago ways but I would get used to it in time. Kent came down from cleaning up, wearing shorts and an IZOD golf shirt and tennis shoes. My "interview" was over for now. We took our leave from Dr. and Mrs. James.

"Where we going, guys," I asked.

"The Abboud's house. Miriam asked us to stop by," Joe said.

"Hey, Miss Toni will cut your hair tonight, Kent," Joe teased.

"Not funny, Sinni," Kent said. Kent had all sorts of nicknames for people. He called Joe "Sinni" and nicknamed me Phillip F. Austin Robertson. He teased me about being a big city blue blood from a highfalutin church prep school you couldn't pronounce.

"If I can go out for the football squad, you can get your hair cut, Kent," I teased back, changing the subject from my alleged pedigree to his locks.

"Dang, guys, Coach Hammond sic you both to ride my ass?" Kent asked. "Nah," Joe shot back. "Not interested in riding your hairy ass! Just want you to be clear around the ears as Coach says. You're starting to look like one of those hippy boys from California," Joe snickered.

"Okay, okay, I give. I will let Miss Toni cut my hair if she offers us mamoul and baklava," Kent replied

Joe gave a stern glance at Kent and said, "Don't make promises you can't keep, Kent James!"

"No, I am good for it. Besides, I know we ate her out of house and home and all her Mamoul and

Baklava last time we were there. And Miss Marguerite only makes that once a month so my hair stays for now," Kent pronounced with confidence.

"I wouldn't bet on that," Joe said as he shook his head with a wry grin. "She may yet shave you like Samson tonight." Joe and I laughed. Kent smiled but with a grimace. This could be a really interesting evening if there was this Mamoul and Baklava in the house and Kent had to eat not only the good food but his cheeky attitude and words.

We drove up to a rambling one-story old house with a huge wrap around porch. This was the Fugali home. Papa C had built this home in 1907. All the Fugali children were born here from 1911 to 1928. The lights were on inside and as we walked up to the front porch we could hear laughter coming from inside the house.

CHAPTER 10

COFFEE AND MAMOUL WITH THE FUGALIS

We rang the doorbell and a short woman with jet-black hair answered the door.

"Kent and joe, come on in. Who's your friend here?"

"Mrs. Toni Abboud, this is Phillip Robertson, Coach Hammond's nephew." I extended my hand and shook Mrs. Abboud's hand.

"Nice to meet you, Mrs. Abboud," I said.

"Oh, come on in guys. Call me Ms. Toni. Miriam is in the back cleaning up. She just got off her shift at Tastee-Freeze. She said you might stop by. My sister, Madeline, is in town tonight from Oklahoma City, so Marguerite has been fixing mamoul and baklava all afternoon for her. So, we have some fresh stuff if you boys are hungry." I saw Joe's eyes twinkle as his face broadened into a big grin. Kent grimaced and cut his eyes at Joe and then looked down at the floor.

"That offer to trim hair still good tonight, Miss Toni?" Joe asked.

"Sure is," Miss Toni said. "Who needs a haircut?" and with that she giggled and smiled as she looked at Kent. "Sampson wouldn't let me touch his curls last time he was here." Kent blushed bright red. This woman had an infectious zest about her. The aroma of freshly baked mamoul and baklava permeated the house; and the house inside seemed more like an historical museum of antiques than a house one would live in. I had never seen so much antique colored crystal bric-a-brac and knick-knacks from the floor to a nine-foot ceiling in my life. The main hall had shelves from floor to ceiling all full of collections of everything imaginable. Furthermore, as you came into the house the floors groaned as you walked across them and gave in just so slightly. In the center of the hallway was a photograph, of a handsome, dapper, well-dressed man with his young bride, in an embroidered frame.

"Who is this?" I asked Miss Toni.

"That is Papa C, my father, and Mama on their wedding day in Beirut, Lebanon, in 1910."

"Wow," I said.

"Come on into the dining room and sit down. My sisters, Madeline and Marguerite, will come up from the kitchen and join us. I just made some fresh coffee and Marguerite just pulled the last batch of baklava from the oven." If Joe, Kent and I had been Labrador retrievers like Joe's dogs, we all three would have had drool oozing from the sides of our mouths. The smell of the fresh baked mamoul and baklava was intoxicating. An older woman came around the corner; and I instantly recognized Marguerite Fugali.

"Good evening, Miss Fugali," I said as she came into the room.

"Which one," another woman shot back at me as she entered the room also. It was Marguerite's younger sister Madeline Fugali. She was smoking a cigar. My eyes widened with amazement at the sight.

"Hey, I know you. You're that young fella I met up on Concharty Mountain when I was walking with the Abbot," said Miss Marguerite.

"That's right," I said.

"Well, hell. Will someone please tell me who in the sam hill he is," Madeline asked, pointing her cigar at me, "and what is this nonsense about meeting him on Concharty Mountain? I hear a story coming on so I had better sit down." And with that Madeline Fugali sat down.

"You boys sit down too. Might as well get comfortable because Miriam is going to be awhile. Let's get these boys some mamoul and baklava. Toni, bring the fresh pot of coffee too," Madeline shouted to Miss Toni, who had gone into the kitchen. She came back with a tray of coffee, mamoul and baklava and sat down.

Marguerite Fugali chuckled, "You boys best sit down as Madeline is right. Miriam will be awhile." Marguerite explained to Madeline how we met on Sunday and my relation to Uncle Raymond and Aunt Louise, and that we were there to see Miriam.

"Well, it seems only fair that Miriam should share these handsome young men with us, Marguerite. There are three of them, so that leaves one for each of us old maids, Marguerite," Madeline said teasingly.

"Say, wait a minute, Marguerite. Are these the three stooges, that were skinny dipping today in Coach Hammond's pond, that you told me about?", she asked, as she puffed on the cigar. The thought of being seen skinny-dipping by a lady like Miss Marguerite was appalling to my big city reserve, much less having it discussed by her family members at the dinner table!

I flushed bright crimson red. I noticed that Joe winced a bit. Kent, though, kept his composure and responded by turning to Marguerite, smiling, "Well, Miss Marguerite, did you enjoy the show?"

"Couldn't really see much," Miss Marguerite replied, smiling. "You all looked pretty small to me from high up on the monastery trails. Just a bunch of young knuckleheads, bare-assed, splashing around in the water, making a ruckus," she relied. "Besides, I didn't see anything I hadn't seen raising eleven younger brothers and sisters," she chuckled.

Kent's smugness melted away from Miss Marguerite's honest assessment of our swimming in the pond. She softened the blow by saying, "have some baklava, Kent." Kent took a piece and started eating. Joe cleared his throat and looked at Kent.

Kent finished eating his baklava and turned to Miss Toni, asking "About that promise. You still good for that offer of a haircut, Miss Toni?"

"I thought you would never ask," she giggled. Kent glared at Joe and me while Toni got up from the table.

Miss Toni went back to the kitchen and you could hear her opening drawers and moving things about. "Kent, you want your hair cut in here or in the dining room?" she asked from the kitchen. Kent had a mouthful of another baklava and his answer of "kitchen" was muffled. He didn't want to be the center of attention, while his locks were shorn with Joe and me in the room.

"You guys stay here and keep your dates company," Kent said teasingly.

"Well, I get your God-son, Joe Corsinni, Marguerite. I have enough conversation for the two of us." She obviously knew of Joe's introverted nature. "You can have the blondie in his Jesus sandals," Madeline added. "Besides, you two already have a thing going for each other," Madeline added, puffing her cigar and grinning at me.

You could have blown me over with a feather. This Fugali family was one for the books. Miss Madeline was blunt and in your face. You knew where you stood or didn't stand with her. Miss Marguerite had more style and class, but she could be dead on blunt also. She was to later tell me that at her season in life she found it more honest to be "truthfully candid and to the point" with folks. That way no one had a misunderstanding as to how things were. But you should speak the truth in love she explained. She had learned that from nearly twenty-five years of owning and running a flower shop. Miss Toni described herself as "Miss Pollyanna"; she always looked for the best in people and had a unique ability to often bring out the best in people. She and Marguerite ran the Haskell Flower Shop and balanced each other very well with their complimenting strengths and weaknesses. Their sister, Madeline, worked for the Oklahoma City newspaper "The Daily Oklahoman." She helped run the business news section of the paper and was used to barking at people to get things done. But underneath all the bark was a good-hearted soul, if one could get past her calloused, exterior mannerisms. In this way she reminded me of Agnes Kotlarski and in many ways I came to see them as kindred spirits; so she didn't intimidate me as I had grown up with such a personality.

I sat around the table with Joe, Miss Madeline, and Miss Marguerite. The usual questions and cross-examination of my family pedigree began again. Only this time I was well rehearsed on how to field incredibly personal questions from strangers. Occasionally, I could hear Miss Toni talking to Kent about how short he wanted his haircut. Miss Toni had once worked in a barbershop and beauty salon in Muskogee, so she knew how to handle a pair of hair scissors. He, however, occasionally let out an "Ouch, Miss Toni. You clipping my hair or trimming shrubbery?"

She retorted with "Keep your head down, Sunshine," and then we would hear clipping sounds begin again.

Mercifully, my interrogation by these two grand dames was interrupted by the arrival of Stanley Abboud. He had just gotten home from his liquor store in Tulsa. I was introduced to him and the usual pleasantries were exchanged.

"Okay, Stanley, go wash up and change. Marguerite and I have some more questions to ask Phillip, " Madeline said. Stanley smiled, looked at Joe and me, rolled his eyes and went to another part of the house to clean up and change.

"Toni, I'll catch you in the back bedroom when you get done with Kent," Stanley said, as he left the dining room.

"Okay, Hon," Miss Toni answered.

Kent came in after Mr. Abboud left the room. Miss Toni was still in the kitchen, cleaning up the clippings. I almost didn't recognize him; he was actually a pretty handsome guy with short hair. That longhaired mop took away from his good looks. The short cut made him look like a Marine corporal, but it was a really flattering look for Kent.

"Hey, whoever you are, tell our buddy Kent we want him back," Joe teased.

"Real funny, Sinni, you are the cause of this," Kent replied with a rather stern countenance.

"Oh, shut up, sit down and eat some mamoul, Kent. You look better with that haircut. It is always good when a man looks like a man and not a girl! So, stop sulking over losing that mop you had on your head," Madeline ordered.

"Never seen a man so vain over something so matted and unkept." With that Madeline drank some coffee, took a bite of mamoul and washed it down with more coffee. She gave Kent a look that would freeze water and then slapped him on the back and laughed.

Joe and I sat transfixed. We didn't dare touch this sensitive issue with Kent. Our stupor didn't last long. Madeline then asked, "What do you think, godson?"

Joe looked at Madeline and then at Kent. "Yeah, he does look better."

"What about you, blondie?" Before I could answer, Miriam came in.

"Well, look what the cat drug in," Madeline said. Miriam looked wonderful. Her dark hair was lightly curled. She wore a pair of culottes with a white Polo shirt and sandals. As she walked by Joe and me, I got a whiff of some exotic-smelling feminine perfume. "Mmmmm, very nice," I thought.

My former Chicago girlfriend, Ann Burns, with all her social graces and aristocratic pedigree, had never made an entrance like that. Miriam had three pairs of male eyes following her every move. She attracted male attention like bees to honey. I then said something totally out of character that was even surprising to me. "Well, the cat sure knew what it was doing when it drug the Miriam bird in."

Madeline arched her eyebrows and looked first, at Marguerite, and then at Miss Toni who had just reentered the room. They returned her knowing look. There was an instant recognition between these three sisters of the import of my statement. Miriam broke the tension and said, "Well, thank you, Phillip. How have you been getting along in Haskell these past three days?"

"A lot has happened. Joe is teaching me the chores at Uncle Raymond's ranch." I then turned to look at Joe and Kent, "and I made two great new chums and decided to go out for the Haskell Haymakers football team."

"Really? That's great, Phillip," Miriam said.

"Thanks," I said. "But you can thank Joe and Kent for that. They have ambitions of making this swimmer into a defensive end. I don't even know what that position does on a football team."

"Turning a fish into a Haymaker. This should be interesting," Madeline said as she puffed on her cigar and looked at Miss Toni.

Marguerite then asked, "Phillip, how much of Haskell have you seen so far?"

"Not much, actually," I answered.

"Would you like to see our store downtown?" Marguerite asked.

"Sure, when?" I asked.

"Now," Marguerite replied, matter of factly.

"Why not. You guys okay with that?" I asked Joe and Kent.

"Sure," said Joe. "Yeah, anything is better than getting slugged by Madeline," Kent answered, arching his eyebrows and cutting his eyes at Madeline.

"Wuss!" Madeline teased back.

"Well. Let's go," Marguerite said. "It's two blocks away so we can walk over there from here. It's a fine night and a walk would do us all good after the coffee and desserts."

At that, Joe, Kent, Marguerite, Miriam and I got up from the table and took our leave of Madeline and Miss Toni.

CHAPTER 11

PAPA C.

We exited through the south door through the formal living room, out the south porch. The evening was warm but there was a nice breeze. The streets were brick. The sidewalks were old concrete that had heaved over time in places. Across the street to the south and west was the Haskell High School. It was an old two-story red brick building built at the turn of the century. Immediately across the street from the school and the Fugali home was a small white clapboard Catholic church. Papa C and Josef Corsinni helped build that church in 1905, two years before statehood. One block down was a red and orange brick church, First Methodist.

"Lots of water under that church bridge," Miss Marguerite said, chuckling to herself .

"How so, Miss Marguerite?" I asked.

"When the Ku Klux Klan took over this state in the 1920's, that church was the gathering place for them in Haskell, where they often burned crosses. Several of the deacons were high up in the leadership of the Ku Klux Klan here. Back then the KKK was anti-Catholic, anti-Indian, anti-black, anti-immigrant and anti-anyone who disagreed with them. The church was only three houses down from us and they often marched in front of our house and the Catholic Church to try to scare the hell out of us. Papa was a leader in the Catholic Church here in Haskell. But Papa was tough. After the massacres he survived in Lebanon by the Turks, nothing scared him much. It scared us kids, though. In 1924, his store in Bixby 'mysteriously' burned down. We believed it was set by the local Ku Klux Klan. They also tried to burn Papa out here in Haskell but he caught the man as he tried to set the fire. Papa was a tough fighter and knew how to box. He stamped out the fire and fought the man trying to restart it. The man got a boxing lesson that evening he would never forget. He tied the man up; called the Muskogee Sheriff's office and spent the night guarding him until the Sheriff's office came to Haskell. He got a full confession out of the man and of those who were involved in this terrorist activity."

"Wow, Miss Marguerite, I never heard that story," Kent said.

"I have," Joe said.

"Why were people doing that, Miss Marguerite?" I asked.

"Oh, there were bigots and boneheads everywhere back then, Phillip. The KKK was very hateful, all in the name of mom, apple pie, religion, and the USA! It was a scary time and people were scared. We had tough economic times starting in 1919. World War I was over and the price of oil and wheat collapsed and our depression started in 1919 in Oklahoma, not 1929 like the rest of the country," Marguerite answered.

"Those were tough times for Catholics," Joe said.

Marguerite continued, "Yes, when I was your age, I had a run in with the Haskell School Superintendent. Looking back, I now realize he was either a Klansman or a KKK sympathizer. He told me that it was a shame a bright young girl like me was not a Christian. Well, that did it. I stopped his bigotry in its tracks. I asked him about his surname, 'Baumgardner' he said. 'That is German, isn't it?' I asked.

"Sure it is,'" he said.

"He was very vain about his 'white' pedigree. I reminded him that as his last name was German, that when his ancestors were running bare-assed in the Black Forest of Germany, worshipping pagan idols in the First Century, A.D., mine were on their knees in Lebanon at the feet of the cross of our Risen Savior."

Marguerite chuckled. "He never crossed me again on that point."

"How sad, Aunt Marguerite, that people behaved like that," Miriam said.

Marguerite turned to Miriam and smiled sadly. "Life is tough, kiddo. Always has been and always will be! That is why it is so important to know where you have come from so you know where you are going. Papa used to tell me that. His life was fraught with peril and challenges. But, mama used to tell me that it was not the absence of hard times that made life sweet, but how with God's help you respond when the storm clouds gather."

We continued walking, all four of us. Miss Marguerite's story had left us all with a heavy spirit. We crossed from the residential district into the commercial downtown district of Haskell. There were several one and two story red brick buildings. Marguerite told us that Papa C had built most of these buildings and I was to learn he was once the wealthiest man in Haskell in spite of the KKK's "reign of terror."

"They even tried to get people to boycott Papa C's store, but it failed. Too many people had depended on Papa C in the 1890's, 1900's, 1910's, until the KKK's time in the 20's. They were not so easily swayed or poisoned after nearly thirty years of trading with Papa C. The Klan used to hold secret rallies on the Concharty Mountain and burn crosses and torment the unlucky Creek Freedmen or Creek Indians who they considered uppity. The sad thing was that the leaders of the Klan in this area tried to use their power to force the Creek Freedmen and Creek Indians out of what pitiful land they had left after the massive probate swindles from 1907 through the 1920's. Papa got wind of what they had been doing up there. Mike Freeman owned that land and was a Klansman. He was in trouble financially due to a morphine addiction. He had mortgaged that land which was going into foreclosure. So Papa bought the note through a straw man in Yale, Oklahoma, and had him foreclose on the lands. Papa used to go out sixty miles west of here to peddle goods to the oil workers' families at the Three Sands Oilfield near Yale, Oklahoma. He had many friends out that way as a consequence. Mr. Freeman never realized what Papa had done, but the Klan's defiling the beauty of that place was stopped." Marguerite smiled as she related the story. "Papa later had the land given to the Catholic Church to found a monastery where weary travelers, regardless of their religion, could find rest and respite, and where a faithful group of men would pray daily for the outside world. He believed there was something magic about these hills and he wanted them preserved for special purposes."

"So that is how the Concharty Hills Monastery was started?" I asked.

"Yes," Marguerite answered as she unlocked the door to her flower shop, turned on the lights, and motioned us in.

CHAPTER 12

HASKELL FLOWER SHOP

As we crossed the threshold into Miss Marguerite's shop it was as if I had stepped back in time. It was a flower shop with every imaginable piece of antique furniture taking up space on the floor, displaying floral arrangements and miscellaneous gift items. There were also antique farm implements hanging on the wall everywhere.

"Papa got these as farmers mechanized their farms," Miss Marguerite told me. Some even dated back to the Civil War era.

"Why did Papa C collect them?" I asked.

"Papa collected stuff like this like a lint catcher in your dryer catches lint," Marguerite chuckled. "He wanted to preserve it for posterity also. Upstairs, the attic is chock full of other items I haven't displayed for years."

Marguerite showed us around the flower shop, explaining everything. But then we came upon an alcove that reminded me of a corner altar I often saw in Episcopal and Catholic churches back in Chicago. There was a picture hanging in this little "religious-like" alcove but no candles. Marguerite carefully took the picture hanging there off the wall and held it facing us.

"This here is a hand autographed photograph of Clark Gable." I squinted my eyes to read a handwritten note on it, "to Marguerite – My most adoring fan in Haskell, Oklahoma. Love and Kisses, Clark Gable." I shook my head smiling. Marguerite explained that a classmate from Haskell ended up working at the MGM Studio in California. She knew of Marguerite's adoration and schoolgirl crush on Clark Gable and got a personalized autograph by Clark Gable himself.

"Most precious thing to me I have in this store," she chuckled. Kent, Joe and I just stood in awe of this store and Miss Marguerite.

"I never knew you had that," Kent said.

"Wake up, Sunshine, Maybe now that your hair is out of your eyes, you will see better. This has been hanging here for twenty-five years.," Marguerite said. Kent gave a slight grimace and looked at Joe and me.

Joe just smiled. He was too shy and too smart to say anything. Joe later told me that if you can't improve the silence by something meaningful to say, he thought it was best to keep your mouth shut. That way no one would realize you weren't as smart as you seemed.

I broke the silent tension by saying, "That is a real treasure, Miss Marguerite. I can well see why you value it like you do!"

"Thank you, Phillip," and with that Marguerite hung the picture back in its alcove.

She finished showing us the store including a 19th Century dentist chair that Papa C had won in a poker game. Apparently Papa C enjoyed the comradery of the guys playing poker and occasionally drinking moonshine.

"Most of his poker and moonshine buddies were Baptist," Marguerite informed us. That was interesting as I had thought Baptist were teetotalers. "I guess you know the difference between Catholics and Baptist?" Marguerite asked in response to my observation.

"No, I don't, Miss Marguerite," I replied.

"Catholics go in the front door of a liquor store. The Baptist pick their whiskey up at the back door where no one sees them!"

"Aunt Marguerite, you've been listening to daddy's jokes again," Miriam said.

"Well, your daddy does tell some good jokes, Honey," Marguerite replied.

We walked out the front door and Marguerite turned out the lights and locked the front door. We started walking back to the house. Marguerite shared stories of Haskell that not even Kent, Joe nor Miriam had heard. But it was her story of the Great Flu Epidemic of 1918 that caught my attention. She had been visiting relatives in St. Louis, Missouri, when the flu struck Haskell. She was quarantined with her relatives for two weeks in St. Louis, at the age of seven. Many folk came down with the flu and died in Haskell. Papa C saved his family by contacting the local bootlegger and buying several bottles of his moonshine whiskey. He ladled that down the throats of his family and friends. Not a one of them died from the flu or its complications.

"Papa C swore the liquor in that moonshine helped their bodies rest and fight off the secondary opportunistic infection," Miss Marguerite said. She told us that when she was finally able to come home, she crawled up into the lap of her mother and cried her eyes out for what seemed like hours.

"I was so traumatized I might lose my mama and family. Everyone was sick and so many were dying," Miss Marguerite said, "It was frightening to a seven-year old child. Took me years to come to grips with that fear."

We then came back to the house. It was 10:30 p.m. Joe said, "Thanks for the coffee and desserts, Miss Marguerite. Please tell Miss Madeline and Miss Toni thanks also; especially for the haircut," Joe winked at Kent. "But Kent and I told Coach Hammond we would have Phillip back by 11:00 so we had better take our leave." Joe gave his winning smile, "Good to see you, Miriam."

"Good to see all three of you guys," Miriam said, looking at us and smiling at me.

"Thanks, Miss Marguerite," Kent and I joined in.

"Come again and see us, boys." Marguerite said.

"Will do, Miss Marguerite," Kent warmly responded.

Miss Marguerite and Miriam went back into the house and we three Musketeers climbed into the cab of Joe's white truck.

CHAPTER 13

ST. CYNGEN CRUSADER TO HASKELL HAYMAKER

"I never knew there was so much history here, guys," I said as we drove back to Uncle Raymond's. "It is like I had a primer for a Haskell social studies course this evening. I had read about the KKK but never met anyone who knew of Klansmen, much less someone who had run-ins with the Ku Klux Klan. It is like my history book lesson of Papa C came alive in the person of Miss Marguerite and her stories."

"Yeah, I heard a lot of stories about the Klan from my grandpa before he died," Joe added.

"Joe, I never knew things were that harsh for Catholic folk here in Haskell. Buddy, why didn't you tell me before?" Kent questioned, almost hurt.

"You never asked me, Kent. Besides, I didn't learn of this till a couple of years ago. Just didn't seem right to bring it up," Joe added, matter of factly.

Joe turned down the Concharty Hill Road to Uncle Raymond's ranch. "Guys, this has been a pretty special evening for me. I feel like I woke up this morning a St. Cyngen's Crusader and will hit the bed as a Haskell Haymaker."

Joe and Kent grinned. Kent put his arm around my shoulder and said, "Good to have you as our pal and part of the team."

"Does that make us the Three Musketeers?" Joe asked.

I laughed, "Well, I think there were actually four Musketeers if I remember correctly. More like the Three Skinny Dipping Stooges, especially after Miss Marguerite spying us out when we went swimming. Next time the shorts stay on!" Both Joe and Kent cut their eyes at each other and laughed.

We pulled into Uncle Raymond's gravel driveway. The time was 10:58. "So, when do I get to see you guys again? I am sort of bereft of wheels down here and it is a long way to ride the Paint into town to see you guys."

"Well, Coach wants us to work out with you to help get you into shape. I will be back here on Wednesday so I guess we will start training then. Make sure you have a good pair of running shoes, gym shorts and t-shirt. Coach Hammond will probably run us three to four miles and then do grass drills. So I will be here at 7:00 AM to workout with you. We will work out for an hour and half, clean up and then get to the chores at the ranch," Joe said.

"Yeah, I will join you guys and be here for you, too. Two a days in August are hell if you aren't used to the heat," Kent added.

"Thanks guys. So I will see you Wednesday morning?"

"Yeah, count us in. 7:00 a.m.! Right, Kent?" Joe asked.

"Only if I get to spend the night with you, Sinni," Kent said. His statement gave me an idea.

"Why don't you dudes spend the night with me? There is plenty of room and Aunt Louise and Uncle Raymond wouldn't mind, I bet. Besides, it would save you both an hour's sleep," I said.

"That could work. Check it out with Coach Hammond and Mrs. Hammond, though! I don't want to overstep my boundaries," Joe replied.

"Never bothered you before, Sinni," Kent teased.

"It is a long walk back home to Haskell, Kent," Joe growled. "See what I have to put up with all the way back to Haskell," Joe whined.

I hopped out of the truck cab and closed the door. Both Joe and Kent were looking at me. "I'll call you about tomorrow night. If I know Aunt Louise, she will slaughter the fattest calf to feed us." With that I said good night and watched the guys pull out and drive back down the gravel driveway, back onto the Concharty Hill Road.

I walked back to the house. I had a sudden moment of panic when I realized I did not have a key to get in the house. I tried the front door and it was unlocked. Aunt Louise had left the front porch light and hall light on for me. I immediately locked the front door as well as the back door and the door to the garage. My big city Chicago ways were pretty set in that regard. No reason to make it easy for someone to try to rob Uncle Raymond and Aunt Louise.

I went to my room and changed into some gym shorts, brushed my teeth and let my head hit the pillow. What in the sam hill was a Haymaker, I wondered. In no time I was dead asleep.

CHAPTER 14

OUTFITTING OF PHILLIP

The next day was chores as usual except Aunt Louise said she was taking me to Muskogee to go shopping at a store called "C. R. Anthony's Clothing" and to "Buck's Sporting goods" after lunch. She thought as she had prodded me into going out for football, she needed to make sure I was properly outfitted. That meant cleats, several pair of gym shorts, jerseys...the list went on. Seemed like she had been down this road before with other athletes.

I cleaned up after lunch and got ready to head to Muskogee. I asked Aunt Louise about Joe and Kent spending the night. She smiled and said, "You really get along with those two, don't you?"

"Yes, Aunt Louise, I do. Never would have dreamed I could have connected so well with those two guys. It is like I have known them all my life and yet it has been less than a week," I replied.

"Sure. Call them before we leave. Tell them to be here for dinner at 7:00. It won't be too fancy, but it will fill up the corners, as they say down here," Louise was smiling. I was later to learn her joy was in knowing many hours of intercessory prayers were unfolding before her eyes. I called Kent who told me that Joe and he would be here at 7:00 sharp for dinner.

"So, I get to see Muskogee! Yeehaw!" I shouted. "I'm proud to be an Okie from Muskogee," I crooned.

Aunt Louise laughed. "You can carry a tune. We might have to put you in the church choir but you can't sing that song."

"Well, I guess all those years of St. Cyngen's Concert Chorus with Father David Rollo taught me how to sing, sort of," I laughed.

We climbed into Aunt Louise's white Chevrolet Impala. It was really hot outside and took a while for her car the cool down. As we drove along, I asked Aunt Louise about her and Uncle Raymond. She explained that she and Uncle Raymond met in high school in Seminole, Oklahoma. Louise's father and mother moved to Seminole, Oklahoma in 1922 to work in the oil fields. Her parents split up in 1936. Her father moved to Austin, Texas, and her mother moved back to Georgia to be near family. She took Louise's two sisters, Edith and Mary, with her back to Georgia. Her oldest son Jimmy Knight still lived in Rome, Georgia. He was my grandfather and Aunt Louise's older brother by nearly 20 years. He had a daughter Mary Katherine, who was my mother. He had stayed in Georgia and never moved to Oklahoma.

Uncle Raymond and Aunt Louise married in 1935. She was 18 and he was 21. He had joined the Marines the year before as things were tough in the oil patch during the depression. They were not able to have children at first. Aunt Louise had three miscarriages before WWII. The doctors told her that they were not even sure she could get pregnant. During WWII she moved back to Rome, Georgia, to be closer to her Mother. She became very fond of my Mother and told me she was her favorite niece.

"Your Mother was always so happy and light hearted. She was more like a little sister than a niece. That is how southern families were back then and families were larger. Families of nine to ten kids were not uncommon. So often the youngest in a litter of ten were close in age to the children of the oldest sibling."

"Your Mother met your Father at Batty Hospital during the war. He was that good-looking Yankee Army doctor from Chicago, Illinois. I think your Mother captured his heart with her fine southern cooking. Of course, I taught her a trick or two on how to cook with fresh lemons squeezed over a plate of fried chicken and then save the rest of the lemons for fresh lemonade," Louise chuckled. "The way to a man's heart is through his stomach."

"In that case, Uncle Raymond has three competitors for your affection, Aunt Louise – me, Joe and Kent," I laughed. Aunt Louise smiled and continued.

"Your parents got married in 1945 and the rest is history, as they say," Aunt Louise said. "Only that fine Yankee doctor, your Father, stole your Mother away to Chicago, never to return to her Oklahoma/Georgia roots."

"Well, maybe I can make up for some lost time down south." We laughed. Aunt Louise told me about moving back to Oklahoma when Uncle Raymond was discharged from the Marine Corps at the end of WWII.

"And I turned up pregnant out of the blue and was able to carry Gerald full term. He was born in 1946 at the Hastings Indian Hospital in Tahlequah, Oklahoma, and we moved to Haskell in 1949."

We pulled up to the C. R. Anthony's Clothing Store in downtown Muskogee. Aunt Louise made sure we got several pair of athletic socks, gym shorts and t-shirts.

"We will get the rest of your gear at Buck's Sporting Goods." We headed over there next and bought the football cleats, a couple of pairs of tennis shoes, some football jerseys and specially ordered some football gear for me. I was going to be number "23" on the Haskell Haymaker Football Team.

"Aunt Louise, how am I going to pay you and Uncle Raymond back for all of this?" I asked.

"Well, in some ways you already are working on the ranch with Raymond," Aunt Louise replied. "But your Father has also made arrangements to cover extraordinary expenses for you this semester. So, you needn't worry about being
a burden to us." Aunt Louise's comment was reassuring.

"Heck, I am enjoying working on the ranch. I love working with horses, even though it is hot. I beat the heat with a swimming break every now and then."

"So I have heard," Aunt Louise said, smiling with arched eyebrows. It was readily apparent to me that there were no secrets in a small town as everyone had a habit of learning everyone else's business.

Aunt Louise added, "One of the reasons Raymond built that pond wasn't just for the cattle, but for him and Gerald! They used to go swimming up there a lot to break the heat during the day."

"Oh, I see! They went skinny dipping, too," I winked at Aunt Louise.

"Yes, but I didn't tell you that," she laughed.

We pulled into the driveway of the ranch. Uncle Raymond was working in the metal garage, repairing some equipment. Both garage doors were open and I noticed a 1966 metallic blue Malibu.

"Hey, I have never seen that before," I said.

"It was Gerald's last car before he was killed in Vietnam in 1966," Aunt Louise said quietly. It looked brand new. I got out of Aunt Louise's car with my purchases. Uncle Raymond had a big smile on his face as he was wiping his hands clean and walking over to us.

"You get everything you need, Phillip?" He asked.

"I think so, Uncle Raymond. Aunt Louise is a good outfitter," I teased.

"Well, believe me, Phillip. That was not my first rodeo outfitting a young football player," she teased back. "I am going inside to get supper ready. You boys have some things to talk over," She smiled a knowing look at Uncle Raymond. Raymond put his arm around me as I was carrying the sacks of equipment and athletic gear. I could smell the sweat of outdoor work and newly oiled machinery about him. He invited me into the garage because he wanted to have a heart to heart talk with me. We walked back into the garage.

Uncle Raymond then said, "Phillip, I've been real impressed with you these past few days. I have watched you in some fairly adverse situations and you have handled yourself real well. Most big city boys could not have handled what you have done. I am impressed with your work ethic and character. You have a winning way about you, Phillip, and you have won both Louise and me over."

That really touched me. I had sensed that but now I actually heard the words. My eyes teared up unexpectedly.

"You can't imagine how much your approval means to me, Uncle Raymond," I replied, wiping a tear from my cheek. Uncle Raymond gazed steadfastly at me and waited for me to regain my composure.

"Well, I talked to your Dad about you going out for football and he is okay with you participating if you want to play. But I talked to him about something else," Uncle Raymond had a grin on his face. I gave Uncle Raymond a puzzled look. He fished some car keys out of his pocket.

"There are the keys to Gerald's blue Malibu. Seems like a young fella like you needs transportation. Louise and I talked about it. No reason for Gerald's car just to gather dust. Besides, he would have liked you too, and wanted you to have it." Now Uncle Raymond's eyes were watering up. He paused and then added, "I discussed it with your Dad and he is supportive of this also. He was steamed up about your Avery Drive prank and initially didn't want you driving down here. But he is cooling down about that now and recognizes you need a car." I was stunned and didn't know what to say. A week ago I was a complete stranger and now I was being treated as a second son. I looked up at Uncle Raymond with tears in my eyes again and thanked him for the trust he put in me for allowing me the privilege of driving my cousin Gerald's car. I assured Uncle Raymond I would prove worthy of his trust. Uncle Raymond gave me a firm handshake and slapped me on the back.

"I know you are good for it, Phillip. You can't be a Marine Drill Sergeant and then coach young men for twenty plus years and not know a diamond in the rough when you see it." He tousled the blond hair on my head.

"Okay, Chief, go put your stuff up and help Louise fix supper for you and your buddies. Tell Louise I will be in after I finish working on the equipment here." He winked at me and returned to his repair work. I turned to leave and headed back to the house. Uncle Raymond silently watched me go, praying to God a prayer of thanks for sending me to him and Louise.

CHAPTER 15

WORKOUT WITH THE GUYS

I put my stuff away in my room and then went back into the kitchen to see what help Aunt Louise might need. It was 6:00 PM and she was a scene of frenetic energy. I had never dreamed you could cut up a head of lettuce and carrots as fast as she did. She had me chopping up an onion and putting the diced onion bits into a frying pan of olive oil. Next she had me snap a large bowl of green beans. She diced three ripe tomatoes into small pieces and then combined the green beans, fried onions and diced tomatoes to all cook together. She added tomato paste, a dash of salt, mashed garlic, chives and cinnamon. I had never seen that done before, but it smelled delicious.

"It is an old recipe of Miss Marguerite. Your Uncle Raymond really likes this dish." So did I. Next she sat another pan on the stove with olive oil and began frying up some "chicken fried steak." An alarm sounded and she pulled out some freshly baked biscuits from the oven. What couldn't that lady cook? The dinner she had prepared may not be fancy but it "ate real well" as Joe would say. About that time the doorbell rang. It was Joe and Kent about ten minutes early.

We put their stuff in my room. There were two beds in there. I was going to give them my beds and sleep on the floor in a sleeping bag I had found in my closet. We went back to the kitchen.

"Boy, something smells real right," Kent said. Joe just smiled as Aunt Louise told us boys to sit down. Uncle Raymond came in and it was apparent he had washed up at the barn. "Hey guys."

"Good evening, Coach Hammond," the guys said.

"Well, I see Louise has fixed something tasty again," Uncle Raymond beamed.

"For sure," we all three agreed in unison. It was a fine dinner with lively conversation by all five participants. It was apparent that Aunt Louise and Uncle Raymond really enjoyed our company and repartee as much as we enjoyed their food! Of course at some point the jock talk began and my schooling began in earnest about football. Aunt Louise kicked us out of the kitchen to the den so she could clean up the kitchen. I learned things that evening in the den I had never even heard of. We stayed up till nearly 11:00 talking positions and football strategy.

"Guys, time to turn in! We will hit the trails at 6:30 A.M. I intend to run you boys three miles. I will be leading you guys. We will do grass drills for thirty minutes and then come back to the ranch to clean up."

"Will do, Coach," Joe said.

Aunt Louise had already cleaned up the kitchen and gone to bed. We guys turned in, too, after the evening ritual of brushing our teeth. I gave Joe and Kent the beds despite their protests. We three continued to talk till nearly midnight.

I shared with Kent and Joe what Uncle Raymond and Aunt Louise had done with the football gear and the car. Kent whistled and then said, "Dude, they must really trust you to let you drive the Blue Malibu."

"Yeah. Coach has never let anyone drive that car. He only takes it out every once in a while to keep it running," Joe added.

The guys then started talking about their goals for playing ball in college. Kent started talking first. "I really want to play football at a small NAIA college. I have been thinking about John Brown University in Siloam Springs, Arkansas. It is a small private non-denominational Christian college. It has a great pre-law program I have been thinking about."

"Really, Kent? You want to be a lawyer? " I then added, chuckling, "You could talk the devil out of his due, that is for sure."

"More like the hind leg off a mule," Joe teased.

Kent threw a pillow at Joe and Joe threw it back. "What about you, Joe?" I asked.

"Lots of my folk want to see me go to the University of Notre Dame, a Catholic school and play ball. But it is too far north and too durn cold. I want to go into business and work in my dad's store. I am thinking about going with Kent to John Brown University, too," Joe added.

"Yeah, playing at OU or OSU would be nice. But you wouldn't get much playing time. If I am going to bust my tail in college working out for football, I want to play," Kent added.

"Why not consider a Baptist college, Kent?"

"I love my church but I have some heartburn about going to a Baptist university. They tend to think only Baptists are going to heaven. This past summer at Falls Creek Baptist Church Camp, I had one deacon tell me Catholics were all going to hell. Well, I know that is not true. My best friend Joe Corsinni is saved. I have sat through many Fellowship of Christian Athletes huddles and prayer groups with Joe. I know in my heart of hearts he is saved." Kent got quiet.

"Yeah, lots of Catholics think only they are going to be in heaven," Joe added.

"Then why go to a religious college at all?" I asked.

"Too much dope, beer and wild partying at the State schools. Coach has leaned on us pretty hard about avoiding that. 'Find a college that suits your athletic goals and education plans and stay away from wine, wild women and song, if you want to be a good athlete!' Coach told us. How often has he mentioned that to us, Joe?" Kent asked.

Joe chuckled, "Yeah. He's pretty big on finding the right fit for your life's goals and hanging out with kids that complement that!"

"What about you, Phillip?" Kent asked.

"Well, I was planning on swimming either at an Ivy League School, Indiana University, or UCLA."

"Wow!" Kent said.

"What do you want to study?"

"Well. After my misadventure on Avery Drive, my Dad told me I either need to make a lot of money to pay for my legal fees or plan on going to law school."

We all laughed. We were all winding down and agreed to call it quits on conversation. Joe rolled over and was out like a light. Kent and I talked for a little bit longer and then agreed to go to sleep.

I heard Joe snoring. I had taken the precaution of bringing some cotton balls to put in my ears so I could sleep in the event one of these two snored. I put the cotton in my ears; however, it was going to be a long night for Kent.

"Dang, I forgot he sometimes snores like a hailstorm." Kent muttered. For a shy reserved guy, Joe made a lot of noise at night. Even with cotton balls in my ears, I could hear Kent tossing and turning. I chuckled to myself, but finally fell asleep around 12:30.

The next morning Uncle Raymond rousted us out at 6:00 A.M. and gave us thirty minutes to get ready. He was wearing running shorts, a t-shirt and cap. We three wearily dragged ourselves out of bed.

"Sinni, you sounded like a sonata in f-flat," Kent said. Joe yawned and just smiled. I was pulling cotton out of my ears.

"Next time bring some for me, Phillip. Dang, Joe, you were sawing logs all night and I hardly slept till three."

"Well, Phillip, just be grateful Kent was not farting after dinner last night. One time at an FCA weekend,

Kent was passing gas continuously all night in the dorm room. He was bunking next to some players from Muskogee and had his backside facing them. All the guys were laughing their butts off and burying their faces in the pillows. Finally at 2:00 a.m., Calvin Miller, a big black Muskogee football player on the bunk next to Kent, said, in a booming voice that woke us all up, 'Dude, either go outside or point that cannon the other way'."

Sinni and I laughed. Kent gave a mocking grin. "Dude, I had a bug that weekend. It wasn't pretty," Kent said.

"Didn't smell pretty either," Joe teased. We laughed as we began getting ready. We all three got dressed for running and joined Uncle Raymond on the back porch. He made us stretch out prior to running. We were soon running after Uncle Raymond, following the cattle trails looping around the lower pasture and then running up to the middle pasture. We ran up to the upper pasture and looped around the edges. It was breezy but not quite yet warm but humid. I could feel sweat pouring down the side of my face. My calves were starting to ache. Uncle Raymond called those shin splints and we were only halfway through our run. Uncle Raymond shouted encouragement to us. He didn't seem to be breaking a sweat. I was to later learn that he had run in many marathons and still ran several miles a week. My sides were now starting to ache.

Both Joe and Kent were sweating profusely. But they showed no signs of pain on their face. Uncle Raymond later told me the secret was to concentrate one-step at a time and not the overall run. It required great discipline to do this and push through the pain threshold.

"No pain, no gain," Uncle Raymond reminded me. Finally we finished our three-mile run and began the grass drills in the upper pasture. He let us take a bit of a break and catch our breath. Uncle Raymond then made a point of teaching us some Marine survival skills and fighting techniques during these workouts after the grass drills. It became part of our workout regimen with him the rest of the summer. He felt that part of his duty was to equip us not only to be well-trained athletes, but also good fighters.

"It never hurts to know some good defensive moves in the event you find yourself where you don't want to be," Uncle Raymond said. We spent upwards of an hour rehearsing some of his Marine fighting techniques. We often had to practice these moves with him and each other. Often this wore me out more than the running did! After we practiced such fighting and defensive moves, it was back to running again!

I thought I was going to die. No swim workout seemed this hard and even voiced this to Uncle Raymond. He said that it was hard for me because my muscles were not conditioned for this workout regimen.

"Joe and Kent would drown if you put them through the workout you swim in a pool."

We exercised for nearly two hours and were soaking wet. All three of us were panting. Uncle Raymond ran us back down to the house. Aunt Louise had breakfast ready for us on the back porch. She had apples and peaches cut up, slices of buttered toast and blackberry jam, scrambled eggs, fried potatoes, chilled water, and a fresh pot of coffee. Although we were exhausted, we were not too tired to eat! There was hardly anything left over when we were done.

Kent took his leave as he had errands to do for his mom. Joe and I cleaned up so that we could be about our ranch chores for the day. Uncle Raymond had me take two Bufferin, but I was still sore the rest of the day. My body aches and pain were compounded by the heartache that hit me this day. I got a letter from Ann Burns basically saying she was glad I was adjusting to

Haskell, but after talking to her parents about me was told they thought it best if we did not communicate any more. Hence, this was going to be her only and last letter. Ouch! One of my links to Chicago had just been severed. However, it was her parents' rejection of me that reinforced my sense of shame at my leaving St. Cyngen. In my mind what a disappointment and failure I must be to everyone back in Chicago! Nevertheless, I dealt with this pain by pushing myself athletically in Uncle Raymond's workouts. The workout regimen with Uncle Raymond gave me something to pour myself into and helped take my mind off my "Dear John" letter and my perceived rejection. Joe, Kent, Uncle Raymond and I would do this three days a week the rest of July. When the two-a-day workouts started in early August, we would stop the early morning routine of running and grass drills with Uncle Raymond.

Uncle Raymond knew this workout routine would strengthen me and prepare me for two a day workouts in August. It also drew Kent, Joe and me into a closer bond. As the three of us bonded as athletes, my homesickness for Chicago faded. It was not uncommon for Joe or Kent or both to spend one or two nights a week at Uncle Raymond and Aunt Louise's house whether working out, working the ranch or going to church. It also allowed me to truly get to know these two guys. Kent and I were a lot alike and both wanted to become lawyers. But Kent had a more winsome personality that bordered being the class clown at times. He loved an audience and was always entertaining to be around. He was the sort of guy that was everyone's friend. Joe was the antithesis of Kent. He did not make friends easily nor did he give his friendship away readily. But I was drawn to Joe as a friend, not so much by what he said but for who he was. I enjoyed working with him and working out with him, too. We were opposites that complimented one another in our strengths and weaknesses. Moreover, I sensed that Joe enjoyed spending time with me, whether working or playing.

I called Dad a couple of times and kept him informed about my adjustment down at the ranch and my progress in football workouts. I told him that despite the heat, I was really starting to like it down here. I still felt that a big city fish in a rural Oklahoman pond at times. Dad laughed at my illustration. He caught me up on Frank, John, and Suzannah. Frank was still working for Uncle Ed; John was thinking of med school in Mexico; and Suzannah decided hoeing potatoes and growing corn on a hippie commune in New Mexico was not all that it was cracked up to be. She and Jacob had broken up and she had decided to work in Aspen, Colorado, to "clear her head."

"Well, as long as that does not cost me too much," Dad grumbled. I could only guess what her new road in life had already cost my Dad. She was always leaning on Dad to bail her out of her latest misadventure. But as she was the only girl, Dad was far more indulgent of her misdirected forays in life. Besides he was grateful she and Jacob Lawrence were no longer a couple. But Dad seemed pleased with my progress and was actually somewhat forgiving of my Avery Drive "faux pas" in that he could sort of laugh about it now.

"The driver of the car was a real jerk," Dad said. "He threatened to sue me for emotional distress." Dad deep sixed that by nailing the guy with questions about any psychiatric care he was receiving as a result of the accident and what medications he was now having to take. The man said none and Dad informed him that there was no money down that legal rabbit trail. Apparently, the man did not know who he was talking to and challenged Dad on this.

"Oh, yeah?" the guy asked. "What makes you so smart?"

"Because I am a psychiatrist and you have just admitted that nearly four months after the Avery Drive prank, you are neither seeing a psychiatrist nor on medication for the trauma of the incident. That won't play well in court before a jury. Besides, we have already paid for the damage to your car. You pursue this any further, we will go after you for fraudulent unfounded allegations in court," Dad responded. With that the man never called Dad again. He could focus on other issues besetting our family and I could prepare for the "dreaded" two a day workouts in the August heat of Oklahoma.

When the two a days started in August under Coach Elliott, I sincerely wondered if I had lost my mind. What was the joy of all this heat prostration and pain for a game where you clobbered the other guy? At least in swimming you stayed cool and were intent on beating your time not another player. Nevertheless, I felt like I had something to prove to myself and I enjoyed the time with Kent and Joe. These guys were becoming my anchors in Haskell. Uncle Raymond assured me the two a days would soon pass and that I would get tougher with each practice. "The pain is still there, Phillip, but you learn to press through it and endure it and overcome it." Kent and Joe handled the heat and pain far better than I did. At times you could tell Kent was hurting because his facial expression would wince in pain from time to time. Joe, however, was an iceman. If he was hurting, you would never know it.

The time the three of us spent together working out drew us together like family. It is hard to describe how you feel about other guys when you are working out together as a team for a common goal. But Uncle Raymond summed it up best, "If you truly want to get to know a fellow, go sweat with him! The real man comes out!" It was obvious that the three of us got to know each other's true personas and, more importantly, that we liked each other. Even now when I think back to that time, it is some of my most treasured memories as a young man.

The football squad itself was interesting. It was composed of young men from all races and socioeconomic backgrounds. That was a first for me to be rubbing shoulders like this with Black, Indian and Mexican kids, many from working class backgrounds. It was certainly different from my lily-white upper middle class experiences at St. Cyngen's Academy.

Thank God, two-a-days only lasted three weeks and then school started. Most of the guys on the football team readily accepted me because Kent and Joe (being the captains of the team) had pulled me into their circle of friendship. But I still sensed my status was that of an outsider, especially with the Black and Indian kids. Thus, my first day of school was like entering an unknown territory. It was strange not being in school with the same kids I had been with since kindergarten; and kids I had almost nothing in common socially, economically, or racially. Time would tell whether I would fit in at Haskell High School.

PART II

HASKELL HIGH SCHOOL

CHAPTER 1

AUNT LOUISE ONE-UPPED BY UNCLE RAYMOND

It was less than five days to school starting on August 22. Aunt Louise eyed me over carefully one evening with the clothes I had brought down with me from Chicago. She had a discerning and exacting eye for how well clothes would fit a man and she said, "Well it is plain as the nose on my face you have grown and gained weight these past seven weeks. Your pants look like they are a half inch too short and I have noticed you complaining about your slacks being a little tight." Aunt Louise had me try on all my clothes and model them for her. It was true. I had gotten bigger in the waist and in the chest. Furthermore, I could tell my legs were bigger, too. The proof was on the weight scales. I had gained twelve pounds in seven weeks.

"Well, with the way you have been feeding that boy, it is a wonder he is not trying out for a lineman at the University of Oklahoma," Uncle Raymond teased.

Aunt Louise whirled around and arched an eyebrow at Uncle Raymond and said, "One more comment like that Raymond Gerald Hammond and I will send you to your room for the evening." Uncle Raymond cocked an eyebrow and smiled. Aunt Louise tried to keep a stern countenance and then she broke out laughing, "I can't help it. I enjoy cooking and he likes what I fix!"

Well, with a cook and conversationalist like Aunt Louise, it was a pleasure to chow down on her food. That was for darn sure. It was easy to eat her cooking constantly! Hence, my weight gain in spite of football workouts.

"Tomorrow we are going back to C. R. Anthony's to hit their back to school sale. No nephew of mine is going to school looking like Tom Joad from the 'Grapes of Wrath'."

It was a bit of a stretch. My clothes weren't threadbare or even worn out. They were now too short in the inseam, too tight in the waist, and getting snug in the chest.

Uncle Raymond leaned against the counter, looking bemused at the spectacle – me modeling and Aunt Louise critiquing. He snickered and said, "Two a days with Coach Elliot will be easier than an evening of shopping for clothes with Louise Hammond."

Aunt Louise narrowed her eyes and pronounced with authority, "You spend time with Phillip, working the ranch and working out. I have no complaints about that. I figure that is your realm to show Phillip how to assume a man's place in the world. But," she held her finger up like she was lecturing a schoolboy, "my job is to make sure Phillip is well fed and well dressed. That is my area of expertise, Coach Hammond."

"Well, you sure are succeeding in the feeding part," Uncle Raymond teased. Aunt Louise poked Uncle Raymond in the chest to drive home a point.

"Raymond, don't mess with me," Aunt Louise replied. Uncle Raymond giggled like a child being tickled and drew up into himself. Then he agilely sprang on Aunt Louise, pulling a Marine survival trick and had her in a wrestling hold he had taught Kent, Joe and me during the grass drills.

"RAYMOND," Aunt Louise shrieked, laughing. He kissed her on the cheek and muttered something in her ear that made her blush crimson. Those two acted more like two 17-year-old lovebirds than a couple that had been married for 36 plus years. He let her go, laughing, winked at her, and slapped her on the rear.

Uncle Raymond went down the hall to his bedroom with a jaunty strut, "Don't stay up much longer, Louise, and keep me waiting. It is already 10:00 p.m."

With that I knew that my clothing and accessory show for Aunt Louise would be over shortly.

"Tomorrow at 3:00 p.m., we were going to Muskogee to buy some school clothes," Aunt Louise said. I thanked her for her time and she excused herself and went back to the bedroom where I heard muffled laughter. I went to my room to hit the hay as I was tired from two-a-days. I could only hope to someday find a gal as good and fun as Aunt Louise.

CHAPTER 2

FIRST DAY OF SCHOOL

Aunt Louise outfitted me very well. My waist had grown from a 30-inch waist to a 32-inch waist and my chest grew from 40 to 42 inches. My sleeve length was now 35 inches and my neck had grown from 16 to 16-1/2 inches and I now weighed 185 pounds. Accordingly, she bought me five pairs of jeans, three pairs of dress khaki slacks, a navy blue blazer, seven long sleeve oxford shirts and several Polo shirts.

She pronounced that should get me through this semester. However, I still had to figure out what to wear my first day of school. Kent and Joe said blue jeans and a short sleeve shirt would be okay.

But I wanted to make the proper impression. Prep was out for Haskell! But I didn't want to dress down, such that I looked out of place. At St. Cyngens it was a uniform-khaki slacks, white oxford button down, red school tie and navy blue blazer. Every day! Here, the sky was the limit. I chose jeans, a Polo shirt, and cowboy boots. Melding my Chicago background with my new found Haskell roots. Chicago boy goes Country!

Aunt Louise said I looked fine as I went to the garage to drive the blue Malibu to school for the first time. School started at 8:10, but Kent and Joe told me to be there at 7:50 to get settled in. They would meet me in the south parking lot.

When I got to the parking lot, Joe was getting out of his white truck. I saw Miriam leave the south porch of the Fugali home and start walking the two blocks towards the school. Kent had not arrived yet.

"Hey," Joe said.

"Good morning, Joe," I responded. "Fine morning for the first day of school. Where's Kent?"

"He's running late because he had to take his little brother and sister to school," Joe said. "But let's head on in anyway. He'll be here soon enough."

The school building itself was an old two-story schoolhouse built a couple of years after statehood. It was a red brick building that Kent had called "Cherokee Gothic." It was a neat looking old building surrounded by ancient trees but it was obvious the school had surely seen better days.

The ceilings were nine feet high and most classroom doors had a frosted glass window above them that a teacher could open to allow for air circulation. The classrooms had the high ceilings and ceiling fans. This was the only air conditioning for the school. Joe and Kent had warned me that the first month and a half of school was not pleasant after lunch.

"Always wear jeans and short sleeved shirts," Kent said. This was especially true if you had a class on the south and/or west side of the building after lunch. The hallways were packed with students, grades 9 through 12. A lot of curious stares were directed my way.

I halfway expected to find an emblem in the floor of a muscular bare-chested young farmer with a scythe cutting through the hay with the motto "Home of the Haskell Haymakers" below it. That is what a Haskell Haymaker was, I thought. However, I was told the name of the Haymakers was really for a punch "The Haymaker."

Joe and I walked to our first class. I saw faces of all colors. That was certainly a new experience. Apparently, the upper classmen get classes on the first floor. The lower classes were on the second floor, which made things very unpleasant particularly as the day wore on. We walked into the homeroom class. It was Miss Belle Dressbach's Modern English class. Joe had cautioned me that Miss Dressbach did not suffer arrogant mouthy young fools. A fact Kent attested to by more than one trip from Miss Dressbach's English class during his Sophomore year to the Principal's office for cutting up too much. Kent came in and sauntered over to where we were sitting.

Miriam came in with a couple of girlfriends. Another girl came into class, following them in. She was a very pretty black girl with light colored skin, straight black hair, fine features like Miriam, and she had light hazel eyes. She saw Miriam and they said hi to each other. But for the skin tone and eye color, I noticed she and Miriam bore a resemblance to one another. But it was her acknowledgement of Joe I found interesting. She held his gaze and they both nodded to one another. Her face broke out into a warm smile and the normally stoic Joe was smiling back at her as she took her seat.

I interrupted Joe's non-verbal repartee with this girl by asking him, "Who's that?"

Joe immediately turned to me and replied, "Sheree Brandt." Before I could inquire further, Miss Dressbach had begun shuffling papers and Joe had warned me that was her way of getting ready to start the class before the bell.

Joe, Kent and I sat next to each other and Miriam sat in the row next to us. She looked beautiful as ever and smiled at me with those emerald green eyes. "Woof!" I thought. My reverie was jolted by the 8:10 a.m. school bell and Miss Dressbach stood up and introduced herself and the Senior English class to us. She took attendance and when she came to my name, she paused. "You're new around here," she stated.

"Yes, Miss Dressbach, I am," I replied.

"Where are you from," she asked, looking at her roll, and then added, "Phillip."

"I am from the Chicago area," I replied.

"Well, I am sure there is a story behind that that we will talk about another time." She continued taking roll. She then handed out the reading syllabus for the semester. Most of the books were ones I had read my freshman and sophomore years at St. Cyngen. I noticed one of the selections was the *Spoon River Anthology* by Edgar Lee Masters. This was one of my favorites. In addition, she included the novel *Rebecca* by Daphne DeMaurier for Modern English Gothic. I heard several students groan at the amount of books we had to read. I thought to myself that this was nothing compared to the reading lists required at my former school.

Miss Dressbach outlined her goals for the semester to us with regard to the reading list, English papers we were expected to write, and expressing ourselves on paper. I have to say that Miss Dressbach made a favorable impression upon me. She was a no nonsense individual who was obviously dedicated to teaching. She was originally from Louisiana, I learned, and could only guess how she ended up in Haskell. She had been gone all summer visiting family back there so she obviously had not been told about me.

The 9:30 bell rang and it was off to the next class. Miss Dressbach caught me as I was getting ready to exit with Joe and Kent.

"Phillip," she said. "Welcome to Haskell High School. I know being new your senior year can be a challenge. If you need any help academically, Mr. John Butts, the Academic Advisor, can line up tutors to help you."

"Thank you, Miss Dressbach," I replied, thinking to myself that she was in for a surprise. Martha Cole, my Honors English teacher back at St. Cyngen, had prepared me well and I recognized this would be a repeat of much of her course work from two years ago.

As we walked into the hallway, Kent nervously nudged me and said, "Oh, boy, Phillip. You are on her radar charts now! You had better perform as well in there as you have been for Coach Elliot on the football field."

"Thanks for the heads up, Kent. I will try my best," I said.

We walked to our next class, Algebra 2, which was just down the hall. The teacher was a man named Mr. Dobe L. Bower. Kent said he was a really tough teacher. He handed out the Algebra 2 books. It was a similar textbook I had had my Sophomore year. Inwardly, I was smiling. The same pattern was repeated throughout the day. I realized just how advanced St. Cyngen's Preparatory Academy actually had been. This semester was going to be a refresher course of my freshman and sophomore years.

CHAPTER 3

MAKING THE TEAM

Sixth hour rolled around and it was off to the field house locker room to suit up for football workout. Mercifully, we only had to practice for three hours, from 2:30 to 5:30, and then clean up. This beat working out six hours a day for two a day. Coach Steve Elliot had been hired as Uncle Raymond's replacement and had been a good choice. A product of Eufaula, Oklahoma, from an old ranching family, he had played football and baseball at Northeastern State University. He had been coaching at Weleetka and Uncle Raymond recruited him as his replacement. He had known the Elliot family from his ranching business and had followed Coach Elliot's high school and college athletic career. That, however, did not translate to making things easy for me. If anything, Coach Elliot seemed to be harder on me. Joe and Kent paved the way with the other football players and we got along okay. But to Coach Elliot, I was an unproven quantity that had yet to earn his respect. I would have to prove myself on the field of "combat" with Coach Steve Elliot. What I didn't realize was that Coach Elliot already knew I was "road worthy," but the politics of this big city interloper displacing a homeboy who had played since he was seven made things difficult and unpleasant. The guy I was up against was five feet, ten inches, weighed 230 pounds; and was not as quick on his feet as me and lacked stamina.

I was a good three inches taller, and faster on my feet and had better endurance. Uncle Raymond's workout regimen helped with the speed and endurance. Coach Elliot had a tough call to make and it wouldn't be easy either way he went. Moreover,

Uncle Raymond unbeknown to me told Coach Elliot not to cut me any slack because I was Uncle Raymond's nephew. So the academic aspect of Haskell High School looked like a cakewalk compared to going out for the football team.

Our first football game was going to be this Friday night against Checotah High School at Checotah. Coach Elliot was going to announce the first string players and backups after workout in the locker room. We assembled in the locker room exhausted, hot and sweaty. Joe was selected as quarterback. No surprise there. Kent was chosen as a wide receiver. He was quick on his feet and had good hands that rarely lost a ball. Coach read off all the positions and then came to defensive end last. I was anxious to know what Coach Elliot would say.

"Defensive end, Phillip Robertson, backup David DeShane. That was the hardest choice I had to make."

Kent and Joe came over and slapped me on the shoulder. The only consolation I felt was that David DeShane was a junior and would be able to have the position after I left in the spring semester. But what a relief after all that work. Coach Elliot let the team elect their captains and Kent and Joe were chosen as co-captains again.   Coach Elliot then dismissed us to shower and clean up.

·

CHAPTER 4

ASKING JOE FOR A FAVOR

As I was showering, Kent was in the other shower stall.

"Phillip, you and Sinni and I need to celebrate tonight."

"What do you have in mind?" I asked.

"Baklava, mamoul and coffee," Joe grinned from the other shower as he soaped up.

"And a raven haired green eyed beauty," I smiled.

"I ain't going if Miss Madeline is there. That old broad nearly knocked a rib loose the last time we were there when she slapped me on the back," Kent protested.

"Remember what Miss Madeline called you – Wuss," Joe teased.

"Sinni, you have Madeline Fugali slap the Baklava out of you sometime and tell me what you think of your Godmother's sister then!" Kent growled.

"She's in Oklahoma City working at the Daily Oklahoman, Kent. So you are coming," Joe firmly said. Joe rarely made pronouncements like that to Kent, but when he did, Kent complied. The thought of going to the Fugali house was appealing to me not because of the Baklava or Mamoul but Miriam. I didn't get the chance to talk to her all day and wanted to see her.

"Great idea, Joe," I said and stepped out of the shower to towel dry off.

We got dressed and discussed a rendezvous time as we walked from the locker room to our vehicles in the parking lot.

"Hey, guys, it is nearly 6:00 now. So let me pick you up in the blue Malibu at 8:00 at Kent's house." Joe and Kent agreed.

"Only thing is though, guys, we can't just show up at the Fugalis uninvited," I said.

"Leave that to me," Joe added as we walked to our cars. What I failed to realize was how close the Fugalis and Corsinnis still were to this day. One phone call from her Godson Joe Corsinni meant an invitation for baklava, mamoul and coffee to whoever Joe wanted to bring.

Joe genuinely liked his Godmother Marguerite Fugali and she returned his affection. They were actually pretty close and she was one of Joe's few confidants. Kent got in his car and said he would see us at 8:00 p.m. Joe and I watched him pull out of the parking lot. I then asked Joe if I could ask him a personal question. "Sure," Joe said.

"Do you like Miriam Abboud as a girlfriend to date?" I asked.

"Nah," Joe replied. "Be like dating my sister. I like Miriam as a friend only. Our families are close and Miss Marguerite is like family to me. But why you ask, big city Chicago boy has a crush on a small town Oklahoma girl?" Joe teased as he flashed me that "Ultra Brite" grin. His blunt candor had me slightly uncomfortable as I shuffled on my feet, not knowing quite what to say.

"Not a crush, but let's just say I am interested to get to know her better and see her more," I added.

"Fluff it up anyway you like, Phillip. I call it a crush," Joe laughed as he slapped me on the shoulder. I was later to learn that Joe and Miriam really were good friends like a brother and sister. Joe kept secrets very well and didn't reveal to me till years later that Miriam had frequently inquired about me. I never learned what he told her about me though.

But that was Joe - stoic and true blue when it came to guarding another man's secrets. That was his character always all his life.

I cut my eyes at Joe with a slight smile and he returned my gaze with a knowing grin. It was the sort of look that only a true friend who had been through a lot and knew you really well could give you. I shook my head. "You know, Joe, we have only known each other for two months, but is as if I have known you all my life."

"My thoughts exactly, Phillip. I'll see you around 8:00 to pick me up," Joe said and began walking off to his truck. I stood there thinking for a minute about Miriam as Joe got into his truck.

I then did something totally unexpected by running after Joe and asking, "So, you will put in a good word for me to Miriam?" I had just put all my cards on the table as Joe got in his truck.

He rolled the window down and shook his head with a grin, locking his steel blue eyes on me, "Thing is, Phillip, I already have. Ever since that first day we worked together. I could tell you were what my grandpa called 'good people'. So, yeah, I have given you a good character reference to Miriam!" Joe paused to let this sink in and then added, "and to Miss Marguerite! and to Miss Toni!" Joe winked at me and said, "See ya at 8:00."

I got into the blue Malibu and drove back home to Uncle Raymond and Aunt Louise's house for dinner, smiling to myself all the way about Joe's revelation.

CHAPTER 5

DEBRIEFING WITH AUNT LOUISE AND UNCLE RAYMOND

When I got back to the ranch, Aunt Louise and Uncle Raymond were like two little kids waiting for their parents' go ahead to open Christmas presents. Throughout dinner they peppered me with questions and they got a thorough debriefing from meeting Joe in the parking lot at 7:50 a.m., to talking about Miriam in the parking lot at the end of the day.

"Well, congratulations, Phillip, on making first string. Coach Elliot is not an easy sell, so you really earned that position of defensive end," Uncle Raymond said.

"Thanks, Uncle Raymond," I said. "So is it okay if I go over to the Fugalis with Kent and Joe at 8:00 tonight to celebrate?" I asked.

Uncle Raymond arched an eyebrow and gave a certain look to Louise as he sipped on his coffee with a slight smile, pursing his lips. He then said, "You going to celebrate or see someone?" I flushed red.

"Raymond," Aunt Louise's expression said it all. Her eyes were as big as silver dollars.

I took the bull by the horns by saying, "You two know me about as well as anyone. So yeah, I want to see Miriam," and then as a weak afterthought I added, "and hang out with Kent and Joe."

Uncle Raymond spit his coffee back into his cup, laughing. "I believed you on the Miriam part. Not so sure about the Kent and Joe part."

Aunt Louise was mildly exasperated at this point. She gave a slight glower at Uncle Raymond and said, "We violating some boundaries here, Raymond? Crossing the DMZ into someone's personal space without invitation to be there, as you are apt to say."

"No, Aunt Louise, really it is okay," I came to Uncle Raymond's defense. "If anyone has a right to know what I am up to and who I like, it is you both. You are the closest thing I have ever had to a real aunt and uncle. Besides, I really don't mind. Sort of welcome your wise counsel and insights," I said.

I turned to Uncle Raymond who arched an eyebrow, smiling at me as I said, "But, yeah, Uncle Raymond, I like Miriam. She has really been nice to me and as my brother John says, 'she is easy on the eyes,' but we are just friends."

That seemed to assuage Aunt Louise somewhat but I sensed a frank discussion between these two after I left. Uncle Raymond said, "If you are with Kent and Joe going to the Fugalis, be back by 10:30. It is a school night. That okay with you, Louise?" Uncle Raymond asked.

"Yes," Aunt Louise said, locking her gaze into Uncle Raymond.

"Thanks," I said and began helping to clear the dishes and clean the kitchen.

At about 7:45, I took my leave of Uncle Raymond and Aunt Louise. Uncle Raymond winked at me and told me to have a good time. I then headed into town to pick up Kent and Joe at Dr. James' house.

Uncle Raymond and Aunt Louise sat at the dining room table, sipping their coffee.

"Well, he had a good day, Raymond," Aunt Louise said.

"In more ways than one," Uncle Raymond mused. "Phillip has good tastes. Miriam is a fine girl. Nothing like a fine looking young woman to enhance a young man's view of life."

"Raymond Gerald Hammond, what am I going to do with you!" Aunt Louise said mildly exasperated.

"Love me?" Uncle Raymond grinned.

"Semper Fi, Sergeant Hammond!" Aunt Louise replied, laughing.

CHAPTER 6

COFFEE AND MAMOUL WITH ABBOT DELAURIER

I picked the guys up at 8:00 sharp. Joe had called Marguerite Fugali and she was expecting us. It seems she already had a guest there and we were just some more mouths to feed her baklava and coffee.

We rang the doorbell and Miriam answered the door. She looked great. She was wearing a pair of shorts, polo shirt and sandals. She looked and smelled wonderful.

"Come on in guys. Aunt Marguerite has a guest here tonight. Abbot Delaurier is here from the Concharty Hills Monastery," Miriam added as she walked us into the dining room.

Around the table sat Miss Toni, Miss Marguerite, Stanley Abboud, and Abbot Delaurier.

"Have a seat boys," Miss Toni said. "Fetch some more mamoul and baklava, Miriam." Miriam excused herself and went into the kitchen to retrieve some more treats.

Miss Toni introduced the Abbot to everyone and asked us to sit down at the dining room table.

"Bon Soir, Phillip," the Abbot said.

"Bon Soir, Abbot Delaurier," I replied. He then asked me how I was adjusting to my new home in Haskell in French. I answered as best as I could in my halting French.

"Perhaps we should speak in English," the Abbot smiled. I agreed.

"Dang, Phillip, I didn't know you spoke Frog," Kent said.

The Abbot looked at Kent and raised both eyebrows. Miss Marguerite frowned and then corrected him by saying, "Mr. Kent James, the language is French not Frog. That is a very demeaning thing to say in the presence of a person of French ancestry. I expect more polite conversations out of you at my dinner table."

She gave him a stern look and he melted under her withering stare. You could tell he meant no offense by his statement.

Miss Marguerite then softened by saying, "Have some mamoul, kid. It will sweeten your disposition and, hopefully, improve your manners." Miss Marguerite would stand her ground to get her point across, but would always give you grace if you were repentant.

Kent took the offer of mamoul sheepishly and said, "sorry," with a mouthful of mamoul.

"Kid, as much baklava and mamoul I have fed you, I expect a lot out of you. Lots of people look up to you as a leader so I need to get my licks in now to bring out the best in you. So don't take an old maid's scolding too personal. Just think of me as your etiquette coach," she chuckled.

Joe and I could only smile. I was about to bust a gut and I could tell Joe was bemused also at Kent's faux pas. But we held our tongue although our body language betrayed us. Kent took Miss Marguerite's correction to heart and even thanked her for her constructive criticism.

"Your mamma has raised you right, that is for sure," Miss Marguerite added.

Miss Marguerite then turned her attention to her Godson Joe Corsinni. Miss Marguerite always enjoyed Joe's company and she was one of the few people who could make Joe open up. Miriam joined in the conversation with them. Kent began talking to Stanley Abboud and Miss Toni. As Abbot Delaurier was sitting next to me, he then inquired about my foray into the American sport of football.

"Well. It is hard and hot. It is a lot different from swimming that's for sure."

"I played European football, what you call soccer," the Abbot replied.

"Really? I was a sweeper in Junior High for my school soccer team at St. Cyngen's Academy." We then discussed the relative differences between American soccer and European football. He then explained he was the captain of his soccer team at his college until the outbreak of World War II.

"What happened, Abbot Delaurier?" I asked.

"I was 24 years old when the Germans invaded Poland. The French army was mobilized for war. I, like the rest of my soccer team, volunteered as did many able bodied young French men. We were so full of confidence in ourselves and the Mighty Maginot line. We placed our faith in man and his devices," the Abbot paused and then continued, "But our confidence and faith were misplaced. Many of my classmates were killed, wounded, or taken prisoners. It was a very bitter time. You cannot imagine how humiliating it was as a Frenchman to see a Nazi swastika fluttering from the Champ d' Eylees and German troops marching through Paris," the Abbot became very quiet and somber.

"Were you also wounded or taken prisoner, Abbot Delaurier?" I asked.

"No. Physically I was uninjured. Only my French pride was wounded. But I allowed my bitterness to take me prisoner and it made for a dark journey of the soul. I joined the Resistance and embraced Marxist ideology," he replied.

"A Catholic Abbot is a far cry from a Marxist revolutionary," I said.

"Indeed it is," the Abbot answered.

"Then how did you transform from a Marxist to a Catholic?" I asked.

"Well, I came from a devout Catholic family in Southern France. I attended the Ecole to study for law. Political Philosophy was a large part of the course of study.   Some of my professors were Marxists and Socialists."

Miriam came over and joined in the conversation between Abbot Delaurier and me.

"So what happened to you during the Nazi occupation of France that turned you to Marxism?" I asked.

"That, my young friend, will be a conversation for another time."   Abbot Delaurier put his hand on my shoulder. "There is no reason to bore a lovely young lady like Miriam with political philosophy and tales of an old man. I think it would be better to talk about the adventures of a young man such as yourself and how you are adjusting to Haskell."   At that Abbot Delaurier arched his eyebrow and smiled.

"Miss Miriam, how do you think Phillip is acclimating to the small town atmosphere of Haskell High School?"

Miriam gave a disarming smile and replied, "I hear he is doing just fine, Abbot Delaurier."

I turned to Miriam and said, "Oh really? And just what have you heard and whose been talking?"

"Names and stories don't mix, Phillip."   Miriam demurely replied. "Let's just say, Abbot Delaurier, he has made a name for himself on the football team by making the team as defensive end."

"How did you know that, Miriam?" I asked. "Coach Elliot announced that only two hours ago."

"News travels fast in a small town, Phillip," Miriam shot back.

"I think, Phillip, that Miss Miriam's wit is a match for your repartee," the Abbot observed. He was right. Miriam was not only beautiful but quick-witted. Not much slipped past Miriam. Her tongue was not as sharp as Aunt Madeline and she always had a way of making people feel at ease.

I turned to the Abbot and said, "I agree Abbot Delaurier, her wit is rapier sharp. A good looking, intelligent woman is a dangerous creature, indeed."

Miriam's face expressed surprise at my remark. "Well, Phillip, I don't know what to say. In one way I am flattered you think I am pretty; but I don't know what to think about being called dangerous."

"I think, Mon Ami, that he means the danger of an intelligent young beauty is that young men do not know how to handle such a woman." And with that remark the Abbot defanged my remarks and redeemed my faux pas. I was to learn that the Abbot was the epitome of tact; he had the ability to tell someone to go to hell in such a way they anticipated the trip. He always had a knack for rescuing people from awkward social situations.

Kent came over and joined in the conversation. "What's going on over here?" he asked.

"Polite conversation involving European football, political philosophy, history, and the relative dangers of the female species to an unwitting male," the Abbot replied, with an awry grin.

"Say what?" Kent asked, perplexed.

"Never mind, Kent," Miriam said, smiling and shaking her head. "It is too long a story to fully explain." Kent gave me a look of "what gives."

"I will tell you later, Kent," I said.

The Abbot and I were smiling. Joe came over and joined us and the conversation took a new turn to discussing the upcoming game with Checotah. Jock talk again. I listened as Joe and Kent became animated. The Abbot engaged them in conversation like a Maestro conducting an orchestra. But the conversation turned from football to family of the respective parties. No wonder this Frenchman was an Abbot of a 40 plus man Monastery. He had a unique ability to engage young men and women and get them to talk about what was dearest to their hearts. It was fascinating to watch him work his magic and I learned a lot about Joe, Kent and Miriam I did not know.

For instance, I learned that Joe's grandfather was from Trentino in Northern Italy and the Corsinni family had cousins living in their ancestral villages. Miriam's great-grandfather had been the Mayor of Beruit and they were still in contact with their relatives who had moved to a more Christian area around Mt. Beshir.

But Kent's family had the deepest roots in Oklahoma as his great-grandmother came over on the Trail of Tears with the forced removal of the Cherokees from Georgia and Tennessee. He had family all over Oklahoma. He was one-thirty second Cherokee as his maternal great-grandmother had been one-fourth Cherokee. Kent, Miriam, and Joe also learned a lot of my background in Chicago. However, there were no deep roots of my family in Chicago like theirs in Oklahoma. Dad had come from Iowa and Mom was from Georgia.

All of these ancestral facts the Abbot coaxed out of the four of us as we sat round the table. I shook my head in amazement. These folks here in Haskell had a greater sense of where they came from, who they were and where they were going than many of my blue-blooded "Bramin" classmates at St. Cyngen. All my Chicago friends cared about was driving new Porsches, drinking Bloody Marys at the Country Club and drawing down on their trust funds when they turned 21. They had very little connection as to where they came from nor did they really care. They were beginning to seem so foreign to me now, as if I had read about them in a book.

Long about 10:00 p.m., Miss Toni reminded all of us we had school tomorrow and to "save some conversation for another time." Joe, Kent and I thanked everyone for their hospitality and took our leave of Miss Toni, Mr. Abboud, Miriam, Miss Marguerite and Abbot Delaurier.

CHAPTER 7

PHILLIP AND AFFLUENZA

As I drove Kent and Joe home, I shared with them how Haskell was continuing to astound me.

"How so?" asked Kent.

"You all have it together. You truly know where you come from and where you seem to be going. My friends were not like that back in St. Cyngen's. They seem almost lost in the midst of all their material affluence."

"They have affluenza," Kent joked.

"Yeah, Kent. They did. That is a good word for it. Here it is like living in a three dimensional world. Looking back, my life in Chicago now seems almost two dimensional." I then added, "I have learned more about where I came from in the last two months living with Uncle Raymond and Aunt Louise than the 17 years of living with my family back home in Chicago It is like I am discovering who I am and learning I have more southern roots than this Yankee boy from Chicago ever thought about!" Joe and Kent were silent as they pondered my rambling.

We pulled up to Kent's house. Joe and Kent hopped out. Joe leaned up against my car door and said, "Well, Professor, we will continue this philosophical analysis of your life another time." He flashed his winning smile and winked at me. "Good night, Phillip."

"Yeah, see you, Phillip F. Austin Robertson," Kent added.

I leaned out of the blue Malibu car driver's side window and said something I had never told any other guys before, "You have no idea how hard it is for me to tell you this, but I feel like I would bust if I didn't. You

116

two are the best friends I have ever had in my life. I really love you guys like you were my own brothers. Thanks for making me a part of your world."

"Back at you, Cowboy." Joe said, wide-eyed.

"Roger that," Kent added.

I said good night and headed back to Concharty Road to go back to Uncle Raymond and Aunt Louise's ranch.

Joe and Kent lingered for a bit, talking as they watched me drive off.

"You know, Sinni, Phillip has been through a lot for a guy 17 years old. Most people would never know he has had some rough bumps in life if you didn't know him. But he seems to have weathered it pretty well," Kent commented.

"Yeah," Joe added. "I am sure glad to have met him and gotten to know him. He has opened my eyes that there is a far bigger world than Haskell, Oklahoma, out there, that's for sure. And it ain't necessarily better out there either."

"Yeah, you wonder what Chicago was like for him, but I keep thinking of his mom. It would be rough to have a comatose mom. I know he misses his mom, he told me that. I talked to my dad about her condition and he said the prognosis was not good. That has got to be rough on a fella," Kent added.

"Well, it would be rough for sure. But I think we have gotten a glimpse of what Chicago was like from Phillip. Lots of money and things, but not much else. Not much family time and love," Joe said quietly.

"Makes you count your blessings that's for sure," Kent replied.

"Well, I agree with you and would add that Phillip has been a real blessing to both you and me. His being here got Coach Hammond revved up to kick start our butts to work out in July. I don't know about you but I can feel the difference in workout and how I am throwing the ball," Joe grinned.

Kent punched Joe in the arm, "just throw the ball right in our opening game against Checotah."

Joe climbed into his truck to go home and replied, hanging his arm out the window like he was throwing a pass, "I will if you will catch my pass." Kent laughed and turned to go into his house.

CHAPTER 8

AN UNEXPECTED VISITOR

The week flew by and our big game against Checotah was looming one day away. I could tell that Uncle Raymond was kind of getting excited for the game. But I also sensed something else was up. Aunt Louise was as cool as a cucumber but she was just a tad bit too cool. That was not quite like her.

When I pulled up after school on Thursday's workout, I noticed a truck in the driveway I had never seen before. Moreover, it had an Illinois license plate, not an Oklahoma license plate on it. That was odd. I came into the house just in time for dinner when I saw my brother Frank at the dining room table, snapping green beans and talking to Aunt Louise as if they had known each other forever. I dropped my athletic bag and books and yelled out, "FRANK!"

"Hey, little brother," was all he got out before I rushed over and almost knocked him over with a hug.

He had a full beard and his hair was long by Coach Hammond's standards. Frank was six feet tall and weighed in around 200 pounds. Unlike John, Sue and me, he had dark hair, eyes and an olive complexion. We joked he was the son of an Italian milkman, but now I knew it was the Indian blood. He had been an all-around athlete in high school but now got most of his exercise running survey crews wherever my Uncle Ed sent them.

"Whoa, Flicka! Don't knock me over, boy. Phillip you have grown since I saw you last and you've gotten big," Frank said in the midst of a bear hug.

It was true. He had not seen me for nearly 18 months. I was now in a growth spurt many young men experienced at my age. "Well, you are about to experience why I have gotten so big, Frank. Looks like Aunt Louise has killed the fatted calf to celebrate your being here." I turned to Aunt Louise, "So that explains the unusual behavior I have sensed in you and Uncle Raymond."

Aunt Louise wiped her hands on her apron, laughing, "Yes, we learned this past Tuesday that Frank was passing through. He wanted to surprise you so your Uncle Raymond convinced him to come on up tonight and stay through Saturday, before Frank had to run a crew in Houston, Texas."

"That's right, little brother," Frank said. "I came to check up on you and see if our relatives were surviving you," Frank teased.

I threw a fake punch at Frank, which he deflected. "So are you coming to the game Friday night?" I asked eagerly.

Frank smiled and tousled my hair, "I wouldn't dream of missing it, Tiger." Younger brothers often yearn for the approval of their older brothers and I was no exception. My sun rose and set on my oldest brother's opinion. He was wise and had much "life experience" as Mom had called it. More than once his wise counsel had served me well in life's difficult situations.

"Awesome," was all I could say. About that time Uncle Raymond came in and introduced himself with a firm handshake and warm smile.

That night at dinner the four of us sat around the dinner table till nearly 8:00, just talking. Frank slowly gathered information about my comings and goings to report back to Dad. But I was to learn about that years later. I could tell Frank liked Uncle Raymond and Aunt Louise and it was readily apparent they returned his affection. Frank was 25 years old and nearly the same age as their late son Gerald. In some ways Frank had similar coloring and body build to Gerald even though they were second cousins.

"Don't you have school work to do, Phillip?" Uncle Raymond asked.

"Yes, sir, I do. But it won't take long to get it done. If you would excuse me, I should be finished by 9:30." And with that I left the kitchen table. I knew the routine. Aunt Louise and Uncle Raymond would still be there in an hour and a half, drinking coffee and talking to Frank. I could get my homework done and still catch another hour of conversation by helping clean the kitchen before going to bed.

I went to my room to knock out my homework. Fortunately, as it was the first week, I did not have much schoolwork. Mainly, Algebra and some reading for English. The laughter of Frank, Uncle Raymond and Aunt Louise filled the house. They were regaling each other with funny family stories and of life's foibles. It felt odd to be left out and I worked quickly so as to rejoin them. My Algebra and reading were soon done. Now it was nearly 9:00 P.M. As I walked back into the kitchen it was great to see these three laughing and drinking coffee as if they were old friends.

Upon arriving, Aunt Louise was sharing a story from their late son Gerald's misadventures as a three-year old one fine summer day in Haskell. At that time, Uncle Raymond had a one-half English Collie and one-half Irish Setter named Doodle. He was Gerald's unofficial baby sitter and playmate when Aunt Louise and Uncle Raymond lived in town. She had put Gerald in the backyard to play with Doodle while she hung up the wash. Gerald opened the side yard gate, taking Doodle with him. They began walking to downtown Haskell. At every bush that Doodle marked, Gerald relieved himself too, much to the horror of some older women who were part of the Haskell Gardening Club. Many a rose bush and flowerbed got watered by boy and dog that afternoon. In addition, Gerald shed an article of clothing at each stop. He reasoned that if Doodle could go naked so could he. When Aunt Louise noticed he was gone and saw the open gate, she followed the trail of shed clothing to find him. She also noticed the disapproving stares of irate gardeners, just as she caught up with Gerald walking through downtown Haskell stark naked.

"I liked to have died," Aunt Louise said almost crying from laughter. "You know how hard it is to chase a naked three year old and dog along the sidewalks of downtown Haskell at lunch, when you have an armful of clothing and shoes? They both decided we were playing tag. I cornered them outside C & C Hardware. Grandfather Joe Corsinni nearly split in two over the sight of me chasing those two. He came out and grabbed Doodle while I corralled that runaway scalawag. I took him into the store to dress him. Unfortunately, the wife of the newspaper owner was in the store. I was the butt of Haskell humor in the newspaper for weeks after that." Now all four of us were laughing to the point of crying.

Frank then shared one of the most infamous family vacations the Robertson family ever had – the trip to New Mexico to get Frank from a summer camp. It was on the way back home that the family moment occurred. It was blazing hot and we were in Mom's 1959 Chevrolet station wagon. The air conditioner broke down on the way home! Thus, Mom was driving with all four windows down. It felt like being in a convection oven, moving 55 miles per hour! Dad was asleep in the back seat on the passenger's side. It was on a back road in New Mexico and the next gas station was 40 miles up the road. We had a little tray that we used for bathroom emergencies. The "dukie" tray is what Mom called it. In any event, Frank asked Mom if she wanted him to empty the tray and she said yes. Frank told our brother John to hand him the tray from the back of the car. John retrieved the tray and handed Frank the tray with all its "contents" and Frank then threw the contents out the front passenger window.

The problem was the contents came flying back into the car on Dad's side of the window and hit him square in his face! Dad woke up cussing a storm. Mom had to pull the car over and stop, she was laughing so hard. All we had was Kleenex and we were all laughing. Dad was totally lacking in humor and I learned a great deal of "Army jargon" that day as Mom called it. All he could do was spit and wipe his face with dry Kleenex, cuss, and then spit and try to wipe his face again with Kleenex. It was a somber drive for the next 40 miles till Dad got to a bathroom and was able to really clean up. He basically took a bath in the service station's sink, Mom used to say.

Uncle Raymond added, laughing, "A good Marine would have known to throw that out the back window! "There were no Marines in the car and Dad was an Army Captain!" Frank added.

Before Uncle Raymond could reply with a retort, Aunt Louise intervened, "Well, as it is drawing high to 10:00, I think we need to carry on this conversation tomorrow. We need to get Phillip to bed. He has a big game tomorrow evening."

"Frank, you can bunk with Phillip in his room tonight," Uncle Raymond suggested.

"Sounds great to me," Frank said.

We helped Aunt Louise clean the kitchen and then took our leave to retire to my bedroom. As Frank and I got ready for bed, he said, "You have a pretty good gig here, Phillip. I like Uncle Raymond and Aunt Louise. She sort of reminds me of Mom. Her cooking is certainly different from Agnes Kotlarski's sauerkraut and wiener schnitzel and dour attitude."

I added, laughing, "I agree." We then got ready for bed and Frank's demeanor turned serious.

"When Dad said he was pulling you out of St. Cyngen and sending you down here to Haskell, Oklahoma, I thought Dad had lost his mind. I challenged him on that and he explained everything.

You unfortunately chose to prank a major donor of Northwestern University who lived on Avery Drive. He had to pull you out of St. Cyngen and get you out of Chicago for political reasons associated with Northwestern University. Once you were out of town, Dad was able to smooth over the ruffled feathers."

Frank then caught me up on the family. "Mom is still in a coma. No progress there. But Dad hasn't lost hope though. John has fallen in love with Mexico and wants to go to medical school there. Susannah Teresa is tentatively planning on attending Colorado State University next year."

"Wow," was all I could say.

"So what are you going to do, Cowboy. Stay here or go back to Chicago? You sure seem to have captured the affection and good opinion of Uncle Raymond and Aunt Louise."

"And they have captured me, Frank. It is like Chicago was another life, but I still sort of miss it. Haskell is still so different from home, but Oklahoma really grows on you, Frank. It is hard to explain but it is almost like there is some sort of magic in the Concharty Hills down here. Heck, the history down here is unbelievable. From Spanish gold miners in the 18th Century to the Belle Starr Gang in the 19th Century to the Ku Klux Klan to the Concharty Hills Catholic Monastery of the 20th Century. What has gone on around here makes your head spin."

"Well, Tiger, if you are going to start football in your first game, the last thing you need is for your head to be spinning on the playing field. So lights out, little brother, and we will talk more tomorrow." With that, Frank turned off the light and we both hit the hay. But I was too excited to sleep. Having my big brother to watch me play against Checotah meant the world to me. Plus, I was anxious about my first football game. It was as if my Chicago world was getting a glimpse of my new life in Haskell. It took me a while to fall asleep, thinking of all this.

CHAPTER 9

FIRST FOOTBALL GAME

Friday, the big day had arrived. I could barely concentrate on classwork through the day. I had told Joe and Kent about my brother Frank being in town for the game. They wanted to meet him after the game.

At sixth hour Coach Elliot briefed us on game strategy from Checotah but we did not suit up. We had to be back at school at 6:00 p.m. to board the school bus to Checotah. The game was to begin at 8:00 p.m., and it was a one-hour drive on the bus. We would suit up at the men's locker room at Checotah and hit the field by 7:30 that evening. I went back to Aunt Louise and Uncle Raymond's home to rest a bit around 3:00. I laid down and slept till 4:30. Aunt Louise was fixing an early dinner around 5. It consisted of a wilted salad with a bacon grease vinegarette and she had sliced some grilled chicken breasts into thin strips and tossed in the salad. She had some sliced peaches and served her homemade sun mint tea. "You need to eat light before the game," she told me. Frank was out working in the pasture, herding cattle with Uncle Raymond. Lord only knew what those two were up to. It was as likely that Frank was trying to assess my situation for dad and Uncle Raymond was probably probing Frank about my family. I figured those two would be somewhat evenly matched but experience and discernment of Uncle Raymond would outweigh the cunning of my brother Frank. The two came in around 5:30 p.m., hot, sweaty and laughing. They obviously liked each other. Over the past six years, Frank had been no stranger to hard sweaty work and enjoyed working with his hands.

"Hey, little brother," Frank said. "Ready for the big game?"

Uncle Raymond then quizzed me about my role as a defensive end and what to watch out for. I fielded his questions rather well, I thought, and then asked him, "Uncle Raymond, can Joe and Kent spend the night after the game? They wanted to meet Frank and since he is leaving early, the best time is tonight after the game."

"Sure, if Louise is okay with that," Uncle Raymond replied.

Aunt Louise looked up and smiled, "We running an unlicensed bed and breakfast here? Of course, my two surrogate sons can spend the night," she teased. Aunt Louise helped me gather my stuff and put it in her car. She was going to drive me to Haskell High School and drop me off and then come back to get Frank and Uncle Raymond after they cleaned up. I later learned she ran a load of laundry for Frank so all his clothes were folded and clean when he left for Houston on Saturday.

As Aunt Louise drove me to Haskell she asked me if she could pray for me and the team. I said fine and bowed my head. She prayed with both eyes open as she drove me to Haskell High School. What a classy lady she was. She was warm, hospitable, engaging, funny and spiritual all at once. No wonder a young Marine barely out of his teens came back from Camp Pendleton to the oilfields of Seminole to marry her.

All the guys and gals and their families were milling around two yellow Haskell High School buses; one for the players and one for the band and gear. The cheerleaders were there but they would be riding in separate cars. The players and band boarded their respective buses and we departed. Most of the players had a double seat to themselves. It was late August and still very hot outside. To make things worse, the bus had no air conditioning.

"The first game is always the hottest," Joe said.

"Yeah, long about the end of September things cool down and it is more fun to play," Kent added.

Joe and Kent sat around me. Kent was sprawled out on a seat, leaning against a window; Joe was on the other side in a similar position. I sat in front of them, doing the same. It was jock talk and lighthearted banter between the three of us all the way to Checotah. It belied our anxiety we all felt at the upcoming game. As the bus had no air conditioning and we kept the windows half down, it was a hot trip that took almost an hour. We finally arrived at Checotah at 7:00.

We got off the bus and each player carried his gear into the locker room to change. We felt like strangers in a strange land and this feeling was reinforced by hand painted butcher paper signs plastered around the locker room stating "HANG THE HASKELL HAYMAKERS" and pictures of a Haskell Haymaker bound up in hay bales in hangman's nooses.

Kent broke the tension of the mildly hostile welcoming by saying, "I hope they play ball better than they paint slogans or we will kick their butts from here to Coweta." At that, most of the guys laughed and we set about the serious business of suiting up in our pads and football uniforms. Coach Elliot gathered the team of players for a brief pep talk and prayer. One thing about Coach Elliot was his serious approach to coaching and playing football. He instilled a sense of purpose in each player and their respective role they would need to play on the field. Yet there was a boyish charm to him also that endeared him to the team. He had the ability to mold twenty-three individual young jocks into a united body of players understanding their respective duties for this evening's game. He closed in a prayer before we left the locker room.

Coach Elliot then led the team onto the field at 7:30 and we began warm ups and stretching exercises. The Checotah band struck up their hometown fight song. This was countered by the Haskell High School band. Thus, the competition began even before the game had commenced.

The game started at 8:00 p.m. sharp, and Haskell won the coin toss. Checotah kicked off to us. Within three minutes into the first quarter, Joe threw a perfect long bomb to Kent who caught it and outran the Checotah defensive halfbacks to score the first touchdown of the game.

This set the whole tone for the rest of the evening's competition between Haskell and Checotah. I even got to sack a couple of players and kept them from scoring. Haskell trounced Checotah this evening by a score of 42 to 7. We retired to the locker hot and tired but elated at our victory. One of the guys ripped down the butcher paper urging the hanging of Haskell, wadded it up and stuffed it into the trash. The guys hooted and clapped. We showered and changed.

The tone and attitude on the bus ride back home was markedly different. The guys were jubilant at our first team victory. Kent, Joe and I debriefed about our respective performance in the game and how to improve as Uncle Raymond suggested. "Always do an autopsy of your performance," he told us back in July when we worked out with him. I was finally learning this new language of "jock talk." Joe and Kent agreed to come back with me to Uncle Raymond and Aunt Louise's house to meet my brother Frank.

We got back to the parking lot at Haskell High School at 11:30. "Joe, why don't you spend the night tonight? You are working at the ranch tomorrow and you might as well. Just grab your work clothes and head on over," I suggested.

"You come, too, Kent. We can put you guys in the guest bedroom and Frank and I will sleep in mine."

"I didn't bring ear plugs," Kent said. "And I am not going through another sleepless night with Joe sawing logs all evening."

I laughed and Joe grinned. "Wuss," is all Joe said, looking at Kent. He then turned to me and said, "Yeah, I am good for that.

"I will come over for a bit, Phillip, but then head home," Kent said. "Mom has some things she wants me to do in the garage and around the house on Saturday. But I want to meet your brother Frank. He might shed some light for me about who this mysterious Phillip F. Austin Robertson really is. Big brothers know all the little brother's dirty laundry," Kent flashed his smile at me. How could you not like Kent! He had a disarming way of teasing you such that you didn't know whether to hug him or slug him.

I laughed and said, "If I know my brother Frank, he will be extracting confessions of a wayward Baptist wide receiver and his Catholic quarterback accomplice." At that we all three laughed.

Joe got into his truck and went to his house to get his stuff. I got in Kent's car and together we went back to Uncle Raymond and Aunt Louise's house. I was looking forward to seeing Frank, having him meet Joe and Kent, and hearing his impressions of this new world of mine called Haskell, Oklahoma. His good opinion carried a lot of weight with me and I wanted his approval.

Kent asked me about Frank, "He do any sports in high school?"

"Yeah, he played football, basketball, baseball and ran track. He wanted to play NAIA football but he broke his ankle twice in the same place. The doctor told him if he wanted to walk the rest of his life, he needed to hang up his football cleats after high school."

"Why didn't you play football, Phillip?" Kent asked.

"I liked swimming and it just came naturally to me. Besides, Frank said I couldn't catch a ball to save my life."

At that Kent laughed and said, "You sure wouldn't have known that tonight."

Changing the subject, I wanted to talk to Kent about something that had been on my mind.

"Hey, Kent, can I ask you a question about Joe?"

"Sure," he replied.

"Who is Sheree Brandt and why do I have a gut feeling Joe likes her?" I inquired.

"Whoa, boy! Phillip F. Austin! You ask a doozy of a question!" Kent replied. "Deserves a doozy of an answer!" I countered. Kent explained to me that Sheree had an interesting background. Her mother had been the illegitimate offspring of a union between Papa C's brother and a local Creek Indian Freedman woman. It seems most blacks in this part of Oklahoma were direct descendants of the slaves the Creek Indians had brought with them over the Trail of Tears back in the 1830's. Many of these Creek Freedmen were a mixture of African, Indian, and White ancestry. Such was the case with Sheree. Technically, she and Miriam would have been third cousins; hence, the family resemblance. Everyone in the school knew that but rarely spoke of it.

"Joe talk to you about this?"

"Nah," I said. "But I have noticed Sinni lights up sometimes when she is around."

"Yeah, I have seen that, too," Kent mused, and then he continued, "but she is a dang pretty girl and really good student. I can see why a guy like Joe would be attracted to her."

"I can see that too, Kent. Thanks for sharing that information with me. Sort of explains a lot about why Joe didn't currently have a girlfriend. It's kind of hard to give your time and attention to a girlfriend when your heart is for another gal!"

"For sure," Kent said.

We turned down Concharty Mountain Road and pulled in the driveway of Uncle Raymond and Aunt Louise's house. The lights were on in the den. Kent helped me take my gear to the garage. Uncle Raymond had earlier told me just to leave it there after the game and we would deal with it in the morning. We came in through the utility room to the den and Uncle Raymond, Aunt Louise and Frank were sitting around the den under the ceiling fan. It was readily apparent they were heavily engaged in discussing something.

CHAPTER 10

FRANK

As Kent and I entered the room, Uncle Raymond got up from his Lazy Boy recliner and said, "Hail the conquering heroes!" Thereby changing the subject.

I blushed slightly and Kent just beamed his winning smile and said, "Thanks, Coach Hammond."

"Frank, this is my buddy Kent James," I said, introducing Kent to my oldest brother Frank. Frank got up from the sofa and extended his hand, saying, "Nice to meet you, Kent. Great game. I really enjoyed watching you play. You and that quarterback played flawlessly. He passed the ball and you always connected. Plus you are fast." Frank gave Kent a firm handshake and slapped him on the shoulder.

"Well, you can thank Coach Hammond for my speed. Coach ran us all over the ranch this summer, toning us up," Kent replied. That was just like Kent too. Somewhat self-effacing, he thanked you for the compliment but shared basking in the adulation with others. Uncle Raymond smiled with satisfaction, knowing he had helped Kent blossom into the wide receiver Uncle Raymond knew Kent could become.

"Well, how about you Friday Night Heroes enjoying the fruits of your victory with homemade blackberry cobbler and vanilla ice cream?" Aunt Louise asked.

"Sure," said Kent.

"I will help you with that, Aunt Louise," I said and went into the kitchen to help scoop the ice cream. Kent, Frank and Uncle Raymond were engaging in their jock talk.

"Your prayers were certainly answered tonight, Aunt Louise," I said as I scooped the ice cream into five bowls. The blackberry cobbler was freshly cooked that afternoon and Aunt Louise had warmed it up in the oven right before Kent and I had arrived.

"In more ways than one, Phillip," is all Aunt Louise could say as she watched me scoop the ice cream as she put cobbler in the bowls.

About that time the doorbell rang. It was Joe Corsinni. I immediately went to the door to let him in. Joe and I took his stuff to the guest bedroom. He hung up his clothes in the spare bedroom and with a wry grin threw a small cardboard box on the bed. I looked at him quizzically and then went to the bed to read the lettering on the side, "ACME Ear Plugs." I immediately glanced up at Joe, laughing. Joe said, "No excuse for Kent not staying tonight. I figure we will be up till 1:00 A.M., so he might as well spend the night. My mom called Kent's mom to make sure it was okay if Kent spent the night. We are good to go if he wants to stay."

"Corsinni, you never cease to amaze me," was all I could say, shaking my head. "Come on, let's get back to the others. I'm starved and hot blackberry cobbler with ice cream sounds awesome right about now."

Joe and I rejoined the others and began eating our cobbler and the ice cream. Joe met Frank and the six of us sat around in the den discussing the high points and low points of the game tonight.

"Guys, I would have never believed my little brother would be playing football in high school. Heck, he couldn't even catch a ball even if you threw the ball to him." Frank took another bite of cobbler; Kent cut his eyes at me and laughed.

"So, Frank, tell us some stories about your little brother," Kent asked, arching an eyebrow as he did so. Frank looked at me, pondering which of my misadventures to share.

"Well, he is a tad bit dangerous with matches. As I recall he lit a match between my toes when I was sleeping after a 24-hour road trip driving back to

Chicago from California. I was beat and racked out on the living room couch. He caused me to have a "hot foot". I almost got reported to the Cook County Department of Human Services for child abuse of my little brother," Frank chuckled as he told the story, and ate his cobbler.

I blushed and winced at the memory. "Yeah, that was a pretty ugly trick I pulled. It's a wonder that I am still alive and that you are even
still talking to me, big brother," I said between bites.

"But, guys, the worst trick was two years ago. I was home over Christmas and had walking pneumonia. Little brother here had been using something called Tough Skin for his feet in a special prescription bottle that looked like cough syrup, "Benzoin Tincture."

"Oh, no, Frank! Not that story." I begged.

"Little brother here watched me pour a tablespoon of that stuff at dinner and ladle it down my throat. I will have to tell you no raw whiskey or straight tequila I ever drank burned like that. The little "rat" just sat there and watched me almost poison myself." Frank had a unique way of storytelling that delighted and amazed his listeners. Uncle Raymond and Aunt Louise were wide-eyed at first and then began laughing. Kent and Joe were just shaking their heads in disbelief.

I cleared my throat and added in my defense, "The rest of the story as that great Chicago spokesman Paul Harvey from Oklahoma says has yet to be told. Number one, Frank took that without asking me what it was. Number two, I didn't tell Frank to take that for his sore throat. Number three, it was not poison and after a frantic phone call by Dad to a local pharmacist, Dad was chuckling and said it was probably not a bad tonic for what ailed Frank." I bored a look at Frank after refuting his "poisoning" story.

Frank forgot contrite, replying "Yeah, but it burned for what seemed like hours. All I could rasp was you little rat; you little rat," Frank reenacted the rasping voice. By now we were all laughing.

"Man, Phillip, it is amazing you survived childhood with stunts like that," Joe said.

"Well, I think that is enough of embarrassing little brother stories, Frank. I wonder if I should share some of your family misadventures. Remember your concept of "mutually assured destruction" or M.A.D. you taught me? Don't rat your brother out or else!" I clinched my hand into a threatening fist as I arched my eyebrow and bored another look at Frank.

"Okay, little brother. I hear you loud and clear," Frank laughed. The conversation drifted back to the evening's game and some of Frank's athletic exploits in his heyday at St. Cyngen's Academy. It was getting close to 12:30 and Uncle Raymond and Aunt Louise announced they were turning in for the night. Joe and I prevailed upon Kent to spend the night with the assurance of Joe's earplugs. We were all laughing at Joe's cunning. The truth was Kent was enjoying the comradery of the four of us together and probably did not want to go home. Hence, the four of us stayed up and continued talking till 1:30 A.M. We had a great guys' "bull session" as Frank called it. Joe and Kent decided to hit the hay and Frank and I went back to our room to go to bed. Frank and I talked as we got undressed for bed.

"I like your buddies, Phillip. They are regular guys and pretty darn good ball players. I like Uncle Raymond and Aunt Louise, too. You know, little brother, what they seem to have here is what I am looking for! I have wandered around the United States for the last six years, living like a Gypsy, doing survey work for Uncle Ed. Sort of wears on a guy. I am tired of this type of lifestyle. I guess what I am saying is that I want a family someday and settle down."

I was stunned. What Frank just told me was like a pail of cold water in my face. I had never heard my happy go lucky older brother say something so serious about his life goals. "YOU want to settle down," is all I could say.

'Yeah, me, Phillip. One of Peter Pan's lost boys that no one thought would ever grow up. Heck, little brother, I am 25 years old. I am not getting any younger. I have seen lots of guys in their 30's and 40's who are rootless and have no ties. I manage guys like that and have for the last couple of years. Dad always said it was best to learn vicariously from other men's mistakes. Well, I have been doing that and have learned that I know what I don't want to become. Sometimes that is as important as knowing what you do want to become. What Uncle Raymond and Aunt Louise have is what I want ... a family and a community of friends."

"A family?" I asked, in surprise. "How do you figure that. They don't have any kids."

"Don't they?" Frank asked, arching his eyebrow. "From what I can tell you are the closest thing to a surrogate son I have ever seen; you and your buddies; plus you weren't up in the football bleachers tonight watching men come up to Uncle Raymond that he had coached over the past twenty years. He was like a dad to a lot of those men. Hell, Phillip, some of those dudes were bringing their kids and grandkids to meet the "Great Coach Hammond." I was introduced to more people tonight than I can count. The folks in this town really love that man. He has a place in their hearts and they have a place in his heart. That is what family and community is about and that is what I want, Phillip."

Frank paused and pondered what he was going to say next, "Mom and Dad loved us. But Dad was swallowed up in his work and he was very successful in his professional career. He just was not very successful as a family man. Mom stepped into the breach and tried to be both Mom and Dad to hold our family together. She was a great Mom but not so great a Dad."

"I agree with you on that, Frank," I said somberly.

"Dad's a good man, Phillip, and he really does love all his kids. He just never took to the role of being a father," Frank was biting his lip now. "But somehow what you have stumbled into down here in Haskell, you are not likely to find in Chicago if you go back, little brother. With all the wealth of money and contacts Dad has, you aren't going to find the people as rich in character and purpose as you have here. Your two buddies are men you can have lifelong friendships with and grow old together raising kids and watching them grow up."

My mouth was gaping wide open. I didn't know what to say. Frank continued, "Dad wanted me to check in on you and make sure the good reports he was hearing about you were true. I have to tell him now that Uncle Raymond and Aunt Louise were understating how well you really were doing. I am proud of what you have accomplished down here, Phillip, and I am not referring to your making the football team; I am talking about how you are finding your stride in becoming a man in spite of what you have been through this past year."

My eyes watered; I was utterly speechless. All I could do was reach out and hug my older brother Frank. I quietly cried on his shoulder. The trauma of Mom's accident and the loss of my life in Chicago as I knew it came flooding back in on me. I had tried to suppress the hurt back in Chicago with distance, new friends, activities, academics and sports, but there was no real anesthetic for the emotional pain confronting the truth of such a loss as an absent father and a possibly brain dead mother. Frank was the closest thing I had known as a surrogate dad when I was younger. Frank held me for a while and then said, "It's okay to cry, little brother. I have cried a lot too the past year over what we have lost in Mom." Frank's eyes were now watering up but he was nowhere near the stream of tears I was letting flow. "Okay, Tiger. We need to buck up and continue on. Remember what Agnes Kotlarski said 'tears are only meant to help bury the past,' and with what she went through in Nazi occupied Poland she ought to know." Frank was right. I had grown up hearing Agnes' stories of her desperate struggles to survive WWII in Warsaw, Poland. The reminder helped me pull myself together.

I sniffed and wiped my nose. "Thanks for everything, Frank! Thanks for being the best big brother a guy could have."

Frank threw a playful punch to my chin like he was going to bust my chops. "You are not so bad yourself, little brother. An elder brother couldn't have a better little brother than you!" We both dried our eyes and hit the hay.

If my head was spinning on Thursday night before the game, I was now in orbit between Jupiter and Mars. There was a lot of information for me to process that Frank had said. I wasn't sure my puerile mind could really absorb all that he had told me. But in time I would realize the impact of what Frank had shared with me.

CHAPTER 11

HIKING CONCHARTY MOUNTAIN

The next morning Aunt Louise put out a spread like I had never seen before for breakfast. She had made blueberry pancakes, blueberry muffins and had baked several loaves of strawberry/banana bread. She cooked some Canadian bacon and had fresh sliced peaches along with some scrambled eggs and grits.

"Geez, Phillip, if Aunt Louise keeps feeding you like this, you will be as big as a house." Joe, Kent and I laughed at Frank's remark. Frank was leaving right after breakfast. Aunt Louise had made a "care package" for Frank of two loaves of her strawberry/banana bread and a basket of blueberry muffins. She presented this care package to Frank after breakfast as we were saying goodbye to him.

"With good food like this, Aunt Louise, I promise you I will be back for more," Frank said. "Thanks for your hospitality and the meals, Aunt Louise."

"I will hold you to that, Frank," Aunt Louise said. "We're family and you know where we are. So don't be a stranger." I knew Aunt Louise meant that too. She cared for her niece's sons as if they were her own. Uncle Raymond told me that was the Southern way about family.

"Thanks for everything, Uncle Raymond. I truly enjoyed working the cattle with you yesterday," Frank said.

"Appreciated the help," Uncle Raymond replied, shaking Frank's hand.

Frank then turned to Joe and Kent and did something totally unexpected. He put his hands on their shoulders and looked at Joe and Kent squarely in the eyes, "Thanks guys for taking my little brother in as one of your buddies. You will never know how much that means to me and how indebted my family is to you for your friendship. You have helped make Haskell a second home to him. I warn you, he is a pretty ornery rascal, but he is a truly good kid at heart." Frank was grinning as he added, "thanks for helping bring out the best in my little brother."

Joe and Kent initially stood there silently, taking in what Frank had said. Joe smiled, "Thank you for loaning us your little brother. He has taught Kent and me a lot but probably doesn't even realize it." I turned and looked at Joe with a quizzical expression.

Frank playfully punched me in the chest, "It's okay, little brother," Frank looked Joe and Kent in the eyes, "They'll explain what they mean in time." I gave Frank one last hug and Frank got into his truck, pulled out of the driveway, and headed south for Houston.

Kent turned and said, "Well, guys, I have to get going. Thanks for bunk and breakfast, Mrs. Hammond and Coach Hammond."

"You're welcome, Kent, to stay here anytime," Aunt Louise said.

Kent got into his car and said, "See you on Sunday at church, Phillip. Catch you later, Sinni," and with that Kent returned to Haskell. Joe and I changed into our work clothes to work the ranch. Uncle Raymond told us we only had to work till noon today as we were pretty worn out from the game the night before. I was relieved to hear that.

Joe and I ran the fence lines and moved the heifers and their calves to another pasture. We checked the oil and gas leases to see if there were any problems. Everything checked out and we finished up around 12:30. Aunt Louise had fixed us a light lunch of sandwiches, cold peach slices and homemade lemonade. Joe left around 1:30 p.m. and I retired to my room for much needed rest. I turned on the ceiling fan in my room to help cool things down. I was so tired that I didn't even shower before I collapsed on top of my bed! The Mexicans, I believed, were some of the most civilized people in the world to recognize that an afternoon siesta was vitally necessary for healthy living. I fell asleep quickly.

I slept till nearly 5:00 p.m. I couldn't believe I had slept for nearly three and a half hours. I took a shower and cleaned up. I changed into jeans and a polo shirt. I put some tennis shoes on. It was nearly 5:30. Aunt Louise and Uncle Raymond left me a note in the kitchen that they had gone to Muskogee and would be back at 7:30. I turned on the TV and caught some of the evening news. The Vietnam War was being waged successfully and the body count of dead Viet Cong after a battle approached 200 casualties. Same old news of firefights and body counts. This only wearied my soul so I turned the TV off as I did not want to hear about the war tonight. I grabbed an apple from the frigerator to eat and decided to hike up to the upper pasture of Uncle Raymond's ranch. I sprayed some tick repellant on my shoes and jeans to go hiking up the Concharty Mountain. A lot had happened in the past 24 hours and I had a lot to process. I left a note on the refrigerator that I had gone hiking up the Concharty Mountain to go walking along the monastery trails. I made sure all the doors were locked and went out the kitchen door, locking it behind me. Aunt Louise said it was not necessary but I don't think she minded my habit that was driven by my big city caution.

I grabbed one of Uncle Raymond's Haskell Haymaker caps from the garage and started following the trail to the upper pastures. Joe had told me that after late August things would dry out so much that late afternoons started to get pleasant because of the lack of humidity. He was right. There was a slight breeze rustling through the trees and the cicadas were singing their loud chorus. Those two sounds made for a beautiful symphony. The higher up I hiked, the breeze picked up and the late afternoon shadows meant I was mostly hiking in the shade. I made it to the top pasture and beheld that incredible view of the river valley. I then heard the 6 o'clock vesper bell from the monastery. I saw the trails Abbot Delauier had once invited me to hike. He had given me a standing invitation to go hiking so I decided to take him up on that. I climbed over the fence and started down one of the trails. I was immediately struck by a couple of things. On this side of the fence the land was heavily timbered but there was not much undergrowth. Further, often the trail was composed of chat that someone long ago had put down so that it made for an easier walk along the trail. One branch of the trail went down to the monastery and the other went higher up on the hill. I chose to go higher up and see where that led. Occasionally there were stations of the cross with benches and a small arbor made of vines and raw timber on this trail. These were usually at scenic spots that were landscaped with small ponds and small flowering trees such as the Wild Dogwood or Redbuds and shrubbery such as Wild Rose or Rose of Sharon. I had hiked for maybe an hour when I sat down at one of these landscaped gardens. It was a truly beautiful setting. I was thinking over what Frank had shared about family and community. I was coming to really like Haskell, but I still wanted to return to Chicago to pursue my athletic career in swimming. My reverie was suddenly interrupted by a familiar voice.

"Bon Soir, Phillip." It was Abbot DeLaurier.

"Good evening, Abbot DeLaurier," I replied.

"I am glad to see you strolling the trails of our monastery," he said.

"I had no idea how peaceful and beautiful they were. How do you keep the underbrush so clear?" I asked.

The Abbot laughed. "What do you think of the hiking trails here? That is quite simple. Some of our brothers manage several herds of goats; they help keep the underbrush under control. The goats eat the underbrush in the areas around our hiking trails. This provides for a better view. This also helps reduce the fire hazard; and our goats then give us milk, cheese and meat in return. It is a very harmonious relationship we have here with God's creation." I asked the Abbot other questions about the monastery and the monks who lived there. I invited him to join me on the bench.

The Abbot sat down next to me as he explained the rhythm of the monastery's operation and life of the monks in response to my questions. To see the monastery through his eyes brought a whole new perspective to me. This man seemed so simple and yet so wise at the same time. I was amazed. We talked about the history and work of the monastery for probably an hour. Finally, the Abbot changed the conversation and focused on me.

"So what brings you strolling along the monastery trails this time of day? It is near dusk." The Abbot's eyes sparkled with a depth of understanding as if he already knew what I had been processing. I was like a ripe fruit waiting to be plucked so I poured out my heart to the Abbot and all I had been through in the past year; the shame of my expulsion from St. Cyngen's Academy; the pain of my Mom's coma; and the loss of my life as I knew it in Chicago.

"There are times when I feel like an utter disappointment and failure to my Dad and my family," I said with my eyes watering. "It is like I am in the midst of my own dark journey of the soul."

The Abbot leaned forward as he listened carefully. He then observed sympathetically, "That is a lot to carry, my young friend."

"How did you deal with your dark journey of your soul, Abbot Delaurier? You never finished your story the other night at Miss Marguerite Fugali's house," I asked.

"It is a long story, Phillip," the Abbot replied.

"I think I could use a long story right about now, Abbot Delaurier," I said.   So the Abbot shared his youthful troubles during World War II with me.   I learned about his work in the French Resistance and the loss of many of his comrades. Things got so hot in Paris that he had to be spirited away for his own safety.

"Many of my friends were killed. It only heightened my bitterness and anger at the Germans but all that did was make me murder men in my heart and my vision was only darkened. I was responsible for many violent acts of terrorism and was on the Nazi and Vichy French wanted list. So they hid me out at the Notre Dame de Fontgombault Monastery. The year was 1942, I stayed there the rest of the war. I met many men who had seen the horrors of World War One and yet had found redemption for their souls. Their life experiences slowly helped clear the darkness clouding my vision.   After six months there, the anger and bitterness lifted from my heart as I lifted my eyes again to the Savior of my youth. All sorts of healing was working through my heart and soul.   I joined the Benedictine Order at the end of the war and was sent by my order to the Concharty Hills Monastery in 1962, where I have been ever since.

"So to answer your question about my dark journey of the soul, it was a slow process. The answers did not come overnight.   And the healing process is still ongoing in that daily I have to still overcome the hurts of the past. A week does not pass that I have to repent of my anger at the Nazis when I recall the faces and names of friends I lost in the war, or seek absolution for guilt of my terrorist activities of my youth. So the truth is, Phillip, we all have hurts in this life, and only your own journey along this path of life with Christ at your side can you work through the injuries that you have experienced in your life."

We both were silent as I thought about what he had shared. Then the Abbot stood up and his eyes sparked as he said, "I must return to the monastery or the brothers will think something has happened to me. You are welcome to hike along our trails any time. Thank you for listening to my tales of a disillusioned youth who found illumination.   May you with God's help find your own path to redemption from this life's injuries.   Good evening, my young friend."   As he walked off, the Abbot turned to me and said loudly, "You must walk with me again sometime and have dinner with us. AuVoir."

At that, the Abbot turned away and continued to walk down the trail leading to the monastery.   I lingered on the bench gazing at the gathering gloom of dusk around me. In some ways, after sharing with the Abbot, I had felt absolved of my shame for the Avery Drive prank but the loss of Mom and my life in Chicago still hurt. Nevertheless, my head was swirling about what the Abbot had shared regarding his dark journey of the soul. How did one journey in this life with Christ at one's his side? How long would my journey take to begin to find illumination? These were heady questions to think about. But as the darkness deepened, I realized these would have to be dealt with later. It was time to head back and I began walking down the trails back to the fence line of Uncle Raymond's ranch. There was a beautiful yellow moon rising on the eastern horizon. It illuminated my way back down the Concharty Mountain. The moonlight made me think of Psalm 119:105, Aunt Louise shared with me one night, "Thy word is like a lamp unto my feet and a light unto my soul." I returned to Uncle Raymond and Aunt Louise's house around 9 o'clock. They didn't ask, but I told them I ran into the Abbot and had a good talk about life. I had some leftovers for a late dinner and then turned in early. It had been an intense 24 hours and I fell asleep quickly.

CHAPTER 12

REVEREND CARMICHAEL'S INVITATION

The next morning we got dressed and went to church. A visiting evangelist was preaching, Rev. Joe Carmichael from Texas. His sermon heading was "Is it Well with Your Soul?" Catchy title I thought as I entered the sanctuary. I saw Kent and of all things Joe Corsinni was with him. I excused myself from Aunt Louise and Uncle Raymond to sit with them. I threw a punch at Joe and said, "You going to be excommunicated for coming to a Baptist Church?"

"Nah," Joe said. "I come with Kent from time to time because I like the music and the preaching. But I am Catholic through and through."

"Well, it is good to see you guys. Mind if I sit with you?"

"Not at all," Kent said.

The congregation sang "It is Well with My Soul," and then Rev. Carmichael began his sermon about the history of that song. I had never heard the story behind that song and learned that the writer lost his wife and children in the sinking of a passenger ship in the Atlantic Ocean. He wrote that song as he traveled on another ship nearly a year later that carried him over that very same spot. Something began nudging my heart as he preached. He then closed up his sermon about how there was always going to be suffering in this life, but we had to press through the difficult trials with Christ's help and the support of the brethren. I could not believe what I was hearing. It was like bells were going off in my head and something deep was stirring within my spirit. The closing hymn was "Amazing Grace" but sung to James Taylor's catchy melody of "Sunny Skies."

Rev. Carmichael gave an invitation to anyone wanting to come to Christ. Without hesitation, I stood up in the pew. Joe and Kent were stunned as I scooted past them and walked down the aisle to the waiting Rev. Carmichael. He had a broad smile and firm handshake. He gave me a hug.

Aunt Louise, assuming Uncle Raymond had a hand in this, whispered almost accusingly to Uncle Raymond, "You know anything about this?"

"No," Uncle Raymond whispered back, wide-eyed in amazement, and then added, "Come on Louise, let's go stand with our boy."

I was totally focused on Rev. Carmichael. He was a handsome guy probably in his early 30's. The congregation continued through all five stanzas of the song. I felt a hand on my shoulder. It was Kent with Joe at his side. They both were smiling. They both shook my hand and gave me a hug. Then I felt an arm around my waist.

It was Aunt Louise with Uncle Raymond. She stood right against me with Raymond at her side. That Sunday morning I made a profession of faith with four of the most important people in my life in Haskell standing with me. Aunt Louise whispered to me that I really caught her off guard. Uncle Raymond chuckled and said to Aunt Louise that the Lord loves to surprise His children by catching us off guard with His blessings. Aunt Louise poked Uncle Raymond in the side. Rev. Carmichael saw this and I thought Rev. Carmichael was going to bust a gut. However, he maintained his composure but just barely. The congregation finished singing the song and Rev. Carmichael then explained the passage of Rev. 3:15 about Christ standing at the door and knocking. If any man would open the door, the Lord would come in to have supper. Rev. Carmichael explained to the entire congregation that a meal in those times bespoke of an intimate relationship. He reminded us that in the four

Gospels the most significant events of Christ's ministry on earth often happened at meals. This passage, he explained, evidenced God's desire for life giving intimacy with us. He then focused his attention on me and asked me if I was ready to invite Christ into my life as an intimate friend and Savior. I nodded my assent. Rev. Carmichael then asked me if I repented of my sins and desired to be part of the body of Christ. I said yes. He then welcomed me into the faith by extending his right hand of fellowship and invited the Church to greet me after the service. He closed up in a prayer as the congregation bowed their heads. At the end of the service I was taken to the entrance to greet everyone as a new member of the Body of Christ. Joe, Kent, Uncle Raymond and Aunt Louise stood with me. I shook countless hands that morning and was greeted into the household of faith.

"Buddy, you continually astound me," Kent said as we stood in the greeting line.

"How so?" I asked.

"You just do man. Too complicated to explain right now," Kent replied. Years later I realized what Kent was really saying. Who really amazed Kent was not me but God. Uncle Raymond was right that God did like surprises; especially ones that strengthened people's faith in His guidance and love in this broken world.

"And heaven knows our weak legs need strengthening," Aunt Louise had once said.

Joe was stoic but smiling. Our eyes locked. Though nothing was said, I sensed Joe understood me. Thus, nothing had to be said. We were brothers not just in athletics but now also in the household of faith. Reflecting back I had never seen Joe at First Baptist before now. I believe it was the Holy Spirit prompting Joe to come to church with Kent that day because God knew what was going to occur and wanted Joe there to stand with me together with Kent; and even now, though I don't see Joe as often as I would like, there is an unusual connection at the heart level whenever we do see each other. Some men never experience an intimate male friendship and it seemed that I had been blessed with two – Kent and Joe.

That Sunday morning was an eventful day for sure. One that would forever influence my life for years to come.

CHAPTER 13

LUCINDA MATLOCK AND THE SUBJECT OF WOMEN

The weeks wore on at Haskell High School. One morning Miss Dressbach was covering the Spoon River Anthology for her Modern English class. She chose some of us to recite the poems from that reading. Kent was asked to read the part of E. C. Culbertson, a very peculiar personality; this he did very well with inflection and enthusiasm. He was a good speaker and there was a magnetism to his speaking ability. Kent would do well as a trial lawyer, I thought. The class briefly discussed this character. Miss Dressbach called on Miriam to read Lucinda Matlock. Miriam came to the front of the class and began reading, "Lucinda Matlock" by Edgar Lee Masters. She began,

"I went to the dances at Chandlerville,
And played snap-out at Winchester.
One time we changed partners,
Driving home in the moonlight of middle June,
And then I found Davis.
We were married and lived together for seventy years,
Enjoying, working, raising the twelve children,
Eight of whom we lost
Ere I had reached the age of sixty.
I spun, I wove, I kept the house, I nursed the sick,
I made the garden, and for holiday
Rambled over the fields where sang the larks,
And by Spoon River gathering many a shell,
And many a flower and medicinal weed—
Shouting to the wooded hills, singing to the green valleys.
At ninety-six I had lived enough, that is all,

And passed to a sweet repose.
What is this I hear of sorrow and weariness,
Anger, discontent and drooping hopes?
Degenerate sons and daughters,
Life is too strong for you—
It takes life to love life."

Miriam had recited the poem with a clarity and enthusiasm that was riveting. If I had been interested in Miriam before, she had ignited a deeper passion in me to pursue her. It was as if she and the character of Lucinda Matlock were merged into one in my mind's eye. I could well see her as Lucinda Matlock that Edgar Lee Masters had described and I was Davis. This stirred me to think about us together. She had a zest for life I was finding irresistible. I tucked this away in my mind for further reflection later. We were about to discuss the character of Lucinda Matlock but the class bell rang and all the students were heading out to the next class

The rest of the day I kept thinking of Miriam. This reverie, however, ended at sixth hour when we suited up for football practice. My mind had to take a new beat with all the physical labor of a three-hour football practice.

We were having a successful year in football and there was talk about making it to the State Playoffs. I liked Coach Elliot and the guys on the team. However, football practice was always a challenge for me. Mentally and physically, my sport of choice was still swimming. Swim workouts were easy for me, compared to football workouts. Haskell High School was somewhat easy for me though, even if there was still a lot of work to do.

In late September and early October the various recruiters of colleges began coming to school. Joe and Kent signed up to meet the recruiter from John Brown University who was speaking during second hour. I knew what that meant; I was going also whether I wanted to go or not. When Kent and Joe ganged up on me to do something with them, it was a sure thing I was joining them!

We were excused from our second hour class with Mr. Bower. No loss there I thought. Ten years from now no Algebraic equation was going to mean anything to me, but hanging with Joe and Kent might. It seemed a better use of my time; even if I was not going to college with them. The recruiter was a young man who was a senior at JBU. He was a winsome speaker and it was readily apparent he was an athlete.

His accent was not at all southern and I at once spotted something very familiar about his appearance. His hair had the sheen that a person gets from prolonged exposure to chlorinated water. He discussed the various college programs and strengths of JBU. He fielded questions about the football team from Kent and Joe very well, I thought. He took their names to turn in to the JBU football coach as well as some of their game stats. There were only five kids who were there to visit with him. He carefully interviewed everyone about their planned course of study and extracurricular interests. He then came to me and noticed my accent was not "Okie" but northern. He asked me where I was from.

"Chicago area," I said.

"Really!" he exclaimed. "I am from Rockford, Illinois. Another Land of Lincoln Man."

"How did you end up down here?" I asked.

"I wanted to go to a small school with a healthy Christian world view. When they offered me an athletic scholarship for swimming, I couldn't turn it down." At that Kent and Joe swung around and looked at me. I could feel two pair of eyes burning into the sides of my head.

Kent cleared his throat and said to the recruiter whose name was Paul Marshall, "Phillip here was an All American swimmer from St. Cyngen's in Chicago." I could have died on the spot. No one knew that except Kent and Joe and Uncle Raymond and Aunt Louise. Now it would be common knowledge in Haskell by sixth hour. I kept a low profile about that because I didn't want to draw attention to myself.

Paul Marshall asked me what my name was. "Phillip Robertson," I replied. He then asked me about various swimmers I might have known in the Chicago area; some of whom I recognized and actually knew.

"In what events were you All American?" Paul asked.

"400 IM," I replied.

"Awesome," he said. "I will tell Coach Cutter about you. Give me some more of your swimming stats. Also, fill out this card with your address and phone number." He closed up the hour by inviting us to spend the upcoming weekend at JBU as a guest of his.

Kent and Joe readily accepted the invitation, which meant I knew that three Haskell Haymakers would be going to Siloam Springs to see the sights and sounds of the JBU campus. Oh, brother. What I wouldn't do for and with these two stooges!

"Well." I said, as we walked back to our third hour, "When are we going to Arkansas?"

Kent slapped me on the shoulder and said "All right!"

Joe just grinned and said, "You knew we would have tied you up and thrown you in the back seat if you had said you weren't going with us."

"Guys, I would be offended if you didn't shanghai me to go with you." We all laughed and began making plans to visit JBU this Saturday. "I will check with Aunt Louise and Uncle Raymond to see if Joe and I can work Sunday afternoon to make up for Saturday." Joe concurred with that and we made plans to leave early Saturday morning and return later that evening.

I knew that Kent and Joe would probably be attending JBU on a full football scholarship but their road was not necessarily my destiny. Doc Counsilman at Indiana University had expressed an interest in me; UCLA wrote me before I left for Haskell; and even some Ivy League schools had expressed an interest. Nevertheless, it would be good to go with these guys to JBU just to learn how to scope out a school and learn what questions to ask.

That evening I talked to Uncle Raymond about going to JBU with the guys on Saturday. He agreed that I could work on Sunday afternoon rather than Saturday so I could go to JBU with Kent and Joe. "I think we can spare you for the weekend," Uncle Raymond said, smiling.

We had an away game Friday night against Morris. It was a tough game but we beat them 23 to 14. We got back to Haskell around 11. Kent and Joe spent the night with me at Uncle Raymond and Aunt Louise's house. Only this time Kent and I exiled Joe to the spare bedroom where he could snore to his heart's content and we might get some rest before we got up to go on our big road trip. We were going to leave at 8:00 a.m. Paul Marshall would meet us at the JBU Student Union to show us around at 10:30 A.M. There was no quick way to Siloam Springs from Haskell.

When we got up, Aunt Louise had fixed a fresh pot of coffee, sliced apples and had scrambled eggs and sausage.

"Mrs. Hammond," Kent said with a mouthful of eggs, "Someday I hope I find a gal as good as you."

"Pshaw," was all that Aunt Louise said, slightly embarrassed.

"Thought you already had," Joe chimed in.

"What was the name of that girl you met last summer at Falls Creek Baptist Church Camp; the one from Bartlesville, Theresa Von Holland?" I asked.

"The way I hear it, you have been burning a hole in Dr. James' checking account with your phone bill," Joe added, teasingly.

"Dang it, Sinni! Don't rat out your friends. Remember what Phillip's brother Frank said. M.A.D., Mutually Assured Destruction! Should I chime in anything about your love conquests?" Kent said, chagrinned.

"There ain't any, Kent, and you know that," Joe retorted, smiling. "But you on the other hand have a fan club of swooning hearts," Joe laughed.

By now Aunt Louise was genuinely amused. I had never seen such a display between Joe and Kent and it was pretty darn interesting. I sat there smiling. I had heard Kent talk about the Von Holland girl but was not aware of his apparent earnest interest.

"What are you smiling about, Phillip F. Austin?" Kent asked.

"You know, Kent, I have never seen you so flustered about women. Heck, half the time you have a pretty girl hanging on your shoulder at school," I teased.

"Exactly," Joe added.

"And what's wrong with that?" Kent asked, defiantly.

At that Aunt Louise arched an eyebrow and was now smiling. In her wise clever way she stayed out of this repartee and let the combatants expose themselves. Her F.B.I. network (that stood for the Family Bureau of Investigation) would be sharing this new intelligence coup. No doubt Kent's mother would hear of this exchange before the morning was over if I knew my Aunt Louise. I was to learn years later that not much occurred in the Hammond or James household that was not the subject of discussion and prayer between Aunt Louise and Kent's mom.

"Hey, guys," I said, changing the subject and limiting the damage from too much gratuitous sharing of personal love life information. "Its 8:00 a.m., we need to get going if we are going to make it to Siloam Springs at 10:30."

I kissed Aunt Louise on the cheek and said I would be home around 10:30 that night. Kent and Joe thanked Aunt Louise for breakfast and we headed out to Kent's car. He drove a new 1971 blue Pontiac LeMans that his dad bought for him his senior year. We piled in and headed off to John Brown University.

CHAPTER 14

VISIT TO JBU

The drive to Siloam Springs was long. There was no four-lane road to get there and the narrow two-lane roads took a long time. But the hills and trees were really beautiful. Siloam Springs sat squarely in the southern extension of the Ozark Mountains. These mountains were really hills that stretched across Missouri, Kansas, Oklahoma and Arkansas. They were heavily forested with beautiful clear flowing streams and rivers. The fall colors were beginning to show and I marveled at the scenery we passed. Finally, we made it to Siloam Springs and drove onto the JBU campus.

Kent followed the directions Paul Marshall had given us and we pulled up to the Student Union parking lot. We got out and walked to the JBU Student Union. Paul saw us and came out to greet us. He had two other guys with him who were obviously football players. I learned they were both seniors. One was the JBU quarterback and the other was a wide receiver. No coincidence there, I thought. Obviously Paul Marshall was impressed with Joe and Kent and wanted to make a good impression on my buddies. They showed us around the campus and the dorms. We ate lunch with a bunch of other jocks who welcomed us. I observed that there were young men and women from all over the United States and many foreign students here as well.

The football players took Kent and Joe to meet the football coach for some coach to potential player talk. I was singled out to meet the swim coach John Cutter and some of the swimmers at Coach Cutter's house. Coach Cutter was a retired Air Force Colonel and his wife Marion was an English Professor at JBU. They were both very engaging and hospitable. She had made a chocolate sheet cake with pecans to die for. The other swimmers peppered me with questions about my times and events I swam. It was a pleasant way to spend the afternoon as I had not been able to talk my swimming jock talk since I had left Chicago.

I was asked about my grades and ACT scores. I had carried a 3.4 at St. Cyngen and a 4.0 at Haskell. My ACT was 29 and I noticed Coach Cutter was favorably impressed. The guys asked if I would like to see the pool and took me to see the swimming facility. I was surprised. I had not expected to find such a good swimming complex here.

Paul Marshall then excused us as we needed to get back with Joe and Kent. It was drawing on close to 4:30 and he wanted to take the three of us to dinner at an Italian restaurant called Mary Maestri's up the road a ways toward an Italian community called Tontitown.

Joe had heard of it because he had some distant cousins from there. "Lots of good eating there," Joe said. Paul took the quarterback Josh Taylor and the wide receiver J. B. Stevens to dinner with us. The six of us had a lively conversation and we learned why these guys chose JBU. All three were very earnest about their athletics, academics and faith. It was really unusual for me to meet guys like this and I was duly impressed. We got back to Siloam Springs around 7:00 and thanked them for their hospitality and time they spent with us.

On the road home Kent and Joe were animated about who they met and what they had seen. There was no doubt in my mind they would go to college here at JBU. There was every doubt in my mind that I would see much of Joe or Kent after the fall semester at Haskell High School.

We got back around 10:00 and Kent dropped me off at Uncle Raymond's house. I came in and saw that Uncle Raymond was still up, but he was reading a biography of Winston Churchill, one of his heroes. We debriefed about the trip to JBU and all that I had seen. I told Uncle Raymond how impressed I was with the JBU swim facilities and swim team. He even asked me if I would now consider applying to JBU. I didn't discount the idea, nor did I commit to this. Uncle Raymond listened to me talk about my collegiate plans for swimming and threw in an occasional comment. Around 11:00 p.m., Uncle Raymond said, "We had better turn in, Phillip, or we both will have a lot of explaining to do with your Aunt Louise." He winked at me and we both headed for our respective rooms to go to bed.

As I lay down on my bed, for the first time it really hit me that I was going to truly miss Kent and Joe. In the space of four months we had become best friends. Heck, the kids at high school nicknamed us the "Three Amigos." I knew that each fleeting day I had down here was precious. Like an hourglass draining sand from the top to the bottom, I knew my time was running out. The Concharty Mountain had worked its magic on me in four months and woven the people who lived around it deep in my heart. That is why I knew leaving for Chicago in less than two months was going to be rough because of the void it would leave, not only in my heart but also in the hearts of the people I had come to care about so deeply. The Abbot had once told me on one of our walks together, that in this vale of tears called life we often had to make journeys away from the things and people we are familiar with and love. This aspect of my life's journey, as Abbot DeLaurier called it, I did not look forward to experiencing. It would be interesting to get his take on how he left his monastery in France to come to an alien land in America.

CHAPTER 15

DANCE LESSONS WITH AUNT LOUISE

It was the week of Homecoming and there was furious activity getting ready for it at school and in town. One night that week after practice, Joe and Kent had dinner with me, Uncle Raymond and Aunt Louise. The subject of the Mixer at Homecoming came up at dinner. Uncle Raymond and Aunt Louise had been chaperones at this event for years. Aunt Louise ferreted out a confession from Kent that a certain Theresa Von Holland from Bartlesville might be coming down to watch the big game and go to the Mixer with Kent. This Joe and I already knew but had kept this to ourselves. This is how the subject of dancing came up. Kent flatly stated he didn't dance. This provoked Aunt Louise to say, "You mean you have invited a girl to travel 70 miles from Bartlesville to watch you prance around high and mighty on the football field, and you can't show her the courtesy of dancing with her at the Mixer?"

Kent defended himself by saying, "Truth is, Mrs. Hammond, I don't know how to dance."

"That can be easily cured young man," Aunt Louise said with authority as she pushed away from the dinner table and stood up. Arching her eyebrow, she added, "Coach Hammond, it is time to teach your ballplayers how to dance not only on the football field but also on the dance floor."

Uncle Raymond smiled and nodded his agreement. "Guys, she's right. If you can entertain the town with your performance on the football field, you can perform on the dance floor for the young ladies. After all, these gals come to support you – now it is your turn to support them. About time you learned the give and take between a man and woman!" With that Uncle Raymond got up from the table and also went to the den to fire up his phonograph player.

"Boys, to the playing field," Aunt Louise ordered, pointing to the den. Joe, Kent and I initially sat stunned in silence. She gave us a look that prompted us to get up and go to the den. I knew how to dance from years of lessons at Skelly Dance Studio to attend the Wintergarden Ball in Chicago. There we had to learn to waltz, fox trot, tango, polka, rumba and the two-step. You could not go to the Wintergarden Ball if you did not know these dance steps. Hence, I had learned my dance steps very well. But this fact I did not disclose to Joe or Kent or even Aunt Louise or Uncle Raymond. Uncle Raymond put on some music, as we came into the den.

"Assume your position, boys," Uncle Raymond commanded.

"What's that, Coach?" Joe asked.

Immediately Aunt Louise took up a position with Kent. Joe and I just stood there but that didn't last long. "Joe, take Phillip in your arms as the lead. Phillip, you play the girl."

"What?" Both Joe and I exclaimed, turning to Uncle Raymond with a look of shock on our faces.

Kent snickered as Uncle Raymond said, "No argument, boys. Besides, Phillip, I know you know how to dance. Your Dad told me you had expensive dance lessons for years back in Chicago. So your secret's out, Cowboy. You're going to help Joe Corsinni. He helped you learn how to play on the football field, now you can teach him to dance at the Mixer in return." I gulped hard. My secret was out!

The most awkward moment in my life was taking position as a dance partner with Joe Corsinni. We were learning the fox trot. Joe was as embarrassed as I was. All he could do was look at his feet as he learned to steps. I took the initiative to truly make Joe into a good dancer.

"Joe, look at me," I said. "You have to learn the rhythm of your dance partner. Always look at the girl in the eyes."

"Yeah, but you're no girl," Joe said.

"Thank God for small favors," I replied, laughing. "Look at me, Sinni." At that I took my hand and grabbed Joe's chin and made him look only at me. I felt Joe's huge hand crush my other hand. I kept a straight face and said, "Good, you are getting it. Believe me, Joe, the girls will appreciate your looking at them. Makes conversation easier, too."

"I don't dance and I don't talk easily to girls," Joe replied.

"Which is why you are driving all the girls of Haskell nuts, Joe. A day does not go by that some girl doesn't hit me or Kent up about you. 'He has the sweetest smile and most beautiful eyes,'" I teased. Joe stomped on my foot and crushed my hand again.

I laughed and said, "You're no gentleman, Mr. Corsinni."

"And you're no lady," Joe replied, laughing. Our dance workout lasted for about half an hour. Mercifully, we changed partners and I got to dance with Aunt Louise. We demonstrated the rumba and tango and Kent and Joe tried dancing with each other. It was hilarious watching those two, dancing something rumba-like with a twist of a tango with each other.

Long about 7:30, we stopped as Joe reminded us we three guys needed to stop by the Fugalis and were running late. The guys had learned the two-step and fox trot. I couldn't vouch for any other dance steps we practiced. We took our leave of Uncle Raymond and Aunt Louise and headed over to the Fugalis. I was on borrowed time as I had to be back by 10:30 since it was a school night.

We arrived late at the Fugali home. Miriam answered the door and the house was full of girls from school who were part of the Pep Club. They were making signs on butcher paper commemorating the upcoming game and Mixer.

"Hey, girls, look who's here. The Co-captains and Phillip." At that the girls got up off the floor from painting signs to come over. I noticed baklava and mamoul on the dining room table.

"What kept you guys so long? I thought you would be here an hour ago," Miriam said.

Without thinking, I said, "Dancing." Joe stomped on my foot and Kent blanched.

"Dancing?" Miriam said.

Several girls cooed at that. "Can we see you dance now?" a cute young coed named Nancy Baker asked.

Before we could answer one girl ran to the Fugali's phonograph and put on some music while the other girls cleared the floor. A cheerleader named Carol Schnelle grabbed Kent while Sheree Brandt immediately grabbed Joe. He didn't resist her advances to dance and they both smiled warmly at each other. At some point, I thought Joe and I needed to broach a taboo subject – his closeted interest in Sheree Brandt! But that thought fled my mind when I turned to Miriam. As I was standing next to Miriam, I asked her to be my partner. A slow song was put on so we could do our easy fox trot. God, it was great dancing with Miriam. It was a pleasure to look into those emerald green eyes. "Bedroom eyes" is what my brother John would have called them. He was the Romeo of our family and knew about these things.

I noticed Joe and Sheree dancing with each other in rather close proximity to one another. It was a safe venue for them to do this and most people would not necessarily infer anything from this. More than once Kent and I pondered how to approach Joe about his sequestered affection for Sheree. There were some social boundaries one did not cross in Haskell, Oklahoma, and racial interdating was one of them in 1970. My thoughts, however, drifted back to Miriam and how good she danced. Gosh, it was great to be with her like this.

But it didn't last long. Other girls began cutting in and Kent, Joe and I danced with every one of those girls that night. Kent and Joe had the fox trot and two step down well. As the evening wore on, their dancing actually improved. We had a great time laughing, dancing, eating baklava and mamoul and just being high school kids. No society soiree' of my classmates back in Chicago was as much fun as I had that evening of an informal get together at the Fugalis with my Haskell friends. Things closed up around 10:00 as Kent and Joe had to have me back at Uncle Raymond and Aunt Louise. We took our leave of the girls and Miriam and headed back to Kent's car.

"You guys picked up those dance steps fairly well. I am impressed. Just don't stomp on the girls' feet, Joe, or crush their hands," I teased.

Joe cut his eyes at me and smiled. "They're prettier to dance with, Phillip."

"No comparison there, Sinni." Kent said.

I laughed and said, "That Bartlesville girl will be impressed with how well you can dance, Kent. You just wait and see." Joe smiled and looked at Kent. "Yeah, you're starting to scoot on the dance floor better than you catch a football in a game."

Kent muttered, "Thanks, I think." Joe and I cut our eyes at each other, grinning.

Kent, Joe and I then chatted about the upcoming game and Mixer. We were all looking forward to Homecoming in a couple of days. The excitement around school and town was downright infectious. I was looking forward to this Homecoming even more than I ever had the Wintergarden Ball back in Chicago. Joe and Kent let me off and I came in. It was two days away till the big day. I got undressed and ready for bed. I yawned, laid on the bed and fell asleep with music going through my head.

CHAPTER 16

THE HASKELL HOMECOMING GAME

Friday, the big game day, comes. It just happened to be my birthday also. Aunt Louise said she would bake me a chocolate cake with pecans for my birthday. Pecans were everywhere down here and were as ubiquitous to Oklahoma cuisine as bratwurst and sauerkraut were to Chicago. There were pecans in your tossed green salad; pecans in your fruit salad; pecans in your green bean casserole; pecan encrusted catfish; and pecans in every manner of dessert. I must admit that I had come to really like pecans. Maybe it was their rich buttery taste that enhanced any dish.

Looking back now, I think it was Aunt Louise's loving touch. She could have thrown in Habanero peppers in a dish and I would have found them tasty. I did enjoy her cooking, but it was her warmth and kindness and spunk that made dining on her culinary creations a hungry jock's delight. It was my 18th birthday and I was looking forward to the game. We were playing the Atoka Wampus Cats. What in the sam hill was a Wampus Cat? I would never hear the end of it from the St. Cyngen classmates back in Chicago when I returned if we lost to them.

The electricity of the game and Homecoming could be felt throughout the school. All manner of kids, teachers and support staff were drawn into the vortex for this one big event. It was as if the whole town was gearing up for this. Letter jackets were popping up everywhere all over town during the week. That day as former Haskell Haymaker alumni broke out the colors to show their spirit. I practically floated through the classes all day. Sixth hour rolled around and we had a pep club rally. It seemed the whole town turned out for this. The band was playing the school fight song when the football team entered the gymnasium with Coach Elliot leading his team with Kent and Joe following as the team captains. Each of the players was introduced. We were all wearing our jerseys and jeans and tennis shoes. Coach Elliot wanted us all to wear the same outfit to be united as a team. The crowd cheered as the name of each player was announced. Joe and Kent were introduced last and they invited Coach Elliot to make a brief pep talk about the team. When he concluded, the crowd came to its feet, roaring support of the homeboys. Coach Elliot led us out of the arena back to the locker room.

"Boys, I want you to go home and rest for a couple hours. No hanging out with a girlfriend or fawning fans. Go home; save your mental, emotional and physical energy for the game. Eat light, rest. I will see you back here at 7:00 tonight." Coach Elliot then had us all put our hands one on top of another and yell "Team."

Coach Elliot walked us out to the parking lot and made sure we got in our cars and left. Any ardent fans who wanted to talk to us were admonished by Coach Elliot to save it for after the game at the Mixer. He projected a stern countenance on this issue and would broach no dissent from players, parents or fans.

I said goodbye to Joe and Kent and headed back to Uncle Raymond and Aunt Louise's house. I got back home around 3:30. Aunt Louise was in the den reading. I could sniff something baking that smelled great. It was my birthday cake.

""Afternoon, Aunt Louise," I said.

"Happy birthday, Phillip!"

"Thanks, Aunt Louise," I said, sniffing the aroma. "Something smells mighty fine, Aunt Louise," I smiled.

"Well, you get some rest now," Aunt Louise said. "There will be plenty of time to celebrate your birthday later. Go rest and I will get you up around 5:30 for a light supper. Talk to you, then." At that, Aunt Louise returned to reading. I turned and went down the hall to go back to my room. I put my books away, took off my shoes, turned on my fan, closed the door and laid down to rest. I dozed off and then was awakened at 5:30 by a light knock on the door. It was Aunt Louise. "Supper's ready, Phillip." I got up and changed.

Coach Elliot wanted us in slacks, shirt and tie for the game. I then walked down the hall back to the kitchen. Aunt Louise had prepared bacon, lettuce and tomato sandwiches, sliced peaches, fresh homemade lemonade and a new pot of coffee. Aunt Louise had made her homemade bread for the sandwiches. I could have eaten two loaves of her wheat bread buttered with her homemade blackberry jam. Joe and I did that one Saturday much to Aunt Louise's shock. I ate two sandwiches, a peach, washed it down with three glasses of lemonade and a cup of coffee. Aunt Louise just shook her head. "I swear, Phillip, I think you have two empty holes in your legs and arms to put that food away," Aunt Louise said, amazed.

I laughed and said with a mouthful of half of a BLT, "Dad says the boys in our family have a fast metabolism and athletics only kick started it to go faster. A faster metabolism makes a guy hungry all the time." And with that I ate the other half of the sandwich. I was up to three sandwiches and started on another peach.

"No wonder you gained 15 pounds in four months. You eat like this back home?" Aunt Louise asked.

"Well, the food was good, but the company wasn't nearly as sweet as you, Aunt Louise. Agnes Kotlarski is a good cook, but you don't want to linger in the kitchen very long around her. I can only handle a dour outlook on life so long. Just kills a guy's appetite. Frank used to call her Eyor in high school until Mom nailed him for being disrespectful. But it wasn't too far from the truth."

"How long has Agnes been with your family?" Aunt Louise asked.

"She has been with our family since Frank was born and actually lives on Mom and Dad's place in a separate cottage attached to the house. She would jump down the throat of anyone who tried to cross our family, but the trauma of World War II permanently affected her view of life. But she was really there for us when Mom had her accident. She went to the hospital every day for hours at a time."

"Hmm," Aunt Louise said. "Give me something to think about and pray about for sure. But thinking about praying, been doing that all day that your team plays their heart out."

"What?" I said. "You are not praying we wallop the Wampus Cats?" I teased. "Nope! Far more important that you play your best. The winning and losing thing I leave in the Lord's hands. Besides, in the eternal scheme of things, it is far better to learn the discipline of practicing hard so you can play your best. That is a good life lesson," Aunt Louise spoke with authority.

I had never heard that angle on winning and losing. Ms. Bea Notly, my Latin teacher, had once made us learn the statement, albeit in Latin, "To be beaten by someone better after you have played your best is to share in their glory." But Aunt Louise had just articulated some homespun wisdom that I later came to realize was not only practical but very profound.

Uncle Raymond came home as I was taking my football gear to the blue Malibu. He helped me load my gear into the car. He put his hand on my shoulder to affirm me and said, looking me in the eye, "Play your best tonight, Phillip. Louise and I will be rooting for you." There was electricity in that man's touch. One felt warm all over and empowered with a sense of confidence that was unexplainable.

Looking into Uncle Raymond's eyes, I replied, "I will play with all my heart, Sir."

Uncle Raymond smiled, "I know you will, Phillip." He patted me on the shoulder and said, "You'd better get going or Coach Elliot will have you running wind sprints all week long if you are late." I got in the car, waved goodbye, and gave Uncle Raymond a thumbs up as I pulled out of the driveway.

I arrived at the playing field at the same time as some of the other players. Kent was already getting his stuff out of his car. Joe was walking into the locker room with his gear. Most of the guys were fairly somber this evening. Everyone felt the weight of the town's expectations for this game. Not even Kent was kidding around or cutting up with the other guys. As we finished suiting up, Coach Elliot came in. We gathered around him and he gave us a pep talk.

He reminded us of each position we played; the role of that position, and how we would play as a team to beat Atoka. He gathered us for a final team prayer before the game. We then put our hands one on top of the other and shouted "Team." Coach Elliot then lined us up to run out onto the field. The Captains, Joe and Kent, were behind him. Then we lined up by age, seniors to freshmen, to run out on the field. We came out of the locker room and got ready to run out on the field. The Haskell High School band was playing the school fight song.

Coach Elliot shouted, "Let's go, men!" and we sprinted out onto the field. The crowd roared and came to their feet, clapping. We warmed up with stretching exercises before the game. The Atoka Wampus Cats then came out on the field to warm up. The visitors' side came to their feet, clapping and shouting for their team. The announcer came on the loudspeaker and asked the audience to stand for the National Anthem. Both home and visitors sang loudly that night, right hands over their hearts. At the end of the song both sides were cheering.

The announcer then introduced the team captains of Haskell and Atoka. This was the most unusual thing about football played in Oklahoma. The team captains would come out on the field, holding hands, for the coin toss for who kicked off versus who received. That spectacle of two guys walking out on a field of athletic combat holding hands would never occur up north. Atoka won the toss so we would be kicking off to them

Joe had warned me that the Atoka guys were a hardscrabble bunch of dudes. They were from a really poor area of the state and often football was their ticket out of poverty via a college football scholarship. Moreover, for others often this was their only means of glory and they fought with every fiber of their being to capture their fleeting moment of fame in their otherwise bleak lives.

And fight they did in this game this night. It was the toughest game we had played up to now. Players on both teams were injured that evening. At half time, the score was tied 14 – 14. We had been playing our hearts out but so were the Wampus Cats. Coach Elliot spoke to us in the locker room at half time to encourage us. He had invited all the fathers of the players to come stand with their sons in the locker room at half time. As the fathers came in and stood with their sons, it was an incredible sight to behold.

Some fathers were hugging their sons; some put an affirming hand on their shoulders; others whispered quiet encouragement to their sons. I was kneeling and looking down at the floor, doing a mental autopsy of my game performance as Uncle Raymond had suggested last summer. My mental review was interrupted by a hand on my shoulder. I looked up and saw Uncle Raymond. He didn't say anything right away but there was a sense of purpose in his eyes. He squeezed his hand on my shoulder and then leaned over and said, "Phillip, this is the roughest game of football I have ever seen played in years. You hang tough, Phillip. Don't lose heart. Focus on what you have to do in the second half. Don't think of the game from the first half."

Coach Elliot then addressed the fathers and sons. He spoke with an almost religious intensity about the game that had yet to be played by the team in the second half. He spoke to each individual player and their role on the team. "Joe, you know what you have to do. Stay with your game, son." And so it went from quarterback to cornerback, to defensive end to wide receiver. By the time he was through, we all had a new sense of purpose and resolve. This was reinforced by the fathers being there also. It was the most unique father-son bonding I had ever witnessed.

Years later guys on the team would reflect wistfully on that moment in time they had had with their fathers at half time in that locker room. Coach Elliot had the players and fathers put their hands together and shout "TEAM!" The players filed out in the same formation of the start of the game. Coach Elliot had sought to bring out the grit we needed for the second half and had succeeded. The Wampus Cats, however, were just as reinvigorated as we were. The second half of the game was as tough as the first except no team was scoring. The ball switched sides throughout the second half. Both teams were determined to win, but we all were tiring. Mistakes were being made because our physical stamina was flagging. We got the ball to the 30-yard line and Coach Elliot played a fast one. He set the line up to look like a long bomb by Joe to Kent when he intended a field goal. Joe could kick the ball as well as he could throw it. The ball was put into play, Kent went deep and the visiting team thought that was the play. But Joe fooled them and kicked the ball. His athletic prowess made the ball go sailing over the heads of the players and scored a field goal. The score moved to 17 to 14 and remained that way the rest of the game. We had won.

We were elated but exhausted. We lined up and shook hands with the other team. Afterwards it seemed that the entire town came down on the field to congratulate us. Then the band played the school song. The players went to the end of the field by the locker room, knelt down on one knee, and held their helmets up in the air as the song played. At the conclusion of the song we got up and went on into the locker room to shower up and change. I had a smile on my face as I thought about dancing with Miriam at the Homecoming Mixer.

CHAPTER 17

HOMECOMING MIXER

We showered and cleaned up. Coach Elliot wanted his team wearing slacks, dress shirt and tie for the mixer. Players who lettered could wear their letter jackets with the slacks and tie; all others had to wear blazers or sweaters. Coach Elliot wanted his players to honor their classmates and the town for supporting them at the game. The entire team was going to enter the Haskell Armory at the same time. Coach Elliot would lead us in. The armory was on the other side of town so the team drove in a caravan. We parked a block away as it seemed that the whole town had turned out for the mixer. There was hardly a place to park within two blocks. There were a lot of men loitering outside the armory smoking cigarettes.

Many of them were wearing Haskell letter jackets. As we walked towards the armory entrance behind Coach Elliot, these guys started clapping and cheering Coach Elliot and the team. We entered the armory. It was packed with people. One side of the armory had tables set up with food and drinks. On the stage a DJ had set up. The crowd started clapping as we entered the armory. We followed Coach Elliot straight to the stage. Coach Elliot took the microphone and spoke to the audience. He made a point of thanking the audience for their faith and support in the young men that composed the Haskell Haymakers. He then turned the microphone over to the team captains. Kent thanked the audience for their support and echoed Coach Elliot's appreciation for the town and then turned the mike over to Joe Corsinni.

"Folks, I have a special announcement on behalf of the team. I have talked to Coach Elliot about this as well as my teammates and we wish to make a special award this evening. As you know, at the Spring Banquet letters are awarded for the past year's athletic performance. We have a teammate who has qualified for a letter, but won't be here then. With Coach's permission, we wish to award him a letter tonight. It also seems fitting because tonight is his 18th birthday. Phillip Robertson, come on over here." Joe handed the mike back to Coach Elliot as I stepped forward. I was absolutely floored. I never saw this coming. Kent told me to take my navy blazer off. He helped me get it off and held it for me. Joe had a letter jacket for me and helped me put it on. "This is my old letter jacket from my sophomore year, Phillip. It is too small for me but I thought it would fit you fine," Joe said. He was right; it fit perfectly.

Kent took the mike and said, "Folks, I think we need to sing Happy Birthday to Phillip." At that a chorus of Happy Birthday was started. I was crimson red and absolutely speechless. That was soon remedied though for at the end of the song, Kent asked me if I had any words to say. I liked to have died, but took the mike.

"Thanks, Coach Elliot, Captains Kent and Joe and my fellow Haskell Haymakers teammates for this honor. I can truthfully say that this is the best birthday gift a fellow could ever want," I paused and then added, "I want to thank the people of Haskell for being so good to me. Joe and Kent, thanks for being the best buds a guy could ever hang with." At that Joe and Kent looked at each other and smiled. And then I saw them, Uncle Raymond and Aunt Louise over at one of the food tables. Of course, Aunt Louise would be somewhere near food to serve to others! "But I especially want to thank my Uncle Raymond and Aunt Louise who have been like a second mom and dad to me. You all know them as Coach and Mrs. Hammond. I know them as family and this honor of a letter is as much an award for them as it is for me." My eyes were starting to water so I gave the mike back to Kent and he gave me my blazer. I then hugged not only Joe and Kent but also Coach Elliot. That caught all three off guard but they were okay with that.

I then left the stage and made a beeline to Uncle Raymond and Aunt Louise. Both of them were wiping their eyes. I gave Uncle Raymond a bear hug and told him how much I loved both he and Aunt Louise. He said, "Back at you, Cowboy." I then hugged Aunt Louise and she started to cry. She told me what a Godsend I had been in both her and Raymond's life. I was too choked up to speak. I just melted whenever Aunt Louise got teary. We just stood there, hugging each other. Uncle Raymond had his hands on both our shoulders. The audience was clapping.

"You know, Phillip, you aren't going to be able to impress the young ladies with your fancy footwork on the dance floor if you stay here, " Uncle Raymond said. I looked up at him; his eyes were red like mine. He threw a fake punch to my chest.

"Okay, Coach Hammond," I said, and let go of Aunt Louise.

She then said, wiping her eyes, "I think there is a green-eyed raven haired beauty expecting an invitation to dance. She then pointed and said, "and you will find her over by the punch bowl serving refreshment."

Uncle Raymond arched an eyebrow as I said, "Thanks, Aunt Louise" and made my way over to the serving table to find Miriam. Uncle Raymond hugged Aunt Louise as I walked off.

"You must be mighty proud of that nephew of yours, Louise and Raymond," a woman said.

"Indeed we are," Aunt Louise answered.

"Our pride borders on sin," Uncle Raymond said, teasingly, as he winked at the lady. His gaze followed me walking over to where Miriam was serving punch.

As for me, I headed straight for the refreshment table where Miriam was ladling out punch to thirsty patrons. I got in the line and grabbed a cup and had a grin on my face as Miriam asked if I wanted some punch. "Punch is okay but I would rather have a dance with you."

Miriam smiled and replied, "I thought you would never ask." She gave the punch ladle to another girl and came from out behind the refreshment table. She was dressed in a dark pantsuit and blouse. A DJ had set up and was playing a variety of songs from the 50's and 60's. The DJ put on a Lettermen tune, "Going Out of My Head Over You." It was a slow dance song. Gosh, it felt great to dance with her. She smelled wonderful and was wearing a perfume called "Charlie," which was a favorite of mine. It felt great to dance with her. I was dressed in my finest khaki; Starched white Oxford button down shirt; red, blue and green striped tie and in lieu of a blue blazer, a letter jacket. I had dressed as if I were going to St. Cyngen so my look was totally prep. I even wore my Sebago tassel Cordovan loafers for the first time in Haskell. We were dancing a slow fox trot to the song. I was putting forth my best effort to dance well and carefully lead her on the floor.

"You know, Phillip, this is the first time I have actually had the chance to talk to you alone," Miriam said.

"Oh, really," I said. She was right. We had never had time alone, just the two of us; but then I had only been here four months and didn't have much time to go out on dates.

"Well, I have had engagements for the past two months on Friday nights and have not had much time to see anyone and as I recall you worked on Friday and Saturday nights before school started," I observed.

"Were you tied up every evening also?" Miriam shot back.

"No," I stammered. "But when school started I usually was recovering from the football practices. Besides, I was usually working on Saturday at Uncle Raymond's ranch so I was pretty worn out by the evening."

"So you place work and sports ahead of anything else?" Miriam inquired.

As we continued dancing, I gazed straight into those emerald green eyes and said, "No reply I can give you will adequately answer your questions, Miriam. I am not really good at a battle of wits. Rather than engaging in verbal repartee, I would rather enjoy the time with you so let's just say I can't think of anyone I would rather be dancing with to one of the most romantic songs I know." I looked straight into her eyes, saying nothing, but telling her how I felt about her by leaning closer into her space and smiling warmly.

"Does that line work in Chicago with girls, Phillip?" she retorted.

"Well, I am not in Chicago; I am not interested in other girls; and I was trusting that it might communicate how I felt about you."

"And how do you feel about me, Phillip?" she asked. At that moment the song hit a new tempo when the lead Lettermen singer sang, "I love you baby and when the time is right I need you baby to hold you oh so tight... trust me baby, let me love you baby."

"The song says it all, Miriam. No guy can improve on that," I replied.

"You, sir, are a hopeless romantic," Miriam said, chuckling.

"And the problem with that is what?" I asked, arching my eyebrow and drawing her closer.

Miriam smiled and said, "Nothing." At that she responded by edging closer to me. The verbal repartee was over and I had won. How could a guy not find such a moment as this intoxicating. The song finished but I kept staring into Miriam's eyes. She looked back; nothing was said. A new song started. A Buddy Holly tune "Every Day," a peppier tune. We danced it and every other song that was played that evening worth dancing to. This magic moment we felt we both wanted to enjoy.

Others came up to us to say howdy but we merely politely acknowledged them as we focused on each other. I vaguely remember seeing Kent dance by with the Von Holland girl and also Joe danced by with a myriad of gals.

The mixer was over at 12:00 but I stayed with Miriam and helped her with the cleanup crew. At 1:00 a.m. I offered Miriam a ride home and she accepted even though the armory was only five blocks from her house. It was chilly outside so I wrapped her in my Navy blazer while I wore my new letter jacket.

We left the mixer arm in arm. As we walked back to my car, I opened the door like a perfect gentleman and then walked around the back of the car. I got in the blue Malibu and she snuggled up close as I started the car. God, it felt great to hold a girl next to me again. I had often done that with Ann Burns when I drove her home from a date and had forgotten how wonderful that felt to have a girl this close. We pulled up to her house and I walked her to the door.

"I really enjoyed this evening, Phillip."

"So did I," looking into her eyes and drawing her closer. I gave her a long tight hug. Her scent was heady. I wanted to kiss her and she probably would have let me. But Miriam was a nice girl; she was not the sort of person one toyed with for a brief fling. I did not want to violate any boundaries and spoil a good relationship. I was leaving in a month and a half so it would be cruel to get something going between us only to have to leave so soon thereafter.

I loosened up on my hug and looked into those mesmerizing eyes. "Thanks for this evening, Miriam, this has been the best birthday of my life and dancing with you this evening was incredible. Thanks for being my friend. I could truly fall for a girl like you, but knowing I am going to be leaving for Chicago in a month and a half, it just would not be right for me to push the envelope with you," I paused and then went on, "Not that I don't want to. But I don't play games with people's hearts and I don't hurt those I care for." I was looking straight into her eyes, those gorgeous emerald eyes. I could spend a whole day looking at them.

She smiled and said, "I understand, Phillip. And you have kept your boundaries with me. Joe said you were a good guy and I see why he likes you. So you will go back to Chicago and back to your girlfriend up there?" Miriam asked.

"There is no girlfriend up there, Miriam," I answered. "We broke up before I moved down here. We thought it best in that we were so far apart," I replied.

"So, you will take up where you left off?" She asked.

"Probably not, Miriam. You see, I am 'damaged goods' now. In those high society circles, fathers don't let their daughters hang out with 'troubled young men' no matter what the circumstances. And based on what has happened in my family, I am regarded as troubled. So my former girlfriend, Ann Burns, will remain just that, a former girlfriend," I said. It didn't sound convincing but was totally true. The "Brahmins" of Chicago were exclusive clubbers who rarely allowed the foolish indiscretions of youth to be forgiven; and Ann was from one of the most socially prominent families from the North Shore. No I would not be forgiven for my Avery Drive prank in those circles. But how does one translate the mores of this alien culture of the upper crust of Chicago to the small town folk of Haskell, Oklahoma? It could not be done unless the listener had lived in both worlds and understood the "polite" slights and snubs of that upper crust world of Barrington Heights that my family had experienced. Eating alone at the country club; no invites for Christmas parties; no one available for lunch or dinner; no partners available for tennis or bridge games; being left off the invitation list for weddings. This my Mom and family had encountered. It was difficult to weather and Mom had paid dearly for it.

Dad did not want that for me either so it had been an act of mercy to send me down here. But my thoughts of all of this were brought to a conclusion when Miriam said, "Someday, Phillip, I want to understand you better. Good night," and at that she kissed me on the cheek. It was all I could do not to grab her and play tonsil hockey right there in her doorway. My eyes were aching to hold her and she sensed that, too.

I caressed her hand as I looked into those eyes again and said "Good night, Miriam. I hope you do come to know and understand me better."

At that we parted and I got back in the Malibu. I was so frustrated at doing the right thing. But I knew in my heart it was for the best. Dang, it was hard, though. Years later I came to recognize that taking up one's cross and crucifying your selfish fleshly desires is rarely easy or pleasant. Another part of my life's journey as the Abbot called it and I did not enjoy it. But in the long run the rewards of such a disciplined life were huge in enhancing the quality of one's life.

CHAPTER 18

SURPRISE BIRTHDAY GUESTS

I woke up the Saturday morning stiff and sore so I went to the bathroom to take some Bufferin. It may have been Homecoming and my birthday the night before but there were still chores to be done on Saturday. I could smell fresh coffee in the kitchen and wandered down the hall. Sure enough, Aunt Louise was up and fixing breakfast. I grabbed a sliced apple and poured a cup of coffee. Uncle Raymond had been up for hours (of course). "So how's the birthday boy this morning?" Aunt Louise asked.

"Tired, sore, and a year older."

"Well, you sure cut a rug last night with Miriam."

"And I am paying for it this morning. Aunt Louise, is this what old age feels like?"

"No," Aunt Louise said. "More like middle age." We both laughed.

"You know, Aunt Louise. Swimming never left me this sore and hurting. Not much glory in sore knees and aching back. If this is the glory of football, I will take the 1650 yard event."

"How far is that?" Aunt Louise asked.

"Nearly a mile," I replied.

Aunt Louise wistfully looked out the kitchen window. "Someday I need to come watch you swim, Phillip," Aunt Louise said.

"Chicago is a long ways away from Haskell to come see me swim," I answered.

"It is. But just the same, that is one part of your life I would like to see some time," she said. Aunt Louise and I both realized I had less than two months left in Haskell. Spring semester at St. Cyngen's was looming ahead but we did not really speak of it. Instead, we relished the time we had together.

"I guess Kent and Joe are going to JBU. They applied and I expect soon they will hear from the Admissions Office at JBU. I won't be surprised if they get athletic scholarships to go there. I am sure going to miss those two."

"They are going to miss you also. Speaking of which, they are coming over for lunch."

"What?" I said, taken aback.

"Yep, for your birthday party," Aunt Louise said.

"What birthday party? I don't know anything about that," I said in astonishment.

"Kent, Joe and Miriam are coming over for lunch and cake to have a belated birthday celebration," she said.

"What time?" I asked, wide-eyed.

"Around noon," Aunt Louise replied.

"Golly, Aunt Louise, it is 8:00 a.m. now and I still have chores to do." I sucked down a cup of coffee and ran back to my room to change. I would wait to shower and shave after my work was done. I had work to do in the barn and cattle to move to another pasture and all of this before 11:00!

Aunt Louise shook her head and chuckled to herself. I got dressed and flew out the door. Stiff and sore or not, I wanted to get my work done so I could hang out with Kent, Joe and Miriam. I raked out the stalls in the barn (yuck) which took about an hour. It was now 9:30 and that left me an hour and a half to saddle the paint, move some of the cattle, come back, unsaddle the paint and shower up. Amazingly, I got that done but not by 11:00, but 11:30! I ran to the house and left my boots on the back porch. I would clean them off later. I flew down the hall, grabbed a change of clothes and hit the shower. Knowing the guys, they would probably be here early! Sure enough they were! They brought Miriam with them and left her with Aunt Louise in the kitchen. Those two buckaroos came back to the bathroom before I finished my shower to talk to me. Kent put the toilet seat down to talk to me while Joe leaned against the bathroom counter.

"Guys, I get no respect from you! Can't a dude take a shower without you two at my side," I said, teasingly.

"Well, we have showered together five days a week this semester. Don't see any reason to stop that now," Kent replied. I threw a wet washrag at Kent and stepped out of the shower to grab a towel to dry off. Only there were no towels or any of my clothes left. Both Kent and Joe had taken them and waited just long enough to see my shocked expression before they darted out of there like two underage schoolboys.

"Happy Birthday, Phillip," Kent said. Both he and Joe were laughing.

"You rats," I shouted. They had me in a dilemma. I could not walk out of the bathroom buck-naked as the hallway was perpendicular to the kitchen. If Aunt Louise and Miriam were there, they would catch me in my "birthday" suit. But I didn't want to give those two much satisfaction at my dilemma. Fortunately, I remembered Aunt Louise had an old stash of towels under the sink. I locked the bathroom door to keep those rag-a-muffins called friends out while I shaved and finished cleaning up. I opened the bathroom door and came out wearing a towel and walked back to my room. And wouldn't you know it, Kent and Joe were there with Miriam! I liked to have died. I had grown up wearing speedos in a pool, but having Kent and Joe there with only a towel was like being a mouse in a cage with two hungry bull snakes. The three of them were decorating my room for my birthday. Kent and Joe had been given the job of delaying my entry while they helped Miriam. They never dreamed I would come out of the bathroom nor did they know of Aunt Louise's stash of old towels.

"Why Phillip, I almost didn't recognize you with your clothes off," Miriam teased. Kent and Joe were busting a gut.

"Well, unless you want to behold me in my primordial glory, would you co-conspirators mind returning my clothes?" I asked, glaring at Kent and Joe.

Kent and Joe took my clothes back to the bathroom where I hurriedly got dressed. I came out and Aunt Louise called me to the kitchen.

"Phillip, stay here and let them finish. Don't spoil the surprise."

"Aunt Louise, this whole day so far has been a surprise. First, I am having a lunch no one told me about; then those two yahoos formerly called friends left me buck-naked in the bathroom. Thank God, they didn't know about your stash of old towels! I nearly died when I went to my room and found Miriam there with those two!"

Aunt Louise laughed and said, "Well, they are making memories for you to take back to Chicago!" At that the three conspirators emerged from my room and invited me in. I growled at them as I walked down the hall. They had tastefully decorated my room with balloons and a Happy Birthday banner. But what surprised me the most was pictures someone from the Yearbook Committee had taken of Joe, Kent, Miriam and myself that Miriam had put on a poster board. It read "St. Cyngen Crusader to Haskell Haymaker." It included candid shots at school, various football games and even pictures from the mixer the night before of Joe putting his letter jacket on me to dancing with Miriam. All I could do was silently take it all in as I crouched down to gaze upon it.

I stood up and said, "Thanks guys. I forgive you for stealing my clothes and embarrassing the snot out of me in front of Miriam. Now I understand what you rascals were up to." I grabbed Joe and Kent by the neck and said, "Thanks a ton, guys. But so help me,

God, if you ever steal my clothes again, I will bust you in the chops!" They were laughing and promised not to leave me without clothes again.

Then I went over to Miriam and, staring into those emerald green orbs, added, "Now I know what you have really been doing in that yearbook class. I know this was your idea cuz these two hairy assed jocks wouldn't know how to finger paint a picture if their lives depended on it."

Kent shot back, "Hey, I resent that remark! Only Sinni's ass is hairy."

Joe was grinning as he punched Kent hard on the shoulder and pushed him playfully. "Yours isn't as baby smooth as you think, Kent James!" Joe teased.

"Don't steal the magic of my moment, boys," Miriam said, arching an eyebrow and sternly giving the guys a look. She then looked back at me and softened her expression. "Now, where were you again, Phillip, about whose idea this was?"

I gave Miriam a hug and kissed her on the cheek. "Thanks for the decorations and this poster, Miriam. It means the world to me!" I said.

Kent and Joe whistled and cleared their throats. "I think it is time we had lunch. I think your Aunt Louise has fried up some chicken and your cake is ready also, unless you want us to leave you two alone in here!" Joe said.

Kent retorted, "Not a good idea, Joe, to leave these two alone in his bedroom. He sheds his clothes too easily every time Miriam is in his room!"

Turning to them, I said, "Okay, you horse thieves. Let's go eat." I took Miriam's hand as I walked out of the room and back to the kitchen. This act was not lost on Kent or Joe. Even Aunt Louise had noticed this, arched an eyebrow and took in the sight. No doubt the Fugalis would know all the details of this morning's escapade in my bedroom with the guys and Miriam. I only hoped Miriam's Aunt Madeline Fugali would not be in town for a long while so the memory of this morning would be ancient history not worth repeating.

It was a wonderful birthday lunch not only because Aunt Louise was a good cook, but also I spent it with five of the dearest people to me in Haskell - Aunt Louise, Uncle Raymond, Miriam, Kent and Joe. We cut the cake and they sang Happy Birthday to me. Kent gave me my own Bible called "The Living Bible." He wrote a wonderful note in it about how he appreciated our friendship and closed it with Ephesians 1:15-16, "Therefore, I have never stopped thanking God for you..." He had been getting more religiously attuned as the year went on and made me wonder if he would someday go to seminary rather than law school. To this day I still have that Bible and it is one of my most treasured possessions.

Miriam had given me the collage of photographs of this semester plus she brought a beautiful birthday bouquet from her mom's flower shop. No one had ever given me flowers before and Aunt Louise put them in a beautiful crystal vase.

Joe gave me the homecoming football. As a team captain, he and Kent each got one at homecoming. He had all our teammates sign it. We laughed and carried on about the game, the mixer and things that had occurred this past semester.

It was a beautiful fall day and the four of us decided to go for a hike up the Concharty Mountain after lunch. We took our leave of Uncle Raymond and Aunt Louise and walked up the trails to the upper pasture. When we got there, I asked the three of them if they would like to go hiking along the monastery trails.

"I have a standing invitation from the Abbot and I haven't gotten to fully explore those trails and I would love it if you three would go with me."

"Okay," said Joe.

"Sounds fun," Miriam said.

"We ain't left yet," Kent said, grinning. At that, the four of us climbed through the barbed wire fence and began following the trails I had walked nearly a month before. It truly was a lovely place; the fall colors heightened the beauty of the place; the red of the Sumacs and Dogwoods, an occasional Maple blended with the yellows of the Ashes, Elms and Hackaberry; and the russet reds of the Blackjack Oak. All the while the wind rustled through the trees. It was a marvelous feeling to be up here with Kent, Joe and Miriam. All at once we heard voices. It was the monks on an afternoon walk. At least thirty of them and they briskly overtook us and nodded their hellos as they went by. The four of us stood to the side of the trail as they walked briskly past in groups of two and three men almost in a precise military formation.

Again, I was amazed at how athletic and virile they looked. We all stood in quiet awe of the spectacle of those 30 young men as they walked past us. Kent broke the silence after they left by commenting, "Makes you wonder why dudes like that commit themselves to silence, celibacy, and prayer when there is so much in the world to live for and experience." All at once a voice behind us said, "Perhaps my young friend, it is because they have heeded a higher calling for their lives from another source than the mere amusements and diversions of this world."

I instantly recognized that voice of Abbot Delaurier as he came walking along the trail. I turned around and said, "Abbot Delaurier, how good to see you!"

He smiled and replied, "And it is always good to see four happy healthy young people exploring the trails of the Concharty Mountain. There is nothing like exercise in a place like this to strengthen the body and refresh the soul. I often come up here to exercise by walking and let God speak to my heart as I journey along these trails."

Kent, who had been developing a deeper spiritual sensitivity these past couple of months, turned to the Abbot and said, "May I ask you a question, Sir?"

"Certainly my young friend."

"How does God speak to you, Sir?"

The Abbot stopped walking and looked at Kent. "In myriads of ways, my son. But the real question is how does He speak to you? What has your life experience up to now shown you how God reaches out to you?"

Kent stood there, silent for a bit, and then said, "Through scriptures; through prayer; through my folks; and sometimes just being alone with God in a quiet time."

"Ah...even so, my young friend, God speaks to me like that, too. But He often speaks to my heart, not my head." The Abbot patted his breast and then looked at Kent with a quiet intensity. It was as if he were listening to an inner voice before he then asked, "And what has He been tugging at your heart, my young friend? What does your heart tell you God is saying to you?"

Kent replied instantly, "To consider ministry as a vocation when I get done with college." Like a head of steam in a locomotive, this had been building in Kent for some time. The encounter with Abbot Delaurier put voice to what had been stirring deeply in Kent's heart! Nevertheless, the three of us were stunned at that announcement.

"A noble calling, but one fraught with a painfully high cost. Have you truly counted the costs of such a choice in life?" the Abbot asked.

"What are the costs?" Joe interjected, looking at Kent. The Abbot raised an eyebrow and smiled at him.

"That short question deserves a long winded answer, Joseph!"

Joe again spoke up, out of concern for Kent as much as curiosity about the Abbot's answer, "What were the costs for you, Abbot Delaurier and what do you foresee as the costs for Kent?"

The Abbot then said, "Will the four of you walk with me a ways? There is a lovely overlook where the five of us can sit down at one of the Stations of the Cross the brothers have built. It will be more pleasant to discuss such a weighty subject there."

'Sure," I said. Joe and Kent readily nodded their agreement.

"We would be honored to accompany you, Abbot Delaurier," Miriam added.

The Abbot smiled at Miriam, "I can see no greater privilege than walking with the four of you this afternoon and discussing the ways of God. My heart was heavy when I started my walk this afternoon and the presence of your company has lifted my spirits. I thank you for that," the Abbot replied.

As we walked with him, Miriam asked him about his life as a young man. He shared more about the bitterness of his youth during World War II and how the sweetness of God's call to intimacy took away that hurt and disillusionment with life. At last we arrived at one of the Stations of the Cross and sat down on the benches. We beheld an incredible view of the river valley. I could see Uncle Raymond's pastures and the spring fed pond where Kent, Joe and I had wrestled last July. I winced at the thought of being seen naked by Miss Marguerite when she was walking along these trails with the Abbot.

"A beautiful view, is it not," the Abbot observed. Joe and Kent then noticed what I had previously spied. They got rather silent at the thought also. As if the Abbot could read our thoughts, he said, "The glory of a young man is his strength Proverbs 20:29. Seeing you three swimming last summer made me miss my youth. Cherish that memory of the three of you working and playing. Don't be embarrassed or ashamed of swimming and wrestling even if you were naked. I have no doubt our Lord did the same with the twelve disciples. Jesus was a 30-year old man and the twelve disciples were young men ranging in age from 18 to 26. I can't imagine that they didn't swim and wrestle like that often."

What the Abbot had shared revealed a depth of understanding of youth that was profound and touched my heart.

"I never realized that, Abbot Delaurier," I said, dumbfounded at the revelation of just how human Jesus and the disciples had been.

"Yeah," Kent agreed. "I never thought of how young they were. Heck, some of them were Phillip, Joe and my age. Wow!"

Joe just looked at the Abbot. You could tell the wheels were turning in his head as he took in the view. He then smiled and added, "Thanks for the insight, Abbot Delaurier. Means a lot to know it is okay to have fun as a guy and be like Jesus, too." As always, Joe's simplicity in such moments was profound. The new knowledge of what Abbot Delaurier shared freed us as young men to be wild at heart yet Godly. It was a strange paradox that this blue-eyed Frenchman had articulated. But there was a clarity to those words that struck a chord deeply in us as young men.

Miriam broke the silence by saying, "Abbot Delaurier, I am not sure that as a woman I will ever fully understand why guys are so competitive and have to wrestle and fight; and why they like to do that sort of thing. But I do appreciate that they need to do that."

The Abbot's eyes sparkled, "That, my dear Miriam, is the beginning of wisdom you will need in order to walk alongside a young man someday as your husband." The Abbot grinned, "But let me return to the question you asked back on the trail. What was the cost of ministry for me and what might it be for your good friend Kent James." The Abbot looked at Kent as he said this.

"Yeah," Kent asked, "What have been these costs to you?"

"Well, there have been many. For me as a Benedictine monk, I chose celibacy. No marriage. No children of my own. I had to give up my dream of becoming a lawyer and politician. I had to say goodbye to my life as I had envisioned it. I had to submit to the authority of the church hierarchy and believe me that at times has been very difficult." He chuckled when he added with a devilish grin, "There have been times when I thought the Vichy French were easier to deal with than church authorities. But I had to often repent of such attitudes and that is another one of the hidden costs of ministry. Sometimes the people you work for in leadership or the people you serve are neither Godly nor good. That can sorely try your faith. The Lord had to remind me that although people would let me down, He never would! Remember the parable of the wheat and the tares. Often the enemy places the tares in leadership of the church such that even the angels cannot tell which are "wheat" and which are "tares."

The Abbot looked pensive. "I have lost many fellow monks and priests who left the ministry disillusioned and wounded souls. These are some of the heavy tolls that ministry can be." We all were silent. Then the Abbot asked Kent, "You are Protestant, are you not?"

"Yes, sir, Baptist," Kent replied.

"Then if you marry, you need a woman who has just as unique a calling on her life as yours. So choose wisely who you marry, my young friend." At that Abbot Delaurier put his hand on Kent's shoulder. "You may make a mistake on what you study in college, or even where you go to college. Don't make a mistake on who you marry." The Abbot's blue eyes gazed intensely into Kent's eyes. Kent held his gaze, soaking in the wisdom of this gentle soul who had the heart of a lion. The Abbot then broke the seriousness of the moment by asking,

"So, where are you young friends going to college next year?"

Kent spoke out, "JBU. I got an acceptance letter today and they offered me a full ride for football. I am going to study religion."

"Congratulations, Kent," the Abbot said.

I looked at Kent and said, "Why didn't you say so?"

"Buddy, it was your birthday and I did not want to steal the thunder from your birthday celebration," Kent replied. Again the true nature and richness of Kent's character were revealed. He would never seek the spotlight to diminish a friend's moment in the sun. Kent was always like that.

"Happy birthday Phillip," the Abbot said. "Where will you go and what will you study?"

"I am not sure yet, Abbot. Maybe Indiana University or an Ivy League school. Pre-Law like you did, Abbot." The Abbot smiled and nodded.

"And you, Joe," he asked.

"I also just got an acceptance letter and full ride offer to John Brown University. I am going to accept that and Kent and I will be roommates. I want to study business."

"Congratulations, Joe," I said, feeling somewhat left out. The three of us had done everything together and now I was the odd man out.

"That's great for both you guys," Miriam said.

"And what about you, Miriam?" the Abbot asked.

"I am going to University of Tulsa to study nursing."

"All four of you have an exciting time ahead of you. Remember your university years as a place where professors use buildings to build students. Relish your time there! And speaking of time, I have overstayed mine and must return to the monastery. Thank you for accompanying an old Frenchman on his afternoon exercise regimen. Au Voir, my young friends!"

At that the Abbot got up to leave but not before Kent stood up and grabbed the Abbot's hand to shake it, and said, "Thank you for the time, sir. Maybe we can talk again about ministry?"

"Of course," the Abbot replied. "It would be my pleasure."

"Goodbye, Abbot Delaurier," Miriam said. We all waved goodbye and watched the black robed figure of Abbot Delaurier walk down the trails back to the monastery.

The four of us lingered there for a bit, discussing our respective plans for college.

"I have to tell you guys that I am going to miss you three. I almost have a hole in my heart at the thought of not being with you guys. But the Abbot has told me that sometimes in this journey of life, choices are made that we don't like but are necessary."

Kent was silent. He always got that way when things were heavy on his heart. Joe locked his gaze on me, saying nothing. Our eyes met and I could sense he felt the ache of my separation from Haskell as much as I did.

Miriam broke the heaviness of the moment. "Well, we four may have less than two months together, but that doesn't mean we can't 'suck the marrow out of life today,' as my Aunt Madeline is prone to say. She is going to be here at Thanksgiving."

At that, Kent perked up and said, teasingly, "Oh, no. Not that old broad. As long as she is free to try to slap the baklava out of me, I ain't coming over to your house, Miriam. I am staying away."

"Wuss," Joe shot back at Kent. It was true that for whatever reason Madeline liked to tease and pick on Kent. Miriam said that Aunt Madeline had a crush on Kent and thus the verbal repartee commenced which lightened our hearts and helped us enjoy the comradery of each other's company. We walked back to Uncle Raymond's pastures and got back to the house around 4:00.

Kent and Joe had to get going but Miriam stayed for a while to talk to Aunt Louise and me. It was a lively banter and the three of us enjoyed ourselves and visited with Aunt Louise. Uncle Raymond had gone into town to get something and was not there.

Finally Miriam asked, "Mrs. Hammond, Aunt Marguerite wanted me to invite you, Coach Hammond and Phillip for Thanksgiving dinner at our house this year."

I arched my eyebrows at this news and Aunt Louise looked at me and then turned to Miriam, saying "Why thank you, Miriam. I will talk to Raymond about your invitation and get back in touch with Miss Marguerite."

"Well, I had better be going. Thanks for lunch and the birthday cake. I enjoyed the hike with you and the guys, Phillip. Happy birthday, again!"

Her emerald eyes were gazing straight into mine. "Easy does it, boy!" I thought to myself. "You are perilously close to losing yourself in those eyes and you are pulling up stakes in less than a month and a half."

"Thanks, Miriam, may I walk you to your car?"

"Sure," she replied. Miriam and I walked out to her car.

"Thanks for the collage, Miriam. Someday you have to tell me how you got all those pictures."

She smiled and said, "Sure. But only if you will go walking again along the trails of the Concharty Hills Monastery with me."

"I will do better that that. Football is over soon and I will start walking you home from school!" What had I just said? My heart was speaking, not my head. Whoa, Trigger! Miriam smiled and leaned into me. I pulled her close and gave her a full frontal hug. Man, it was heaven! I had not hugged a girl like that for almost six months but it seemed like a lifetime. But even hugging my former girlfriend Ann Burns was nothing compared to this. I was relishing the moment perhaps too much as Uncle Raymond turned onto the Concharty Hill Road.

I let her go and said, "See you at school on Monday."

"Sure," she replied as she got into her car.

She pulled out of the driveway as Uncle Raymond was pulling in. She waved at him and he returned the greeting. I just kept looking at her car as it pulled out of the driveway. My daydreaming was interrupted by Uncle Raymond's voice, saying, "Boy, you got some explaining to do!" He chuckled and slapped me on the shoulder. He came along side me and put his arm around my shoulder as we walked back into the house.

"You could do a lot worse than being attracted to Miriam Abboud, Cowboy! They don't make them much better than her."

Looking at Uncle Raymond full square in the eye, I replied, "You know, Uncle Raymond, you are one wise old bird! I wholeheartedly agree with you. Problem is I am leaving in a month and a half. I have tried to keep my boundaries with Miriam and not get too involved. But dang it, Uncle Raymond, I just start to melt when I am around her. I go weak in the knees whenever I hold her hand and could explode when I hug her."

"Sounds like you need a cold shower, young man!" Aunt Louise chimed in as we came into the den.

"Cold shower wouldn't do any good, Louise. All young men are like hot water tanks. There is always a burning flame warming the tank. That is how God made all men and you wouldn't want Phillip any other way. Problem is that he can't go throwing kerosene on that flame or he will burn up the hot water tank!"

At that, Uncle Raymond looked squarely into my eyes, "And you know just what I meant, don't you, Cowboy?"

"Yes, sir. I expect that I do." Uncle Raymond had a grin on his face and Aunt Louise shook her head and said, "Well, I can see you two need some man-to-man time, so if you will excuse me I am going back to my bedroom to do some reading."

Uncle Raymond and I then discussed the proper boundaries I needed to observe to protect not only myself but also Miriam. He shared stories of his days as a Sergeant in the Marine Corps and the trouble many young Marines got into with girls and unwanted pregnancies.

"Don't screw up a good friendship, Phillip. There are reasons why there are certain social taboos about a relationship between a man and a woman. Don't cross that boundary unless you are putting a gold ring on a girl's hand and you truly know her really well; and you are prepared to stand by her through thick and thin!" He winked at me and I knew our heart to heart talk was almost at an end.

"If you ever need to talk about this, Phillip, remember I was once a lively young buck like you, only I knew the girl I wanted and came back and married her when I was 20 and she was 18, Miriam's age! Hang tough, Tiger!" He punched me in the arm and went back to his bedroom to talk to Aunt Louise.

Well, our talk wasn't as bland as the sex education lectures we got in the 8th grade, but Uncle Raymond made a whole lot more sense about keeping the boundaries reinforced emotionally and physically. "Nothing good happens after 10:00 alone with a girl, Cowboy," Uncle Raymond had once said.

I took that message to heart and would be careful with Miriam on that point.

CHAPTER 19

THE FIRE ON CONCHARTY HILLS

One morning in Miss Dressbach's English Class we were discussing the characters from the book *Rebecca* that was on our reading list. Miss Dressbach was asking some fairly thought provoking questions to the class. Miss Dressbach said, "So what did you think of the contrast in characters between the First Mrs. DeWinters who was Rebecca and the second Mrs. DeWinters?"

Miriam raised her hand and Miss Dressbach called on her. Miriam opined, "Miss Dressbach, Rebecca was beautiful and socially charming on the outside, but horribly selfish and wicked on the inside. While the second Mrs. DeWinters lacked self-confidence in herself and was not described as a beauty; she nevertheless was a solid redeeming force in Maxim DeWinters' life that he needed."

"What about the character Mrs. Danvers?" Miss Dressbach asked. Joe raised his hand and Miss Dressbach called on him.

"She had an unwholesome devotion to the memory of Rebecca," Joe said. "It was as if she was keeping the spirit of Rebecca alive to spite the second Mrs. DeWinters and Maxim DeWinters." As always, Joe had concisely stated a complex issue. He didn't speak out often, but it was readily apparent those wheels in his mind were always working.

"That is a keen insight, Joe," Miss Dressbach commented. She then observed, "The author does seem to make Rebecca larger than life to 'haunt' and overpower the other characters. Anyone know, for instance, 'What was the second Mrs. DeWinters' first name?'"

"They never identified the second Mrs. DeWinters' first name. It almost added to her diminished importance in the shadow of Rebecca's memory," Miriam commented.

Miss Dressbach then discussed the other characters in the book and asked, "What about the character of Maxim DeWinters?" I raised my hand and Miss Dressbach called on me.

I spoke up on this one as I could no longer contain myself, "Like Mr. Rochester in Jane Eyre, Maxim DeWinters had a secret tormented past that a young woman of character had to redeem," I then looked at Miriam when I said, "He had to press through the pain and endure the vicissitudes of life and the spite of enemies." Then looking back at Miss Dressbach, I continued, "But, in the end, both men weathered the tough times with the hope of better times ahead with a good woman at their side." I obviously was not the unlettered jock she initially took me for!

Miss Dressbach, who noticed my obvious focus on Miriam, was taken aback by my reference to Jane Eyre. She raised an eyebrow and said, "That's a very interesting analogy, Phillip, a young woman as an instrument of redemption. Does anyone have any thoughts on this?"

Various classmates commented on this theme. The bell rang and the class was over. As Joe and I got our books, Joe had a wry grin on his face.

"What?" I asked.

"Don't play dumb with me, Phillip," Joe replied. "You know what I mean."

"You haven't said anything!" I replied, exasperated.

"Don't have to. I know what that comment implied and who it was intended for."

Kent caught up with us and said, "What's going on here?"

Joe cut his eyes at me and replied, "Let's just say if Phillip hustles on the field as well as he does in class, we should win State!" I rolled my eyes and Kent smiled as we headed to second hour. I kept a low profile the rest of the day and focused on the tasks ahead.

That evening after football workout and dinner, I was sore and stiff as usual. Swimming was never like this! But my aches subsided as I focused on Miss Dressbach's discussion of the characters from *Rebecca* and her take home assignment. Part of her take home work was to write an essay on "Why did the author utilize fire as a symbol of purging the past?"

It was at that moment I noticed the sunset out my window. "That's odd," I thought. It was now nearly 9:00 p.m., yet there was an odd glow in the distance as I looked out my window. About that time the phone rang and Aunt Louise answered it. She immediately called Uncle Raymond to the phone. I could hear him getting mildly agitated as he talked on the line. He hung up and made some other calls. I came out into the hallway to see what was going on plus it was time to raid Aunt Louise's frigerator.

"Phillip, get dressed in some old clothes," Aunt Louise said. "There is a fire that got started on the far side of the Concharty Mountain and all able bodied men are needed to help fight it."

"Can I call Kent and Joe?"

"Raymond has already called Bill Corsinni. So I expect he, Joe and Jimmy will be out here to help fight the fire."

"What about Kent?" I asked.

"He has called Dr. James, so I expect them to be here, too." Uncle Raymond told us that a man named Hayes Freeman had been operating an illegal moonshine operation down a ways from the Concharty Mountains in a ravine. Something had gone wrong and the still had exploded earlier in the evening starting the fire.

"Hayes Freeman. Who is he?" I asked.

"He is the grandson of a notoriously corrupt businessman and politician from the early days named Michael Freeman. He swindled a lot of Indians out of their land and was very involved in the Ku Klux Klan. His grandson Hayes Freeman has been a bootlegger and moonshiner in these parts since the 1940's. This isn't the first time one of his stills has exploded."

Uncle Raymond put on a heavy coat and wool hat and told me to do the same. He grabbed two pair of leatherwork gloves and handed me one pair of the gloves. Aunt Louise soaked some old handkerchiefs in water and put them in a baggie for us.

"You wrap these around your mouth and nose if the smoke gets too bad, Phillip," Uncle Raymond told me.

Aunt Louise was to stay at the house and man the phone. Uncle Raymond and I re-parked the cars on the driveway away from any trees or poles where the grass was kept mowed. We also moved his farm equipment out of the barn onto the gravel driveway and made sure the horses were not in the barn but the pastures.

"They can run down to the lower pasture or creek to get away from the fire if it comes down this far."

The fire was about a mile north and west of Uncle Raymond's ranch but it was moving this way. The winds were out of the north in November, so the fire would spread and come our way.

"Most times the fires burn out about the time they reach the monastery lands. The monks have done a good job of controlling the underbrush growth with their goats so the fire tends to die out. The hickory and black jack oak trees don't burn easily without that dry underbrush."

"Is that why you let the monks sometimes graze their goats on your pastures for free?"

"Yep! They clear out a lot of that undergrowth for me. That way I don't have to spend money on herbicides and it is part of being a good neighbor. Their goats have good grazing and I get a less fire prone pasture. Those monks have been very helpful to me at times so it is my way of returning the favor. Plus, I like to think there is more to this life than dog eat dog that some men advocate. Sort of 'you scratch my back, I will scratch yours!'" Uncle Raymond slapped me on the shoulder and said, "Let's go, cowboy."

I helped Uncle Raymond load an empty water trough onto the back of his truck. He then filled it full of water and stacked dozens of old gunny burlap sacks in the bed of his pickup.

"We soak the gunny sacks in water and then smother the fire with them," Uncle Raymond explained. About that time I saw Joe's truck drive up and park on the gravel driveway. Bill Corsinni and his two sons hopped out of the cab. Shortly afterwards, it seemed like half the town had either pulled into our driveway or parked on Concharty Hill Road. These men knew the drill as this had not been their first forest fire to fight. A good many other men had gone on up to the monastery up the road and were assembling there to fight the fire. Apparently, Kent and Dr. James were directed to go up there to help fight the fire.

Uncle Raymond spoke to the men about the buddy system. Everyone had a "buddy" and could not be out of earshot of his buddy. Uncle Raymond and I buddied up. Joe and Jimmy Corsinni buddied up. Bill Corsinni buddied up with the Chief of Police of Haskell, Pat Calhoun. There were maybe thirty men who came to Uncle Raymond's ranch to fight the fire. All of them brought flashlights, burlap gunnysacks and many had empty water troughs in the back of their truck beds, which we filled up with water at Uncle Raymond's ranch.

We left the hoses running and let them water the yard. We strategically placed the hoses so the ground could create a "water break" if the fire came this far.

The hoses drew water from his well he used for livestock and not the rural water district lines that served his house; hence, so there was no danger of depleting the water pressure in the Rural Water District lines that served the monastery and surrounding homes and ranches.

The men loaded up on the trucks and we drove to the upper pasture to assist the monks in fighting the fire if it came this far. Years ago, Uncle Raymond had roads cut to every pasture on his ranch so it was a fairly easy drive and we didn't slosh much water out of the troughs. When we got to the top, you could smell the smoke of burning brush. But it wasn't so thick yet that it caused your eyes to water.

The fire itself was still a good mile away to the north and west. I could hear men shouting and the sound of machinery. The monks were literally creating a firewall by cutting trees and bulldozing dirt. Uncle Raymond saw one of the monks he knew, a Father Anderson, and went up to discuss firefighting strategy. Father Anderson was from Oregon and was a seasoned fire fighter from his youth as well as a former Marine.

I saw Uncle Raymond nodding his approval and Father Anderson barking orders like a drill sergeant. Next thing I knew, Uncle Raymond's fences were being cut between the monastery lands and his ranch. He gave his approval to allow the monks to cut some of his trees and scrape the dirt on his lands to build a firewall the length of the pasture. The smell of smoke and diesel fumes filled the air. Someone yelled timber and I saw one tree after another fall so as to create that firebreak.

Next a bulldozer pushed the fallen trees aside with newly scraped dirt. This went on for about an hour as they tried to build a firewall in anticipation of the fire's path. Joe and I stood next to each other, watching the spectacle. Occasionally, we joined in to help push a fallen tree out of the way with several other men.

Joe had warned me to be careful around rocky ledges. Joe told me that sometimes the heat and smoke of a fire can revive the snakes and they would slither out of their dens. Moreover, if they were poisonous, they were more dangerous in that they had venom stored up from hibernation. Plus, with the fire, smoke and people running everywhere, it made for a very agitated snake.

"So be careful," Joe warned.

The smoke in the air was getting thicker and I could hear men coughing.

Now we could see the orange glow of fire and began to feel the heat from the fire on the lower slope. The property owner, Hayes Freeman, refused to allow the monks or Uncle Raymond to clear out any of the underbrush on his land. He didn't like the monastery given the history of Papa C foreclosing on his grandfather's land back in the 1920's. Plus, he didn't want anyone wandering on his land given his history of illegal activities. The more dense and thick the underbrush, the less likely strangers were to trespass on his land. Only this time his illegal act had clearly started the fire and his body burns from the still explosion would be impossible to explain away in a court of law. He had been taken to the Burn Center at Hillcrest Hospital in Tulsa.

Hillcrest Hospital kept very good records and the State Fire Marshall would be investigating the cause of this fire. The legal consequences of Mr. Freeman starting this fire would very likely cost him lots of money, civilly and criminally. Joe and I overheard some of the men speculating that Hayes Freeman would probably have to sell this land to pay for the damages this fire had caused to his neighbors!

"Everyone, listen up!" I heard Father Anderson say. "Re-park the trucks with the water troughs facing the fire. Get ready to start soaking the gunnysacks. Remember, gently place the gunnysacks on the brush in the area that is burning. Don't beat the fire as you only fan the flames.

Uncle Raymond and I stood next to each other. "You okay, cowboy?" he asked.

"Yeah. But I feel like I do before a football game or swim match - that hard knot in your stomach. Only the competition this time is a fire that plays for keeps," I responded.

Uncle Raymond put his arm around me and said, "You're safe with me cowboy! Stick close by! This isn't my first rodeo, Phillip. I have fought many fires successfully. We'll get through one this, okay!" he said, confidently. His confidence allayed some of my anxiety.

The men started soaking the gunnysacks as the fire came up to Uncle Raymond's fence line and the Concharty Hills Monastery land. I could hear some of the monks audibly praying that the winds would die down to allow us to fight the flames. The men waited till the fire crossed the fence and began placing the gunnysacks down along the fire. The smoke was intense but the intensity of burning began to subside when it reached the top of the hill. There was not much to burn and there was now no wind pushing the flame up the hill. Some of the trees on down the hill were burning but the hickory and oak trees by and large did not readily burn without a lot of underbrush to ignite them. Slowly it seemed the fire was petering out before the firewall, and the gunnysacks seemed to be working. Looking back now, I have often wondered about the efficacy of the monks' prayers. But the smoke was overpowering at times.

Even with my wet handkerchief over my face, I was choking at times. I could feel my body sweating as I ran from the truck to the fire. As I put down my last gunnysack, I ran back to the truck for another. I then noticed that I did not see Uncle Raymond at the truck or on the fire line. I became anxious and shouted his name "Uncle Raymond." No answer. I started looking around and retraced my steps to where I had last seen him. I silently said a prayer that I would find him! He had placed a gunnysack down at the east end of the fire line. So I began my search over there.

I pointed my flashlight around, hunting for Uncle Raymond. As the time went by, my anxiety level increased. Joe then noticed my frantic running around and became concerned for me. "Phillip, what's wrong?" he asked.

"I don't know where Uncle Raymond is and he's my fire buddy! I haven't seen him in fifteen minutes," I said. Joe whistled at Jimmy and he came over to us.

"We need to help Phillip find Coach Hammond!" It was more of a command than a request; the sort of order an older brother gives a younger sibling.

Joe and Jimmy Corsinni then joined me in the search. We each fanned out, looking in the smoky darkness. The smoke stung my eyes and made me cough. The other men kept up their work fighting the fire. You could hear the shouting of men and the sizzle of wet gunnysacks on the fire. It seemed their efforts were succeeding in stopping the fire along the boundaries of the monastery and Uncle Raymond's lands. As a consequence, there was now not as much light from the flames but much more smoke.

"Oh, Lord, please let us find Uncle Raymond!" I said out loud in desperation. Jimmy suddenly yelled out, "Joe, Phillip, over here!"

Joe and I immediately ran over to where Jimmy was calling out and there he was, lying on the ground. I lost it and cried, "Uncle Raymond!" I ran over to his side, but he was passed out. I checked his breathing and his pulse and I was relieved somewhat.

Joe, cool in the heat of a crisis, said, "Let's get him in the truck and take him back to the house." Joe, Jimmy and I carried him to his truck. We placed him in the cab while we removed the almost empty water troughs from the truck bed. We then laid Uncle Raymond in the truck bed and I climbed in the back and held Uncle

Raymond's head in my lap. My anxiety grew again over his condition. He was breathing but I had no idea what was wrong. I became worried that Uncle Raymond had had a heart attack or been bitten by a snake.

"Please, Lord," I said quietly through tears from the smoke and concern for Uncle Raymond, "Please let him be okay!" All I could do was to plead with God as I held Uncle Raymond.

Joe drove the truck back to Uncle Raymond's house while Jimmy helped me with Uncle Raymond. We got home and they both helped me carry Uncle Raymond inside and laid him on the couch in the den. Aunt Louise was on the phone in the kitchen and was shocked to see us carrying him into the den. She got off the phone and immediately came over to check on him.

"Raymond, Raymond," she said as she felt his head and checked his pulse.

His pulse and breathing appeared to be okay but he was still unconscious. We decided to call the hospital and request an ambulance in Muskogee just to be sure. There was nothing more the Corsinni boys or I could do.

"Aunt Louise, I need to get Joe and Jimmy back to fighting the fire but I will be right back!" She turned to me, ashen white and nodded her assent. There were tears in her eyes. God, it killed me inside to leave them both, but the Corsinni boys needed to get back to helping the other men fighting the fire.

I ran Joe and Jimmy back to fight the fire and Aunt Louise called a nurse she knew and began describing the symptoms for a possible diagnosis. At about that time Uncle Raymond started to stir and regain consciousness. She told the friend on the other end of the phone she would call her later and hung up the phone.

"Where am I? Where's Phillip?" Uncle Raymond slurred.

Aunt Louise murmured, "Thank you, Lord," as she came over to Uncle Raymond's side and then said, "Raymond, it's me, Louise. Are you all right?"

"What? What am I doing here?"

"Phillip and the Corsinni boys found you and brought you back here. Phillip took them back to fight the fire and will be back. You gave us quite a scare, Coach Hammond!" Aunt Louise did not tell Uncle Raymond she had ordered the ambulance and knew it would be about thirty minutes until they got here. She knew he would object. I came back to the house nearly twenty minutes later and saw Aunt Louise attending Uncle Raymond with a cold compress. Her eyes were red but her color had returned.

"Uncle Raymond, are you okay? Coach, I was so worried about you!" I came over and gave him a hug as he laid on the couch. "What happened to you?"

"I think I got overpowered by the smoke, Phillip, but I am okay now, cowboy! I told you this wasn't my first rodeo!" he smiled weakly.

"You did not get bit by any snake, did you?" I asked anxiously.

"No. I didn't see any snakes this time, Phillip, but that waft of heavy smoke hit me and I was trying to get to better air. I was trying to run away from it and I guess I passed out from the exertion and smoke."

"Well, Raymond Hammond, you gave me quite a fright! I might let you work out with Phillip and the boys at 60, but I'm not so sure about your fighting fires anymore. That may have been your 'last rodeo' as far as I am concerned with firefighting!" Aunt Louise said sternly.

"Louise, you're getting all worked up over nothing," Uncle Raymond said, coughing. About that time we heard ambulance sirens and saw the lights pulling up to the house. There was a knock on the door and Aunt

Louise invited the emergency ambulance team in to check on Raymond. After a cursory examination, they recommended he be taken to the Muskogee Hospital. Of course, Uncle Raymond vehemently protested, but both Aunt Louise and I put our foot down.

"Raymond Hammond. You are going to the hospital!"

"I AM NOT," he protested.

"Uncle Raymond, you once taught me that when a commanding officer is no longer deemed competent to command, he is relieved of his duty and a subordinate officer is to take over. I am invoking that rule now. So, Uncle Raymond, you and Aunt Louise are going. I will stay here and make sure things are okay. THAT'S AN ORDER, SOLDIER!" I barked at him.

Uncle Raymond was wide-eyed and his mouth was gaping open. He then smiled and said, shaking his head, "You just made it as a drill sergeant, Phillip! Carry on, Sergeant Robertson!" and he then saluted me. I know he didn't want to go, but I caught him off guard with his own Marine training and logic. The ambulance staff put him on the gurney and Aunt Louise followed them to the ambulance. I walked her out there and watched her get in as they loaded Uncle Raymond in the ambulance.

"Everything is going to be fine here, Aunt Louise," I assured her. "You just attend to Uncle Raymond and call me if you need anything. I don't think I will be at school tomorrow, given this crisis." I could see a protest rising up in Aunt Louise.

"I will call the school attendance office and explain to them, Aunt Louise. You can confirm this tomorrow with them so the Truant Officer doesn't come after me!" She looked at me and squinted her eyes as if she was mounting another objection. I headed her off by adding, "Someone has got to repair the fences and attend to the ranch while you get your 'patient' checked out. We both know they will probably keep him for a day or two, so I will watch over things till you both get back."

She reluctantly agreed and I watched them pull out of the driveway. I was still anxious for Uncle Raymond, but I was relieved to know he was in good hands. I got in Uncle Raymond's truck and drove back to where the monks and other men were still fighting the fire. It was now 11:30 and we continued stomping out the remnants of the fire till nearly 2:00 A.M. It had really gotten cold outside but the wind had totally died down now.

Father Anderson called the men together and said we would reassemble here at 9:00 A.M. to assess the damage and see if any smoldering remnants needed tending. Joe, Jimmy and I had buddied up as fire buddies. All three of us were sweating and looked as if someone had smudged soot all over our faces and clothes. Joe turned to me and asked with an air of concern, "Coach Hammond okay?"

"Yeah," I said. "The ambulance came and took him and Aunt Louise to the hospital."

Joe then asked me, "You going to be okay, Phillip?"

"It has been an interesting evening, Joe! As much as I like working out with you at Uncle Raymond's ranch, I don't want to ever do this again!"

Joe laughed and said, "I agree." I asked Joe if he wanted to spend the night and help me repair the fence in the morning. I told him I was not going to school tomorrow and he checked this out with his dad. Bill Corsinni gave his okay for Joe but took Jimmy home with him.

Joe and I went back to the house and we stripped down naked in the laundry room and threw the sweaty, smoky clothes into the washer. We looked like two Vaudeville performers in black face with lily-white bodies! I sent Joe back to take a shower and clean up while I attended to the laundry. I gave Joe an extra pair of my gym shorts to sleep in as we both had about the same waist size. When Joe was finished, I showered off to get the smoke and soot off my body and out of my hair. "Man, this was a night for the books, Phillip!" Joe said after I finished showering and was drying off.

"That's for sure, Buddy." I wrapped a towel around my waist and walked back to my bedroom. As I put on some guy shorts I asked Joe, "You see any snakes?" I asked.

Joe smiled and said, "Yeah, just one," and then he showed me the rattles from the tail of a rattlesnake he had.

"What the ....." was all I could say.

"Don't get too worked up! I saw the charred body of a rattlesnake and cut off the tail earlier in the evening!"

"Think we ought to rename you Rattlesnake Corsinni!" I laughed.

"But where was Kent?" I asked.

"Dad said he and Dr. James went to fight the fire a ways closer to the monastery. Seems like the fire was spread out a ways and guys were all along the line of where the fire was spreading to." Joe said.

I heard the washing machine beep and I checked on the clothes. I put them in the dryer and both Joe and I headed to bed. We both collapsed onto our respective beds in my room, too tired and exhausted for further conversation this night. It had been one heck of a night. But I was glad to have Joe with me to spend the night and it was comforting to have one of my closest friends with me during a traumatic event like this even if he did snore!

In some ways that fire really brought home to me the things most precious to me, Uncle Raymond, Aunt Louise, Joe, Kent and the Concharty Mountain. It was amazing how that small town rallied to help each other out during that fire. I would have a lot to write about on Miss Dressbach's essay on the theme of the purging effect of fire from Rebecca. I was to realize years later that the Concharty Hills fire had just about burned away the last of my big city Chicago belief that it was a totally dog eat dog world out there. That night cleared the way for a paradigm shift in me from big city suspicion of others to small town trust of your neighbors. I was embracing the values and mind set of small town America and shedding my big city attitudes without fully realizing it.

When we got up the next morning I treated Joe to a full "Aunt Louise" breakfast ala Phillip Robertson style. This meant scrambled eggs with sausage, cheese and mushrooms, fruit on the side in the form of sliced bananas, and we washed it down with fresh coffee. I then asked Joe something I had never had the nerve to ask.

"Joe, may I ask you a personal question?"

"Sure," Joe said.

"You really dig Sheree Brandt, don't you."

Joe cut his eyes at me, smiled, and said, "There's not much you don't miss, do you, Phillip!"

"So, is that a yes?" I asked.

"Dang, you ask hard questions!" he chuckled, and then added, "I like her. She is a mighty fine gal. I like her a lot but there is no way I could ever date her. But I have enjoyed getting to know her as a friend. She's a good gal and really neat," Joe said wistfully.

"I agree. She does seem sharp." I paused and added, "Sort of like her cousin Miriam." Joe about choked on a piece of fruit.

"You've been talking to Kent again!" he shot back.

"Yeah. There aren't too many secrets about the three of us that we don't know or find out about each other," I said. "But I know how you feel, Joe. When you like someone or they like you and neither of you can return that affection!" I looked straight into Joe's eyes as I said this, reflecting on my own experience with Ann Burns. I then shared everything with Joe about the failed relationship between Ann and me, and her parents' disapproval of us as a couple after the Avery Drive prank. He listened carefully, nodding and grunting occasionally as I shared my story.

When I had finished, he said, "Thanks for sharing, Phillip. Means a lot that you understand me; hard for a fella to find a bud like that!" He held me in his gaze and I could discern pain in his eyes.

Joe explained that he had talked this over with his dad and his father had encouraged him to be friendly but not romantic with Sheree. "The times they are a changing, Joe," Bill Corsinni told his son, "But they ain't changed that much. It is best to observe certain social customs and taboos for now."

So Joe had adhered to his father's advice regarding restraint in pursuing a relationship with Sheree; but his heart was not in this and thus he had his own inner turmoil to deal with. He had to crucify his own desires relationally, not so much for spiritual reasons, but for social taboos. He had shared with me how tough it had been for him. I saw a side to Joe's soul that few men have ever glimpsed and it drew us closer as friends.

Now that I realized Joe had his own hurt in life, we became fellow wounded wayfarers. Me with my sense of failure and rejection in Chicago; Joe with his secret crush he could do nothing about in Haskell. After this time there was nothing Joe and I could not talk about or share with one another of an intimate personal nature.

"You ready to get to work now, Professor?" Joe asked. He had a boyish twinkle in his eyes. He often called me professor when we talked about weighty subjects to lighten the moment.

"We ain't left yet?" I responded, stealing a line of Kent's and we headed out for the upper pasture to meet Father Anderson and the other monks.

Father Anderson had a meeting with some of the men from the night before at 9:00 A.M. at the firewall.

Joe and I joined the men in our clean clothes. All of us hiked through the charred areas checking for smoldering fires. By and large the fire was out. It was interesting hiking down this side of the mountain as it was fairly steep with no clearly defined trails to take you to the bottom. More than once Joe and/or I would slip and fall on the soot going down the hill. We would then help each other get back up. We made it to the base of the hill and then we hiked to the ravine where Hayes Freeman had hidden his moonshine operations. We saw the remains of the still that had exploded and started the conflagration. It was a mess of melted coils and twisted metal everywhere. Apparently the moonshine had helped ignite the fire much like gasoline. The State Fire Marshall was there, inspecting the scene also and we gathered from what we heard that Mr. Hayes Freeman was probably going to be charged criminally for some sort of arson crime. He was in Hillcrest Hospital in the burn unit, recovering so he was not a flight risk. We hiked back to the top of the hill. The monks were there clearing the damage from the firewall on the monastery lands and on Uncle Raymond's ranch. Some of them even offered to help us repair Uncle Raymond's fence.

The Monks were pretty handy with a hammer and it was the first time I really got to be up close to these guys, working with them. You would think these guys were regular dudes not men who chose a life's vocation as monks. They offered to chop up the fallen trees in the firewall and stack them next to Uncle Raymond's barn. I agreed to this. Joe and I got the fence repaired in no time with the help of the monks. After we got the fence repaired, we checked for any evidence of still smoldering fires. We found none so we began to spread the dirt from the firewall back on the pasture where it had been bulldozed. The monks were harvesting the downed trees. They chopped Uncle Raymond's downed trees into firewood and began taking the wood down to Uncle Raymond's barn to stack.

When we got back to the house, Uncle Raymond and Aunt Louise had returned in an ambulance. Joe and I came in and saw Uncle Raymond being put in his recliner by the ambulance staff. They made sure he was okay and then left.

"Sergeants Robertson and Corsinni reporting for duty, Sir." Both Joe and I gave Uncle Raymond a full Marine salute.

Uncle Raymond laughed and shook his head. "You two knuckleheads should be sent to the brig for two days on rations of bread and water for going AWOL from school!"

"Only if that is Mrs. Hammond's homemade bread, Sir!" Joe shouted, maintaining his at attention pose and salute. At that both Aunt Louise and Uncle Raymond were laughing. We relaxed our Marine pose and then debriefed Uncle Raymond about the extent of the fire damage and the repair to the fence. We also told him about the ruined still in the ravine and what the Fire Marshall said.

"Louise, get me that woman attorney from Bixby, Janice Beesley. Seems it is time to call our attack dog attorney about our damages from the fire; she's more Rottweiler than woman in situations like this." Uncle Raymond then told us all he had was smoke inhalation and was okay.

"Raymond Hammond! That is not all the doctors said," Aunt Louise admonished.

Uncle Raymond looked sheepishly at Aunt Louise and rolled his eyes and added, "And my heart was racing but not necessarily dangerously."

Aunt Louise arched an eyebrow at that.

"We got the fence repaired and checked for any smoldering fires. We're going to have to finish spreading the dirt on the firewall. The monks are harvesting the downed trees. They are chopping yours into firewood and told Joe and me they would help stack the wood by the barn," I said.

Uncle Raymond nodded his approval and Joe and I got back to cleaning up the mess from the fire. I was greatly relieved to know Uncle Raymond was okay. Joe and I worked the rest of the day and quit around dinner time. Joe took his leave despite offers to feed him and life began returning to normal except that Uncle Raymond was under doctor's orders to rest for two days. Aunt Louise made certain that his regimen was strictly adhered to.

"You might as well put me in the brig, Louise," he grumbled.

"That can be arranged, Coach Hammond!" she replied, sternly.

Uncle Raymond did not make a good patient despite the good nursing skills of Aunt Louise. So it was a relief to all parties on the third day when he got back up on his feet. But he had not sat idle during this time. Janice Beesley, his attorney from Bixby, came out and met with him about a damage claim. She fired off a demand letter for damages to Hayes Freeman.

"If I know that gal, the monks and I will own the rest of the Concharty Mountain when it is all said and done!" Time was to prove Uncle Raymond correct on this point.

CHAPTER 20

A WALK WITH THE ABBOT

Life returned to normal on the ranch and the weeks flew by repairing the fire damages to the upper pasture. Football season was coming to a close and we had played two more games before state playoffs. At the state playoffs, we got knocked out by Tahlequah Sequoyah, Oklahoma. This was a high school run by the Cherokee Nation and had operated since before statehood. Cherokee or not, it was still a big disappointment to the team and school. After football season was over, I often walked Miriam home from school as there was no more football practice. She was so easy to talk to and an avid listener. She asked me to describe my life back in Barrington Heights. Thus, I got some more talking time one on one with Miriam and began to explain to her the world I came from.

So Miriam would get a daily snoot full of life among the privileged upper crust of St. Cyngen's and Barrington Heights. She learned about my social activities, including the Wintergarden Ball, Skelly's Dance Studio, and Millerwood Riding Stables; and about some of the significant people in my life, Agnes Kotlarski, Coach DeGarza, my brother Frank, Mitch O'Nalley, Ann Burns, and other key players of that world. She heard my stories of going to Camp Lincoln in Minnesota as a boy, and traveling all over the U.S., Canada and Mexico for vacations. But she also heard about the underbelly of this world. She learned about the lack of family life in the midst of "society events" and work demands. I explained to her that the competitiveness and meanness of some of the kids jockeying for positions was not unlike what their parents did in the corporate world. She heard me discuss the wave of drug usage and abortions that were rampant in my world although swept under the rug by "hush" money and well paid abortionist doctors.

How no one I knew of 18-25 years of age ever went to Vietnam. Most young men went to college then and grad school on 4-F deferments. This, however, was not the case in Haskell. Many young men such as my cousin Gerald Hammond went to Vietnam only to return a dead hero. How we never saw any black people or dark skinned people unless they were servants at homes or country clubs. How my school was lily white as opposed to Haskell High School, which had Black, White, Brown, and Indian. How they were only now "integrating" the country club by letting Jewish people join. Catholics had broken that barrier starting in the 1920's because the mob controlled the booze and most of them were Catholics. Many had made a fortune in bootlegging and money seemed to be the great social equalizer to the upper class rather than a person's character.

Miriam asked me about the house I grew up in. I think she didn't believe me at first. It was a four-story structure consisting of 10,000 square feet. There were three half baths downstairs, and four full baths and five bedrooms upstairs not counting the two bedrooms and bath on the third floor servant's quarter. There were three stairways to the second floor and a full attic and basement. The house had three fireplaces and had buzzers to call butlers or a maid throughout the house. The den had a 20-foot ceiling and measured 50 feet by 25 feet with floor to ceiling Phillipine Ribbon Mahogany. It had been built in 1933 by an oil magnate who made his fortune around the world in that business. It was built with steel girders and had thick plaster walls clad in the most beautiful and expensive Indiana Grey limestone.

I couldn't blame Miriam if she didn't believe me when I told her about the house. Even now it seemed like a castle from a Disney movie. It was on a two-acre estate called Greystone Acres. The house sat on the top of a hill and part of our yard had steep slopes and a lower area we used as a playing field. There was an attached "cottage" of 1200 square feet where Agnes Kotlarski lived and her cottage adjoined a three-car garage attached to the main house. It had a tennis court in the back yard, which I had played on a lot. We didn't have a swimming pool because there were several beautiful trees that Mom did not want to cut down. In addition, she was concerned about the pool being an attractive nuisance to kids in the neighborhood and didn't want that responsibility.

I brought an aerial shot of the house one day to school that I showed her when we were walking home. Her mouth was gaping at the photograph. She just shook her head in disbelief. But she was catching a glimpse through my eyes of the world I came from and the world I was returning to in a short while.

I started a regimen of running and weight lifting to get ready for swim season next semester. The weather was growing colder outside as the Thanksgiving holiday approached. Nevertheless, by Chicago standards, it was relatively warm. I had written Coach DeLargza back in August about going out for football and he was okay with that. He did recommend certain exercises to do once season was over. Running was part of the regimen to strengthen my stamina. Sometimes Uncle Raymond and I would go running around the pastures during the day checking the fences; that way we could work and get a workout at the same time. It seemed to be a go to return to St. Cyngen's Prep School. The school principal who had wanted me expelled last year had taken another job over the summer and had moved to Massachusetts to run a prep school there. The successor principal was an old family friend who greased the wheels to get me readmitted.

I refused to think about what it may have cost my Dad financially or politically to pull that off. I just focused on the upcoming final semester at St. Cyngen's and the State swim championship. Agnes Kotlarski had forwarded a lot of the schools interested in me as a recruit for their respective swim program. I corresponded with a number of schools but realized much ultimately hinged on my performance at State this year. One of the schools that expressed an interest in me was John Brown University and I even had a note from Coach Cutter. On a lark I went ahead and applied to JBU together with Indiana University, UCLA, Princeton, Cornell, University of Illinois and University of Missouri. I posted these the week before school let out for Thanksgiving.

One Sunday afternoon in November, I was working out by running on Uncle Raymond's ranch. Sometimes I would climb through the fence and run along the trails on the monastery land. The path was better and made for a smoother run. Plus the views were awesome at times. It made me want to run further which I often did. As I was running on the monastery trails I saw a familiar figure walking ahead of me. It was Abbott DeLaurier. Often I would see him when I went on runs along the monastery trails; and I always enjoyed talking to him. Today was to be no exception. There was something about working out and running that made me do a lot of thinking; and many times Abbott Delaurier ended up being a very good sounding board for my thoughts. This afternoon in early November I was thinking about returning to Chicago. My heart was heavy at the thought of leaving Oklahoma. As I came running up on Abbott Delaurier, I slowed my pace and shouted to him, "Bon Jour, Abbott Delaurier!"

He whirled around just in time for me to come upon him like a cat springing on a June bug. I grabbed him and gave him a sweaty hug – all 6'2" of me hugging his slight 5'9" frame.

"Phillip!" he exclaimed. Both the Abbott and I were laughing. "It is good to see you, my young friend!"

"It is always good to see you, Abbott Delaurier."

"So what brings you out on a cold November day to the monastery trails?"

"Work out, Abbott!" I replied, panting. "I am in training to return to Chicago."

"I see," the Abbott replied.

"May I walk with you, Abbott?"

"Please do," he replied. As we began walking, the Abbott explained the purpose of the various trails and rest stops.

I sought to change the subject, "May I ask you a question, Sir?"

"Certainly, Phillip."

"Do you miss home at all?" I asked. The Abbott arched an eyebrow at that and smiled as we continued walking.

"If by home you mean France, certainly! But in many ways the Concharty Hills Monastery is my home now. But yes, a part of my heart will always be in France!"

"How do you deal with that, Abbott?" I asked. The Abbott smiled as we continued along our path.

"That my young friend, is just part of the cost in this veil of tears we call life. But, as we have discussed before, the Lord often sends fellow wayfarers in this life to walk with me on this journey to share my burden. Often times they have experienced woundings and sorrows in this life and need someone to help carry their burden. Such men and women are gifts of God. And they have helped me deal with my homesickness and sorrow at my parting with my native land of France as I have often helped them carry their burdens." I listened intently as he shared his experience in life.

"You see, Phillip, we were never meant to live this life alone. Even at this monastery the brothers are here to support and encourage one another. Life will always have pain this side of eternity. So, if you have issues in your life, pray that God sends such men and women to walk with you and help you carry your burdens as you help them carry theirs!"

"You mean guys sort of like Joe Corsinni and Kent James."

"Precisely! It is friends like that God will send your way to encourage you and support you."

"Wow," I said. "Never thought about that."

"Our Lord is everywhere, my young friend, and works in a myriad of ways to demonstrate His love and power to us. Friends are but one expression of His love to us."

"So, may I ask you a question, my young friend?" the Abbott inquired.

"Sure," I replied.

"Why do you ask me such a question?" the Abbott inquired with a twinkle behind his blue eyes.

"I guess because I, like you, was an outsider who now feels at home in Oklahoma. It's like my heart is in two places. Does that make any sense?" I asked.

"Yes. Perfect sense. But sometimes, my young friend, that is the way of life. It is hard at first to understand, but somehow there is a deeper mystery at work; the Lord intends to weave a life lesson in our hearts and we must place our trust in Him. But it is not an easy journey, my young friend. And separation from those you love, things and places you are familiar with is neither easy nor pleasant."

At this point we had reached a fork in the trail. "I must return to the monastery now, Phillip. Thank you for the time today."

"No, thank you, Abbott Delaurier. I always enjoy walking and talking with you. So, Merci Beau Coup, Monsieur, Abbott Delaurier."

The Abbott chuckled at my fumbled attempt to speak French, "Au Voir, my young friend." I watched the Abbot walk down the trail back to the monastery and then turned to run home, back to Uncle Raymond's ranch. Abbot Delaurier had given me a lot to chew on and running home helped me process this.

CHAPTER 21

THANKSGIVING AT THE FUGALIS

Aunt Louise had accepted Miss Marguerite Fugali's invitation to come to Thanksgiving Dinner. Uncle Raymond was going to smoke a turkey and some beef ribs to take to the Fugalis and Aunt Louise also made a pecan pie and a pumpkin pie. It seemed that this was going to be a grand affair. Several Fugali relatives plus family friends had been invited. The three of us brought the number to nearly 25 people. It was going to be a potluck Thanksgiving supper. Miss Toni and Miss Marguerite were polishing all her sterling silver serving pieces and flatware. Miriam told me one day at school she felt like slave labor in that the house was being cleaned and repainted for the big event.

"I love my family soirees! But it is the preparation for them that makes you homicidal! If mom tells me to re-polish one more silver piece or wash any figurines and dust one more corner of the display cases, I will scream!" Miriam said, laughing as she leaned her back against her locker after class, holding her books against her chest. I put an arm alongside her with my hand flat against her locker by her head, looking at those emerald orbs dancing in her head as she talked about the furious Fugali family efforts to prepare for the Thanksgiving feast. I leaned over her as she talked and smiled at her.

"Phillip Robertson, are you listening to what I am saying?" She asked.

"Drinking up every word," I replied, grinning and leaning closer. She and I had agreed no more frontal hugs, no serious kissing. We wanted to keep certain rules in place to protect us emotionally and physically as Uncle Raymond had suggested. I, however, was pushing the envelope!

"Boundaries, young man!" Miriam said, pushing her books into my chest and knocking me off balance. I almost fell down but Miriam caught me from falling. We were both laughing and then I said, "I get lost when I start gazing into those green emerald jewels."

"I am sure there are plenty of girls with green eyes in Chicago, Mr. Robertson!" Miriam said, mildly exasperated at my response as she started to walk off.

"Yeah, but none are named Miriam Fugali," I said as I caught up to her and grabbed her hand.

"May I walk you home? Aunt Marguerite might need a tall guy to pull down some dusty figurine for you to clean."

"You do and I will slug you!" Miriam said, teasingly.

"If she does, I will buy you dinner at a restaurant of your choice," I replied.

"Heaven help me!" I thought. "Good grief, Phillip, you are leaving in less than a month yet you are acting twitter pated around this girl," I thought, recalling the scenes from Walt Disney's <u>Bambi</u>. Not that it was all that bad. Actually, it felt pretty good and I was confident she felt the same way. But we both tried to maintain our guard up to protect ourselves.

I had never felt this way about a girl before. Uncle Raymond had once told me the story about how he knew he was going to marry Aunt Louise. "All I could do 24/7 was think about that gal! And, Phillip, when you get to that point, quit wasting time and go marry the girl. I got my chops busted in the boxing arena one day because I was thinking of Louise instead of concentrating on how to throw my next punch. My sparring partner made me see stars with that hook. I decided then to marry her. On my next leave from the Marine base, I made a long distance call and proposed to her on the phone and she said yes! Well, Cowboy, the rest is history as they say."

I was not there yet with Miriam but it was not totally beyond the range of possibility at times; but we kept our emotions in check with playful teasing. We also made a pact not to be alone after 10:00 at night.

"It would be too tempting, Miriam, and I am not strong in this area," I had confided to her. "You have to help me be a gentleman and keep my hands off you." She agreed to that and we kept the physical out of our relationship.

We got to her house, which was a scene of frantic activity with Miss Toni and Miss Marguerite cooking and cleaning. Sure enough, I got put to work pulling down objects on the higher shelves to dust and clean.

Miriam cut her eyes at me and we both started laughing. Thanksgiving was two days away and I would swear there was not one speck of dust left in that house even now!

"What in the hell is so funny about dusting porcelain?" A familiar voice asked. It was Aunt Madeline.

"Oh, no," I thought. "She is going to bust me in the chops verbally no matter what I say." Miriam came to the rescue by saying,

"Phillip just lost a bet to me, Aunt Madeline!"

"Oh really?" she replied. "What did you wager?"

"A dinner at Jamil's Steakhouse in Tulsa before he returns to Chicago."

I looked at Miriam with my mouth gaping open and said, "Never bet with a woman! A guy always loses."

Madeline Fugali grunted her agreement and returned to the kitchen where she, Marguerite and Miss Toni were cooking up a storm. Kibhi, cabbage rolls, homemade yogurt, green beans, mamoul and baklava. The aroma made me hungry. I stuck around till 5:00 helping clean and wipe down the top shelves in the display cases and built-in bookshelves.

I was invited to dinner but knew I needed to get back as I still had some chores to do. I took my leave and headed home to Uncle Raymond's ranch. That didn't stop Miss Toni from sending me home with some freshly cooked cabbage rolls and a dollop of their homemade yogurt to put on them. I brought these into Aunt Louise, which she promptly made part of our evening's supper.

I watched Uncle Raymond and Aunt Louise as they carried on a conversation at dinner. I noticed that he followed her around the kitchen with his eyes as they talked. But, then I remembered he often was like this whenever he was with Aunt Louise. "Seems like he still thinks about her 24/7 after nearly 30 years of marriage." I thought, making a mental note to myself. In two days I would be dining with the Fugalis at Thanksgiving, and I would be following Miriam like that with my eyes. Would her family spy me out? Those Fugali sisters didn't miss a trick. Time would tell in a couple of days, but I was coming to the point where I didn't care who knew that I was falling hard for Miriam.

School was out for Thanksgiving break and the big day had arrived and we gathered the smoked turkey and beef ribs to take to Miss Fugali's house. Uncle Raymond had cooked nearly 20 beef ribs that he had marinated and rubbed down with a secret recipe.

I had tasted his smoked meats before and Uncle Raymond was a great cook on the grill. He had cooked them that morning so they were still warm. He had them in an aluminum pan and the aroma was great. Aunt Louise had put the turkey on one of her finest platters covered in aluminum foil. I would carry the pies in a pie carrying case. I stole a pinch of pie to sample when Aunt Louise was not looking. The taste was sweet and made me want to eat more! That, Aunt Louise confided to me, was the mark of a good pie.

We arrived at the Fugali house at 11:30 a.m. Cars were parked up and down the street and I could hear laughter of people as we came to the front door. We rang the front door and Miriam answered the door.

"Come in, Phillip, Coach Hammond and Mrs. Hammond. Let me help you with that turkey." At that Miriam whisked the turkey off to the kitchen. She returned and took the ribs back to the kitchen and I followed her with the pie carrying case.

It was a lively group of people. Both of Miriam's older married sisters and their husbands, with kids in tow, were there. Aunt Madeline was there together with a couple of other members of the Fugali clan. Several friends of Miss Marguerite were there from Tulsa, Muskogee, and Okmulgee. Ages ranged from two to 71.

There were several younger children, ages from five to 14, and Miriam and I ended up with the role of keeping them victualed and entertained. I had brought Joe's birthday gift – the Homecoming football together with some Frisbees. Although it was chilly outside, the sun was shining so it was great to take these seven kids outside to run and scream to their hearts' content before supper. We walked over to the high school.

This was much to the relief of the adults, not having rambunctious kids underfoot. Miriam and I got a light game of Frisbee tag going and kept the kids busy until supper was ready. One young teenager was 14 and attached himself to me. His name was David Flowers who was a blond haired handsome young jock. He was a good kid and played football at his junior high in Okmulgee. He liked to pass the football as we discussed football jock talk. He had a good arm for football and could really throw the ball. However, it was encroaching upon my "Miriam" time. I was able to observe her with the kids and was impressed. She was a natural with children. David threw the football as I was looking at Miriam playing with the kids and he nailed me in the chest due to my inattention to tossing the ball.

"Oww!" I said. He had a firm toss and it hit hard when it connected to my chest. "Dude, that hurt!"

"Sorry," Dave said. But it gave me an excuse to shift the focus of our activity from tossing the football to helping Miriam.

"Hey, Dave, let's help Miriam with the other kids!" He readily agreed as he did not want to offend me. His faux pas gave me an excuse to hang around closer to Miriam. "That's a relief," I thought. Dave was a good guy, but he was low priority to me compared to Miriam.

Miss Toni called us in for dinner and we lined the kids up with plastic plates and forks, marched them through the serving line, and took them to the den to sit down on the floor to eat. They were happily victualed so Miriam and I could go through the serving line. I loaded up my plate but Miriam ate like a bird; however, I took Miriam with me and slipped out to sit on the front porch to eat alone.

It was all good and when we finished I told her to put down her plate and invited her to go for a walk around the neighborhood. She was wearing jeans, a white turtleneck under a pink wool sweater and looked great!

I had my letter jacket and turtleneck on also. I had brought a wool cap to keep my head warm, which Miriam quickly snatched off my head. She put it on her head as we walked through the neighborhood and reflected on the past semester.

"You know, Miriam, you were the first person I met when I arrived in Haskell," I said. "You made quite an impression on me."

"Oh, really? How so, Mr. Robertson?" Miriam asked as she snuggled up to me to stay warm.

"It was the eyes. Those windows to your soul. You were very warm and friendly but I was entranced by your green eyes. Believe me, when I say you would turn heads among the men at St. Cyngen and stir up some jealousy with the girls there."

"Is that so?" she asked smugly.

"And what did you first think of me?" I asked.

"Hmmm." She responded. "Well, you were tall, tanned, blond, and handsome."

Mimicking her earlier response I said, "Is that so?"

She threw a fake punch to my stomach, which I fended off. "So you have a thing for blond guys?" I asked.

"Yes," she said smiling. Her eyes were sparkling as she gazed back at me.

"Cool," I answered. "Because I have a thing for dark haired green-eyed beauties who like blond guys!" At that I earnestly looked at Miriam as we were walking along and said in all seriousness, "And I am not sure if I will ever meet another girl as good as you back in Chicago." Miriam returned my look and studied my face.

Miriam was silent at my last statement. She broke off her gaze at me as we walked for a while. "I don't know what to say, Phillip. You are a wonderful guy. It is almost like you are from another world who has crossed my path for a short season of my life. There is so much I admire about you; but you are heading back to Chicago and I am staying here in Oklahoma. I have so tried to protect my heart by not letting myself go to you." She got quiet as we continued to walk. "Not that I have not thought about it and wondered if our worlds could be merged; but I am a small town girl from Oklahoma. All I want to be is a nurse and a mother someday. I don't think I would fit in real well with your North Shore crowd at St. Cyngens."

"I am beginning to think that I am not sure I fit in there either, Miriam, or if I ever did. I have learned so much by being here with you all. I have lost a lot of my big city caution and feel like I am becoming a small town guy! What you have here is hard to describe. Uncle Raymond once told me the Creek Indians thought there was magic in the Concharty Hills. Aunt Marguerite says she feels something so special when she often walks the trails with Abbot Delaurier. Your grandfather thought it was blessed by God. And I have come to love riding or hiking up to the Concharty Mountain. It just seems to draw you back again and again. There was nothing like that for me in Chicago."

We continued walking in silence only this time I took Miriam's hand and put it through my arm so we walked closer together. Not much was said for a couple of minutes as we walked and just enjoyed our time together. Even to this day, I fondly look back on that as one of the most wonderful experiences I ever had with a girl. Miriam and I had connected as friends deeply. There were romantic feelings but we didn't allow them to totally overpower us and blind us to the painful reality that this season was approaching its finale.

Nor had there been a physical relationship, which totally would have obscured the clarity we needed in the days ahead. There was a freedom I experienced in my friendship with Miriam I had never known before. Too often in the past, things got too romantic with other girls (and invariably physical); one or the other got possessive or did not desire the intimacy and out of the wreckage of that relationship two wounded teenagers would emerge. Only most did not realize how wounded they were most times. I experienced none of that dysfunctional cycle with Miriam.

Out of the blue, I said, "So, where do we go from here, Miriam?" I turned to her and gazed into her eyes. It was a fine late afternoon in November; a chilly but beautiful day.

"I don't know, Phillip. Where do you want it to go?" she replied.

"Could those beautiful green eyes ever fall for a guy like me?" I asked sheepishly, looking at the ground.

"In a heartbeat, Phillip," she replied, looking back into my eyes. "But don't take that as a yes...yet!" Then changing the subject "and speaking of eyes, I can't tell if yours are blue, green, hazel or what! They are almost cat like. That is what I first thought about you."

"Oh really!" I said.

"Yes, really! Mr. Cat Eyes!" she continued. "Several of the girls and I nicknamed you that. Did you never hear us talking about you?"

"NO!" I said emphatically. "With Kent James and Joe Corsinni attached to me at the hip all semester, it is a wonder I even got to dance with you at the mixer." I laughed. "Cat eyes, huh? Fair enough. I call you emerald eyes so I guess I need a nickname for mine. Only most guys don't like to be called cat like, we are more dog like!" I grinned. "But, to answer your question, I want to stay in touch. May I call you once a week? I will write you if you like. Will you promise to write me a letter once a week?"

"Yes, I will write if you do!" she responded, coyly.

"I am going to miss Haskell, Miriam," I said, looking around. Then turning to her, "And I shall dearly miss you, too, Miriam."

Miriam looked at me and replied, "Kent, Joe and I will truly miss you also. It is like you grew up here with us. And, yes, Mr. Romantic, the loss of your presence will be sorely felt by many, especially me," she threw a fake punch to my arm. "And speaking of sorely missed, we had better get back or I will have grief to bear for abandoning my charges." We walked quickly back to the house and gathered up our plates from the porch and went back inside. We did not seem to have been missed much. The adult men were watching a football game and I was drawn in there. Miriam and the women were in another room.

The guys were watching a football game. It was a pleasant way to spend the afternoon while the women talked and the kids played. I didn't get any more one on one time with Miriam that day. The guys stayed glued to the game until it was over. Whereupon, there was much washing of dishes and packing up what food remained. It was a memorable and fun Thanksgiving. Families began leaving after thanking the Fugali sisters and the Abbouds.

We took our leave also and headed home to spend the rest of the evening together, just the three of us, Aunt Louise, Uncle Raymond and myself. We talked into the evening about things we were grateful for and I heard many a story about past Thanksgivings those two had shared. I truly understood what Frank meant about wanting a sense of family and community now. I was so blessed to have that in Uncle Raymond and Aunt Louise.

CHAPTER 22

DINNER WITH THE ABBOT

I had less than three weeks left before I returned to Chicago. Kent had hit me up about accompanying him to have dinner with Abbot Delaurier. Translated that meant I had to set up the time by contacting Abbot Delaurier. This I did and we set a time on a Saturday after Joe and I got the ranch work done. As Kent and I were going, Joe got drawn into our adventure with the monks also. I chuckled to myself that I would miss these two knuckleheads since it was fun to do things with them and experience new places and things. Aunt Louise and Uncle Raymond thought it was good that the three of us were going to have dinner with the monks.

"It will broaden your perspective about life, Phillip. It will also help you to appreciate the lifestyle and sacrifices men such as these monks have made," Uncle Raymond had shared.

The day came and the three of us drove over to the monastery that evening. I did not know what to expect. We arrived and went to the main dining hall. Abbot Delaurier was there with two other monks. As we entered the dining hall, they greeted us. The other two monks had a bowl and towel. They washed and towel dried out hands as a symbolic greeting like washing our feet as Jesus had done. We were instructed that monks and guests observed a rule of silence. Translated, we were eating in absolute silence.

That would be no problem for Joe, but would present challenges to Kent and me. We were seated at a table on benches. The dinner consisted of vegetable soup, homemade bread and butter, sliced carrots, one-half baked potato, and pumpkin pie. Kent's expression was one of shock at the small servings and no meat! Throughout the dinner one monk was reading from the writings of a Pope Leo XIII, interspersed with readings from the New and Old Testament. At one point, Kent asked Joe to pass more bread. He was tapped on the shoulder and a monk shook his head "no" with his index finger over his lips. I had to stifle a snicker. Joe's eyes were as big as silver dollars at Kent's silent scolding.

Joe, Kent and I made up for the paucity of meat by eating an entire loaf of bread, much to the surprise of the monk serving our table. When the monks were dismissed from the dining hall, the Abbot came up to show us the monastery compound. It was fascinating to hear the philosophy and history of the Benedictine Order.

At the end of the tour, we had the opportunity to talk to Abbot Delaurier alone. Kent had many questions for the Abbot about ministry, God's call on a man's life, the pros and cons of ministry, and the Abbot's greatest frustration with ministry. Joe and I hardly got a word in edgewise but that was okay. We were there to support Kent as well as get a glimpse of some of the routine of the monastery. At the conclusion of the conversation we took our leave of Abbot Delaurier and thanked him for the courtesy of the invitation for dinner and the time he spent with us. I was not certain how Kent was processing the interchange with Abbot Delaurier.

"Seems every time I talk to that old bird, he raises more questions about ministry than he answers," Kent observed.

"He is making you carefully gauge the costs, Kent," Joe replied. "And what better person to challenge you on that than a man who has spent nearly 30 years of his life doing ministry," Joe observed. As usual, Joe profoundly and succinctly summarized what the Abbot was doing with Kent. I could not have stated it plainer, but that didn't satisfy Kent.

"Still, there must be more to ministry than what he described," Kent stated, thinking out loud.

At that Joe rolled his eyes and said, "Kent James, I am not prepared to argue what is the meaning of God's call on your life. This is a tough life issue and you are not going to get it resolved in one night bull session with Phillip and me."

I concurred and added, "Rome was not built in a day and your questions about ministry won't be answered in one night. Joe's right. This is a question you are going to have to pursue and ponder for years to finally find your answer. But right now I am pondering what is in Aunt Louise's frigerator because a bowl of soup, carrots, bread and a meager slice of pie aren't going to cut my hunger right now."

At that, the gravity of the moment was lifted and both guys were smiling in agreement. Aunt Louise didn't know it, but her refrigerator was about to be raided, not unlike what the men of Rome did to the Sabine cities, except for the raping and pillaging. When we arrived home, we were still hungry as we came through the front door. Aunt Louise and Uncle Raymond were in the den, reading and Aunt Louise asked, "How was dinner?"

"Not nearly enough," I said as the three of us marched straight into her kitchen and took plates of leftover fried chicken and Mediterranean green beans out of her frigerator to eat.

Aunt Louise came into the kitchen and said with amazement, "Land sakes alive! You boys would eat the house down around you if you were termites." She had us sit down while she warmed up the chicken and green beans. When the chicken was warm enough she took a fresh lemon and squeezed it over the warm fried chicken to enhance the taste. It was a fitting ending to our culinary adventure at the monastery.

"I am definitely a carnivore!" Kent said, biting into a chicken breast. Joe and I nodded in agreement. Uncle Raymond joined us at the table and quizzed us about our evening's activities and meal, or the lack thereof from a jock's perspective.

"No wonder they were about to carry away your frigerator, Louise! These boys have worked hard today but were hardly fed by the good monks," he said, grinning.

"Well, I am glad I am not a monk," I added. "If I ever had questions about being one, it was answered in the negative tonight at dinner. I might give up marriage, but not talking and eating," and I winked at Aunt Louise.

"You've created a monster with all your conversation and cooking, Louise," Uncle Raymond teased.

"Yeah. Phillip will never find a girl who cooks as good as you, Mrs. Hammond," Joe added. And that was most likely true, too. I didn't think any girl could match the culinary skills of Aunt Louise.

Aunt Louise blushed and said she could teach all three of our future wives to cook as good as she did.

"I for one will take you up on that, Aunt Louise," exclaiming that between bites. Something struck a chord in Aunt Louise as she immediately looked at Uncle Raymond with a smile. She seemed both happy and sad at the same time.Kent spoke up, "Will you teach my future wife to cook, too?"

"You mean that von Holland girl?" Joe teased. Kent shot back. "Yeah, it could be her," slightly glaring at Joe, knowing full well this would be reported back to his mom. Kent was really close to his parents but he was at an age that he didn't share everything with them when it came to girls. His mother was not shy about delving into this area of Kent's life and he knew he was now going to be asked about this.

Aunt Louise broke the tension by teasing him when she remarked, "Well, when do you want to set up some cooking lessons with her, Kent?" Aunt Louise then took the teasing a step further and nailed both Joe and me when she added, "Phillip can invite Miriam and if Joe doesn't have a gal picked out, we will invite Sheree Brandt for him."

At that I blushed red and Kent choked on a bite of chicken, trying not to laugh. Aunt Louise was a keen observer of events and what occurred at the mixer did not slip by her with regard to all three of us. Joe turned red and said, "Ha Ha!"

"Try suggesting Phyllis Long, Aunt Louise. He might be more responsive; only from what I hear he mangled her feet on the dance floor at the mixer," I added.

Joe's eyes opened wide and his mouth was gaping. Kent spit out some green beans and I got slugged in the shoulder by Joe, lecturing me, "M.A.D., buddy! I am invoking your brother's Doctrine of Mutual Assured Destruction! No more! Capiche!" What I did not fully appreciate was that Joe's parents were bilingual and Joe understood and spoke some Italian. At that all of us were laughing.

"Well, there ain't any secrets at this table, Louise," Uncle Raymond added, chuckling.

"Only don't go rat out the boys to your 'Stitch and Chat' circles at the church. What has been revealed at this table should stay here! Well, at least until tomorrow! " At that he winked at Aunt Louise and looked at Kent. "But, yeah, Kent, that von Holland gal is a looker and a keeper." He then turned to me and said, "Phillip, you will never find any gals as good as Miriam." He paused then, put his hand on Joe's shoulder and said, "As for Joe, I think that Phyllis Long would be a better fit for him than Sheree Brandt but what does an old retired coach know." Although Joe still had an interest in Sheree, as of late a spunky little sophomore by the name of Phyllis Long was capturing his attention and affection. That was somewhat new to Joe and us. Joe cut his eyes at Uncle Raymond and then at me as if pleading for respite.

The conversation then turned to discussing the relative merits of these various young women in our lives. We opened up about everything we three guys felt about these girls. I think my candor about my feelings towards Miriam surprised Kent and Joe. Uncle Raymond and Aunt Louise had a pretty good hunch as to the depth of my feelings. Not much slipped past them when it came to Phillip Robertson. Joe, however, only opened up about Phyllis and the taboo subject of Sheree was not touched. Aunt Louise and Uncle Raymond sat there listening and guiding the conversation. They had just ferreted out all the information about the significant girls in our lives yet we almost felt relieved that they had done this. Joe and Kent opened up in ways I had never heard them do before. Probably we all needed a good sounding board. Obviously, we needed the wisdom of a Godly older couple and what better two than Uncle Raymond and Aunt Louise. The three of us guys talked later that we did not feel as if they had invaded our privacy at all. This repartee lasted till the fried chicken and most of the green beans were gone.

Joe then concluded the meal by saying, "Well, the price of squealing on each other about women we like was worth your green beans and fried chicken, Mrs. Hammond."

Aunt Louise nodded her head smiling and replied, "Your secrets are safe. We appreciate your opening up to us."

We helped clean up the kitchen. Kent and Joe thanked Aunt Louise and Uncle Raymond and I walked them back to Joe's truck.

"Thanks, guys," I said. "This was a good evening tonight."

"Yeah, it was good to get that out in the open. Appreciate you guys sharing and listening," Joe said, "and I think Coach and Mrs. Hammond are not as prone to share all that either with our folks."

"You are right, Joe. Besides that is your job to tell your mom and dad, not Uncle Raymond and Aunt Louise's responsibility."

Kent added, "Yeah, that is right. Guess I had better talk to Mom about Theresa." Kent paused, had a gleam in his eye, and then teasingly said, " But guys, I still have questions about ministry!"

Joe and I rolled our eyes and both pushed him into the truck, laughing and we said goodnight. The guys drove off and I went back into the house to turn in.

CHAPTER 23

SETTLING A BET AT JAMIL'S

School was finally out for Christmas break and I was fairly sure I had pulled a 4.0. I had a date with Miriam to take her to dinner on Tuesday night in Tulsa at Jamils. It would be our last date together as I was leaving on Friday. Tuesday evening came. I was dressing up for this. I starched my khaki slacks and ironed them myself. I wore a white shirt and a blue/silver/green stripped tie with a navy blue blazer. I even polished my Sebago Cordovan tassel loafers. I was going all out prep tonight. I even put on my All-American ring I had earned at the State swim meet last year.

Aunt Louise saw me and approved of how I looked. "You look really fine for your date with Miriam."

"Yeah, he is one cowboy who cleans up well for a girl," Uncle Raymond joked.

I took my leave and headed over to the Fugalis to pick up Miriam. Miss Toni answered the door and invited me in. Miriam, as usual, was not ready. I liked this girl, but she was rarely ready when I came to get her. That meant conversation with Miss Marguerite, Miss Toni and Mr. Abboud. This evening it was more like an interrogation about my return to Chicago and my plans for the future in terms of college. Mercifully, Miriam came in and my cross examination was over. We excused ourselves and headed up to the restaurant.

"Thanks for rescuing me, Miriam. Your family was really grilling me tonight."

"Do you blame them?" she asked. "In walks a guy from Chicago with pedigree, good looks, athletic, and ambitious; and he is interested in hanging out with your daughter. I would say that might have them slightly on edge."

"Am I a dangerous criminal?" I asked.

"No, just an amorous teenage male athlete and that spells danger to a parent," she teased. And Miriam was right. I did have strong feelings for Miriam and had often pushed the envelope with her playfully. I was shooting straight for the heart and Miriam knew that. Only she was not an easy target as she herself was uncertain how compatible we truly were. The more aloof she became at times the more determined I was to pursue her. But the pursuit of such a woman as Miriam required style, grace, timing and wisdom. A guy had to play his cards just right or he was out of luck.

I didn't really want to push the physical with Miriam. I would honor my word and her integrity on that. I wanted her to want me as much as I was beginning to want her. Joe was right. I had a crush on Miriam. Only now it had grown into something more intense. Yes, sports fans, I was truly falling in love with this girl! It made no sense. It was poorly timed, seemed illogical, but there it was. I had started thinking about her 24/7 as Uncle Raymond had warned.

"An amorous teenage male? You make it sound like I am a werewolf or something that on a full moon is going to stalk its designated prey for dinner." Ironically enough there was a full moon rising as we drove north into Tulsa. It made for a stunning sight on the horizon.

"I am not worried." Miriam replied. "Mother gave me a garlic necklace to wear to ward you off, and Daddy supplied me a pistol loaded with silver bullets to shoot you with if you start to change into your true character and attack," she teased.

"Ahrooo" I howled in reply. But the truth was I did feel more amorous during the full moon cycle, and being with Miriam only heightened that. She looked awesome. She had worn a jade green blouse with black pants. Her Aunt Marguerite had loaned Miriam her fur coat to wear to stay warm in this cold weather.

"You look more like a werewolf than me!" I joked, referring to the fur coat.

"Aunt Marguerite skinned the last werewolf who made overtures at a Fugali girl," she bantered back.

I shook my head, smiling to myself. There wasn't a single girl I knew on the North Shore society circles that was as beautiful as Miriam nor as quick witted. How could a guy not admire this girl. Plus her family was awesome. Her mom still had a very nice figure after nearly 30 years of marriage and three pregnancies. Dad had often told me to look at the mother because that is what you are married to in 30 years. In Miriam's case then, she would be as beautiful then as she was now. Dang, I was feeling weak in the knees. Fortunately, we pulled up to the restaurant and I was able to think of other things.

Jamil's Restaurant was a Lebanese steakhouse in an old 1940's house. It had a family feel to it and a reputation as one of the finest steakhouses in Tulsa. We had a great meal of hors d'oeuvres, consisting of humas tahini, tabouli, pita bread, salad, cabbage rolls, barbeque bologna and ribs and then a filet. Now that was a dinner worth remembering.

But it was the conversation that was the best part of the evening. At one point in the evening I took my All American ring off my finger and asked Miriam to keep this for me.

"Whatever for?" she asked, taken aback.

"To keep alive our friendship and give me a reason to come back to Haskell." I said as I gazed intensely into her lovely face.

"For a ring?" she asked, incredulously.

"No, for you!" Miriam sat there dumbfounded at my reply. I took hold of her hand and said,

"Miriam, I am not asking you to marry me...yet! But I am asking for a commitment for a special friendship from you. I guess in your grandfather's day they called it courting. Nowadays, it is to go steady. Been there, done that, got a t-shirt! I don't want a 'steady thing.'" Looking into her eyes, I said, "I want you."

"You are asking for a serious commitment shy of marriage, Mr. Robertson! That is a big deal for this small town girl to ponder. I can't answer you just yet. But I will keep your ring for you and thank you for your gift of friendship in entrusting this to me." She looked at me almost trembling. It was the most vulnerable that I had ever seen Miriam. Her warmth and self-confidence usually flowed out of her like a spring. But tonight she was totally discombobulated. My request had totally caught her off guard. That was okay. She looked at me with those warm green eyes and we held each other's gaze as I held her hand. The magic of that moment, however, was broken by the waiter bringing the bill. I paid the bill, helped her put coat on and walked her back to the car.

Miriam snuggled up to me as we slowly made our way back to Haskell. God, it felt great to hold that girl like this. I dropped her off at her house, walked her to the door, and gave her a hug and kissed her check. It was nearly 10:00 and I was not going to press any further. I was after her heart and soul, not merely her body. The physical could come later in the event things turned serious and we got married. Until then I observed boundaries. Besides, I knew I was weak in this area and did not want to tempt fate. Sexual activity before its time soiled a relationship, Uncle Raymond said and I believed him! I did not want to spoil things with Miriam. I said good night and would talk to her in the morning. I was not certain what Miriam would say, but I knew she had some feelings for me. Time would tell how things would play out when I returned to Chicago. But I was willing to wait for a girl as good as Miriam.

CHAPTER 24

SAGE ADVICE FROM MS. MARGUERITE
AND AUNT LOUISE

Miriam immediately went into her house and hung up Aunt Marguerite's fur coat. Marguerite was still up and asked Miriam how her date was.

"Aunt Marguerite, I really need someone to talk to right now."

"Talk away, honey. You look flustered! You okay? Was Phillip a gentleman?" Marguerite asked in rapid fire staccato.

"Phillip was polite as always, Aunt Marguerite. It is just that he asked me something." Miriam replied with a look of consternation. Marguerite's eyes opened wide and she said, "Asked you what?"

"Aunt Marguerite, he wants to court me. Me! I'm only 18," Miriam protested.

"Land sakes alive, girl. You scared me." Marguerite said, chuckling. "You are a grown woman and he is a grown man. What's wrong with him courting you?" Marguerite replied matter of factly.

Miriam's mouth was gaping open. "But, but...." She stammered.

"Honey, you don't want to end up an old maid like your Aunt Madeline and myself. The boy likes you. There is no harm in that as long as he is not fresh."

"No, he has never been physically forward with me," Miriam said. "But we are from two different worlds. A fish may love a bird, but where would they make their home?"

"Oh, I see," Marguerite replied, rolling her eyes. "He's not Catholic and he's from Chicago. Two strikes against him and he is returning to Chicago next semester. Third strike. He's out." And Marguerite mimicked an umpire calling a baseball player out.

"No, no, that is not it." Miriam countered.

"Then what?" Marguerite asked, mildly exasperated.

"I just never thought I would ever get serious with a boy till after nursing school, is all." Miriam stated in frustration.

"Is that what is really eating you up about him?" Marguerite asked. "Honey, lots of people get married and go to college."

"But I can't live in Chicago," Miriam countered.

"Who said you would? Honey, you have no idea where Phillip will go to college. I have known plenty of couples that were separated by wars and distance and yet today are happily married."

"What should I do?" Miriam asked, cutting to the chase.

"I saw that question coming," Marguerite chuckled. "Invite him to the Senior Prom."

"What?" Miriam gasped.

"Why not? He's a good dancer; he is a good young man from a nice family. And I know you like him more than you will admit to! So there." As always, Miss Marguerite was blunt and to the point. She really liked her niece and she had grown fond of me almost as much as she liked her Godson Joe Corsinni. It had not hurt that she and Joe had talked a lot about me so she had a pretty good read on me. But she also recognized before Miriam did that she was falling for me, too!

"That's it?" Miriam asked.

"What else is there to discuss? He likes you; you like him. Take him to the Prom. He will come back to take you, even if he is in Chicago, it will allow you two to get to know each other better. You will have a better idea about things then, too."

"But we come from such different backgrounds," Miriam protested.

"Doesn't mean you two are that different or incompatible. Honey, you think it over. I will remember you in my Rosary tonight before I go to bed. It will turn out all right. Now, it's time to go to bed." Marguerite had had enough conversation in this subject and turned in.

If Miriam's head was spinning at her house, my heart was roaring. I came into the house and Aunt Louise was still awake.

"You have a good time?" Aunt Louise asked, looking up from her book..

"Yeah," I said, coming into the den and pulling up a chair. "Aunt Louise, may I ask you something?"

"Sure," she said, putting her book down.

"Aunt Louise, how did you know you loved Uncle Raymond enough to marry him?"

Aunt Louise's mouth was wide open in astonishment. She squinted her eyes and said, "Phillip Robertson, what have you been up to this evening?"

"Nothing, Aunt Louise. Really. But I think I am going to court Miriam over the next four years. I have never met another girl like her and don't want to lose her."

"Well, she is one in a million and waiting four years till you get out of college is wise. But are you sure you are not speaking out of romance because it is a full moon and you are leaving in two days?"

"Nah, it is nothing like that," I said.

"Well, you have put your foot in it, Phillip. I like Miriam, but getting this serious at your age is fraught with peril."

"Peril!" I said. "You married Uncle Raymond when you were 18!"

"But times were different then, Phillip. Raymond had a job, you don't! Besides, he was 21 and you are still barely 18. It's the man's role to support his wife, not vice versa. You are going to college and then maybe law school. That is seven years before you can support a wife and family. Besides, people change a lot from 18 to 25."

"Hmmm. You may be right about that. But still, I gave her my All American ring to keep for me as a pledge of our friendship. Did I do wrong, Aunt Louise?"

She smiled, shaking her head, and said, "No, there is nothing wrong with what you did. But that is a serious step, Phillip. Count the costs."

"I have, Aunt Louise. I am sure I will never meet a girl as good as Miriam."

"Well, what is done is done. We will think about it and pray about this. What you are talking about is a serious matter, but a blessed thing if the time is right and God is in it. But I think we need to sleep on this for now." At that we both got up and went to our rooms. I was a little taken aback in that I would have thought Aunt Louise would have been more excited. But that was okay. We would have more time to talk about this. In the meantime it was lights out. I only had two more nights here and then it was back to Chicago.

CHAPTER 25

THE BLESSING OF FRIENDSHIP

The next day was my last day to work with Joe on the ranch. It was a Wednesday. We worked the cattle on the lower pastures in the morning and worked in the barn in the early afternoon. We saved checking the fence for last because I wanted to go hiking on the monastery trails and wanted to take Joe with me. We got our chores done so it was off to the Concharty Mountains to go hiking. It was really chilly outside so we were both warmly dressed and wore gloves. The smell of the fire was still evident in the air from the burn site when we got to the fence where the monks built the firewall.

When we got to the upper pasture, it was a pretty sight to behold. I turned to Joe and said, as we climbed through the fence, "I am going to miss this view, Joe. But I am really going to miss working with you, bud. Besides my brother Frank, there is no other guy I feel this close to and someday I want you to be in my wedding as a groomsman, both you and Kent."

Joe's eyes widened when he asked, "You getting married or something, Phillip?"

I looked at Joe, man to man, eye to eye, putting my hand on his shoulder, "not yet, buddy. But I think I know who I want to marry," I answered.

"Miriam?" Joe asked, stunned.

"Yeah, buddy. Miriam," I replied, grinning like the Cheshire Cat from *Alice in Wonderland.*

"Whoa, dude. I got to take a minute to let this soak in." And Joe did just that as we continued walking silently down the monastery trails. We came to a clearing with bench seats and sat down.

"Phillip, I knew you had a crush but, buddy, this is serious stuff." Joe replied, shaking his head.

"I know it is, Joe. I gave her my All American ring to keep for me. There is no other girl I am interested in. I wanted to share this with you, Joe, because I wanted your blessing," I said, excitedly.

"My blessing?" Joe asked in astonishment. "What do I have to do with this?"

"Joe, your good opinion means the world to me. If one of my best friends in Haskell who knows both Miriam and me doesn't think this is the right thing, then I need to retrench. That is why I want your blessing, Joe. You are like a brother to me and you know me. There is a heartfelt connection between us, Sinni, that is hard to explain. Half the time I only have to look in your eyes to know what you're thinking and, what's scary, you can look at me and read me like a book. Now, if two friends have that sort of connection, then that is why I say I need to know I have your blessing to proceed." I had become rather animated at this point and Joe sat there stoically as ever with a wry grin on his face as he listened. It was true. There was a heartfelt connection between us and he had sensed it, too. He looked at me with those steel blue eyes that communicated understanding.

He leaned forward and said, "Well, bud, then there is only one thing I can do." At that moment he did something totally unexpected and un-Corsinni like, as he wrapped his left arm around my neck and put a hammerlock on me with that huge arm. He then said, "Go for it. You have my whole hearted blessing," giving me a Dutch rub with his free hand.

I almost got dizzy from Joe squeezing my neck like that, but all I could do was smile and hoarsely say, "Thanks, Buddy. Joe, you will never know what that means to me. If I ever have a son, I will name him after you and I want you to be his Godfather."

Joe immediately let me go and looked troubled. He asked, "No one is pregnant, are they?"

I punched him hard in the shoulder and said, "I am a red-blooded American male, alright, but no procreational activities have been occurring. Besides, with you and Kent attached to my right and left sides, when would I ever have had time? But, no, I would never do that to Miriam. She is too fine a girl. For her, I would wait till our wedding night and then it is Katy bar the door!"

At that, Joe started laughing, looking at me. "I am going to miss you, too, Phillip. Your zest for life is downright infectious at times. You have been the best bud a fella can have. You are right. We do have a connection here." Joe patted his chest where his heart was and continued, "and you have taught me a lot and did not even realize it. I really thank you for that!" I could only wonder what Joe meant."

As we looked out over the view, I remarked, "Uncle Raymond said the Creek Indians thought there was something magical about these hills. There is something special about this place, all right. I am just not sure what it is."

At that point, we both heard a familiar voice to our backs, "Perhaps it is because the 'magic' as you call it is not magic at all, but answered prayer. Answered prayers of the Creek Indians safely making it to Indian Territory; answered prayers of settlers trying to eke out a living; answered prayers of Papa C that this mountain could be a blessing to weary travelers; and the multitude of answered prayers of my fellow monks that this would truly be a haven for spiritual and emotional refreshment to wounded souls hurting from life's injuries."

We had both turned around and stood up. "Abbot Delaurier," I said with a smile, and immediately went up to the Frenchman and gave him a bear hug. This caught him off guard and he said, "I am glad to see you also, my young friend, but what is the meaning of this most exuberant greeting? I have never known you to be a man who is prone to throw Abbots of a monastery around in expressing affection."

I immediately put the Abbot down and answered the Abbot in French about the last day's events with regard to Miriam and the fact I was leaving to go back to Chicago to finish high school. I switched back to English.

"I will sorely miss seeing you strolling along these trails, Abbot Delaurier. I have so appreciated your stories of how you have lived your life. It has truly given me guidance."

The Abbot was smiling now. "I am glad to hear that, Phillip. Amor, that is a powerful intoxicant. Drink carefully and wisely from that cup mon amie! I will certainly pray for you on that and I, too, will miss your youthful enthusiasm and hunger for living. You will always be welcome to walk the trails of our monastery. Would you both walk with me now?"

"Sure," I said.

Joe smiled and nodded his agreement. The Abbot invited us to walk with him and put his arms through our arms as we walked beside him, Joe on the left and me on the right.

"May I pray for you both?" the Abbot asked.

"Why not," I said. Joe nodded his assent.

"Lord, may my young brothers, your sons, find your paths to follow all of their lives. May they, with your help, find the right helpmate to walk with them in this life. And may my young brothers, your sons, always be a blessing wherever they go and whatever they do, and may their brother and young friend Kent find answers to all his questions about ministry; and may we all have patience and understanding for his spiritual journey." And with that both Joe and I said, "Amen and Amen."

The Abbot caught us off guard with that and we were both smiling and chuckling.

"So, you see, Abbots can be practical as well as spiritual in their prayers. The Lord loves his children to be real in their conversations with Him.   And I should have been praying these past few weeks for patience and wisdom for you both in dealing with your young friend and brother Kent."

Joe and I cut our eyes at each other and laughed. "He is spiritually hungry and he is an honest pilgrim. But spiritual pilgrims can sorely test your patience on their journey! And it is a sin to bore others with the gospel, is it not?" the Abbot asked, arching his eyebrow and looking at Joe and me. We smiled, nodding our agreement as he continued, "But I think he has the true grit to be a good minister, but it will not be an easy road for him. Your young friend makes me think of a prayer I read some time ago. It was from your Civil War. It is called 'The Prayer of a Confederate Soldier.' Are you familiar with it?

"No," Joe and I answered.

"Let me recite it for you. I believe it applies to your young pilgrim.

> I asked God for strength, that I might achieve;
> I was made weak that I might learn humbly to obey.
> I asked for health, that I might do greater things;
> I was given infirmity, that I might do better things.
> I asked for riches, that I might be happy;
> I was given poverty, that I might be wise.
> I asked for power, that I might have the praise of men;
> I was given weakness, that I might feel the need of God.
> I asked for all things, that I might enjoy life;
> I was given life, that I might enjoy all things.
> I got nothing that I asked for, but everything I hoped for;

Almost despite myself, my unspoken prayers were answered;

I am among all men most richly blessed.

The Abbot continued walking with us but none of us said anything. That prayer was thought provoking and the Abbot wanted to give us time to let that sink in. He then continued after a bit.

"You both must pray for your friend Kent on this point of his spiritual odyssey; he is somewhat naïve and his expectations of ministry may not match the realities of a life devoted to ministry. He desires to be a shepherd but he will find herding people is not an easy task to take them to green pastures, as the Psalmist wrote."

At that the Abbot had a fire burning behind those blue eyes. He spoke with an intensity and conviction on that such that even to this day I still pray for Kent and his ministry.

"We will," Joe said.

"Well, my young friends, this has been a pleasant respite." He then looked at me and speaking fluent French told me how he had been praying for me since our first meeting and prayed for the blossoming of my friendship with Joe and Kent when he saw us skinny dipping; and that he had prayed I would journey home to the heart of God and find illumination to my path after our conversation that night back in September. He then switched to English, "And I have been given the privilege of seeing all those prayers answered in my lifetime before my eyes. For that I above all men am truly blessed and will remember to thank our Lord for this privilege." I had a tear in my eye by now and hugged the Abbot again. But it was tears of appreciation and farewell.

"We will meet again, my young friend. I am sure of it." The Abbot's eyes were dancing as he spoke. "Something in my heart tells me this. So it is not goodbye, my young friend, only auvoir for now." The

Abbot was touching his chest as he said this, and turning around continued on his way back to the monastery. Looking at Joe, I saw he was red in the eyes, too, with tears streaking his cheeks.

"Sinni, we both can't be crying babies. One of us has to be a real man."

"Hey, real men cry, too, Phillip," he teased, wiping a tear himself as we headed back to the fence to walk back to Uncle Raymond's.

"In that case, I am a real man, Joe, because I have cried a lot this past year," turning to him and teasing him, "Does crying put hair on your chest?" Joe punched me and said, "No. But, hey, I will race you back to your Uncle Raymond's barn"

"You're on, Cowboy," and away we ran. Not that that was a smart thing to do in cowboy boots, running down rocky tree lined trails through uneven pastures. Joe, of course, won. But I managed to stay on his heels and almost beat him. We were both winded, panting and leaning over with our hands resting on our legs. We both stood up at the same time.

Joe extended his hand, "You're a good man, Phillip Robertson. Don't let those rich uppity Chicago kids tell you otherwise. I have worked with you, worked out with you and seen how you weather tough new places. You're all right! And, yeah, I count you as one of my best friends, too." At that he grabbed me into a bear hug. "And I will miss your hairy ass, too"

Laughing, I replied, "My ass isn't hairy."

"You ain't seen your backside in a shower," Joe replied.

"You should talk, Sinni. It ain't for nothing Kent sometimes calls you 'sasquatch'."

We started laughing and walked back inside after we took off our boots. Aunt Louise had fixed us a fine supper and we relished the time together, laughing over the past five months. The phone rang and Aunt Louise went to answer it. It was a long distance call from Agnes Kotlarski in Chicago. I took the call and Agnes firmed up the details of picking me up at O'Hare Airport. She reported that there had been a snow blizzard in Chicago and she warned me to dress extra warm.

"God willing and weather permitting, I will see you at 3:30 on Friday," she said. I finished the call and returned to our conversation.

Uncle Raymond came in as we were finishing and joined the lively conversation. Joe stuck around for about thirty minutes and then left after thanking them both for dinner. I then had the chance to thank Uncle Raymond and Aunt Louise for all they had done for me these past five months. I had to pack up tomorrow as well as get some chores done. Plus, I wanted to say goodbye to a lot of different people.

They both then quizzed me about Miriam and my plans with her. I explained that I really did love her and wanted to wait till after college to get married.

"That's a good plan," Uncle Raymond said. It also seemed to satisfy Aunt Louise. For her, the proof would be my actions in the next four years. She cared for me deeply and I knew that. But she also wanted me to be wise; hence, her concern about my intentions towards Miriam at the tender age of 18. Of course, I still did not have a firm commitment from Miriam but I believed it would come with time.

"Uncle Raymond, Aunt Louise, can I ask you something?" I said tentatively, looking at the floor.

"What is it?" Uncle Raymond asked with a look of concern.

"These past five months have been the best five months of my life. May I come back and live with you in the summer and maybe even bring a friend? I promise not to be much trouble and to continue working chores on the ranch!" I looked up at both of them.

"Good Heavens yes, son!" Uncle Raymond replied with a smile.

There was a look of genuine relief on Aunt Louise's face. She added, "You're family, Phillip! As I told your brother Frank, family is always welcome. But you especially have captured a special place in our hearts. I know both Raymond and I are going to miss your enthusiasm and your hard work on the ranch. It is like the Lord knew we needed you to help fill some of the empty places in our lives."

My eyes started to water up at this. The truth was they had both filled what seemed like a yawning chasm in my heart. It was more like the "Good Lord" (as Aunt Louise called Him) knew I needed them to help me through the difficulties I had encountered.

"You will never know how much I love you both and words are inadequate to express what you mean to me," I said as I hugged Aunt Louise and then Uncle Raymond. I maintained my composure with Aunt Louise, but totally lost it with Uncle Raymond. All I could do was cry as I hugged him. He quietly held me and let me just release my grief at so much loss this past year. What I didn't realize is that he was crying too, albeit silently. That was his Marine way of saying goodbye and identifying with me as a man.

Aunt Louise beheld the spectacle of two grown men bonding in their respective grief from previous personal losses and my upcoming parting. She came over to us and put her hands on both our shoulders and said a prayer, "Oh, Lord, thank You for Your gracious blessing of life. Thank You that You understand our pain and hurts in life. Thank You for the gift of Phillip in our lives these past five months. Thank You for the continued healing You have worked in our lives through Christ over the loss of our own son Gerald. Thank You for the honor and privilege of serving You by hosting Phillip in our home. Thank You for how You have answered prayers of so many people on behalf of Phillip that he would fit in well here and make new friends. Thank You for his friendship with Joe, Kent, and Miriam. May he and Joe and Kent always be friends. Give both he and Miriam wisdom as they pursue their relationship further. And help Phillip always see Your hand in his life and always seek Your Presence wherever he goes. Always raise up Godly friends for him to run with who pursue righteousness out of a pure heart. Amen."

Both Uncle Raymond and I had stopped crying at this point and joined Aunt Louise in saying Amen. We let go of each other and just looked at each other, man to man. Uncle Raymond put a fatherly hand on my shoulder and said, "You are like a second son to me, Phillip. I would lay my life down for you. If you ever need anything, you call me 24/7! You got that, Cowboy?"

His statement was more like an order. I gripped Uncle Raymond's hand on my shoulder and answered, looking him straight in the eyes, "Yes, sir! I will! Be assured of that!" I answered him.

"You had better finish packing or you aren't going anywhere!" Aunt Louise interjected.

Uncle Raymond let go of my shoulder and added, "She's right, you know! You can always tell when a woman's advice is good if it is a touch practical and just slightly irritating that a man didn't think of it first!" Uncle Raymond was grinning and Aunt Louise poked him in the side.

"Uh-oh! Before I start a fight, I had better finish packing!" With that I excused myself and went back to my room to get my things together.

Uncle Raymond went over to Aunt Louise and hugged and kissed her, and said, "It's been an incredible ride these past five months, Mrs. Hammond."

"I wouldn't have missed it for the world. I am humbled that God chose us to be there for Phillip; and

I am humbled at how He has answered so many prayers for Phillip and for us. It is as John Newton wrote in his song *Amazing Grace.* The Lord has been good to me."

"Well, speaking of good, why don't you let me help you clean up the kitchen!" At that, he and Aunt Louise finished up in there and retired to the den to read awhile before going to bed. I finished packing, came out to say goodnight and then turned in for the night. I slept really soundly.

CHAPTER 26

FAREWELL TO HASKELL FRIENDS AND FAMILY

Friday had come. It was time to go to the airport. I had talked to Aunt Louise and Uncle Raymond about Kent, Joe and Miriam taking me back to the airport. Uncle Raymond thought that was a good idea.

"It would be an awfully lonely drive home without you," he said. I came out of my room for the last time and touched the "P" on the door. Aunt Louise was watching me from the kitchen. I turned and smiled as I walked down the hallway to her. I hugged her and kissed her on the forehead.

"Thanks for being my family, Aunt Louise. I don't know where I would be without you both."

She hugged me tight and said, "You have been a real gift to us, Phillip. The Good Lord knew we needed you as much as you needed us. That's the way in life, Phillip," she said as she let go of me. "Relationships are always two way streets."

For the second time in my life, I saw Uncle Raymond's eyes water. "It just won't be the same without my ranch hand checking on things for me." He reached out his hand and I took it; and then I pulled Uncle Raymond into me to hug him.

"I love you, Uncle Raymond. Thanks for being a second dad to me and speaking life and wisdom to me." Uncle Raymond didn't say anything but hugged me tighter.

"I hope to make you both truly proud. I am becoming the man I am because of you both."

Uncle Raymond turned me loose, wiping a tear and said, "You are becoming the man you are because Louise overfeeds you." We both laughed and Aunt Louise rolled her eyes. Uncle Raymond was standing beside Aunt Louise, hugging her. "Just kidding, Phillip. We know you will make us proud."

"And I still want to see you swim in a meet," Aunt Louise said, reaching out to touch my arm.

"I will send you a swim schedule."

The doorbell rang and it was Kent, Joe and Miriam. Aunt Louise made a point of getting some woman-to-woman time while Joe, Kent, Uncle Raymond and I moved my stuff to the truck.

Aunt Louise and Miriam went into the den at Aunt Louise's invitation. Aunt Louise immediately cut to the chase.

"Miriam, may I talk candidly, woman to woman?"

"Yes, Mrs. Hammond," Miriam replied.

"I want to talk to you about Phillip," Aunt Louise said.

"Okay."

"You know, he believes he is in love with you," Aunt Louise said.

"Yes, Mrs. Hammond. He made that perfectly clear at dinner."

"You realize that in his mind he intends to marry you?"

"I know, Mrs. Hammond, and I have done nothing to encourage that or to lead him on. I would never hurt Phillip."

Aunt Louise smiled, "I believe you, Miriam, but our Phillip is a very single-minded young man when he sets his sights on a goal, and he is relentless when he pursues something or someone! And he has his sights definitely set on you. What do you want to do?"

"I am not sure, Mrs. Hammond. Phillip is a wonderful guy. He is handsome, smart, and good-hearted; any girl would welcome a catch like him. But we come from such different worlds."

"That does not necessarily mean you are different people, Miriam. Do you think you might love Phillip?" Aunt Louise put her hand on Miriam's arm.

Miriam bit her lip and stared at the floor; she then looked up with her eyes watering, "Yes, I expect I might love him, Mrs. Hammond and I have only now realized this, just as he is about to leave for Chicago."

Aunt Louise hugged Miriam and said, "Miriam, I could not bear to see my Phillip with any girl that was not as good as you. He's been like a second son to me and I don't want to see him hurt. He has had enough hurt in his life already. I have been anxious about him going back to Chicago and getting mixed up with the wrong sort of girl." Aunt Louise let go of Miriam, but continued talking, "You will be like an anchor to help him keep his focus and priorities straight."

"Aunt Marguerite says I should invite him to the Prom. Is that okay?" Miriam asked.

"Is that okay? By all means! Give him something to look forward to, Miriam; and bring him back home to Haskell, even if only for a weekend."

"Mrs. Hammond, I think I started to like Phillip the first day I met him at Tastee Freeze."

"Well, I know my Phillip and he was attracted to you the first day he saw you, too. I watched him follow you with his eyes. That's a secret tip I give you about Phillip. Always watch his eyes; that will be a clue as to what he is thinking."

"Thanks, Mrs. Hammond."

Both Aunt Louise and Miriam had tears in their eyes. They went to the kitchen where Aunt Louise dampened a paper towel and they both wiped their faces to freshen their looks.

"Shall we go check on how the men are coming along?" Aunt Louise asked.

"Let's," Miriam replied and the two of them went outside, arm in arm.

Aunt Louise and Miriam came out of the house, arm in arm, and walked to the car. Obviously, Aunt Louise was pleased with the conversation and was smiling. Miriam gave her a hug and a kiss on the cheek and off the four of us went in Joe's truck to the airport. It was snug but I didn't mind. I put Miriam on my lap. It was somewhat uncomfortable but I got to hold her the whole way.

This was the closest physically I had ever been with this girl and enjoyed the ride the whole way from that standpoint; even if I was lacking blood circulation to my legs. That meant I was shifting her from thigh to thigh. I could feel that Miriam was strong. She had back muscles, I could tell. Woof!

We arrived at the airport and Joe let us off at the concourse with TWA to check in my bags and went to park his truck. Kent and I got everything unloaded and checked. It was cold outside and I was wearing the letter jacket Joe had given me. I did that to honor both Kent and Joe.

The bags were checked in and the four of us walked to my gate. I had my boarding pass but they had not let the passengers board the plane yet. Kent started talking nervously, "You're not going to forget us when you get back to your high fallutin friends back in Chicago are you?"

I looked at Kent grinning and said, "You may talk the hind leg off a mule, just don't preach it off. The Abbot said it was a sin to bore people with the gospel."

Kent had a puzzled look on his face and then Joe popped off, "Not another word about God's call for ministry, Kent."

I laughed and hugged Kent. I whispered in his ear, "The Abbot also said you would make a good minister and he prayed for you." Kent was a mixture of surprise, shock, joy and sadness at this news and at my departure.

"Love you, man. You stay in touch, you hear?" Kent said.

"I will, Kent," I replied, turning him loose.

Next it was Joe's turn. We just gazed into each other's eyes for a bit. Joe then smiled, reached out and hugged me. At that my eyes started to water. There were no words that could express the friendship between two men like Joe and me.

"I love you like a brother, Joe, and I would lay down my life for you!" We released each other and I caught Joe wiping a tear from his eye.

"I feel the same way, Phillip," Joe said.

Finally, it was Miriam's turn. The delight of my eyes! "Miriam, I don't know what to say..." I got lost in mid-sentence as I gazed into her emerald eyes. She pulled a chain out from around her neck. It was a beautiful gold filigree chain with my ring through it. My eyes opened wide.

"Will you be my date to the Senior Prom?" Miriam, was all that she asked.

"A thousand times yes," I answered, too thunderstruck to fully appreciate both her request and her gesture. Then it hit me and I asked, "Does this mean you want to be my girlfriend or something more?"

Miriam arched an eyebrow and smiled, "It means, Mr. Robertson, I think you scored a touchdown in the man on woman football game, you have been trying to play with my heart. I am wearing your ring so it is near to my heart. And..." At that moment she drew me into her and kissed me long and hard on the mouth. My body immediately responded and I wrapped my arms around her to hold her as we kissed. It was if the two of us melded into each other. All the pent-up desire came flowing out of both of us to each other in that embrace and kiss.

Coming up for air, "Am I violating boundaries?" She said nothing verbally but drew me back into her. It was pretty odd kissing her like that between Joe and Kent, but mercifully they said nothing.

Suddenly, the stewardess announced, "Ladies and Gentlemen, we will now be boarding Flight 267 from Tulsa to St. Louis, continuing on to Chicago." I let

Miriam go. Joe and Kent's eyes were the size of silver dollars. Kent was smiling and Joe was looking at the floor.

"Will we ever see you again, Phillip F. Austin Robertson?" Kent asked, anxiously.

"YES!" I said. "Why don't you three come to Chicago and stay with my family for a month this summer. Come to my Barrington Heights and see where I came from. Will you do that? Let me show you my world. I could maybe even help you get a job to working up there." I looked hopefully at the three of them.

"Do you have room for all of us?" Kent asked.

Miriam cut her eyes at Kent and answered, "They have plenty of room, Kent." Miriam then added, "Yes, we will come, all three of us."

"Guess we are coming," Joe added, looking at Kent with an expression that brokered no dissent. Kent silently nodded his assent.

"Awesome!" I said. "We will work out the details later." I gave Miriam one last hug and kiss; and shook Kent's and Joe's hands and said goodbye. I turned and followed a line of people to board my flight. It finally sunk into me that I was finally returning to Chicago. I could not believe it. But I was so excited at the thought of going to the Senior Prom, hosting the three of them in Chicago, that it took away the loss of leaving.

When I took my seat on the jet, I saw Kent, Miriam and Joe standing at the gate looking out. Miriam had obviously been crying and was wiping her cheeks. I waved at them from my seat. They saw me and waved a last farewell before my plane began to taxi to the runway. The jet was soon in the air flying me back to Chicago.

PART III

THINGS PAST

CHAPTER 1

<u>BACK IN CHICAGO</u>

As the flight approached O'Hare Airport, we finally broke through the cloud cover. It was nearly 2:30. I looked down and saw a heavy blanket of snow on the ground. Agnes Kotlarski had called me yesterday and warned me that Chicago had been hit by a major snow on Wednesday and more was expected. It was, indeed, a change from Oklahoma. As I deplaned I was instantly reminded how brutal the winters could be in Chicago. I had brought a wool cap and put it on. Agnes was picking me up at the gate and I looked around for her.

Suddenly I felt a tug at my sleeve. It was Agnes. She had a look of stunned surprise on her face.

"You have grown! I almost didn't recognize you!" Agnes said in her Polish accented English. It was true. I was nearly two inches taller and had gained nearly twenty-five pounds. "Oi vey, you've gotten big! You are not going to fit into your clothes you left at home."

We gathered my luggage at the baggage claim. I had to rent a roller to put my bags on while Agnes pulled the car up for passenger pick up and drop off. The scene at the airport was sheer chaos. The snowstorm of two days ago had resulted in many cancelled flights and stranded travelers; hence, O'Hare was not a happy place. It was a relief to get out of that madhouse. Agnes was driving Mom's Cadillac, which was a dark green 1970 Fleetwood. Riding with Agnes on Chicago freeways was a trip one rarely wanted to repeat. She had two speeds, fast and slow. She drove slow in the fast lanes and fast in the slow lanes. Often younger drivers would fly by us, waving the universal three-fingered salute of disrespect. Mercifully, Agnes either couldn't see this or didn't comprehend this cultural phenomenon of the younger generation. Either way it was a long and embarrassing ride home from O'Hare to Barrington Heights.

We got home after 4:30. Dad's driveway was full of snow with a set of car tracks. We got my bags into the house by trudging through the snow and I went to the garage to get a snow shovel. I came back through the house with the snow shovel.

"Where are you going?" Agnes asked, somewhat out of concern.

"There are chores to be done, Agnes," I said, winking at her.

"Chores? What chores?" Agnes asked with a shocked expression.

"You'll see," I said, grinning as I went out the den door. I immediately began shoveling the stoop there next to the driveway. There snow was three feet deep in places and I slowly made progress. I shoveled off the side stoop and worked my way down to the driveway. I cleared two car lengths. Next I shoveled clear the pathway to Agnes' cottage to the house. Finally, I started working on the front stoop and shoveled clear the walkway to the driveway. It was then I heard a voice calling me. I must have looked like a handyman dressed the way I was – old jeans, cowboy boots, letter jacket and wool cap.

"Young man! Oh Young man!"

I turned around and said, "Yes, Ma'am."

There she was. A doughty dark-haired looking matron in snow boots, a fur coat and ear muffs, maybe 5'2" tall. She came to the curb and said, "I will pay you $5.00 to shovel my driveway and front stoop. I am hosting a holiday open house this week and I need my driveway and front stoop shoveled." I looked at what she wanted shoveled.

"That is a $20.00 job, Ma'am." I said in my best Oklahoma drawl.

"You must not be from around here," she said, noticing my accent, trying to size me up.

"No, Ma'am," I answered.

"So what brings you around here?" she asked, curiously.

"Agnes Kotlaski is a family acquaintance and needed some work done," I replied.

"Oh, you're a handy man then?" she surmised.

"In a manner of speaking, you could call me that," I answered, leaning on the snow shovel.

"Seven dollars for the job," she then shot back.

"Eighteen," I replied, just as quickly.

"What! You're trying to take advantage of me," she answered, in disbelief.

"I have plenty of work, ma'am, and there is hardly any daylight left," I replied, looking around at the growing darkness.

"Ten dollars," she said almost spitting out the number.

"Fifteen," I replied, with a straight face.

"What! You think I'm made of money. Ten is more than generous."

"Then Ma'am, you can show your generosity to someone else." I turned and started walking back up the driveway.

"No, wait! Twelve dollars," she shot back at me.

"Make it $12.50 and I will do it. My last offer," I replied.

"All right. You drive a hard bargain. I will pay it when you get done."

"No, ma'am, I get paid first or I don't work," I replied.

"What? You don't trust me?" she looked shocked.

"Ma'am, I don't even know who you are! So until I know a customer, I get paid up front," I answered matter of factly.

"How do I know you will do the job?" she asked suspiciously.

"Look for yourself, what work I have done for Agnes Kotlarski's employer. My work speaks for itself." I swept my arm, pointing at my snow-shoveling job.

She then muttered some Yiddish phrases that I was familiar with from Agnes Kotlarski. Agnes was Polish Catholic but her husband had been Jewish. It was a mixed marriage, which was unusual for the times back in Poland in the 30's. As a result, Agnes was well acquainted with the Jewish subculture and many phrases in Yiddish; and she had made a point of teaching us some of the more emphatic expressions. I chuckled to myself.

"Stay right here. I have to go inside and get the money." She then made another Yiddish remark that translated roughly as swindler/hard bargainer. I continued shoveling some snow in the driveway at the entrance to the street. We lived on a hill and this would make it easier to get in and out.

The woman came back and handed me the $12.50. I immediately began working on her front stoop and walkway, and then her driveway. It took me about 45 minutes and I was through. She hung around for a bit to make sure I was good for my work. No doubt Agnes Kotlarski would hear about this.

"So you know Dr. Robertson."

"I have been acquainted with him, Ma'am," I replied, honestly.

"He is a good doctor. My husband Dr. Aaron Horowitz works with him at the hospital. It is such a shame such a fine man has had such difficulties in life."

I arched my eyebrow as I shoveled more snow and said, "Difficulties?"

"Oh yes. So tragic. His wife was in a car accident and has been in a coma ever since. They say she was a real beauty!" I nodded my agreement.

"And his kids. Oi vey gevault! Such a heartache and mess they are. Spread out all over North America like some sort of diaspora.

"Oh really," was all I could say. It was as I told Miriam, others' perception of myself was "damaged goods." I didn't realize they perceived my two brothers and sister in the same vein. The thought of this made me quiet.

"Oh yes, one son traveling all over the United States working on a survey crew, never finished college; a daughter who ran away from home and is now living on a hippie commune; one son expelled from St. Cyngen's School; and his wife's tragic accident. If that man didn't have bad luck, he would have no luck at all." The woman added.

I redoubled my efforts and shoveled the snow harder.

"So, where are you from?"

"Oklahoma," I answered, venting my humiliation and frustration in shoveling her driveway.

"So have you never heard anything about the Robertson family from Agnes?" she asked, pointedly.

"I make it a point, Mrs. Horowitz, that if I am not part of the solution, not to ask about other people's problems. But, no, Agnes has said nothing to me about such things while I have been here this holiday in Chicago. And if she had, I certainly wouldn't repeat the private pain of others for public scrutiny." I was almost finished and this Betsy Horowitz was starting to get under my skin now with all her probing questions.

"Oh... wise boy, I see," she said, somewhat sarcastically.

"Not wise. Just tend to my own business, Mrs. Horowitz." My accent on that last phrase slipped from Okie back to Chicago. But she didn't fully catch that as she obviously thought I was some country bumpkin from a wild hillbilly place called Oklahoma.

"Well, nice visiting with you. Be sure to shovel that walkway there to that side door," she said condescendingly as she went inside. We had not agreed on that but I went ahead and did it after she went inside. I finished the job and returned home. It was nearly 7:00 now. Agnes immediately called me into the kitchen.

"Phillip, I need to see you."

She was in the kitchen fixing a light supper of potato soup.

"Yes, Agnes?" She looked at me all hot and sweaty.

"What have you been doing?" she asked in amazement.

"Chores. I shoveled our stoop and driveway and then a lady hired me to shovel hers off," I replied.

"What lady?" she asked.

"Betsy Horowitz," I said.

"She may be the wife of a doctor, but she is no lady!" Agnes replied, sourly. "I know her type. She came from a working class background and now has all the bad habits, airs, arrogance and attitudes of the Noveau Riche. I hope you charged her."

"I did. She wanted to pay me $5.00 but I quoted her $20.00. We settled for $12.50."

"You should have started at $30.00," Agnes then muttered some Polish phrase to herself and then added, "Oi, I almost forgot. Your father called and wants to take you with him to a holiday open house at the hospital. He said he would pick you up at 7:30. It is 7:00 now. Eat some soup and clean up. I have already unpacked your things and put away your luggage while you were shoveling the driveway. Pick out a shirt and slacks and I will press those for you while you shower."

I did as Agnes commanded. I had forgotten that one of her gifts was efficiency and organization, not to mention making good potato soup. That hit the spot after working so hard. After a quick bowl, I went upstairs and retrieved a white oxford button-down shirt and some khaki slacks. I had a red and green Christmas tie to go with it and a red pullover sweater. I delivered these to Agnes downstairs in the kitchen.

"Go, shoo! I will hang these on the outside of your door. You should probably shave as well as shower."

I had totally forgotten that I had not shaved today. How did Miriam put up with kissing a face that felt like sandpaper? I used to be able to shave every three days but now I had a full beard coming on by 5:00 every day. In addition, I noticed I had started growing a rug on my chest and stomach.

As I started up the long spiral staircase in the foyer to the upstairs landing, the splendor of my home amazed me. Five months in Oklahoma made me forget what an incredible place I had grown up in. Between the wood floors, oriental rugs, chandeliers, antique furniture and paintings, it felt like I was in an art museum or furniture showroom.

I went to my room and stripped down for a shower. It was incredible, the shower had a huge head on it and was attached to the ceiling, which was eight feet high in the shower. The bathroom itself was completely tiled in aquamarine with kasota stone countertops. I showered off and then shaved. Uncle Raymond told me it was always better to shave after a shower as it softened the whiskers.

Agnes knocked on the bathroom door and told me she had laid everything out. I said, okay and would be out in a minute. She recused herself from my bedroom and I heard the door close. When I came out, the shirt, slacks and tie were all where she said they would be.

But Agnes had gone a step further and had polished my cordovan loafers and even laid out a matching pair of socks. I had forgotten how efficient she was at making herself indispensable to your every need. I quickly got dressed and came downstairs.

I was in the den when I saw Dad's headlights pull in the driveway. Dad drove a 1968 gold Lincoln Continental with a black interior. I went to the door to let Dad in. He had immediately noticed the clean steps and driveway by the door. Mom and Dad's driveway was nearly 250 feet long. I had cleared the area fronting the street and the sidewalk to the front door and the den door. The den door was the entrance we mainly used to come into the house.

As I stood in the doorway my Dad registered a look of surprise.

"Phillip! My stars, you've changed. Frank wasn't kidding when he said I might not recognize you."

I smiled and gave Dad a hug, something I had not done since I was a little boy. I could tell he was somewhat uncomfortable with that.

"Good to see you, Dad. Good to be home for Christmas!"

Dad returned my hug and patted me on the back. "Good to have you home, Phillip."

Agnes stood at the top of a short flight of stairs above the den, looking on approvingly. There was a hallway adjacent to the stairs that took you to the kitchen. She had come out of the kitchen to tell Dad something.

"Dr. Robertson, your Phillip cleaned the front stoop and driveway without me saying a word. He came home and said he had chores to do. Oi vey! And he shoveled a path to my house, too. Such a nice boy!"

I blushed and Dad let go of me and asked, "You did? This is not the Phillip I knew. You sure you aren't some look-a-like imposter?"

"No too many imposters have a scar on their left knee from the age of four! Nor would the imposter know you picked me up and carried me to the car or know that their dad helped sew me up at the E.R. after falling on a piece of broken glass when they were four years old....." I shot back.

Dad grinned and just looked at me. He had the most piercing ice blue eyes; Mom's eyes were brown and mine were sort of a gray-greenish blue. But Dad's eyes were hauntingly blue. Mom called them wolf eyes and had once confided to me that it was those eyes that entranced her to marry a Yankee. He had a full head of graying blond hair.

"Well, you ready to go, Chief?"

"Yes, Sir. Where are we going?"

"There is an open house holiday reception at the University Hospital. It starts at 8:00 and we should be done by ten."

"Let's go Papa Doc!" I said. That was a nickname Frank came up with when he studied world history and learned about Papa Doc Duvalier of Haiti. He had been an absolute dictator for a couple of decades and Frank thought it an appropriate nickname for Dad. Dictator for life!

Dad smiled and said, "Keep that up and you will be walking home tonight, Buckaroo." That was a nickname Dad called me as a boy. As we drove over to the hospital, Dad caught me up on the comings and goings of my brothers and sister. Susannah Theresa was working at a ski resort in Aspen and rooming with a couple of other girls. She was actually earning a living for the first time in her life and not costing Dad too much money. She had met a promising young man out there who was also a ski instructor and operated a business. He actually had been to college and had a military background. Hence, he took advantage of the veteran's benefits for college. This impressed Dad.

Frank had gone to Utah on a survey job and was going to spend Christmas in Aspen with my sister. She had arranged several days of free skiing for him as well as setting him up on dates while he was out there. "He has a bird's nest made on the ground," Dad remarked.

John was staying in Mexico City, preparing for admission exams to the University of Guadalajara Med School. It seemed not only had he fallen in love with the Mexican culture, but also a Mexican senorita. "I think our Romeo may have found his Juliet! She is a really pretty thing from what I can tell from the pictures he has sent me." That was a startling bit of news. Moreover, John was spending Christmas with the family of Franchesca Incarnacion Mendoza-Garcia of Morelia, Mexico. Things were starting to look serious and Dad said we might be looking at a Mariachi style wedding in Mexico.

"So, it is just you and me this Christmas, together," Dad told me. Wow, just the two of us in that big old house with Agnes Kotlarski; now that would put the Charles Dickens in anyone's Christmas! Only Dad would hardly be there and Agnes would be around all too often together with her "woe is me" attitude. Now, that was a scary thought, alone with Agnes over Christmas break. Sheesh!

We pulled up to the hospital and Dad parked in the doctor's only parking garage at the hospital. It was a brisk walk to the side doors to go to the reception that was already taking place. We walked down several corridors and then caught an elevator to where the Holiday Open House Reception was occurring. The elevator doors opened and we went to the reception hall filled with people.

Dad was immediately greeted and I was introduced as his youngest son home for the holidays. It was an evening of glad-handing, fielding questions, and receiving compliments. Not unlike what I had experienced in Haskell, only not so sincere and more politely sophisticated.

"At least in Haskell, people really wanted to know who you were and were genuinely interested in carrying on a conversation. Here, people were on the surface polite, but did not carry the conversation much beyond initial pleasantries," I thought to myself.

It was about that moment Dad introduced me to a new colleague of his. A man by the name of Dr. Aaron Horowitz. He was a very cordial and charming man and seemed delighted to meet me. Moreover, he told me that he and his family were now our new neighbors, having bought their home across the street at an estate sale. "We got such a good deal on the old place!" Dr. Horowitz beamed with pride at his business savvy.

He then called to his wife, "Betsy, come over here and meet Dr. Robertson's youngest son." As fate would have it, there she was decked out to the tees. Betsy Horowitz. You could visibly see a smile freeze on her face when I was introduced to her. It got even more interesting when Dad said I had arrived from Oklahoma that day .

"Is that so," was all she could say, looking at me like a cornered animal trying to assess its hunter's next blow.

"Dad, Mrs. Horowitz and I met earlier today. We had a nice conversation." I winked at her. She knew I had caught her red handed trying to snoop and pry into my family's business and private pain. But, I think she also sensed I was not there to punish her for her faux pas.

"Well, it was nice meeting you, Phillip, and I hope you enjoy your holiday break," and she extended her hand to shake mine. She tried to squeeze my hand hard but I squeezed back, smiling all the while. Joe, Kent and I had played this game with Uncle Raymond and I had learned how not to wince even in pain. Her hand was smaller but she had the most wicked flesh piercing rings on her fingers. She never got the satisfaction of knowing she made my hand bleed as I kept a perfect poker face.

"Thank you, Mrs. Horowitz, and I will look forward to seeing you in the neighborhood. Happy Holidays!" I said with much Christmas cheer gushing in a smile. Dr. and Mrs. Horowitz went off to greet someone else. And so it went for the next two hours. Dad and I made the rounds of doctors, nurses, support staff and their spouses. Around 10:00, Dad asked me if I had had enough and I said yes. We took our leave and headed back to the car. On the way home we discussed Mom. Agnes had suggested I let Dad bring this subject of her health up. This I did and Dad talked at length about Mom's prognosis in our 45-minute drive home. He explained that many coma patients could actually hear things being said to them so Dad had retained hospital staff to attend to Mom by talking to her, reading to her, and exercising her legs and arms.

"Her medical condition has not changed much since you left for Oklahoma, Phillip. But Dr. Timmerman, the neurologist, says people revive all the time from comas. Sometimes it may take years."

"May I see her, Dad?" I asked.

"Yes. But let me make arrangements with some of the nursing staff attending your mother. She has lost a lot of weight. You will need to prepare yourself for that, Phillip. It may be disconcerting for you. You sure you are ready for that, pal?"

"Yeah, Dad. It might be rough for me to see her like that, but how rough is it for her if, as you shared earlier somehow coma victims sometimes can hear or sense another person talking to them. How much more important is it for them to have those they love to talk to them or touch them?"

Dad looked at me and gave me a wry grin. "You may be right!" We arrived back home at 10:45. After we went inside, we sat down in the den and talked awhile.

"So, tell me about your time in Haskell," Dad said.

"What do you want to know?" I replied.

"How did the big city kid adjust to rural Oklahoma?" Dad asked, quizzically.

"Well, it was different, that's for sure. But Uncle Raymond and Aunt Louise helped me a lot in the transition." I replied, yawning.

"Did you miss Chicago at all?" Dad asked.

I laughed, "Of course," and then added, "but they kept me so busy at the ranch that Chicago sort of faded from memory. Plus, I started making new friends and that helped me settle in."

"Who were your friends?" Dad asked.

"Mainly Joe Corsinni, Kent James, Miriam Abboud, and others." At the mention of the name Miriam, Dad arched an eyebrow but said nothing inquiring about her.

"How do you feel about coming back to Chicago?" Dad asked.

I thought for a bit and then said, "I am glad to be back, Dad, and excited for the State swim meet. But it is like I left a part of my heart in Haskell. Does that make sense at all?"

Dad smiled and said, "Yes it does, and that is a good sign that Haskell was the right choice for you. I know how you feel when a part of your heart is left somewhere else."

"Has it been rough for you, Dad, with Mom's coma?" I cautiously inquired. At that Dad put his hand on my shoulder. I could tell his eyes were full of emotion.

"It has been lonely at times, Phillip, I miss the good conversations and company of your mother," Dad paused and looking at me added, "but you have discovered a secret for medicating your pain, stay busy!" I could see his eyes were starting to water.

At that point I got up, grabbed Dad and hugged him. "I miss her too," I said, my eyes beginning to tear. If there was one thing I had learned from my time in Haskell, men needed to hug each other and often times cry together. I couldn't say anything else as I was too choked up.

Dad patted me on the shoulder, "it's okay, Phillip. We will weather this storm!"

I let go of Dad and saw that his eyes were somewhat red, too. "If you ever need to talk, I'm here, Dad."

"I will, son," Dad added. "But I think it is time to turn in. We can save some conversation for tomorrow."

The conversation I had just had with Dad was the first man-to-man talk I ever truly had with my Dad. In some ways it began to radically change my boyhood perception of my father as a benign tyrant I called Papa Doc to another man with just as many hurts and pains as any other guy.

I said good night to Dad and went back to my room. I got out some stationery and wrote a letter to Miriam describing in detail the day's events. I also wrote a letter to Aunt Louise and Uncle Raymond. I would have Agnes post them tomorrow. At midnight I finally turned in. There was more snow in the forecast for Saturday so I anticipated more snow clearing on Saturday. I could tell my shoulders and back were a little sore. I took some aspirin to help cut the pain before I went to bed.

CHAPTER 2

MY OLD FRIEND MITCH

The next morning I woke up at 6:30 and could have sworn I heard Uncle Raymond walking across the gravel driveway to the barn. I remembered I was back home in Chicago and immediately got out of bed and went to my window. Sure enough, it had snowed last night and the sky was heavy laden with another round of storms heading our way. I went ahead and took a shower. I shaved and got dressed for the day. I took my dirty clothes downstairs to the utility room. I went to the kitchen and made some coffee. I knew Dad had hospital rounds to make and would be leaving around 8:00 to go to the hospital. I knew Dad liked to eat breakfast so I decided to whip together one of Aunt Louise's culinary creations for him. Not only had I eaten Aunt Louise's cooking, I had also learned how to cook her recipes. In less than thirty minutes I had biscuits in the oven, fried up some sausage; saved the grease to make sausage gravy; cracked several eggs to make a breakfast casserole; and sliced up some apples.

Agnes came into the kitchen at 7:30 and was amazed at the scene and exclaimed, "What is this? Someone has taken over my kitchen!"

"Sit down, Agnes, and let me feed you Aunt Louise Hammond style," I replied.

About that time Dad came into the kitchen and said, "What in the sam hill is going on in here?"

"Sit down, Dr. Robertson and eat! We are having an Oklahoma breakfast compliments of a Mrs. Louise Hammond's recipes!" Agnes said, with a toothy grin.

Dad did as she suggested and then said, "The smells remind me of meals your Mother's family used to fix when I was dating your Mother Mary Katherine." He had a sad smile on his face as he recalled better times.

"You should remember this, Dad. These are all Aunt Louise's concoctions she said they used to prepare for you during the war when you were stationed at Batty Hospital in Rome, Georgia. It seems her cooking helped sway your good opinion of Mom." Dad merely nodded as he smiled.

I served both Dad and Agnes. Agnes verbally expressed her approval of the breakfast while Dad's actions spoke his approval - double helpings of biscuits and gravy with more of the egg casserole; some of the fruit with coffee to wash it all down. Dad ate heartily while Agnes ate more gingerly. He had one last swig of coffee and then excused himself as he had to get to the hospital.

He told me as he was leaving, "Agnes told me you might need some new clothes this semester. I left her the charge card for Macy's. You should hit the stores this morning. There may be some pre-Christmas sales going on." I walked Dad out to the garage.

"Thanks, Dad," I said. "Is there a ceiling on what I can spend?"

"Well, not the national debt!" Dad teased. "Agnes said you may need several pairs of slacks and some new jeans at least. You might need some more oxford button-down shirts, too, so limit your purchases to those items." He said goodbye and went to the garage to get his car to go to work. I returned to the kitchen to find Agnes busily putting away the extra biscuits and gravy. There was not much egg casserole left or hardly any apples.

"No wonder you got so big! It is amazing you didn't eat your Aunt and Uncle out of house and home!" Agnes marveled.

"I tried," I teased back.

"Seems like you nearly succeeded," Agnes shot back. She could be dour at times but that did not dampen the speed of her retorts. Moreover, underneath it all, Agnes was a dear soul who was devoted to our family. She even went to the hospital at least three times a week and sat with Mom for several hours a day. She would talk to her; read her letters; and tell her the news of the world and our family in general. She also often would hold Mom's hand and pray for her in Polish.

As I started to wash the dishes, I asked her to post my letters to Miriam and the Hammonds. She replied, "This I will do. Now, you go! This is my job to clear the kitchen! You go shovel snow and hobnob with your new girlfriend Betsy Horowitz."

"You said she wasn't a lady and Mom would never approve of me dating a girl who was not a lady!" I shot back.

Agnes arched an eyebrow and replied "Oi, Vey! You got me there. But speaking of ladies, who is that girl you have in that picture frame on your bedside table?"

"She is quite the lady, Agnes. I think even you would approve of her," I replied with an air of confidence.

"Approve of her for what?" Agnes' eyes narrowed as she looked at me suspiciously.

"Let's just say that she is everything that Betsy Horowitz pretends to be, a classy girl!" I replied, toying with Agnes.

"Classier than Ann Burns? That is hard to believe!" she said in disbelief.

"Believe it, Agnes," I said firmly.

"What have you been up to down there?" Agnes asked. "Oh heavens, not another Romeo like John. I don't think the good doctor your father could weather two such sons in one family!" Agnes said, rolling her eyes. I sensed a dour attitude of woe and lecture coming on.

"This gal is as good as they come, Agnes, and she is a good Catholic!" I replied smugly.

At that Agnes softened somewhat and said, "Just make sure she stays that way, Phillip." Agnes gave me a hard knowing look with that statement and added, "She certainly has pretty eyes, like green crystal. Such a beauty! Now, off you go. We can't have two cooks in my kitchen! We will continue this conversation another time."

I was starting to the garage to fetch the snow shovel when I heard Agnes call me back. "Phillip, I forgot to tell you. You have several letters from colleges."

I returned to the kitchen and got the letters. One was an acceptance to the University of Illinois at Champaign Urbana with a partial offer of scholarship, tuition and books; another was an acceptance to Indiana University, no scholarship offer there though; but there were also rejection letters from Cornell, and Princeton. So much for my Ivy League ambition! That really hurt and was a blow to my ego. It was very disappointing and took the wind out of my sail. But there was one last letter from John Brown University. It was an acceptance letter containing another letter from Coach Cutter. He was offering me a full four-year swimming scholarship! I was dumbstruck. So far JBU was the only college that had even offered me a full scholarship. That school was not even in my gun sights before last October! It was not even an NCAA athletic program, but only NAIA! Nevertheless, I tucked the letter away in my pocket and went back to the garage. I shoveled the stoop by the den and cleared a path from Agnes' front stoop back to the house with great vigor. I had disappointments to work out of my system. I did not shovel the driveway or front door entrance. I didn't want to get flagged down by Betsy Horowitz. I was in no mood or state of mind to deal with her today.

When I was done, I got the credit card from Agnes and the car keys to my car that I had left behind. It was a yellow convertible 1969 MGB. I put the hard top on and dusted the seats; the car had sat in the garage the entire time I was gone. Great car in the summer with the top down but it was a virtual icebox on wheels in the winter till its heater warmed up. The heater usually didn't fire up till you had driven it for 15 minutes or so. That meant a chilly ride at first. I started the car and pulled out of the garage into the driveway. I let the car warm up and ran inside to tell Agnes where I was going today.

I called an old classmate of mine, Mitch O'Nalley, who had been my best friend up here. There was no one like Mitch who could cheer me up! Both Mitch and his brother Mike attended St. Cyngen on an academic/athletic scholarship as they were from a working class background. Mitch and I had known each other from grade school forward and had become really close chums. Dad really liked Mitch and had sort of taken him in as a surrogate fourth son. Mom approved of him too. Often Mitch would go with my family to Mackinac Island on our summer vacations. He and his brother had played football at St. Cyngen's but Mitch was also a swimmer. His brother Mike was a couple of years older and Mitch was my age. He was the youngest son of seven kids, which is probably why Mitch and I got along so well. His brother Mike was always serious while Mitch was Mr. Happy Go Lucky. He was going to meet me at a local restaurant. After I got my shopping done we were going to hang out together. I hit the clothing store and bought two pairs of jeans, five pairs of dress slacks, and six oxford button-down shirts. The slacks had to be tailored but would be ready after Christmas.

It was the old "nab it, sack it, and buy it" routine guy style and I was done in less than 30 minutes. To this day I never understood why girls could not run a mile but could spend an entire day walking ten miles through shopping malls, meticulously inspecting every possible article of clothing for sale. Going shopping like that with a girl could be an experience in sheer hell for a guy my age.

Mercifully, I was not shopping with a girl today. When Aunt Louise took me shopping, she had an eye for what looked good on me and could cut to the chase fairly quickly. The clothes store I went to was a store where we usually bought our clothes so I readily knew where to look and what I liked. I charged my purchases on Dad's card and they called Agnes at home to verify my use of the card. They knew who Dad was but the sales associate was part time Christmas help. He didn't know who I was and my Oklahoma Driver's license only heightened his caution about me. It took more time than I thought such that I was running 20 minutes late to meet Mitch at the restaurant. This was a teenage hangout that served great burgers and sandwiches. Knowing Mitch's propensity to eat, I knew he would be well fed and, besides there were several attractive waitresses our age who usually worked there.

If I were a betting man, Mitch was already engaging one or more of them in a conversation. Mitch was a handsome dude and was easily six feet, three inches tall with a muscular athletic build. He was half-Irish and half Italian. He had blue eyes and fair skin from his Irish side, but had dark hair and a winning smile from the Italian side. Plus he had that "cute" puppy dog look about him that girls liked. Hence, he had cut quite a swath through the female circles we had run in. His brother Mike was not nearly as tall or muscular and had dark eyes, skin and hair. The Italian influence certainly dominated in Mike's DNA; however, he had all the seriousness of an Irish Jesuit priest and the two of them were a contrast in personality as well as looks. As I walked into the restaurant, sure enough there was a lively interchange occurring between Mitch and an attractive redheaded waitress. As I walked up, Mitch stood up and said,

"Geez, Phillip! What happened to you! Aubrey, this is my buddy Phillip I was telling you about."

"Aubrey McCaslin," she said, extending her hand. "I'm a junior at the High School nearly!"

"Nice to meet you, Aubrey. I am Phillip Robertson, lately of Haskell High School."

"Mitch, you didn't tell me your friend had a cute Southern accent!"

"He's not a Southerner, believe me. I have grown up with this guy and he is 100 percent Yankee!" Mitch replied.

"Are you so sure?" I said in my finest Oklahoma drawl I had picked up from Kent James.

Mitch slugged me in the shoulder, saying, "Dude, talk right."

"What's wrong with how I talk?" I asked, rubbing my shoulder mocking Mitch's punch.

"I think it is cute," Aubrey said.

"See! There you have it, Mitch. It is two against one!" I said winking at Aubrey.

"Maybe, but he is 100 percent Yankee," Mitch replied.

"Actually, I am not. My Mom was from the Deep South in Northwest Georgia, so I am only one-half Yankee," I said, smiling at Aubrey.

"Well, I have got to get back to waiting other tables. I hope to hear from you, Mitch," and with that she went about waiting on other tables.

I leaned across the table, smiling and slapped Mitch on the shoulder, saying, "Another one bites the dust."

Mitch replied, shrugging his shoulders, "A man's got to do what a man's got to do."

"Yeah, but polygamy is not legal in these parts of the USA," I teased back. Mitch ignored my jest.

"Damn, Phillip! It is good to see you. I have missed you buddy, and what in the hell happened to you? You've grown two inches and you look like you've gained 30 pounds."

He was right about the two inches but was off the mark on the 30 pounds; it was only 25 pounds I had gained. I explained about playing football this past semester as a defensive end for the Haskell Haymakers and working on the ranch of Uncle Raymond and Aunt Louise. I also told him about Kent James and Joe Corsinni.

"There are Italians in Oklahoma?" Mitch exclaimed.

"Yeah. It is not the backward place most folks around here think it is," I replied.

"Meet anyone named Joads?" he teased.

'Uh, no. Besides they moved to California," I shot back. "But it is not the *Grapes of Wrath* sort of place at all. I saw plenty of forest, hills, lakes and rivers."

"What?" Mitch replied in amazement.

"Yeah, it is true, and the women down there are gorgeous!" That remark got Mitch's attention.

"Oh really?" he said, intrigued. "Big city Chicago boy hook up much with some local yokels down there?" Mitch teased. At that remark, I pulled out my wallet and showed him a picture of Miriam. Talking about her took the pain away from my Ivy League rejection letters. He let out a wolf whistle.

"Buddy, who is this? Man, those eyes! A guy could get lost in those eyes. She your main squeeze?" he said, grinning.

"There was no 'squeezing' of this girl. Her name is Miriam Abboud and she is as bright as she is pretty. She has a rapier wit and could dance circles around most guys up here or anywhere else. But she is a good girl and is the sort of girl you would take home to meet mama for her approval." I looked straight into Mitch's eyes and gave him a Mike O'Nalley look expressing my seriousness about her. The disappointment of my college hopes for a swimming scholarship enhanced my serious demeanor as I discussed Miriam.

"Dude, you are scaring me. You have a thing for this girl?" he asked, almost unnerved by my statement.

"I don't have a thing for this girl, but admire and respect her tremendously. She has been like a cool breeze coming off Lake Michigan in the summertime."

Mitch looked at me dumbfounded and then asked, "Phillip, are you falling for this girl?"

"Hmmm. Good question. Am I falling for this girl?" I looked pensively and then added, matter of factly, "kind of hard to fall for someone when you have committed yourself to wanting to marry her." It was then that I realized that somehow my rejection by some of the schools might not be such a bad thing if it meant I might be closer to Miriam!

"Wait a minute. This can't be happening. You have fallen for some girl from some backwoods town in Baja Arkansas? Mr. Barrington Heights who dated only society girls from the better families along the North Shore?" Mitch looked perplexed. "This isn't the Phillip Robertson I have known! I can't believe it."

"Believe it, Mitch," I shot back, looking straight into his perplexed face.

"Ann is not going to like this!" he warned.

"Ann and I aren't a couple, buddy. If you recall, we redefined our status as being 'just friends'. Besides she only wrote me one time while I was in Haskell and it was a matter of fact sort of letter, encouraging me to 'have a good life,' and let's not write each other anymore. Translates 'I am not interested in you.' So we had some good times together, Mitch, and probably did things we shouldn't have done..."

At this point I looked at him earnestly, "But the past is just that! The past. So we move on with life. I have moved on and met this wonderful person called Miriam Abboud. Mitch, you are probably my best friend up here. We have grown up together and you know me pretty well and there aren't too many secrets about each other we don't know." Mitch nodded his head. He had once come to me when he discovered Mia Farronte, his girlfriend, was pregnant. He was only 16 and she was 18. He didn't know what he was going to do. He was so distraught at the thought of bringing shame to his family. Mitch came from a devout Roman Catholic working class family.

I had asked Mitch if I could talk to my Dad about his dilemma; even though Dad at times was distant from me, I had observed how he earnestly tried to help his patients. Thus, I risked seeking his help for Mitch! Mitch told me he was cool with that so I talked to Dad about Mitch's predicament. Mitch was a sophomore and his girlfriend was a senior. She went to public school in the neighborhood where he lived. Mia had been Mitch's first serious girlfriend and things had gotten carried away between the two of them. Mia had informed Mitch that he was not her first rodeo but to her shock it was her first pregnancy. Being an unwed mother was not her intended paradigm for life. She had wanted to be a beautician and a baby would wreck her career plans. Also, she was from a broken family and was raised by her grandparents. She knew firsthand this was not what she wanted for a child. Dad intervened immediately. It seems this was not the first time he had done something like this. He talked to Mia and arranged for her to live in an unwed mothers' home. She carried the baby full term and had agreed to allow the child to be adopted. Dad knew of a good North Shore family looking to adopt a child and Dad helped arrange that, too via a downtown law firm that specialized in adoptions.

Dad helped cover the medical costs of this pregnancy but never said a word about that to me. Mitch told me about that years later. Although he was disappointed in this chapter in Mitch's life, Dad, nevertheless, recognized the good qualities in Mitch.

Dad had a unique ability to often bring out the best in people who had no confidence in their own goodness. He saw to it that Mitch got a lot of help in his troubled time from fellow colleagues, gratis. He supported my friendship with Mitch and that meant Mitch ended up spending a lot of time with our family.

After that, Mitch was a devoted friend and ardent supporter of the Robertson family. At times I called Mitch my "Irish Sheep dog" because he tended to steer me away from trouble. If he had been with me the night of the Avery Drive prank was planned, he would have put his foot down and stopped it. Dad recognized this and was grateful I had a friend like Mitch in my corner. Dad did lecture me sternly about learning from other people's mistakes. I took this life lesson to heart and tried to keep my pants on when it came to girls no matter what! So Mitch and I had no secrets between us. But it was strange that I now felt closer to Kent and Joe than I did with Mitch.

Mitch and I had more time together growing up but it seemed as if Joe and Kent and I had had more life experiences together. Hence it was hard to explain in one afternoon how I had changed this past six months and what Miriam had come to mean to me. Heck, for that matter, what Miriam, Uncle Raymond, Aunt Louise, Joe, Kent, Abbot Delaurier, the Fugali sisters, and the Concharty Mountain had come to mean to me. It had to be lived and experienced in order to be explained and understood. Nevertheless, I saw that searching look in Mitch's eyes wanting to understand and be part of this new paradigm I was experiencing.

"Mitch, you are going to have to go back with me to Oklahoma and work on Uncle Raymond's ranch to understand me on this," I said.

"Fair enough. We going back there this summer?" he asked earnestly.

"I am planning on it and they gave me permission to bring a friend. You were the buddy I was thinking of. Besides, you would really dig working on the ranch. You, Joe and Kent would hit it off and I want you to meet Miriam and her family.

"Dude, when are you setting the wedding!" he replied in amazement.

I rolled my eyes and said, "You confounded lump of one-half Italian Garlic and one-half Irish potato, I am not even engaged...Yet!" I laughed. But I knew I could marry Miriam; more importantly, I wanted to make her my wife! But this was no laughing matter to Mitch. After his almost brush with fatherhood, he was genuinely gun shy about the subject. As one of his closest friends, I had just reminded him that our irresponsible days of boyhood misadventures were going to have to be replaced by mature responsible manhood!

That was as great an adjustment for Mitch as if he were ten years old transformed to a 22-year-old man in an instant. The shock of that reality change takes some getting used to.

"We're not boys any more, Mitch. You of all people should recognize that. We have the bodies of men so we need to assume the responsibilities of men," I added, quoting a conversation I had once with Uncle Raymond.

"You sound like my dad, Phillip. He is always reminding me that God didn't give me these broad shoulders to be a babe magnet in a bathing suit, but to handle responsibility," Mitch replied somberly.

"He's right, you know," I added.

"Geez, Phillip! Seeing and being with you has aged me emotionally ten years today!" he said, sarcastically teasing me.

"Good. That means your emotional age almost matches your chronological age," I punched him in the shoulder.

"Ha,ha! Real funny. I forgot to laugh."

"Well, catch me up on the St. Cyngen, the swim team, Coach DeLagarza and anyone else you think I need to hear about." At that, Mitch opened up like a sieve. Being one-half Irish, he had a gift of conversation and more. He soon educated me on the comings and goings of all our classmates.

Ann Burns had dated around quite a bit but nothing serious. "Emily Palmer says she still has a thing for you! And she ought to know, she is one of Ann's best friends," Mitch said. "Stockton Daniels has Ann in his sights and has been trying to spend time with her." I rolled my eyes. Stockton had a bad boy reputation and sullied the reputation of many an ostensibly "good girl." Moreover he passed around his "conquests" to his fellow teammates on the St. Cyngen wrestling squad when he broke up with the girl. The swim team called them the "Coyote Squad" and there was often bad blood between the swimmers and wrestlers about this. If Stockton was hanging around Ann, that could not be a good thing.

Mitch went on to say that the swim team had an okay season last semester and that Coach DeLagarza was looking forward to having me back on the team and thought we had a good shot at an all-city championship. Mitch then went on to say that Brian McWilliams was having a Christmas Open House and I could go along with him. Several of the other guys on the swim team would there, too. The party was this evening at 8:00 p.m. I said okay. It would be great to see the St. Cyngen gang.

Aubrey McCaslin brought us our orders, which we polished off quickly. Mitch then said, "Hey, I bet Coach DeLagarza is at St. Cyngen. The team is going to work out this afternoon at 3:00. Why don't you join us in our workout?"

"Sounds great to me. I could use the exercise, but I will need a new speedo since I have nearly a 34-inch waist now.

"Hit Anderson's Sporting Goods Store. They should have some suits that would fit you!" Mitch suggested.

"Okay," I answered. "I will see you at 3:00. Only don't tell anyone I am back yet. I want to surprise Coach DeLagarza." We then parted after lunch and I ran to the sporting goods store to get a new speedo. By now it was nearly 2:00, so I headed straight for St. Cyngen's Academy. I arrived there around 2:20 and saw Coach DeLagarza's truck in the parking lot. I went in the door leading to the Natatorium and took the hall to the swim coach's office. I saw a light on in there and knocked on the door.

"Come in," I heard a muffled voice say. I opened the door and saw Coach DeLagarza. "May I help you," he said and then stood up with his eyes wide open.

"Good God, is that you, Phillip? I heard you had grown but, holy smokes, you have gotten huge!" he came over and felt my arms.

"They are real, Coach," I answered.

"The question is, can you still swim as fast?" he said with a concerned look on his face.

"I brought a suit, Coach. You want to time me?"

"Sure thing." He then threw me a towel and said, "Suit up, Stud. Let's see if that Oklahoma heat has melted my All-American iceman!" That was a nickname he had for me because he said I was so cool under pressure. I quickly changed and came into the pool. Although I had gained weight, it was muscle not fat. My arms and chest had gotten a lot bigger and my legs were stronger. As I mounted on a starting block, Coach DeLagarza commented, "Phillip, you left here an adolescent but you now look like a grown man on the starting block." It was true not only was I taller and filled out, I was growing what seemed like a shag carpet on my chest and stomach.

He clicked his watch as he said, "Go." He wanted to time me on a 60-yard free style and 400-yard free style. Although it had been awhile since I was in a pool, my workout regimen with Uncle Raymond served me well. My 60-yard free style time matched my time from a year ago. But it was my 400-yard time that impressed Coach DeLagarza. My time was a good three seconds faster. My bigger size meant more muscle mass. Uncle Raymond had trained me such that my stamina for longer haul swimming had strengthened. About that time the guys started coming into the pool. They had questions as to who was in the pool talking to Coach DeLagarza.

"Can I work out with the team, Coach?" I asked.

"Sure. The guys are going to swim 3000 yards. You good for that?" he asked.

"You ever run three miles a day in Oklahoma heat in July or practice two a days in August, Coach?" I asked, smiling.

"Does physical training with the Marines in Camp LeJeune in North Carolina count?" he asked.

"It might," I answered, smiling. Coach DeLagarza had to return to his office to get his clipboard and notes from the afternoon workout and left the pool for his office.

About that time I saw Mitch walking in on the pool deck, tying the strings on his speedo. He was grinning ear to ear. He hopped into the pool next to me and said, "Hey guys, look who's back." He had his arm around my neck as he flagged attention to me. All of a sudden I had a dozen guys in the pool around me, giving me a Dutch rub or slapping me on the shoulder.

Brian McWilliams, the swim team captain, came onto the pool deck, tying his speedo string and said, hopping into the pool, "Guys, you know the rules. A new guy needs to be initiated!"

"Like hell," I said and broke free of the crowd of guys. A race was on and I knew what would happen next. In no time I was denuded of my speedo.

Coach DeLagarza returned to the pool deck; saw what had happened and was laughing. He said, "Okay,

guys. Let's get serious. Give him his speedo!" I
quickly grabbed my suit and put it back on.

"Thanks a lot, guys! I guess this makes me a St.
Cyngen Crusader again!"

Mitch looked perplexed and asked, "Was there any
doubt?" I smiled to myself, thinking actually there was.
I had become a Haskell Haymaker and now was to be a
St. Cyngen Crusader again. It seemed surreal. We
swam 3000 yards in two hours and then hit the
showers. Bryan McWilliams came up to me and invited
me to his Christmas Open House at 8:00. I readily
accepted and got dressed. I invited Mitch to spend
the night and suggested I follow him to his house to
pick him up and take him home. He was okay with
that but needed to check with his parents.

"Besides, mom and pop would love to see you.
They always liked you. They believed you were a
wholesome influence on me."

I laughed, "I don't know how wholesome anyone
thinks I am after almost getting expelled from St.
Cyngen!"

"Nah, no one cares!" Mitch replied.

"Don't be too sure of that," I replied. We drove on
over to Mitch's house where he dropped his car off and
we went into talk to his parents.

CHAPTER 3

COACH DELAGARZA

Circumstances were to prove that my assumption about people was correct. There were some guys on the swim team who did not want me back because it meant I knocked them back a notch in the line-up. Coach DeLagarza got a phone call that evening from a Mr. Jim Bolt regarding me and his son Remington Bolt. The Bolts originated in South Chicago and Bolt was an Anglicized name of a Slavic name of Baltarski. Mr. Bolt's father had built a family business in electrical contracting. Mr. Jim Bolt managed the success of his father quite well and had grown the business. Moreover, as the Bolt family fortune grew, he relocated the family to the more affluent Barrington Heights. His son had been at St. Cyngen for the past four years and Mr. Bolt had great ambitions for his son's swimming career. Dad told me that Mr. Bolt intended to live through his son's swimming achievements. However, like so many circumstances in life, there was an impediment to these ambitions. In this instance it was me! Mr. Jim Bolt was not going to sit idly by and watch his son's chance at success eclipsed by "damaged goods" as he called me to Coach DeLagarza.

"Listen, DeLagarza, I have given a lot of money to St. Cyngen and I expect my son to be in the 400 IM line up."

"Not if Phillip Robertson beats him out. The kid was an All American last year and helped secure a fourth place finish in state for St. Cyngen's. A coach can't ignore that," DeLagarza retorted.

"You will if St. Cyngen's expects to get a $20,000 donation from Bolt Electrical Contracting!"

"There are some things that money does not buy, Bolt! And my decision is one of those items that is priceless," Coach DeLagarza countered, his anger rising.

Bolt loved to provoke people much like a cat playing with a wounded mouse before he struck the deathblow. "Oh yeah? Well, let's see what your Headmaster Moore says!"

"No threats of higher authority or withholding of money matter to me, Bolt. I did not go through the Korean Was as a 19-year old Marine fighting off hordes of Communist Chinese just so I could be pushed around by a sleazy Southsider trying to throw his weight around!" Coach DeLagarza was shouting now.

"You will regret that statement, sir. You don't know who you are screwing with. I have taken out better men than you! I will get your job!"

Coach DeLagarza calmed down and said, "I have job offers all the time to go elsewhere. I had a job before I came here and I damn sure will have a job when I leave. Your threat is meaningless. Good night, Mr. Bolt!" And at that he hung up the phone. Coach DeLagarza immediately called Headmaster Hugh Moore and apprised him of my possible return and the implications based on Mr. Bolt's threat.

"Merry Christmas, Headmaster Moore!" was all Coach could say at the end of his explanation of the confrontation.

"Tony, there are assholes everywhere in the world. Unfortunately, we have more than our share of arrogant rich assholes at St. Cyngen's. I will back whatever decision you make. Bolt's alleged $20,000 gift be damned. He never disclosed that to me or the Board. The guy's a jerk. Don't give it a second thought! Have a good evening and Merry Christmas to you also, Coach!" And Headmaster Moore meant that too. He was not easily swayed by money when it came to backing his staff. He did not believe in micromanaging their decisions or second guessing them in the classroom. However, Bolt spun a distorted view of the conversation and made it sound as if Coach DeLagarza had threatened Bolt's life and his son when he talked to Headmaster Moore later that evening. He was a master spinmeister and had learned that lying was like rat poison. Ninety-nine percent was good corn, but it was the other one percent that would kill you. Hence, he would tell 99 percent of the truth with one percent distortion. He had utilized this spinmeistering to his great advantage in the business world and would now try to employ such activities to secure his son's place on the team; DeLagarza be damned. But what he didn't know is that he had met more than his match in Headmaster Moore and Coach Tony DeLagarza. Moreover, his reputation for fraud and trickery was well known in contracting circles in Chicago, so he did not get favorable play with his spinmeistering to Headmaster Moore nor were his pleas later to the Board of Directors met with success. He did succeed in spreading a lot of untrue gossip about me in the hopes of turning the tide of St. Cyngen families' opinion against me. In this, he ultimately did not succeed. But, it was one of a myriad of things that would negatively color my view of coming back to Chicago, reinforcing my desire to go back to Oklahoma.

CHAPTER 4

CHRISTMAS OPEN HOUSE

When Mitch and I came into the O'Nalley house, only Mrs. O'Nalley was there. At first she didn't recognize me but was stunned when I said hello.

"My heavens, Phillip! You have changed!"

"Thanks, I think!" I replied, smiling. I then asked her if Mitch could spend the night after the Christmas Open House at Bryan McWilliams. Christmas was still a couple of days away so she had no objection. Mitch grabbed an overnight bag and threw in some changes of clothes. He also packed some khaki slacks, loafers, a turtleneck and sweater to wear to the party tonight and headed back to my house. We got in and put Mitch's stuff up. We went down to the kitchen and Agnes was preparing a light dinner.

She saw Mitch and exclaimed "Mitchell O'Nalley!" she exclaimed. "Oh, it is so good to see you!"

"He is spending the night tonight, Agnes. What's for dinner?"

"For you, soup. For him, pirogis!" This dish was one of Mitch's favorite. It took her about 30 minutes to whip together this dish. Mitch and I wolfed down dinner before you could say Merry Christmas.

"What am I feeding here? Boys or wolves?" Agnes exclaimed.

Mitch and I answered together, spontaneously, "Wolves! Ahroooo!."

Agnes chapped her hands and laughed. "It has been too long since we have had laughter of young men in this house."

"Merry Christmas, Mrs. Kotlarski!" Mitch said and we helped clean the kitchen.

"Mitch we need to get ready for the Open House. Thanks for dinner, Agnes," I said, finishing the last pot.

"Yeah, thanks for dinner, Mrs. Kotlarski," Mitch added.

"What? This is a new Phillip and Mitchell thanking old Mrs. Kotlarski for dinner and cleaning the kitchen! I think I like this change. You boys get going now! I will finish cleaning up in here." And with that we headed upstairs to change. We didn't have to shower or clean up because of showering after workout earlier that day. It didn't take long to get ready.

The outfit Mitch picked out actually matched mine. Khaki slacks, white turtleneck, red sweater and cordovan loafers. When we came downstairs Agnes exclaimed, "What are you two? The Bobbsey Twins?"

"Yeah, we are Humpty and Dumpty!" Mitch teased.

"Well, don't go falling off any walls tonight!" Agnes shot back.

We put on our overcoats, took our leave, and headed out to the Open House. It was slow going but we made it to Bryan McWilliams' house fashionably late, around 8:20. A lot of our classmates were there already. Many did not recognize me at first. The conversation was on the surface polite and even cordial at times. However, in time the focus of many classmate's conversation centered on what they were getting for Christmas or where they were going for a Christmas vacation. I was immediately struck at the difference between the kids in Haskell and the kids at St. Cyngen.

The kids in Haskell had less material affluence but seemed to possess more richness in character; very few had things given to them and they had to work hard to afford things. Hence, they were more frugal with their money and took good care of their hard-earned purchases. They had a totally different attitude towards money, people, and things. No one gave them anything and they didn't expect life to owe them a living. The kids in St. Cyngen were pretty wealthy but most were poverty stricken when it came to character. They had no appreciation for what things cost or taking proper care of anything they bought. Mom and dad always had money to buy them something new. The St. Cyngen kids at times expressed an attitude in their conversation that such gifts and trips were owed to them in this life. I was pondering this contrast when Ann Burns arrived. She was with Stockton Daniels, of all people! Sheesh! She looked like a million dollars but in my mind Miriam in a Tastee Freeze uniform had more radiance than Ann decked out like Grace Kelly.

She said hello to Mitch and when I said hello, she had the look of a deer in a headlamp.

"Phillip?"

I extended my hand and said, "Merry Christmas, Ann." I then offered to shake Stockton Daniels' hand. He would not take my hand so I merely said, "Merry Christmas."

Stockton retorted, sarcastically, with "Since when did skinny squids grow into men?"

I laughed and looked him straight in the eye and answered, "When you work hard, exercise, eat healthy and live right! Stockton, it has a positive effect on a man."

Stockton winced at my reply. He knew full well what I was driving at.

Ann, sensing the tension between Stockton and me, defused our repartee by asking, "When did you get back into town?"

"Two nights ago," I answered.

"Do you intend to return next semester to St. Cyngen?" she asked.

"That has been my initial plan," I answered.

"Well, I am sure your fellow squids could use all the help they can get!" At that remark Stockton said to Ann, "There's Jerry Holder and Beth Caldwell. Let's go say hello to them. Catch you later, Phillip. Ann and I have friends to talk to." He added as much condescension as his arrogance would allow.

Ann looked at Stockton with a disgusted look I well knew. Ann was not a mean spirited person and did not like people who intentionally slighted others. She would go over there as he suggested so as not to make a scene, but he was going to get a snootful later. Ann was a gracious young lady who had been raised on courtesy and tact. However, she did not suffer fools or jock dunderheads lightly, no matter how popular or good-looking they were! Her parents had schooled her well in that regard. I often thought she could be a governor's wife or the wife of a CEO of a major corporation; she appeared easy going but it belied a backbone of iron and a sharp tongue. These she carefully employed only out of necessity when the occasion arose. It would seem that Stockton had provoked her to employ these at some point this evening. I chuckled to myself about this. He obviously thought she was a pushover and an easy mark. I knew from experience she was going to pin his ears back. What I didn't know is how the volatile temper of Stockton Daniels would react to being verbally chastised.

Mitch accompanied me in making the rounds of the party. We talked, joked and laughed. Mitch always had a knack of spreading Irish Christmas cheer with Italian enthusiasm and it made for an enjoyable evening. What was not so enjoyable was the confrontation between Ann and Stockton at the end of the party. Stockton's usual ploy of seduction was to go to an after party hosted by some alumni old enough to buy booze, get the girl drunk, and then have your way with her. That was the usual method except Ann would have none of that. She was wise to that trick and had had enough of his bad boy manners, slights and bullying. Moreover, she had the nerve to tell him so at the front door as he was leaving and that she would find a ride home with someone else. He grabbed her wrist to try to take her to his car but she broke loose of his grip and slapped him.

"You don't know who you are messing with, Mister!" she angrily said as she turned to walk back inside; and she was right. Stockton didn't fully appreciate who her family was and how they could forever influence a young man's destiny. Stockton insisted they talk this out in the driveway. Ann said she would walk him to his car but was not going with him.

At that point, Emily Palmer came running into the room where Mitch and I were and informed us of what Stockton was trying to do. She had seen Stockton grab Ann in a rough way right before; Mitch and I ran immediately to the front door. I heard Ann scream "NO" and ran towards where I heard her and Stockton arguing. Mitch and I came upon him arguing with her to go with him.

"Stockton, so help me, God, if you grab my wrist again, I will see to it that you are expelled from St. Cyngen and run out of Chicago!" A threat her family could follow through on in part. Her great-grandfather was a charter member of St. Cyngen and her family had been perhaps the largest donor to the school throughout its history. I was not certain about the second part of her threat.

"Stockton, leave her alone, man!" Mitch said, inserting himself in their argument.

"Mind your own business, squid," Stockton said. "Come on, Ann! There is another Christmas Party we need to go to!"

"She is my business," I said, stepping forward. "Be a man, not a bully, Stockton, and leave her alone. She doesn't want to go with you anywhere tonight and Mitch and I will see her home." One thing I had learned in life is that bullies will try to have their way with their intended victim unless they are confronted. The same was true of Stockton. By now, a crowd from the party had gathered and witnessed Stockton trying to force Ann against her will to go with him. He saw this and let her go.

"I will settle up with you later, squid," Stockton said, angrily pointing his index finger at me. He got in his car and pulled out of the driveway heading down the street.

Ann recovered herself and asked if Mitch and I would take her home.

"No problem," I said. "Mitch take Ann inside and get our coats. Tell Bryan thanks for inviting us! I will get my car and warm it up; it is down the street about a block. When it is warm enough, I will pull back in the driveway and come inside to get you both."

Mitch walked Ann inside while I went to get my car that was parked down the block. Ann thanked Mitch for coming to her rescue. Unbeknownst to me, Stockton had not really left. He parked a block away and waited for me to come out. He knew my car and had parked not far away. When he saw me walk toward my car, he got out of his. He crouched down as he was lurking behind some bushes to ambush me. As I bent over to unlock my car, I heard a voice right behind me and then felt a hand on my shoulder.

"We have a score to settle, squid!" I whipped around to see Stockton pulling back to throw a punch at me. Employing some Marine survival techniques Uncle Raymond had taught me last summer, I dropped and rolled just as he threw a punch. Stockton missed me but connected full force with my MGB driver's window. The collision of his fist with my window resulted in a broken window. But it also severely cut up Stockton's wrist when he pulled his arm back, he screamed and cursed in pain. I was furious at this attack and wanted to deck him until I saw the red stains on the snow and then realized that Stockton was bleeding badly. He was on the ground, rolling around, holding his wrist. My anger turned to resolve to help him even if he was a jerk. I would deal with him later about his sneak attack, man to man in a fair fight, if necessary.

"Let me get you a towel out of my trunk and bandage that hand, Stockton. That looks serious." I popped my trunk and got a towel out of my gym bag; I helped Stockton to his feet and wrapped Stockton's hand and wrist in it. "Man, we need to get you to a hospital." Stockton was panting and breathing hard, looking warily at me like a wounded animal in pain. He wasn't sure he wanted my help, but I could tell he was also getting dangerously lightheaded.

"Stockton, it looks like you are hurt badly." I saw that the towel was turning red. I continued, "Buddy, now is not the time to be macho. Let's get you to a hospital. We can go to my Dad's hospital, it is only 30 minutes away. You okay with that?"

He finally nodded his assent. I then said, "Hop in, Stockton, I am going to pull in the driveway and tell Mitch what's up. You cool with that?"

"Yeah, I guess," he said. He was resigned to my helping him. I opened his door, cleared the glass shards off the passenger seat and helped him into the car. I opened my door and cleared off the glass shards from the driver's seat, got in, and drove into Bryan McWilliams's driveway. I left the car running as I ran inside the house and asked Bryan for a spare towel and told Mitch what had happened.

"I am going with you. I don't trust that bird alone with you, especially if there is some broken glass in the car; no telling what he might try to do. Bryan can you see to it that Ann gets home?" Mitch asked.

"Will do, Mitch," Bryan McWilliams added.

"Tell your folks thanks for having us," I added.

I ran out to my car with Mitch beside me and he climbed into the narrow space behind the seats.

"You okay, Stockton?" I asked. "We have an extra towel for you."

"Thanks," Stockton said. I noticed the towel looked really red. This did not bode well for Stockton. We wrapped the other towel around the soaked one and drove straight to the hospital. I turned the heat on as the wind blowing through the broken window made my car feel like a frigerator. Stockton was getting woozy and I was afraid he might pass out. We kept talking to him and made him answer us. We pulled into the E.R. and Mitch hopped out; he got a wheelchair from an orderly and we both helped Stockton into it and pushed him inside. I asked for Dr. O'Melia, the ER doctor, and told them I was Dr. Robertson's son. This got Stockton treated immediately. He appeared to have lost a lot of blood and there was blood in his lap, staining his slacks. Stockton by now was really weak from the loss of blood.

It was a slow night at the E.R. so Stockton got immediate attention. His fist had smashed my window and lacerated his wrist severely when he retracted his hand. Stockton was checked in that night and emergency surgery was performed on his right wrist. He apparently also had some nerve damage to his hand. We called Stockton's mom and step dad and let them know where he was. It was now nearly 1:00 a.m.

Mitch asked, "Phillip, what are you going to do about your window?"

"Get it fixed," I said.

"That's not what I meant. What are you going to tell your dad and Stockton's parents?" Mitch asked, mildly exasperated.

"My Dad, the truth, his parents, I will say we were horsing around and he got hurt. That is somewhat true." I replied, yawning.

"Yeah, but you didn't start this, man. It was Stockton's drive to get laid and his wounded pride at our stopping him that got us into this," Mitch said. I noticed he had said "us", meaning he was going into this mess by my side, no matter what.

"Yeah, but if I have learned anything, it is to give a guy a second chance. His wrestling career this year is probably screwed, based on what I heard the ER doctors say. He was counting on some athletic scholarship to get through college. You know he was on a scholarship like you at St. Cyngen. His parents don't have a lot of money. This may have dashed that," I said. "He doesn't need me to pour salt in his wounds."

"You are as good as gold, Phillip. I am glad to call you friend!" Mitch said, slapping me on the shoulder. The truth was Mitch was better than gold to stand with me in this mess. It made me really grateful to have him as a friend.

We waited for Stockton's step dad and mom to get there. We told them he got injured by horsing around and then took our leave. They were not pleased with this news and obviously thought this was my fault. I knew that only family would be allowed to see Stockton so Mitch and I left the hospital for home. We got in after 2:00 a.m. We went in through the back door and went up the back stairway quietly. Dad's house was so large that you could sneak up the back stairway and no one else in the house even knew you were there! We got ready for bed. This meant we both were brushing our teeth at the sink. We were rinsing out mouths, when Mitch said, "Dang, Phillip, looks like you've got a rug growing on your chest."

"Yeah, more to shave for State. But you have a black patch growing on your pecs!"

"Yeah, I have a small patch growing there," he said, fingering his black down on his chest.

"Uncle Raymond says part of being a man is being in the 4-H Club."

"4-H Club? You're kidding, right?" Mitch asked quizzically.

"Nope. 4-H. Hairy legs, hairy ass, hairy chest, and hairy face! He said that hair was part of God's heritage to us as men and never been ashamed of it."

"I like your uncle and never even met the dude," Mitch said, chuckling.

"You and he would hit it off, Mitch. That's why I want you to come back next summer to work the ranch with me," I said as we climbed into our beds. I had two twin-size beds in my room.

"But I have something else to tell you, Mitch." I added.

"Oh, no. Not another secret! Don't tell me that girl is pregnant!" Mitch shuddered.

I laughed. "Mitch nothing like that has happened. Believe me, when I marry that girl, your hairy ass will be standing with me as a groomsman."

"I would be honored to do that, Phillip." Mitch promised.

"But I want you to do something for me." I said.

"Sure, what is it?" he replied, curiosity getting the best of him.

"I want you to apply to John Brown University in Siloam Springs, Arkansas, and go out for the swim team with me."

Mitch sat up in bed and said, "What did you say? Are you for real?"

"Like a heart attack, Mitch," I replied.

"ARKANSAS?" he said in amazement. "You have to be kidding."

"What if I can get you a four year scholarship? I know what your finances are. I have been offered a full ride and I am giving serious thought to taking it. Come with me, Mitch, and join me."

"You really are serious, aren't you, man?"

"I think our times in the 400 IM would land you a scholarship there. What have you got against a four-year scholarship? They have a great business college and liberal arts school. I have seen the campus and met the swim coach. I think you would like the coach and the guys. I have an extra application for admission."

"My grades haven't been the greatest. I only have a 2.8," Mitch added.

"What was your ACT?" I asked.

"26," Mitch added.

"Yeah, but a 2.8 at St Cyngen's would be a 3.8 elsewhere. Will you do it?" I pressed him on this.

"How can I say no to your enthusiasm at 2:30 in the morning, bud?" he said with sleepy sarcasm and then added, "Yeah, I will apply and if I get a scholarship, I will join you." He yawned and rolled over to go to sleep. "Nite, man."

"Awesome," I said. I hopped out of bed and pounced on him, putting him into a full nelson.

"Phillip," Mitch said in a muffled voice as I forced his face into the bed, "you do this to Miriam?"

I tickled him under the arms; I knew he was particularly vulnerable there.

"Cheap shot, dude! Cut it out!" He was getting ready to slug me so I released him and climbed back into my bed.

As he gathered himself back together from my pouncing, he said "You sure you're not part Italian? You pounce on her like that you will have seven kids in no time. Promise to name your second son after me."

"Deal, buddy." I eagerly replied. My response surprised Mitch.

"Whoa, Trigger! You might want the input of Miriam on that," he said, laughing. "Let's get some sleep, Phillip. It has been quite a day."

My head was spinning. The altercation with Stockton and the ride to the hospital was enough to keep most guys up but having the possibility of Mitch joining me at JBU put me over the top. I eventually fell to sleep after 3:00 a.m.

CHAPTER 5

<u>SWIM WORKOUT</u>

Dad came into my room at 7:30 a.m. and turned the lights on. "Phillip, you want to tell me what happened last night?"

Both Mitch and I sat up in bed.

"Oh, Mitchell! You're here; nice to see you, son." Mitch immediately intervened even if somewhat groggily, "Dr. Robertson, Phillip was attacked by Stockton Daniels who broke out Phillip's window on the driver's side. Phillip drove him to the hospital and made sure he was taken care of. He even called Stockton's parents and let them know. He waited till 1:00 a.m. for them to come to the hospital. After they arrived, we came home."

Dad looked at me and said, "Is that true, son?"

"Yes, Sir," I answered.

Looking at Mitch, he said, "Anyone else I would not have believed. But Mitch's word I would take to the bank." Mitch smiled groggily at that remark.

"Dad, one more thing. It is true he attacked me and I dodged his punch and he cut his wrist when he knocked out my window. I told his folks we were horsing around and he accidentally knocked my window out. I didn't want to get him in more trouble than he is already in. I am willing to pay for the window." I said to Dad.

Dad smiled and said, "Stockton has already somewhat confessed to Dr. O'Melia's staff about last night's events. I just wanted to hear your perspective. If you want to pay for the window that is your call, son."

"Well, I think a guy should have a second chance. I had one and I turned out okay. It is the least I can do for someone else."

Dad lingered at the door pondering my statement and then said, "Phillip, if you want to see your Mom today, I can make arrangements for you to see her this afternoon."

"Thanks, Dad," I said. "What time? It would probably have to be after swim workout. I couldn't get by there till after 6:00."

Dad looked at Mitch and said, "Mitch, will you go with Phillip and make sure he is okay after he sees Mrs. Robertson? Seeing your Mother injured can really take a toll on a young man. I don't want Phillip to do that alone."

"Yes, sir, Dr. Robertson," he answered.

"I will see you later tonight, son."

"Sure thing, Dad." Dad then turned off the light and closed the door. Mitch and I collapsed back to sleep and didn't get up till 9:30. We cleaned up and had a quick breakfast. Around 10:00 a.m. I got a phone call from Ann thanking me for helping her last night. I told her she was welcome and we concluded our conversation as I had errands to run. What I didn't know till years later is that she told her dad about Stockton's bad behavior and my intervention to rescue her. After that, Mr. Burns' opinion of me changed and he became a staunch advocate on my behalf when misinformed people wagged their tongues with half-truths. He was one man in Chicago no one wanted to cross and much of the accusations began to diminish with the "Bramin adults" of Chicago; but that did not stop some of their kids at St. Cyngen from continuing to tell the half-truths.

Mitch then helped me run my car in for repairs; he drove Mom's Cadillac and followed me to the repair shop. I then drove Mitch home and told him I would see him at 3:00 for workout.

"Don't forget your dad said I am going to the hospital with you," he reminded me.

"Okay," I answered. "See you at the pool."

When I arrived at the Natatorium, Coach DeLagarza called me into his office. I had to recount what happened last night and told him Mitch O'Nalley could affirm my story. He then told me about potential issues with Remington Bolt. He had heard some wild concoction of a story about last night that I had jumped Stockton in a fit of jealous rage over Ann Burns. That was the story circulating among students and parents of St. Cyngen. He had already had a couple of phone calls about that.

"Coach, Ann Burns, Mitch O'Nalley and Bryan McWilliams can refute that!"

"I will check it out, Phillip. Don't worry!" Coach said. "Suit up."

I hit the pool and swam hard. I noticed that some of the guys were standoffish after workout. Bryan McWilliams was not at workout to set the story straight as he had to be somewhere else. But Mitch was there. Mitch even confronted some of the guys and was told they wanted nothing to do with a guy who had just ruined Stockton Daniels' wrestling career. Mitch called bullshit on that. Apparently, Remington Bolt was wagging his tongue. It was rather interesting considering he did not come to the open house but was the "absolute authority" on what occurred last night.

"He sure has a knack for making a guy feel welcome," I sarcastically said to Mitch in the shower after workout.

"He does not want you on the team" Mitch said, as he soaped up. "You knock him out of the line-up. He's not too keen on that."

"Yeah. But I have a scholarship to college whether I swim at St. Cyngen or not. So I don't need it now but it still hurt to hear lies being said about you, Mitch. If you weren't here as my friend, I don't think I would stay here. Speaking of which, did you send that application off this afternoon to JBU and your stats to Coach Cutter?"

"Yes, I did. So no more riding my ass or pouncing on my body when I am sleeping or you get Mr. Hammer," Mitch playfully answered to lighten my mood as he rinsed off and teasingly threatened me with his clinched fist.

I laughed and directed my shower at him as I turned the water from hot to ice cold. The cold water hit him full force in the chest, stomach and crotch. "Cut that out," Mitch said, turning sideways to evade the cold shot of water and shielding his crotch with his hands. I turned off my shower and we both towel dried off.

I then said, "Well, now you have given me something to pray about with regard to your getting a scholarship. But, Mitch, I have to tell you, I have been here in Chicago for four days and I am really homesick for Oklahoma; at least those people wanted me there! I miss Uncle Raymond and Aunt Louise, and Joe, Kent, Miriam, the Abbot..." At that my eyes began to water but I don't think he noticed. I gathered myself and changed the subject, "You still want to go to the hospital with me tonight?"

"If I am applying to Baja Arkansas University to attend college, I am sure as hell going with you to the hospital tonight." He punched me in the shoulder. "When are we heading out?"

"Now," I said; and with that we got dressed and went by his house. We dropped off his car and then headed over to the hospital to see Mom. I didn't know what to expect, but I had a lot to tell her about the last six months.

CHAPTER 6

NURSE O'CONNOR

When Mitch and I dropped his car off at his house, he explained to his parents what we were doing and they said okay. I was somber the whole way to the hospital. Even Mitch was not his usual happy go lucky self. We arrived at the hospital and parked in family member/patient parking and went inside. The hospital was clean and well lit. It was a long walk to the elevator and was a scene of all sorts of human activities ranging from joy at the birth of new babies to grave expressions reflecting serious illness of loved ones.

We got off on the fifth floor and went to the nurses' station; Dad had told me to ask for a nurse named Gail O'Connor. Nurse O'Connor was paged and came to the nurses' station shortly thereafter. She was a short wiry woman in her 40's but her demeanor indicated she was a take-charge sort of person.

"May I help you?" she asked with a serious expression.

"Yes." I extended my hand. "I am Phillip Robertson, Dr. Frank Robertson's son." At that revelation her expression softened.

"Dr. Robertson mentioned you might be coming around today. Good to meet you, Phillip. Who is your friend?" she asked.

"This is Mitch O'Nalley, my best friend. He is like family to the Robertsons, Nurse O'Connor. He grew up with me and practically lived at our house." I said this because I knew that only family members would be allowed to go into the ICU ward.

"You know the rules for ICU. Only family!" Nurse O'Connor said, sternly.

"I understand the rules, Nurse O'Connor, but Mitch was like a fourth son to my Mom, and a brother to me." I turned to Mitch who stood there silently and put his arm around my shoulder. "Nurse O'Connor, I need him there for me." We both looked at her, straight in the eye. On this point I was dead serious. I did need him to be there for me emotionally. Mitch gave her his best puppy dog look. Nurse O'Connor stared hard at the two of us.

"Come with me," she said. We obeyed and followed her to a washing area.

"Both of you scrub your hands and arms down and put on these gowns over your clothes. We have to be careful of visitors bringing in an infection. Either of you have a chest cold or runny nose?"

"No, ma'am," we both answered.

"Good," she said.

We washed up and put on the gowns.

"Follow me," she said and walked at a brisk pace; we almost had to jog to stay up with her.

"Phillip, when did you last see your mother?"

"In late June," I said.

"You may be in for a shock. She has lost weight after a bout with pneumonia in October," Nurse O'Connor said.

"I didn't know anything about that," I said, stunned.

"Your father did not want to worry you," she replied. She then focused her attention on Mitch.

"You have got to be strong for Phillip. If I let you go in, you are there to buck him up, you understand?" It was more of an order than a question. Dad had told me that Nurse O'Connor had been an Army nurse and employed all the military discipline in running her unit.

"Yes, ma'am" is all Mitch could say.

She opened the doors to the ICU unit and we followed her. The smell of medicine and antiseptic was in the air. We were checked in at the nurses' station and then taken to Mom's room.

Nurse O'Connor said, "Phillip, if you have any questions, I am available to answer them for you. I will be right over there when you are through." She had a softer less military bearing when she said this and patted me on the shoulder. Mitch and I opened the door and went into Mom's room.

CHAPTER 7

MOM IN ICU

As Mitch and I went into the room, the first thing I noticed was all the medical equipment and there were tubes connected to both these machines and Mom. There was buzzing of some of these machines, faintly audible. I was shocked at what I saw. Mom had become pitifully thin. She reminded me of a victim from the World War II films of the Japanese POW camps. I gripped Mitch's shoulder as I walked forward and sat down in a chair next to her. By now my eyes were watering as I took her hand and gently massaged it. This wreck of a body was a mere shell compared to what my Mother once was. Even Mitch's face betrayed his shock at the sight. He put a hand on my shoulder and said, "Talk to her, buddy. Let her know you are here."

I turned to Mom and leaned over to kiss her forehead and then said, "Mom, it's me, Phillip. I am home from Oklahoma." I then opened up like a sieve and told her everything I had done these past five months. Mitch was shocked to hear I was one-sixteenth Cherokee, could ride a horse, cut cattle, and had come to love working the ranch with Joe and Uncle Raymond. I talked about Abbot Delaurier and our many walks and talks about the difficult paths in life. How his life's journey had intersected with mine and set me on a new course after he shared his dark night of the soul.

Mitch learned of my decision to embrace the Christian faith and sat there dumbfounded as I recounted Rev. Carmichael's sermon after my talk with Abbot Delaurier. He heard the full story of my friendship with Joe and Kent and began to enter into my world of the Concharty Mountain. He stifled a snicker about the skinny dipping episode and marveled at the Fugali family's survival in the face of the KKK in the 1920's; he heard me speak at length to Mom about how I had come to love Uncle Raymond and Aunt Louise as my second set of parents. How Joe gave me his letter jacket on my birthday; how Kent had accepted me into his fold of friendship; how so many people I did not even know had been praying for me and my family. I told her I initially had dreaded going to Oklahoma, but now clearly missed being there; and finally I shared about Miriam. This greatly interested Mitch and I shared all my feelings about this girl.

"Mom, she is as good as gold! She is so like you in some ways. You would truly like her, Mom. And, yes, I someday want to marry her after I finish college and start law school."

At this Mitch's eyes popped open and he let out a whistle. I looked up at Mitch, smiling through my tears, "And, Mom, that lug of an Irish potato called Mitch O'Nalley is here with me. He has heard everything I have shared. So there truly are no secrets I have now that this lug doesn't know. But, Mom, I think you would give me the okay to mash that potato if he spills the beans on anything I have shared here tonight." Mitch was staring at the ceiling innocuously acting as if he had not heard a thing! We had been in that room for nearly an hour.

"Mom, we have to go now. But we will be back real soon! I love you, Mom!" I bent over and kissed her. I stood up, tears running down my face and looked at Mitch. Tears were silently welling up in his eyes as he felt my pain. He reached out and hugged me. All I could do was silently sob on his shoulder till I could cry no more.

"I think it is time to leave, Phillip," Mitch said, patting my shoulder, and I nodded my agreement. We came out of Mom's room and saw Nurse O'Connor. She came over to us and said, "You guys okay?"

"It's been sort of rough, Nurse O'Connor," Mitch said.

I nodded my assent to this.

Nurse O'Connor could see my eyes were pretty red. "It's okay to cry and cry a lot, Phillip," she said touching my shoulder. She then turned to Mitch, "I let you in because Phillip said you were like a brother. Now you can prove yourself true by sticking to him closer than a brother. He is going to need you all semester. Capiche?" she said.

Mitch answered, "Yes, Ma'am!"

"I expect a lot out of you, Mr. O'Nalley, for Phillip's sake. I have known Dr. Robertson for over 12 years now and watched him work wonders in people's lives. If you don't follow through as a brother to Phillip, I will come looking for you to kick your ass." At that, Nurse O'Connor had me smiling. The thought of a 5'2" nurse kicking 6'3" Mitch in the ass was too much. I started laughing.

Mitch sort of laughed too, but he was understandably wary of this woman and her threats! Somehow that was the perfect icebreaker to lighten the mood.

"All kidding aside guys, here is my business card, Phillip, if you want to come up and see your Mom. Call me and we will arrange things." She gave us both a hug and walked us to the elevator. "Phillip, I am glad to meet you. I am so sorry it had to be under these circumstances; Mitch, likewise. I trust both you guys will have a Merry Christmas!" At that point an elevator door opened and we got in. I waved goodbye and wished her a Merry Christmas, also.

Mitch and I silently rode down the elevator and exited on the first floor. We walked out of the hospital back to my car. "Thanks for coming, Mitch."

Tales of the Concharty Hills

"Phillip, thanks for having me come. I am so sorry about your Mom. She didn't look good, dude!" He then added, "I am beginning to understand why you want me to come to Oklahoma! Dude, no wonder you love the place!" He then got a mischievous grin, "Does Miriam have any sisters?"

I rolled my eyes and said, "No." But I then, cutting my eyes at him, I mischievously added "But she did have some attractive cousins, all Catholic too!"

"Hallelujah!" Mitch retorted, laughing. I shook my head. If I took Mitch back with me to Oklahoma, I needed to write Miriam and make sure both her cousins and Aunt Madeline were at the Fugali house at the same time, The cousins to entice him and Aunt Madeline to verbally cage him. Between the baklava, mamoul, friendly banter and good coffee, Mitch was as good as married to one of Miriam's cousins. Somehow the thought of us both fathering children related to one another was pretty cool. Only he didn't know that his best friend had a streak of Yenta (matchmaker) in him as wide as the Arkansas River in Oklahoma.

If her family thought I was an amorous teenager, I was toothless compared to full fanged, smiling Mitch. My next letter would warn Miriam to make sure she had a necklace of garlic cloves and a derringer loaded with silver bullets when I brought Mitch O'Nalley to Oklahoma. He was not your run of the mill wolf!

CHAPTER 8

CONVERSATIONS WITH DR. ROBERTSON

We left the hospital and drove Mitch back to his house. "You sure you don't want me to hang around and maybe spend the night?" Mitch asked.

"I appreciate the offer, Mitch. But Dad and I have some talking to do about things. I think he and I need to discuss my summer plans and probable college choice; and I probably need to do that one on one with him. Plus, I want to talk to him about Mom and he probably won't discuss that subject with non-family members present. He is pretty private on serious family issues. But why don't we plan on tomorrow night if that is cool?"

"That's cool," Mitch said. "But call me if you need anything or someone to listen to you. I mean that! Cuz, so help me, God, I will wallop your ass if I find out you needed something or someone to talk to and didn't call me!"

I laughed and replied, "You're the greatest, Mitch. I will catch you later." With that he headed back into his house as I pulled out of his driveway to head home.

I knew there was a basketball game tonight that Dad wanted to watch so I figured we could both watch that together. I pulled back into our driveway around 8:30 and went inside. Sure enough, Dad was watching a basketball game so I sat down to watch it with him. It was a lively game and we watched it to the end.
I then spoke up and said, "Dad, can I talk to you about something?" He turned off the TV and turned around to talk to me.

"What's up, son."

"I think I have made a decision about college, Dad!"

"Really?" Dad replied. "Where are you going to go?"

"I have been offered a full scholarship at John Brown University in Siloam Springs, Arkansas, and I think I am going to accept it. I have already met Coach Cutter and toured the swimming facilities as well as the campus. It has a great pre-law program, also. But it is a NAIA college, not a NCAA school, is that okay?" I looked at Dad, anxiously.

"That question is one for you to answer, Phillip, not me. Do you want to go to a NAIA school rather than a NCAA college? As for a full scholarship, that is okay by me. Glad to know I have at least one child who won't cost me an arm and leg to get through school!"

"So you are cool with my choice of college?"

"Unlike Remington Bolt's father, I am not trying to recapture my lost youth through my son!" He then explained how parents sometimes tried to relive their lost youth through their children. He also discussed Coach DeLagarza's altercation on the phone with Mr. Bolt.

"Whoa!" I said. "Coach DeLagarza talked to you about that?"

"Yes he did," Dad replied. "Don't fret about bastards like the Bolts. They are sniveling opportunistic frauds and cheats. Jim Bolt may chisel and cheat his subcontractors and others, but he is playing with fire when it comes to messing with my family. His complaint about you was meritless and he burned a lot of bridges with his unfounded allegations. As for Stockton Daniels, I have already met with his parents. The story was fully laid out to them and they are grateful Stockton's macho performance with Ann didn't get him expelled. Her dad wanted that too, but I calmed him down!"

"You did?" I said.

"Yes, I did!" Dad replied.

"How?" I asked. Ann Burns' dad was the CEO of an international company and didn't traffic in Dad's sphere of influence. I had never seen then together nor had Dad ever talked about him.

"That, Mr. Phillip Robertson, is a privileged communication I ethically cannot divulge," Dad replied, authoritatively.

However, years later I was to learn that Mr. Darrel D. Burns was a patient of my father. I would only discover this at a 20-year high school reunion when Ann disclosed that to me by saying, "I would never know how much my father meant to her family."

"What?" I replied.

"You didn't know your Dad was my father's psychiatrist for 30 years?" Ann replied.

"No. Dad never told me stuff like that." I was to have many such conversations over the years with classmates of mine.

It didn't register with me when Dad refused to divulge his conversation that Mr. Burns might be his patient. Dad talked to a lot of important and influential people. So nothing would surprise me. I then said to Dad, "So you have checked out my story about Stockton Daniel's incident?"

"Yes, I did and from several sources." And Dad had done just that. He had talked to the ER staff, Stockton's parents, Headmaster Moore, Coach DeLagarza, Mitch and Ann. I learned about this when Mitch told me Dad had called him at home. Ann also apprised me of this over Christmas break, as did Coach DeLagarza. But that was like Dad, leave no stone unturned when he searched out for the truth. "You handled the situation wisely and you comported yourself like a gentleman. I would have been tempted to let Stockton bleed himself into oblivion for pulling a stunt like that. But it appears his wrestling career has been wrecked by his own action. That's going to be a tough life lesson that may hurt more than his cut wrist and banged up hand."

"You know, Dad, since I came back, it has been a really mixed reception for me. Some people like to have me here, but others want me out of their way. Remington Bolt doesn't want me on the swim team and Stockton Daniels does not want me at St. Cyngen. Dad, I have to tell you, there are times I wish I could finish school at Haskell rather than St. Cyngen."

"What?" my Dad exclaimed, almost in disbelief. "If you left now it would vindicate the naysayers like Jim Bolt that you could not fade the heat. Plus, it would make it seem as if you had to run away because you were at fault with Stockton Daniels. Finally, you would let down Coach DeLagarza, Headmaster Moore, and Mitch O'Nalley, who have all stuck their necks out for you. You're going to let the likes of Jim Bolt or Stockton Daniels run you off?" Dad was stern in his countenance on that. I was taken aback at the vehemence in Dad's countenance. It reminded me of my boyhood perceptions of him as the benign tyrant "Papa Doc."

I held Dad in my gaze firmly, replying, "No, Sir! I would never let them down. I will stay and finish up this semester." What Dad did not add was he had really gone to bat for me also. He had as much invested in this as any of them did. However, he did not tell me this till many years had passed.

"Good," he replied. "I always thought you were made of sterner stuff to weather difficult times. Phillip, I have had to deal with people like that, too, in Chicago all the time. So you are not alone, son!" He put his hand on my shoulder to emphasize the last point.

"But," looking up, "I have another thing to ask you."

Dad looked at me cautiously and said, "What."

"I want to go back to Haskell later this summer and work for Uncle Raymond," I said.

Dad arched an eyebrow and smiled. "You sure it is not to see that pretty young thing on your bedside table?" I was surprised at Dad's statement. It was obvious that he and Agnes had been talking.

"That pretty young thing is a girl named Miriam. And yes, she is part of the reason but not all of it," I answered. How could I even begin to explain the past six months to Dad? Abbot Delaurier, the Fugalis, Uncle Raymond and Aunt Louise, Miriam, my affirmation of faith and my new journey as the Abbot called it. I had found faith, but Dad wasn't religious at all and didn't even like Baptists.

"Agnes tells me you are pretty smitten with this girl. You haven't promised her anything serious, like marriage, have you?" Dad asked, narrowing his eyes. I knew that look. It was his cross-examination mode. However, I stood my grounds, man to man, with Dad.

"Promise her to marry her?" I exclaimed. " No, not yet, Dad, but she is one I could certainly marry!"

"Young men change a lot from 18 to 22, Phillip! And so do young women. I would not go seeking a serious girlfriend at this point in your life!"

"Dad, you would like her. She reminds me of Mom in some ways," I said. This softened my Dad's interrogation demeanor.

"Oh, really," Dad said. "Tell me more about this girl." That gave me the lead in to talk to Dad about Miriam. I talked at length about her family and how Uncle Raymond and Aunt Louise thought she was the nicest girl in town. She wanted to be a pediatric nurse someday and that drew Dad's interest. I also told him about how we tried to observe boundaries and keep the relationship unsullied with the physical aspect. Dad listened intently but did not give any indication of what he was thinking about all this.

"She sounds like a good girl, Phillip, but you are hundreds of miles apart!"

"Though far apart, near at heart when you are on your knees in prayer," I blurted out, quoting Aunt

Louise. I realized how naïve that sounded to Dad. Dad shook his head and said,

"Ever hear the phrase, 'out of sight, out of mind,' Phillip? You run that risk with Miriam being so far apart."

"Well, she invited me to the Haskell Senior Prom and I am going!" I said, almost defiantly. I then softened my demeanor and added, "And, Dad, I am thinking of inviting her to mine!" Dad arched his eyebrows at that revelation.

"And, uh, Dad, I invited her, Joe and Kent to come spend a couple of weeks with us this summer to see Chicago in June. I will get a job after swim season is out and work through June. Then I will go back to Uncle Raymond's and work his ranch in July and August. We report to school after Labor Day in September."

Dad eyed me pensively. I knew he was cautiously trying to figure out how to respond to this and then added, "I have no issue with you going to her Senior Prom or her coming to yours." He stopped and pondered something for a moment, "It might be nice to have a fresh female face around here for a while. Agnes says you have brought laughter back into the house. She might add a nice touch. What would she and your buddies do if they come for a month?"

"I was thinking I could talk to Coach DeLagarza about getting them jobs as lifeguards at the Country Club. He runs the pool and what he says goes. Kids would love Miriam, Joe and Kent and we could all four work together for the month of June!" I was getting really excited now. I explained to Dad the gift of the letter jacket on my birthday and their embrace of me as a friend. "Dad, all three of them did so much for me in Haskell; I want to show them my world of Chicago. Heck, Joe has never been north of Oklahoma, yet!"

Dad was gauging me very carefully. He then, slightly smiling, said, "They can come here in June,

Stephen P. Gray

Phillip. If they did even half of what you said they did for you, they would be welcome to come here anytime."

"You kind of sound like mom, Dad!" I exclaimed, half surprised at Dad's statement.

"Well, I sort of have to be both Mom and Dad now, don't I? I can't always be the cold-hearted dictator known as 'Papa Doc,' now, can I?" he said with a wry grin. "But Miriam would stay with Agnes, you understand." Dad was always understated in his dry wit and would catch you off guard at times.

I nodded my head. "Susannah Theresa (my sister) is right; at times you are downright amazing! Only I never really saw that till tonight. But, Dad, I have another question for you."

"Yes," he responded.

"What about Mom, Dad? What is her prognosis? Really. And why didn't you tell me she got so sick in October? I was shocked at her appearance!"

"That is why I didn't want you to go right away. Nurse O'Connor told me she broke the rules in ICU to let Mitch go with you. Some song and dance that he was like a fourth son to me!" Dad looked amused at this point. "Well, Mitch is as good a kid as they come, although a little wild when it comes to women. But he is a lovable rascal all in all! I would claim him as a son, no argument there!" Dad hesitated and then continued, "I am glad he was there with you. What you experienced was rough. Your Mother had a severe bout with pneumonia. She was gravely ill and I didn't want to worry you. There was nothing you could do anyway. Your Mother received great medical care and we beat the pneumonia. But it caused her to lose a lot of weight. As to her prognosis, only time will tell, Phillip."

I looked at Dad. The thought of maybe losing Mom hit me hard. In effect, it was wait and see for now. There were no good answers as to the prognosis of

Mom's condition. "So that's how it is, Dad. We wait and hope something happens."

"That is about all we can do, Phillip!" he replied seriously.

"Well, I can pray and ask others to pay for her, too!"

"It certainly can't hurt, Phillip!" was all Dad would say on that point. "Any other questions, Phillip?" He had an earnest look in his eyes as he asked that.

"No, Dad. Not tonight. I think I have exhausted my quota of questions for you tonight. Thanks, though, for letting me invite my friends up. May I write them about this?"

"Sure. But the boys stay in the house and Miriam stays with Agnes! Capiche?"

"Yes, sir," I replied.

"Let's turn in now, though." And with that, Dad and I turned off the lights in the den and went upstairs to our respective bedrooms. I penned a letter to Coach Cutter accepting his scholarship offer. I also put in a comment about Mitch O'Nalley applying to JBU and that he was an anchor for the 400 IM that won State last year. I also wrote Joe, Kent and Miriam a letter inviting them to visit for a couple of weeks in June and told them about accepting the JBU offer. I explained the living arrangements as set down by Dad. I then turned in after midnight. I would have Agnes post the letters tomorrow.

CHAPTER 9

MITCH LEARNS ABOUT THE CONCHARTY HILLS

Agnes got my letters posted and I went to the last swim workout before Christmas. When I got home, I had letters from Aunt Louise, Joe, Kent, and Miriam. I even put off dinner so I could read them. I hungrily devoured their news in the letters. All four letters spoke of love and friendship. It made me miss them all the more. I would write all four of them again after Christmas.

That evening, I called Miriam before Mitch came over to spend the night. She was not in but I got to talk to her Aunt Marguerite. She would have Miriam call me later when she got off work from Tastee Freeze. The last thing I wanted was to have Mitch hovering around during my precious phone conversation time with Miriam! I knew I would not get a word in edgewise with that Irish wolfhound present.

Sure enough, Miriam called back at 10:00. Mitch was there and got on the phone with her. Thirty minutes later I finally got to talk to her. But not before he had set before her my whole life history and dating misadventures. He got slugged for that. But he also interrogated Miriam about some of her good-looking cousins I had told him about. He was such a hound dog when he was on the scent of an attractive woman! Events were being set in motion, I thought, that could bring wedding bells sooner to Mitch than to me. The truth was that although Mitch was a lady's man and a flirt, he truly was a one-woman man. He just hadn't found her yet! He also got serious at the end and questioned her about her intentions towards me. I liked to have died. If he had not been bigger than me, I would have beat the hell out of him for that.

I cut that off and got the phone away from him, yanking hair off his chest as I did so. He whined and playfully slugged me on the arm. Miriam was laughing and told me she looked forward to meeting Mitch. I explained that he was not your garden-variety rattlesnake when it came to women. Miriam retorted, "And what are you?"

"More like a garter snake," I replied. She laughed and told me about Joe, Kent, the Abbot, and Aunt Louise. She was spending time with Aunt Louise and enjoying getting to know her better. I related all the events of the past week with the Bolts and Stockton Daniels.

"I am going to stick it out, Miriam, but I sure miss Haskell! But I have something to ask you."

"What's that?" she asked.

"Will you come to my Senior Prom in May?" I asked.

"I have to check with Mama and Papa," she replied. "But I will let you know!"

"Cool. And one more thing. I have accepted a four-year scholarship to JBU, so the three amigos will ride again!"

She laughed and said, "That's wonderful. Joe and Kent will be so excited. Do you want me to tell them?"

"Yes, if you would. I have written them about this but if you see them, tell them. Okay?"

"Sure thing."

"Well, I had better get going. Merry Christmas, Miriam! I miss you, kiddo," and I hesitated not wanting to say this in Mitch's presence but did anyway, "I love you girl!"

"Merry Christmas to you, too, Phillip. I miss you too, cowboy! I will call you about the Prom."

With that we hung up the phone and Mitch was grinning from ear to ear.

"What?" I said.

"I love you girl?" he snickered. I threatened to slug him for that comment.

"No wonder you dig this chick! I have never seen you so worked up about a girl before. Not even Ann Burns got to you like she does and you say her cousins are good-looking women? I am looking forward to our Concharty Ranch time in July and August now for sure!" Mitch put his hands behind his head on the bed, fully stretched out. He was relaxed and even crossed his legs.

"You know she gave me three names of cousins," he smiled.

I pounced on Mitch to catch him unaware and we wrestled around. Only this time he got the best of me and had me in a near fall and then in a full nelson. "Hey, if you marry this girl and I marry a cousin we would be related," he said, holding me down.

"Heaven help us," I said with my face eating carpet. He ground me into the carpet for saying that and then let me up. We were both panting, sweating, and laughing.

"Actually, that would be pretty cool," I said.

"Yeah, it would," he replied, slapping me on the shoulder. "Tell me more about Uncle Raymond, the Concharty Hills, and this mysterious Abbot you are always talking about."

So, for the next two hours, I shared with Mitch about Uncle Raymond, Aunt Louise, Abbot Delaurier, Joe, Kent, and the Concharty Hills. I shared about my decision about fully embracing the Christian faith, not merely with my head but my heart and actions.

It was a rich time of reflection over the past six months. Long about midnight Mitch said, "I would never have imagined you would have experienced what you did, Phillip. I am jealous and it makes me feel like I have not lived at all. So the hills have magic in them," he said pondering it all.

"The Abbot told me the magic of the Concharty Hills was answered prayer; I am starting to believe that."

"Hmmm. You're starting to sound like my Italian grandmother," Mitch said.

"Well, grandmother or not, it is time to hit the hay," and with that we both turned in.

CHAPTER 10

CHRISTMAS BLESSINGS

Christmas Eve had arrived and I had offered to take Agnes to Midnight Mass at her Polish Catholic Church, Holy Trinity Polish Church, on North Noble in Chicago. We arrived at her church and it was bitterly cold outside and it was not much warmer inside, either. The entire service was reverent and the candles gave a soft ambiance to the church. It was a beautiful neoclassical Baroque Church inside and out. However, the Mass was spoken entirely in Polish and I did not understand a word. My thoughts drifted back to Abbot Delaurier and the Concharty Hills Monastery. How I missed walking those trails with him. I realized years later what a wise older man he was and how his wisdom had blessed my life. At one point during the service the congregation bowed their heads for prayer. I bowed mine also and prayed for the Abbot and thanked God for his influence in my life. I also thanked God for Joe and Kent and the chance to be with them for four years in college. I prayed for Kent's ministry decision also. Finally, I prayed for Miriam that God would bless her this Christmas. I so longed to see her again and spend time with her. May seemed so far off to see her again. I shot a quick arrow prayer, as Kent called them, and prayed that we might get to be with one another sooner than that. The service ended and I met some of Agnes' friends.

We drove back home and she thanked me profusely for taking her to the Midnight Mass. "At my age, you don't feel so safe to go out this late at night in Chicago," she said.

"Agnes, anyone would be a fool to try to mess with you!" I said, teasing her.

"Mess with my tongue, yes! But my tongue and wit are no match for a gun with bullets! So old Agnes thanks you again for taking me!" We pulled up to home after 1:30 a.m., and I walked Agnes to her cottage before turning in.

On Christmas Day I received a long distance phone call, person to person. It was from Kent James. Miriam had called him that day and told him I was going to JBU. He was so excited he called me to wish me Merry Christmas.

"Buddy, Sinni and I are so pumped you are going to be with us at JBU; things just aren't the same without you around here. Heck, Sinni has even gotten quieter than usual! And you know how dull a monologue is with him when you are doing all the talking!"

I laughed and added, "Yeah, it can be a pretty lonely conversation, one on one with Sinni!"

"Phillip F. Austin, you have given Joe and me the best Christmas present! We can't wait to see you again," Kent gushed with enthusiasm.

"Kent, you don't know how much I miss you guys." My eyes began to water, "If I had my way, I would complete school at Haskell High School with you, but I have some 'unfinished business' as my Dad calls it. So I need to man up to the tasks ahead and stay the course up here." I was quoting Dad on that point.

"How are things up there for you?" Kent asked.

"Dad and I are reconnecting in a really neat way – more man to man like. But believe me, there are people up here who wish I had stayed in Oklahoma. It's no fun having to put up with some of their attitudes and lies they say about me. It really hurts, Kent! That's some of the 'unfinished business' I have to attend to. Sometimes it is downright painful to go to school. I have done nothing to some of these people but they want to put me down and keep me there!" I was expressing the pain I felt as a disappointment and failure for my almost expulsion from St. Cyngen last semester.

"Phillip, the best revenge for folks like that is to live well! Part of living well is keeping your faith in Jesus not people's opinions about you. If I know you, Phillip, you will blast those folks out of the water," Kent said reassuringly.

I laughed and said, "If you pray for me daily like you wrote in the Living Bible you gave me, then I will for sure!"

"You got it, buddy," Kent replied and added, "Just remember Philippians 4:13, 'I can do all things through Christ who strengthens me.'" Kent asked me if he could pray for me on the phone and I said okay. He then prayed for strength and comfort for me and that God would provide a special friend up there to stick closer to me like a brother this next semester. He finished with an amen and then we concluded our phone call. I felt so much better to hear his encouraging words and it meant a lot to me that Kent had called. He always had a way to make a guy feel like you were his best friend. For me, Kent was like an anchor to help me keep my eyes on the prize – faith in God not people or circumstances. He would call at least once a week to make sure I was weathering my time in Chicago successfully. In some ways I grew closer to Kent while I was up in Chicago through those phone calls than when we were together in Haskell. I always looked forward to his phone calls and believed if he ministered to me like that, he was going to be one heck of a minister! He was what Uncle Raymond called a true Barnabas, "Son of Encouragement!"

Looking back, I have no doubt Kent in his religious fervor did pray for me. My swimming was greatly improved over last years' time. The people who were against me failed to intimidate me or stop my readmission to St. Cyngen. I still experienced their slights and attitudes, but I learned to endure and ignore them. It was like Uncle Raymond had explained to me about football workout, the pain was still there, but my endurance to press through the pain strengthened. So it was with the more adverse influences and people back in Chicago.

The Christmas break had flown by, as well as the months of January and February. I wrote many letters to Joe, Kent, Miriam, Aunt Louise and Uncle Raymond, and even the Abbot detailing my struggles, hurts, and hopes for this semester; and they frequently wrote back, especially Kent. I kept them all apprised of my weekly activities. It was as Aunt Louise once wrote me, "Though far apart, near at heart when you are on your knees in prayer!" So it was with them! They all often encouraged me with scripture and common sense to carry on! It really empowered me at times!

There was an incident in February where their encouragement made all the difference to me to persevere. I was at St. Cyngen before class one morning getting my books out of my locker. I had been at school since 6:00 A.M., as we had morning workout. It was now nearly 8:00 a.m., 15 minutes before school started, some girls were on the other side of the locker and thus they could not see me. I recognized the voice of one of the girls. It was Pam Williams. She was a "society" girl who was as mean on the inside in contrast to her good looks on the outside.

"Well, I think it is unfair that Phillip Robertson went unpunished for destroying Stockton Daniel's wrestling career! He and his family are such losers! Mom doesn't understand why they even let him back in school. His mother was a notorious alcoholic and she was drunk the night she had her accident!" The girls continued their conversation as they walked away from their lockers. I stood there alone, embarrassed and ashamed. What they said about the incident with Stockton was blatantly false but the sting of truth about Mom hurt! I felt sucker punched in the gut. I allowed a cloud to hang over me all day. Even Mitch noticed this but didn't press the issue.

That evening after I got home from swim workout, I had a letter from Uncle Raymond and Aunt Louise. It was like an answered prayer to take the dark cloud of shame off my shoulders from the mean spirited comments of Pam Williams. Their letter spoke to me of their continued love and encouragement through tough times. Aunt Louise closed the letter with a verse from the Second Letter of Corinthians that was appropriate to my circumstance. II Cor. 4:8-9 reads "We are hard pressed on every side, but not crushed; perplexed, but not in despair; persecuted, but not abandoned; struck down, but not destroyed."

She wrote in closing, "Remember, Phillip, tough times don't last, but with our Lord's help, tough people will!" The letter was then signed by both her and Uncle Raymond, closing with "We love you, cowboy!"

Tears welled up in my eyes. I was so grateful for this letter. I then and there shed the mantle of false shame I had allowed to weigh me down this day. Dad had once told me never to empower persons who did not have my best interests at heart. His statement was beginning to make sense to me now! I resolved to finish strong that semester at St. Cyngen despite the Pam Williamses of the world!

CHAPTER 11

ALL DISTRICT SWIM MEET SURPRISE

It was now early March and we were in a three-day meet called All District. Mitch, Bryan McWilliams, Aaron Buerge, and I were getting ready for the 400 I.M. Race. We were hoping to better our time and set a new All District Record as well as win the race. Mitch was backstroke, Aaron was butterfly, Bryan was breaststroke, and I was the free style anchor.

As we were loosening up, Mitch came up to me and said, "Is that Agnes up in the stands with an old lady friend of hers?"

I shrugged my shoulders and replied, "She said she might come." I was totally focused on the upcoming race.

"Dude, she's waving at you and pointing at her friend."

I looked up, squinting my eyes, but couldn't see her. "Where?" I asked.

"Right there," Mitch pointed. I then saw Agnes and she was pointing at her friend. It was a silver haired lady that looked familiar. And then it hit me.

"OH, MY GOD!" I exclaimed out loud, not believing my eyes.

"What's wrong?" Mitch asked, alarmed.

"It's Aunt Louise!" I said, pointing at her and waving back at her. She then responded by gesturing down at the lower rows in the bleachers. I followed her arm and then was stunned by who I saw. It was Miriam! I was floored and my heart was in my throat! She was smiling and waved at me.

"Dude, what's wrong?" Mitch asked, concerned, noticing my obvious agitation. I grabbed Mitch's arm and then excitedly I put my arm around Mitch's shoulder and pointed where Miriam was.

"MIRIAM IS HERE!" I exclaimed, excitedly. Mitch almost had to restrain me from climbing over the railing to hug her.

"Dude, you have a race to swim," he said, turning me back towards the pool. Mitch did see her, smiled and waved. She returned a greeting.

"Phillip, she is easy on the eyes in person that is for sure! Just let your enthusiasm translate in swimming your butt off and setting a new State record!" Mitch said as he herded me like a sheepdog back to the starting block.

Our heat was called and we lined up for our race. I knew that it was going to be a tight contest; I made up the last leg of the relay and swam my heart out. I was up against another All American swimmer anchoring his team but I had something to prove and someone to perform for! I wanted to perform for Aunt Louise and Miriam like there was no tomorrow! I swam like I had never swam before and beat the other guys out by two arm lengths and we were not favored to win this race either! When I was through, Mitch, Bryan and Aaron jumped in the pool to slap me on the back and hug me. We had not only won, but set a new State record. Later, we would all be given All American rings for our times. Another treasure for Miriam to keep for me!

All I could do was lock eyes with Miriam the whole time. I raised my arms up and hooted with the guys when it was announced we sat a new record. I pointed at her and said, "That was for you!" I knew she couldn't hear me but hopefully she would get the drift of what I meant.

I climbed out of the pool, grabbed a towel and flew over the wall separating the bleachers from the pool deck before anyone could stop me. I knew Coach DeLagarza would bust my chops for this and I would have to swim 400 yards of butterfly, but this was worth it! Mitch said that Coach was pretty agitated at my stunt. Mitch did tell Coach that the girl I was head over heels with had flown in from Oklahoma unannounced to see me swim and pleaded with DeLagarza not to bust me.

"Okay, wise guy. If you will swim it with him, I will only make it 200 yards, butterfly for you both!"

"It's a deal, Coach, I will do it," Mitch said.

DeLagarza shook his head, smiling and said, "Just be sure you get that love bird back down on deck for the awards ceremony!"

I ran up to where Miriam was sitting and gave her a full body wet hug. I picked her up off the ground with my six foot, two inch frame holding all five feet, five inches of her. We were quite a sight; me in nothing but a speedo while she had on a jade green sweater and black suit pants. She was wearing a gold necklace with my ring around it on the outside of her sweater. I so wanted to kiss her but thought better of that here with all those people around us. That would have been too controversial and inappropriate behavior. I had already created quite a stir.

"What in the sam hill are you doing here?" I asked with a smile as big as Chicago as I put her back down.

"To see the legendary Phillip Robertson set a new State record," she coolly replied with an effusive smile, regaining her composure. I hugged her again, picking her up off the floor. "Do you know how much this means to me to have the most important girl in my life come to my world," I asked, whispering in her ear. God, I could just eat this girl up! It felt so good to hold her before she could answer; I felt a tap on my shoulder. It was Aunt Louise. I let go of Miriam and picked Aunt Louise up off the floor and hugged her, too.

"PHILLIP," she exclaimed, rather startled. "PUT ME DOWN!" I obeyed immediately and put her down. Aunt

Louise wiped the wet spots off her blouse where I had dripped on her.

"You came to Chicago! You really flew up here to see me swim!" I exclaimed. I had tears in my eyes; I had never dreamed Aunt Louise, not to mention Miriam, would come to Chicago to see me swim. The emotion of the moment choked me up.

"I told you I would," Aunt Louise replied, smiling coyly. "And congratulations on a new State record." I heard Mitch's wolf whistle to me and pivoting around saw him motioning me to get back down on deck now!

Turning back to Aunt Louise and Miriam, I said, "Listen, I have to get going. But after the awards ceremony I will clean up and meet you outside here." I hugged Aunt Louise, kissed Miriam on the cheek and then quickly climbed over the rail to get back on the pool deck. I wiped the tears from my eyes before I caught up with the guys. The awards ceremony was brief and the top three teams were allowed to stand on the platform. The four of us crowded on the First Place stand and waved at the audience. After the announcement, I knew the All District Meet was over and we could hit the showers. I literally ran into the showers to clean up so I could get back to Aunt Louise and Miriam; but I also did not want the team to see the redness in my eyes from crying. As I was soaping up, the guys from the team came straggling in. It was obvious they had seen my performance in the stands and who the object of my affection was, but they had not noticed how emotional I had become.

"Hey, Robertson, you always hit on old ladies?" Aaron Buerge asked me, teasingly.

"Too long a story, Aaron. You wouldn't understand," I replied, rinsing off the soap. Aaron was a great guy with an eye for pretty girls, but I did not want to hang with the guys right now. I had one thing on my mind – Miriam.

Mitch came in whistling the Wedding March tune by Felix Mendelson; he had a grin from ear to ear. He was shaking his head when he said, "She is more beautiful in person than her pics indicate, buddy! Woof! Woof!" Mitch then apprised the guys who Aunt Louise was and who Miriam was, and why I was hurrying to get the hell out of there! The guys threatened to denude me and throw me buck-naked in the pool.

"You try to do that and you won't have any teeth left to smile with," I replied, quoting Joe's half-serious threats not to cross certain boundaries.

"She got any sisters?" Bryan McWilliams asked, changing the tone of the teasing. The other guys laughed.

"None that are available," I said, exiting the shower for the locker room to get dressed. I toweled off and was getting dressed when Mitch came in.

"Hey, wait up for me, buddy. I want to meet this girl."

"I have to dry my hair and brush my teeth, but hurry your ass up, then. I get to see you every day, I only see her hardly ever. 'Never keep a woman waiting' is what Uncle Raymond schooled me on." I went to the sink bare-chested to brush my teeth. We always dried our hair with a blow dryer with our shirt off. It felt better and if you started sweating, you could towel it off before you put your shirt on. I had finished drying my hair when I saw Mitch again. He skipped the shower and was fully dressed. He had only towel dried his hair. He pulled out a wool cap and said, "I am wearing this when we go outside."

"Come on. Let's get our stuff and go," I said. We said goodbye to the other guys and went upstairs to find Agnes, Aunt Louise, and Miriam. Then I saw Miriam looking like a million dollars. I had my warm up bag in one hand and almost ran over to greet her; this time with a full kiss even if Agnes and Aunt Louise were there. God, it was heaven! And by the way she responded with her body, I could tell she had wanted to kiss me, too! We embraced each other like that for a while. Mitch told me later that Agnes was in a state of palpable shock at my display of affection with Miriam.

"Uhhhmmm," Mitch said, clearing his throat as he walked up to us. "Come up for air, sports fan, and introduce me." I let go of Miriam and said,

"Miriam, I want you to meet the guy who put the R in romance, Mitch O'Nalley."

Mitch arched an eyebrow and, with his puppy dog look, said, "He may give you the wrong impression of me."

"No, I think I have a fairly good picture of who you are and I have already warned my cousins about you," turning to me and gazing at me with those emerald eyes, she added, "Aunt Madeline will definitely have the garlic necklace and a gun loaded with silver bullets," she winked at me as she said this.

"Huh?" said Mitch, taken aback.

"Inside joke, Mitch." Turning to Aunt Louise as I hugged Miriam with my right arm, I said, "And Mitch, this is our hostess for July and August, Aunt Louise. She single-handedly fed me so well with her Southern cuisine I gained 25 pounds."

"Nice to meet you, Mrs. Hammond. I have heard wonderful things about you and your husband; and awesome things about your cooking!"

Aunt Louise blushed and said, "I look forward to cooking for you if you come this summer to work on the ranch."

Agnes added, "While you are here, you need to teach me some of your recipes; the good doctor would like that! And speaking of that, your father wants to take you all to dinner tonight at the North Shore Country Club.

"Me, too?" Mitch asked, begging, almost.

346

"Of course, you, too, Mitchell O'Nalley. The doctor even told me to include you if I saw you!" Agnes added.

"Great, but I need to swing by home and change, then. If my 'Godfather' Dr. Robertson is taking me to dinner at the club, I need to dress up! I will meet you at your house and we can go from there!" Mitch said. He took his leave and headed home to change. Aunt Louise rode home with Agnes and I took Miriam in my MGB, "the frigerator" as I called it. We rode home together and I talked incessantly, pointing out buildings, parks, and monuments along the way.

"Miriam, I can't believe you are here. I feel like I am in a dream. How long will you stay?" I asked, excitedly. It was Saturday and they had flown up that morning, arriving in the early afternoon, but would fly back on Monday morning. "We are only here for a short while, Phillip." She said and then added, "So I really only have 24 hours to spend with you." We talked about what she might want to see on Sunday.

"Surprise me," she said. "This is your city, Phillip."

"I will," I said. "But welcome to my world, Miriam. You have seen me now in football at Haskell, but now you have seen me in my real sport, swimming."

"Well, I like you in every athletic endeavor I have seen you in," she replied. If she was trying to curry favor with me by saying that, she had my heart in my throat. As we drove down the interstate, I would occasionally gaze at her. As we were in bucket seats, we couldn't snuggle together, but that didn't stop me from holding her hand most of the way! We arrived at home and drove up the driveway. Agnes had picked Aunt Louise and Miriam up at the airport so they had not been to the house yet. Miriam was stunned.

"It is just as you described it. I feel like the second Mrs. Max DeWinters when she first arrived at Mandalay for the first time in *Rebecca*!"

"Oh really?" I said, roguishly. "Married already and I haven't officially proposed." We both laughed at that. Well Agnes is no Mrs. Danvers and there will be no fires at this Mandalay," I added. I could tell Miriam was stunned at what she saw. Even today it is hard for me to believe I lived in such a house!

We parked the car and I took Miriam inside. No one was home so I availed myself of a full body hug and another passionate kiss. Damn! Kissing Miriam was downright addictive. She came up for air and said that was enough for now. I heard Agnes drive up about that time. When Agnes arrived with Aunt Louise, I brought their luggage in and took it upstairs to Susannah Theresa's room. Aunt Louise and Miriam went directly to their room. Dad called and let me know he was running late. After I got off the phone, Agnes pulled me aside and asked me what Aunt Louise and Miriam might want for breakfast. We discussed a couple of menu ideas and she sent me to the grocery store to pick up some items. This I did and returned home lickity split. I brought in the groceries and bounded upstairs to change.

Miriam told Aunt Louise she felt like she was in a palace with the high ceilings, marble floors and all the rich furnishings.

"It is palace like," Aunt Louise confided to her. "It is sometimes amazing to realize our Phillip grew up here." They freshened up and then got dressed for dinner. They came downstairs before I was done changing.

Mitch rang the doorbell and Agnes let him in. He was dressed in his best suit. She told him where I was and sent him upstairs; he came into my room as I was getting dressed. He helped me tie my tie and I joked that he was the most athletic valet in the history of the North Shore. He commented what an impression I had made with the other swimmers hugging Miriam like that in the stands at the Nautorium. "Tongues are wagging all over St. Cyngen now. A new State record, an All District Championship, and a mysterious beautiful girl from some God forsaken place called Oklahoma! You are busting all sorts of false assumptions about you, Phillip."

"I could care less what other false assumptions are about me!" I retorted, but then asked, "Mitch, do you really think she is pretty?"

"Pretty is an understatement, buddy; more like gorgeous!" he laughed. "You're truly Prince Charming to this little Okie Cinderella! Let's go down, Bud." He patted me on the shoulder as he finished checking my collar.

Dad was downstairs with Aunt Louise and Miriam. For once she was ready before me! Mitch and I came downstairs. I could tell that even Dad was impressed by how poised and beautiful Miriam was and that was a promising start to the evening. There were six of us so we rode in Mom's Cadillac. Dad drove us to the North Shore Country Club for dinner. There I learned that Dad had been part of a secret conspiracy and had known about the two of them coming for a month. Dad, as usual, had kept his counsel and not even told Agnes till the day they flew into Chicago. Agnes was not so good at keeping important events like this secret for very long. Hence, I knew nothing of this till I saw them on the pool deck late this afternoon.

The dinner at the Club was excellent, but the conversation and company was better still. It was a grand evening. We saw several St. Cyngen families having dinner at the club. Ann Burns and her family were there and she saw my obvious attention to Miriam. She nodded to Mitch and he waved back. I, however, was too absorbed in Miriam to notice anyone else! At one point Miriam and Aunt Louise excused themselves to go to the ladies' room. When they were gone, Agnes said to me in the presence of Dad, "I like this Miriam! Phillip, she is just what you described." and turning to Dad, said, "She is a good girl!"

Mitch looked at me and smiled. He winked at me and whispered in my ear, "Remember, sports fan, the second son is named for me!"

I replied, whispering back, "For you I will father twins with Miriam! One boy named Mitchell, the other named Joseph for your middle name and Joe Corsinni." Mitch smiled at me and slapped me on the back. Dad noticed this behavior and gave us both a curious look of "what are you two young rascals up to!" We regained our composure and talked to Dad about the swim meet. Miriam and Aunt Louise returned and rejoined the conversation.

We lingered at the table for a bit so Aunt Louise could savor the coffee they had at the Club. It was a special brand called Gevalia. "That's the best coffee I have ever tasted. That alone is worth the price of a country club membership," Louise said.

"I have to agree, Aunt Louise. It does go down smoothly compared to some of Uncle Raymond's coffee!" I added.

Aunt Louise laughed and remarked that all those years in the Marine Corps had taught Uncle Raymond to drink coffee grounds! "Part of being a Marine," she said. He was not particular about his coffee as long as it had caffeine! We all laughed. We then finished our coffee and left the table to the Porte Cache.

We ran into Ann Burns and her family. I immediately introduced Miriam and Aunt Louise to Mr. and Mrs. Burns and Ann. Pleasantries were exchanged. Miriam was very charming and cordial to the Burns family, but she also recognized who Ann was and was well aware from our talks last semester that this was the "other woman" at one point in my life. However, she showed no insecurity or discomfort with this reminder of things past in my life. Dad was watching the interplay between Ann and Miriam with great interest. No telling what he was thinking. Mitch interjected himself and helped avoid any unpleasant tension with his good-natured teasing and schmooze. Plus, I knew that his handsome looks were disarming to most girls and Ann was no exception. In many ways as I reflected back on this chapter in my life, Mitch was an answer to Kent's prayer for me last Christmas that God would bring a buddy to stick closer to me than a brother back in Chicago. Once again, my Irish/Italian wolfhound came to my rescue in what could have been an ugly social moment as we called it at St. Cyngen's.

The valet brought Mom's Cadillac and we took our leave of the Burns family. Dad drove us back to the house. It was around 9:00 by now and I asked Dad if I could take Mom's car so Mitch and I could show Miriam Chicago. Dad threw the keys to me and said,

"Be back by midnight. Mitch, I assume you are spending the night as you are like a 'fourth' son to me, or so I have been told." By this time Dad arched his eyebrows and was grinning, "And I expect you will chaperone these two!" At this, Dad looked straight at Mitch with a look that tolerated no dissent.

"Yes, Dr. Robertson!" Mitch answered like a soldier responding to a higher up's command.

"I will call your parents and let them know you are spending the night with us. If you need to go to Mass you can go with Agnes in the morning," Dad added, knowing that Mitch's folks were devout Roman Catholics.

"May I go also?" Miriam asked, "I would not want to miss Mass either!"

"Of course, dear! Old Agnes would welcome another young Catholic to go with me."

"Count me in! I may not be Catholic, but I will go also!" I added, looking at Miriam.

"Oi Ve! What will Father Tarchalski say with so many guests!"

"He'll say good job, Agnes Kotlarski," Mitch added, winking at her. "But moonlights burning! Let's get going you two. Cinderella's time is running out so if the Prince is going to show Cinderella his kingdom before midnight, let's go!" Mitch said.

Miriam, Mitch and I took our leave and headed out. We left Aunt Louise with Dad and Agnes. Aunt Louise then told Agnes, "If you will get me some paper and a pen, I can write out some of my recipes for you, Agnes."

"Good idea!" Agnes said. "Let me run to my cottage and get my recipe folder. I will be back in a bit." And with that Agnes left Aunt Louise and Dad alone.

"Thank you for dinner this evening, Frank. It was a lovely time and I think the kids really enjoyed it," Aunt Louise said.

"I am glad. It allows me to have some time alone to debrief with you about Miriam and Phillip."

"What do you want to know?" Aunt Louise asked.

"What do you really know about Miriam?" Dad asked.

"I know she is about the finest young lady in Haskell. She's worked hard all her life and she is going to be the Salutatorian in her class and she has a full President's Scholarship to attend the University of Tulsa. She intends to be a pediatric nurse."

That seemed to impress Dad, but then he asked Aunt Louise, "She appears to be a very capable young lady that is for sure. But what do you think of the two of them? You know he is smitten with this girl?"

"Yes, it is obvious, isn't it? He told me that right before he left. Frank, I told him to wait and give things time. Young people change a lot from 18 to 22."

"What do you think she wants?" Dad asked.

"She is very cautious, Frank. She recognizes that she and Phillip come from very different worlds. She wants to take things slow. She intends to get her nursing degree before she gets married. But she does care for him."

"Nothing will be slow going if I know my son!" Dad muttered out loud and then added, "You know, Louise, Phillip looks up to you as a second mother since Mary Katherine's accident. Your opinion carries a lot of weight."

"Raymond and I love him like he was a second son! Thank you so much for sending him to live with us in Haskell at the ranch," Aunt Louise said. "We got to know him very well. He is very single minded when he has a goal in mind and I have advised him to finish school before he makes a serious commitment like that."

Dad was thoughtful, "That is sound advice for Phillip. Well, she is stunningly beautiful. Those eyes would capture most guys. No wonder he is attracted to her. She has good social polish and Phillip says she is very quick witted. She handled herself very well this evening when we ran into Phillip's old flame and her family; and that was no easy task, I could see that."

"She can run circles around most young people her age," Aunt Louise added.

Dad then asked a question that was on the forefront of his mind, "but I wonder how well did they get to know each other?"

"Frank, they got to know each other by spending time with each other as friends and nothing more. She is very close to one of Phillip's best friends in Haskell, Joe Corsinni. He is an outstanding young man and he told her that Phillip was one of the most together young men he had ever known. He knew that Phillip had had a lot of upheaval in his life and yet was not defined by those experiences," Aunt Louise said. "So I think she got to know Phillip fairly well from spending time with him and from reports of his close friends."

"He did seem to carry on somehow in spite of everything he has been through this past year, that is for sure!" Dad observed.

"What do you think of Miriam and Phillip, Frank?" Aunt Louise asked.

"Well, they are young but there could be a potential there. Agnes says he is faithfully writing her and she is replying. He has been single-minded about school, swimming and her! So, if they take it slow, who knows! From what I have seen, they do seem to have compatible personalities, but she is so very far away – how will they develop a relationship?"

"You know Phillip wants to come back and work on the ranch this summer?" Aunt Louise asked.

"Yes. He told me. But is it just for Miriam, do you think?"

"No," Aunt Louise answered, shaking her head. "She is a large part of the reason, but he also wants to be with Kent, Joe and Raymond. He wants to go walking again with Abbot Delaurier; he loved that Frenchman's insight on life. Phillip has written me that he genuinely enjoyed the time with all those men and dearly missed them. You might say he fell in love with Haskell and Haskell fell in love with him," Aunt Louise added, her eyes watering.

Dad smiled and said, "I well know that you are a lot of that, Louise! Phillip loves you dearly, too, Louise. You have been a Godsend to him."

"Amen," Agnes Kotlarski said as she came down the stairs to the den. "Forgive me, Dr. Robertson and Mrs. Hammond, but I could not help overhearing some of your conversation and I for one want to thank you, Mrs. Hammond, for the impact you and your husband have had on Phillip. He is a changed young man. He makes his bed; does his own laundry; and I have to kick him out of the kitchen half the time or I have no job fixing supper!"

Dad laughed. "It is true he does like to help more around the house now."

"But it is more than that! He is respectful of authority and more appreciative of what he has been given," Agnes added.

"As for Miss Miriam, I like her. That little girl is the real deal! I can tell she has character as rich as her eyes are beautiful. I never thought anyone could be as classy as that Ann Burns, but this little girl has her beat in spades! Did you see how she handled herself when she met the Burns family? That could have been a really tense moment so I watched her like a hawk! But she talked to Ann Burns with courtesy and kindness, no female cattiness at all! That impressed old Agnes. I think she has such poise she could handle the devil in such a way to tell him to go to hell such that he would look forward to the trip."

Dad chuckled and said, tongue in cheek, "Well, as you can see, Louise, Agnes rarely has a strong opinion on anything or anyone!" He then got serious and added, "But Agnes, you think she is a good fit for Phillip? You know him as well as anyone."

"Emphatically YES," Agnes said. "She appears to be his equal intellectually and more importantly, they appear to be drawn to one another. I think there is chemistry there!"

"Well, Louise, Agnes is no easy sell. If you have Agnes Kotlarski's good housekeeping seal of approval, you are in like flint!" Dad said.

Aunt Louise responded, "But they still both need to take things slow and easy, Frank. I have cautioned them both on that. They both need to finish college, but they can get to know each other better to see if they are truly a match for each other. Will you allow Phillip to work for us in July and August then? It might give them more time to get to know each other better."

"You think I could stop him?" Dad asked earnestly.

Aunt Louise smiled and replied, "Probably not." Dad then asked, "You know Phillip has chosen JBU for college?" Aunt Louise nodded yes. Dad stated, "It would be good for him to reacclimate to the climate and culture in that part of the country. Would you mind if he could spend some of his college breaks with you and Raymond as you are so close to Siloam Springs, Arkansas? I know firsthand how lonely college breaks can be when you don't have the means to go home!"

"Not at all," Aunt Louise answered. "We'd love to host him and any of his friends over break! You know he may bring Mitch O'Nalley to work on our ranch this summer."

Dad laughed and said, "Then you had better be prepared for Phillip and Mitch O'Nalley to eat you out of house and home this summer then."

Aunt Louise laughed and said, "As we say in Haskell, Frank, that wouldn't be my first rodeo in feeding the boys."

"Well, speaking of feeding the boys," Agnes interrupted. "Excuse me for changing the subject, could you write out your recipes now? I especially want the Mediterranean Green Beans. Phillip won't tell me how he makes that. He says he needs an excuse to come into my kitchen to cook!" Agnes' eyes were smiling at that.

"With pleasure. They are Miss Marguerites' recipes, actually." And with that Dad excused himself and said goodnight. He had a phone call to make to the O"Nalleys and then was turning in. Aunt Louise and Agnes stayed up for nearly two hours talking and swapping recipes like two old friends.

CHAPTER 12

CINDERELLA IN CHICAGO

"Hey, buddy, I have something to share with the both of you," Mitch said. We had spent nearly two hours driving around downtown Chicago. We had stopped at a coffee bar/bookshop to get something warm to drink and all three of us were trying to warm up with some Godiva hot chocolate.

"What's up, Mitch." I asked as I was sipping my hot chocolate. I was so happy, I felt like I was in heaven having Miriam with me and showing off Chicago to her. She sat close to me and snuggled up, trying to stay warm. It was heaven!

"Will you be my roommate in college next year?" he asked coyly, as he leaned forward to take a swig of his hot chocolate. He arched his eyebrow, smiling at me.

"What!" I exclaimed. "You're going to JBU next year?" I asked, wide eyed.

"Yes, sir, Mr. Robertson. You are not rid of me yet! When I went home this afternoon to change I had a letter from Coach Cutter at JBU and he has offered me a full four-year ride! My parents were really excited about that for me, and now they are good to go with me working for your Uncle Raymond and Aunt Louise this summer."

"Wow! Congratulations buddy!" I leaned across the table, furiously shaking his hand and then slapped him on the shoulder. Turning to Miriam, I jokingly said, "Miriam, tell Aunt Madeline to make it a double row of garlic cloves on that necklace when he comes to Haskell."

Miriam saw my obvious joy at Mitch's announcement and, laughing, she added, "Don't forget the silver bullets!"

Stephen P. Gray

"Hey, what gives you two with the garlic necklace and silver bullets? Am I a dangerous criminal or something?" Mitch asked perplexed.

I was hugging Miriam tight and said, "No, just a testosterone over charged teenage male!" And then I kissed Miriam spontaneously.

"Whoa, sports fan, that is the kettle calling the pot black!" Mitch retorted.

"Indeed it is, Mr. Robertson," Miriam said, coming up for air. She was not expecting that kiss and looked at me with those piercing green eyes as if she were scorching my soul. I leaned forward and kissed her again. She took my face in her hand as we kissed and welcomed my advance.

"Awkward," Mitch said, looking at the ceiling. "Third wheel here."

I came up for air and said, "No, you're not. You are our chaperone, to ensure my good behavior as a gentleman. Remember Dad's instruction to you, 'brother'?" I said that to tease Mitch about being the fourth son of the Robertson clan.

"Funny," Mitch said, rolling his eyes.

As always, Miriam defused Mitch's disaffection by saying, "Mitch, I promise to set you up with my cousins but you have to comport yourself as a gentleman! But no hairy out of control werewolf, Mister! Or it is the woodshed with Aunt Madeline for you with the garlic cloves and silver bullets!"

"Trust me, Mitch, you don't want to cross that Fugali woman! She'll slap the Irish out of you and verbally lacerate the Italian in you for bad behavior," I added.

"Hey, pal, I am not the one playing tonsil hockey! Miss Miriam, I think your hairy werewolf is Phillip, not me! Have you noticed he is the one sprouting a rug on his chest? He's your wolfman, not me." Mitch slugged me playfully and winked at Miriam.

Miriam countered, "Papa says a good woman makes a boy into a man."

Mitch laughed at that remark and said, "Now I know why he's sprouting hair!   All Fugali women have that effect on young guys?"

"Yes," Miriam answered, also laughing.

"Great! I will be as hairy as my Italian grandfather and my Uncle Luigi Delsandro by September," Mitch teased back.

"Hey, guys, it is nearly 11:30 and we need to get heading home or Dr. Robertson will cut me out of his will as his fourth son."

How could you not love a friend like Mitch. He was a kid held hostage in a man's body with his playful zest for life, but he also had a strong sense of duty. He had really taken Dad's charge to him to heart this evening with Miriam and me.   Mitch admired and appreciated my Dad; hence, that admiration and respect brought out his sheepdog herding instincts when it came to me. Looking back now, I realize that Dad long ago recognized this character quality in Mitch and knew he could be a good friend who helped set boundaries for me.

"Okay, let's go," I said. "But first, I need to hit the bathroom. I have a full bladder and it is too long a drive home not to relieve myself. I'll be right back." I left the two of them at the table. Mitch leaned across the table and said,

"So what's the verdict Miriam? Does Chicago pass muster with the Haskell Cinderella?"

Miriam laughed and replied, "It's more like does Chicago's Prince Charming's royal family approve of me!"

"You handled a truly awkward moment with the Burns family amazingly well! So, I think Agnes Kotlarski likes you and that is huge with Dr. Robertson. As for Dr. Robertson, he can be a hard bird to read sometimes.   He likes to carefully consider things before making a decision. He does not make quick judgments; he carefully observes people and he was watching you closely. But he mostly keeps his opinion to himself or at least that is what I have experienced with him," Mitch said earnestly.

"Really," Miriam said. "Phillip is really a contrast to his father then. I am not sure what Dr. Robertson thinks of me, but Phillip is fairly outgoing and friendly and you know where you stand with him. He certainly has made that clear to me." At that remark, Mitch arched an eyebrow.

Miriam then asked, "So is Phillip more like his mother than his father?

Mitch answered "He has his mother's warm extrovert nature. His dad is much more reserved as you saw at dinner tonight. But, once you have his dad's friendship, you have a man who will be like a second father. Believe me, I know. I gave Dr. Robertson every reason to throw me away like garbage when I made a mess out of my life and Dr. Robertson intervened on my behalf. In some ways, he really is like a second dad to me and there isn't much I wouldn't do for the Robertson family!" Mitch held Miriam's gaze with that statement.

"Hmmm, there is a story that I would like to hear sometimes if I am going to set you up with my cousins!" Miriam gave him a look that was half-serious and then added, "You are really devoted to Phillip, aren't you?"

Mitch smiled and said, "Miriam, I love this guy like he was family."

She replied, "What a blessing you two will be in college together."

"Yeah, I am pretty excited about that! But, hey, I have a question for you!" Mitch said.

"Okay," she answered. "I may or may not answer."

Mitch cut straight to the chase by asking, "Do you love Phillip?" Mitch was not smiling now and had a serious look on his face as he leaned across the table waiting for her reply.

"Mitchell O'Nalley, I don't believe that is something I can answer! I am not sure what you mean by 'love.' If you mean do I love him enough to marry, that is way too premature. There is a lot for us to explore to see if we are truly meant for each other. But if you mean do I have feelings for Phillip and am fond of him, I think I have answered that question by coming here." She looked him straight in his baby blue eyes with a serious countenance.

Mitch backed away and said, "Geez, Miriam. How does Phillip handle himself with those mesmerizing eyes. I can hardly look at you without losing it! How does he do it?" Mitch paused, looking down, and then added by facing Miriam again, "But thanks for answering my question. Good answer. You see, as I said, I love that guy like he was a brother. So forgive my Irish/Italian protective nature. I get territorial about people I care for!" Mitch shrugged his shoulders and sat back in his chair as he said this, looking at his half-empty cup of hot chocolate.

Miriam smiled and broke the tension by leaning forward and touching his hand, saying, "Mitch, I would set you up with any cousin of mine. I admire and appreciate your devotion to Phillip. That speaks volumes of him and his family and of you. It also makes me feel better about coming up here to see Phillip with Mrs. Hammond and see his world he always talked about back in Haskell."

"How so?" Mitch asked.

"Gives me a fuller picture of who this wonderful guy called Phillip Robertson is," Miriam replied. She was quiet for a moment and then opened up to Mitch by saying, "When I first met Phillip. I thought he was a nice looking guy. But we have a saying in Oklahoma, 'handsome is as handsome does.' I did not know what his character was. Oh, he was bright and charming and at times witty!" Mitch snickered at that remark.

"Yeah, sometimes he is not that quick on his feet with verbal repartee!" Mitch added.

"But, Mitch, I got to watch and observe this big city guy slowly fit into the small town of Haskell. He and my best guy friend Joe Corsinni worked together all summer. Joe is an incredible guy who is like a brother to me. He came to admire and deeply respect Phillip as a friend. They worked together on the ranch and Joe was a major reason why Phillip went out for the football team."

"Yeah, that really threw me for a loop when I heard that he went out for football!" Mitch said.

"But Joe came to really love Phillip like he was a brother. We all did! Kent, Mom, Aunt Marguerite, Dad, Coach and Mrs. Hammond. He really captured out hearts! When he left to come back here, he left a big void in all of us. It was as if a friend had died. Kent and Joe mope around, missing their 'Third Amigo', as we called him. And I know that Coach and Mrs. Hammond truly took Phillip to heart as a gift from God for the loss of their son Gerald. Mrs. Hammond is one of the reasons I came to see Phillip. She invited me to come up to Chicago with her; she so wanted to see Phillip in his element – the swimming pool doing what he loved most – swimming. I wanted to see Phillip also and try to figure things out with him and me."

"And are you figuring things out?" Mitch asked.

Miriam smiled, sipping her hot chocolate, and replied, "Mitch, Phillip asked me for a serious commitment before he returned to Chicago. I wasn't sure if that was the emotion of the moment or something else. Phillip's actions in staying in touch with me by writing letters and weekly phone calls speaks volumes to me. Plus, I saw Ann Burns before you did. I knew who she was from the pictures Phillip had shared with me. He never took his eyes off of me or even acknowledged she was sitting three tables over from us. You did, though, but Phillip was totally focused on me. So I know he is for real in his intentions; but we both have a lot to do education wise before I take his surname!"

Mitch's mouth dropped open. That lug of an Irish potato with garlic cloves sat there, thunderstruck. "He asked you to marry him?"

"Not quite," Miriam said. "But his intentions and actions speak of a serious commitment. My grandfather Papa C would have called it 'courting' a girl."

"Miriam, I am telling you, you couldn't find a better guy than Phillip. But, dang – marriage? And at our age! Geez!!!" Mitch was speechless.

Miriam laughed, "He has not proposed; I haven't accepted and my parents haven't been consulted! And yes, we are way too young for that now. But I think the next four years would give us both time to grow up and get to know each other really well enough for marriage. I want to know more of his character. Mamma says marry a man with character not just for looks or money. She says the flower manhood fades and too many guys get bald and fat! And money is easily lost! But character will stand the test and trials of time!"

I then came up behind Miriam. I put my index finger to my lips so Mitch would not give me away. Mitch was unusually quiet as I put my hands over her eyes, saying, "Cold hands, warm heart."

"Phillip Robertson!" Miriam answered, flustered. I removed my hands and she scolded Mitch. "You saw him coming and didn't give him away."

Mitch regained his composure and replied, "Sorry, Miriam! I have only had the pleasure of your acquaintance for one-half day and I have known Phillip for nearly ten years. So when all things are considered,

Phillip wins! Besides, he put a finger to his mouth as he snuck up on you so I couldn't rat out my buddy."

"I am glad to know where your loyalties are, Mitch," I said. "Let's get going now." I put my hand out to Miriam to help her up. Dang, she was lovely. She moved as gracefully as a gazelle. I was totally entranced in watching her. I just stood there, holding her hand. She returned my gaze.

"Earth to Phillip. Come in, please! Over?" Mitch teased.

"Sorry, let's get going," I said.

We busted the midnight curfew by 15 minutes but I knew that was okay. Mitch went on up to my bedroom and I walked Miriam to the door of her bedroom where Aunt Louise was.

"Goodnight, Miriam," I said.

"See you tomorrow, Phillip," and I gave her a hug. I didn't think it wise or appropriate to kiss her with Aunt Louise on the other side of the door and Mitch possibly lurking nearby so I went back to my bedroom. Mitch was lying on top of the bed with his arms behind his head. He had gotten ready for bed and was smiling at me.

"Dude, I like that girl. She's great!"

"You think so?" I asked.

"I know so," he said. He sat up in bed and said, "If I had any questions about this girl and her character, they were answered this evening."

As I got undressed and pulled my shirt off, I said, "Oh really? How so?"

"I think she's attracted to who you are inside, not just your family's wealth and connections. She's no gold digger like Jacob Lawrence was. She wants a man with character and grit. Ann is a good gal, but Miriam outshines her. Like comparing silver to gold – both precious metals, but silver tarnishes; gold never does. Sort of like how I see Ann and Miriam." Mitch paused for a moment and then added, looking at me with that impish smile of his, "All those phone calls and letters meant something to her. I think you have proven to her that you may just have the character and grit she is looking for. Plus, she handled the situation with Ann Burns with poise and confidence. That was no small feat, Phillip! You made her feel absolutely secure in your intentions towards her, so even though Ann looked like Grace Kelly, Miriam was not threatened!" Mitch paused again and then looked wistfully at the ceiling, "And you say her cousins are as beautiful as her? Are they as good as Miriam?" he asked.

"Yes," I answered.

"Wow." Mitch just sat there dumbfounded at the thought of meeting one of Miriam's cousins. He had the funniest grin on his face like a love struck puppy.

"You dawg," I said, teasingly.

"AHROOOOO," he howled back at me.

"Keep it down, Mitch! Aunt Louise and Miriam's room is next door!" I admonished him on that.

I shook my head and finished undressing while we kept talking. "So you really like her?" I asked as I brushed my teeth.

"Yeah, I do. She really likes you, too, buddy. I quizzed her pretty hard on that. She wouldn't commit to marriage but she does care for you, Phillip. And any gal who likes you like that is good by me. Plus she's sharp, Phillip. No air pockets between her ears!"

I turned off the bathroom light and climbed into bed. "Mitch, I think I have fallen in love with this girl and I would marry her in a minute if we were both out of college. God, I forgot how awesome it was to be with her. I could just gaze into her eyes for hours and be happy! So, she's not yet ready for marriage? Hmmm."

Mitch sounded alarm at my reverie and said, "Give it time to play out though, dude! I don't think we ought to be eating wedding cake till you do get out of college. Don't put any gray hairs on my head by worrying about you over the next four years! I am not ready to be an uncle to any of your children yet!" he said, half-serious and half-teasing.

Laughing, I said "I will try, Mitch. But as you say all the time, a dude's got to do what a dude's got to do."

"Yeah, but this is no red headed waitress like Aubrey McCaslin wanting a Friday night fling. This gal is for keeps and you treat her right," he added.

"Mitch, I have found a pearl of great price. I will only treat her right!"

"You better or I will bust your chops if you don't." We both laughed and then turned the lights out and went to sleep.

CHAPTER 13

48 HOURS IN CHICAGO

The next morning Aunt Louise and Miriam had a talk before church. It was obvious to Aunt Louise that I was as moonstruck as ever, if not more so with Miriam. She was concerned that the excitement of the new surroundings and apparent wealth of Phillip's family would make Miriam act like she was carried away, too. She had a talk with Miriam in their room before breakfast.

"Falling in love with love is falling for make believe," Aunt Louise said.

"I don't think I am in love with love, Mrs. Hammond. And I do think as I get to know Phillip better, I could fall in love with him enough to marry him. I am drawn to him and, yes, I am being careful. But I am beginning to get a clearer picture of him. I don't believe his declarations to me when he left Haskell were emotions of the moment. He has proven to me with his letters and phone calls he is in this for the long haul. He really proved it last night when his old girlfriend showed up. Mrs. Hammond, he never noticed her or took his eyes off of me. I don't play games with people and I would never do anything to hurt him, Mrs. Hammond."

Aunt Louise listened carefully and patted Miriam on the arm, smiling, "I know you wouldn't hurt him. Take your time, Miriam. I agree with you, honey. He is playing for keeps, but you both are awfully young and you have so many thing to achieve before you say 'I do,' but we can talk more about this later. I want to fix everyone a real Haskell breakfast! Do you want to help me?"

"Sure," said Miriam. She got showered and ready for the day and came downstairs with Aunt Louise to the kitchen.

Aunt Louise had gotten up early so she could fix us a home-style Haskell breakfast. She fixed bacon, sausage, sausage gravy fried eggs, homemade biscuits, fresh coffee and juice and fried up some potatoes. The aroma woke us up and we went downstairs unshaven and unwashed. Dad even came down. About that time Agnes came into the kitchen, mouth gaping open at the sight of Aunt Louise and Miriam fixing breakfast.

"Now, I understand where Phillip gets his culinary skills," she said, smiling.

"Sit down and join us, Agnes," Dad said.

Eating like this, Mitch thought he had died and gone to heaven. Dad was bemused by Mitch's reaction and told Miriam that any of her cousins could pluck Mitch for the taking if they knew how to cook like this. Miriam smiled at this and Mitch nodded his head vigorously.

After breakfast, Mitch and I hightailed it back to our room to shower and shave.

"Dude, that was an incredible breakfast. If the way to a guy's heart is through his stomach, just point out which of Miriam's cousins is the best cook!" I laughed at this and almost cut myself shaving as Mitch stepped into the shower.

"Hurry your ass up, O'Nalley! I need to take a shower, too!"

Mitch started whistling and took his sweet time while I waited. Finally he came out, dripping wet, and grabbed a towel.

"Ahhh. Nothing like a good hot shower after a meal like that!" he said, drying himself off.

As I stepped into the shower, I teased him, saying, "Only cold showers for you cowboy when you get to Oklahoma and meet Miriam's cousins. We have to rein in that wild stallion in you. I don't want to be an uncle to your kids before I am out of college." If I was having a hard time with my physical drive with the girl I loved, I knew Mitch would spread his genetic material a little too easily if the right girl came along that he would fall in love with. He would have little self-control in this area of his life, given his track record.

"Neighhhh," Mitch retorted and stomped his foot like a horse. We both laughed at that.

I finished up and we got hurriedly dressed for Mass.

We went to the Polish Catholic Church with Agnes and then came home. Mitch took his leave of us to go home and left me with the afternoon and evening with Miriam and Aunt Louise. Dad had to make his hospital rounds so I kept them entertained. I took them to the Chicago Art Museum. Aunt Louise had wanted to see that and we then went driving along the North Shore. I drove them around St. Cyngen's and they saw where I went to school. Aunt Louise asked me to drive down Avery Drive where the prank occurred. This I did and shuddered at the memory.

"My, my, my, Phillip Robertson," was all she could say when I explained the extent of damage of my dastardly deed. "If Gerald Hammond had done that, he wouldn't have been able to sit for a week after Raymond Hammond got done with him!" Somehow I thought Aunt Louise was not kidding.

Aunt Louise then asked me if she could see Mom. I asked her, "Are you sure about that, Aunt Louise? It is pretty shocking to see her at first."

"Yes." She replied, firmly. "I would like to see my niece Mary Katherine."

"What about you, Miriam?" I asked.

'I would like to meet your mother, Phillip, even if she is frail."

"She is still in the coma, Miriam, but we aren't far from the hospital and it is still visiting hours." I then headed to the hospital. We parked and went to the ICU; I asked for Nurse O'Connor and she came to the Nurses' station to meet us.

"Phillip, how are you, pal?" Nurse O'Connor said. We had become good friends from my weekly visits to see Mom this past semester. "This an unscheduled stop?"

"Yes, Nurse O'Connor, we have come to see Mom."

"Who are these people with you?" she asked.

I replied, "Nurse O'Connor, this is my mom's aunt, Mrs. Louise Hammond." Aunt Louise looked a lot like Mom.

"I can see the family resemblance but who is this? Another fifth son to your father?" Nurse O'Connor asked, arching an eyebrow, teasing me.

I laughed and looked straight into her eyes as I hugged Miriam, "Better than that. Maybe a future daughter-in-law!"

That disclosure choked even tough old Nurse O'Connor. Her eyes popped wide open. All she could do was shake her head, "Phillip Robertson, you're killing me! I suppose the next non-family person you will bring here will be your son!" She sighed and said, "Come with me. Dr. Robertson may bust my chops for this!" We walked down the hall to the scrubbing station. All three of us scrubbed up and put on a gown. Nurse O'Connor then walked us into ICU and took us to Mom's room and ushered us in. "I will be right over there if you need me for anything." Nurse O'Connor then went to the ICU Nurses' Station and Aunt Louise, Miriam and I went into the room.

I walked up to Mom's bedside. I took Mom's hand and kissed it. I then leaned forward and kissed her forehead. "Mom, it's me, Phillip. I am here with Aunt Louise and my girlfriend Miriam Abboud. She's the girl I have told you so much about. I am going to step back and let them talk to you now."

I stepped back and let Aunt Louise in. I could tell Aunt Louise was visibly shaken at Mom's appearance. As I looked at Aunt Louise talking to Mom, I was struck by their close family resemblance. Aunt Louise could almost pass for Mom's sister. Miriam was holding my hand tight but she kept her composure. The condition of the room was unnerving at times to me and I could not imagine what it did for a stranger.

Aunt Louise motioned Miriam over and introduced Mom to Miriam. Miriam held Mom's hand and carried on a conversation with her as if she were in Miss Toni's dining room, drinking coffee and eating baklava. I marveled at her composure in this setting. After nearly an hour, our time with Mom drew to a close. I leaned over and kissed Mom goodbye as did Aunt Louise and Miriam. We left the room and Nurse O'Connor escorted us out of ICU. I could tell Aunt Louise was visibly shaken and had teared up after we left her room. Nurse O'Connor had wise words of comfort that seemed to help shore up Aunt Louise. Nevertheless, the drive home was rather somber compared to earlier in the day.

We went back home and had a Polish dinner prepared by Agnes. It was delicious and even Agnes' dour attitude had softened somewhat with these guests. Dad came home and joined us. I let him know we had gone by the hospital to see Mom. Dad, Aunt Louise, Miriam and I stayed up till 10:30 talking about Mom, my brothers and sisters, and his work in Chicago.

Miriam and Aunt Louise were flying out at 11:00 A.M. on Monday and Agnes would take them to the airport. I offered to do this, but Aunt Louise would hear nothing of me missing school. Nevertheless, Miriam and I stayed up another 30 minutes after Aunt Louise and Dad turned so we could have some time alone. We sat on the couch in the library, holding each other, watching the logs burn down in the fireplace. I had lit the fire in the library room. It was more like a small office with a fireplace, a couch and two chairs. It was not as huge as the clubroom and had a much more intimate feel about it. Miriam had her head on my shoulder.

"Thanks for coming, Miriam. It means the world to me," I said, holding her close against me.

"I am glad I got to glimpse your world of St. Cyngen's and Barrington Heights. It gives me a fuller picture of who you are. I wish I could have seen your mother in better times, Phillip, but I am glad to have met her. Your father seems like a good man. I am not sure what he thinks of me, but it is apparent he loves you and he is very protective of you, Phillip," Miriam said.

"Hmmm," I answered. "Never saw him as protective."

"Well, he is protective of you and your family based on the conversation I heard at dinner."

I then changed the focus of our conversation by asking Miriam, "And the verdict about my family is?"

"They are good people as Aunt Marguerite would say."

"What about me?" I asked.

"I think the jury is still out, Mr. Robertson. But things are looking promising. We just need to give things time."

My face betrayed me with a smile. "Let's just say I am looking forward to the summer, Miriam. I think we can get to know each other better."

"I agree, but boundaries, young man. We have kissed each other several times now. We need to be careful with that. My Aunt Madeline says kissing too much is merely an invitation to a lower invasion," Miriam said.

That statement triggered an amorous side of me and I said, roguely, "Most guys would welcome the chance for such an invasion," I was looking longingly into those green orbs. Miriam rolled her eyes at that statement. Uh-oh, I thought. Did I just blow it? I tried to recoup myself by adding, "Miriam, I could fall head over heels with you and run away with you now." I leaned into her to hold her tighter. I so wanted to kiss her.

Miriam pushed me back a bit, "And I am flattered, but let's save the physical for a wedding night! So I am honoring your earlier request to help you keep your hands off me. You are too amorous tonight for either of our good. You know that and I feel it, too!" At that she stood up from the couch to separate us from each other physically.

"This is our last night together in Chicago!" I protested, reaching out and grabbing her hand to pull her back next to me.

"We will have all summer in Haskell, Phillip, to spend time together," she replied, pulling her hand away.

"May is a long ways off before the Prom," I pouted.

"Then we will both wait till then," she said, walking over to the fireplace and looking at the dying embers, "If we are meant to have something so precious as marriage, the physical is well worth waiting for, Phillip. Let's not spoil it with false romance and emotion of the moment." She looked at me pleadingly to honor her request. I got up from the couch and walked up to her before the fireplace. She gazed into my eyes steadfastly. But, if I wasn't careful and pushed the boundaries, I would forever blow it with Miriam. That was not an option for me – losing Miriam. Dang it! She was right about spoiling things! She was a keeper and well worth having but I would have to wait!

"Well, if Jacob could wait 14 years for Rachel, I guess I can wait four years for you!" I sighed. I had remembered one of the sermons from last summer from Aunt Louise and Uncle Raymond's Baptist Church.

"What is that supposed to mean?" Miriam said, inquiringly.

"It means I am prepared to wait four years till we both get out of college to marry you! You are the most important person in my life and I don't want to lose you because I tried to do something stupid. So, yes, I will patiently wait for you!" I said this holding her hand in the glow of the dying embers of the fireplace as I gazed into her emerald eyes. They almost looked amber in the twilight of the glowing embers.

"Are you proposing to me, Phillip Robertson?" She narrowed her eyes and looked hard at me.

"Not officially! If I were officially doing it, I would be on one knee with a diamond to put on your hand, saying Miriam Antoinette Abboud will you have me, Phillip Robertson as your husband?" I stood next to her and gazed back into her eyes. "But I am prepared to wait no matter how long it takes. I feel like we are soul mates, Miriam. I am no card player. I have put my cards on the table so you know my intentions," and I kissed her hand and then lingered, gazing again into those gorgeous eyes. "May I walk you home, Cinderella?"

"You may, Prince Phillip!" she said, relieved at not having to ward off any more physical advances. And at that I walked her back to her room and hugged her goodnight. Dang, she smelled so good. I turned and went back to my room. As I was getting ready for bed it suddenly dawned on me that God had answered my prayer to see Miriam before May, and journaled that before I went to bed. I also wrote Kent a short note about arrow prayers and how they worked. Boy, would I have a lot to share with him in our next phone conversation. I turned out the light and hit the hay.

The next morning before school both Aunt Louise and Miriam came downstairs for breakfast to say goodbye. Dad had already left at 6:30 that morning and I had to head out by 7:30 and it was 7:10 now.

"Goodbye for now, Phillip," Aunt Louise said as she hugged me. "I am glad to have seen you compete in swimming."

"Thanks for coming, Aunt Louise. It was an incredible surprise. Please tell Uncle Raymond hello and that I really want to get some man to man time with him." Aunt Louise smiled and said, "I will. He would like that."

It was Miriam's turn now. I just looked at those eyes and then said, "Four years will fly by in no time at all! I will be patient and wait till then." This statement caused Agnes Kotlarski to turn around from cooking eggs on the skillet. Even Aunt Louise's eyes were wide open. I gave Miriam a full frontal body hug and saw their astounded looks. "Yes, you two, I do love this girl and someday plan on marrying her if she will have me. But we both have to finish high school and then college." Turning back to Miriam, gazing into her green eyes, I said, "And if she will have me, then you are looking at the future Mrs. Phillip Robertson!" Miriam held my gaze and didn't resist the frontal hug. I could tell she sort of welcomed the idea.

Agnes Kotlarski was stunned. "What did you just say?" she asked. She stood there as if she had been hit by a truck.

"Agnes, you're burning the eggs," Aunt Louise anxiously pointed out and then added, "Well, you certainly know how to take one's breath away, Phillip."

Miriam then broke the tension and added, "Well, he has not officially proposed; my parents haven't been consulted, and I haven't said yes." She then put her hand to my face. God, she had the sweetest hands and said gazing straight into my eyes, "But he is the most wonderful and amazing guy I have ever known. And, yes, I would wait four years for a man like you to marry!"

Agnes's eggs were burning again and smoking up the kitchen. I was as high as a kite at this revelation by

Miriam but the scorched eggs brought me back to earth.

I let go of Miriam and said, "Out of the way, Agnes! Here, sit down. I will fix some more eggs after I get rid of the burnt offerings to the Lord." At that I dumped the now somewhat blackened eggs down the garbage disposal; washed the skillet and started a new batch of eggs; and then put the heat on simmer.

Agnes was crying now. Aunt Louise, sitting next to her, was holding her hand. "I cannot believe what I am hearing," was all she could initially say. "Your mother, God bless her soul, would be in such joy at news like this. My heart aches that she is not here. I will tell her today at the hospital about this. Her little Phillip, such a grown man, and not a mischievous boy anymore!" I blushed at that. It was true that I had gotten into a lot of mischief. Miriam arched an eyebrow at that.

"I merely stated my intentions, Agnes. Nothing is set in stone," trying to reassure her.

"Not set in stone? Phillip Henry Robertson, I have known you since you were born! I know that when you make up your mind to do something it is done! Miss Miriam, he is bull-headed and stubborn as a mule. You better be ready for that! He will push you and badger you till you give in. How many cookies have you eaten before supper – huh? How often you come into the kitchen of Agnes and press me for dessert? And most of the time he got it!"

Agnes was right and had revealed the game I played with her before dinner when I was a boy. I often pushed Agnes to exasperation such that she would give me a cookie or dessert just to get me out of the kitchen. That stubbornness and determination had served me well at times.

"Yes, I have experienced that also, Miss Agnes!" Miriam replied. "And I thank you for that warning, but I think I can handle Phillip. My Aunt Marguerite says although the man is the God-given head of the house, the woman is the neck. And the head often goes only where the neck wants it to go." Miriam was looking at me with an arched eyebrow. "So, Mr. Phillip Robertson, do you think you can live with that?" She said that with full confidence as to what my response would be.

"I would sure like to give it a try, in about four years after college. But in the meantime, I have got to get going so I can finish high school." I hugged Aunt Louise goodbye and kissed Miriam on the forehead and whispered in her ear, Two months to May, then ma habibi." She nodded her head yes. Ma habbibi meant my love and Miriam had written to me about various Arabic phrases expressing affection, so others would not readily know what we meant.

"But you haven't had breakfast," Agnes said.

I got a banana and said, "This will do." I grabbed my books and headed out, feeling like I was on top of the world.

"Well, that was a whirlwind of a goodbye," Aunt Louise said, shaking her head.

"More like a Tsunami," Agnes chimed in. "But he was always like that. His father once called him the human Tsunami of activity! Oi, I need to finish those eggs now. You both hungry?" She turned to Miriam and said, "Such a pretty girl. He says you are more beautiful inside than on the outside. I believe he is right! You've captured his heart and somehow you are now capturing mine! I will be praying for you a lot these next four years. The Robertsons are a wonderful family but strong like garlic. That can be good and bad. But you will have the next four years to discover that. Now, who wants eggs?" At that Agnes served Aunt Louise and Miriam breakfast.

As they were packing their things, Aunt Louise simply stared at Miriam, smiling. Miriam looked up and said, "What is it, Mrs. Hammond."

"You know, you may call me Aunt Louise. If you are going to potentially be my Great Niece-in-law, you might as well call me by a family name."

Miriam came over and hugged Aunt Louise. "I would like that," she said.

"But Miriam, take it slow. That love struck boy is ready to run off to the nearest Justice of the Peace and marry you! And he has strong physical drives! Can you hold him off till then."

"All I can do is try, Aunt Louise. I don't want to sully the relationship. My mom says love is like a flower, never allow it to bloom before it's time. So, yes, I think I can." Miriam then added, "But I need your help in corralling those passions. He listens to you but takes his cues from Coach Hammond or Joe. I like his Dad, but he is reserved and not overly affectionate. But you can see he loves his son. He just doesn't really know how to affirm Phillip like Coach Hammond does."

"That is probably true, Miriam. Raymond said early on there was something good about Phillip he really liked. And Raymond does have a way in affirming young boys to be men and bringing out the best in them so they can assume their God-given responsibilities."

"Well, we had better get finished packing," Miriam said. "I sure have a lot to talk to my mother and father about. They aren't expecting what I have to tell them. They like Phillip, but I am not sure they want a new son-in-law just yet, but Aunt Marguerite had a hunch that things might get real serious with us!"

"Marguerite is an astute observer of people, honey," Aunt Louise said.

"That she is, Aunt Louise! But she also has pipelines of information and Joe Corsinni has told his Godmother a lot about Phillip and his intentions. She asks a lot of straightforward questions Joe rarely refuses to answer her. So I think Marguerite has a pretty good picture of who Phillip is and what he would do!" she added, chuckling.

Aunt Louise smiled, nodded her agreement and the packing was then done in no time. Agnes took them back to the airport and after a tearful farewell from Agnes, they boarded their plane and returned home to Oklahoma. That night Agnes debriefed Dad at length of my intentions with Miriam. Dad listened carefully but said nothing.

"And Dr. Robertson, I think she is a good girl for your Phillip. I believe your boy has found his match. She is his soul mate!"

"Hmmm," Dad said. "You don't think their being so far apart will cool things down?"

"Not for him," Agnes said. "There is no other girl who turns his head like she does. He never noticed Ann Burns three tables over. I watched the boy the whole time at dinner. He rarely took his eyes off Miss Miriam. Plus, I post two or three letters a week for him to her and he writes long letters cuz the envelope is often thick and she often writes back!" Agnes then added, "I think, Dr. Robertson, you have had the privilege of meeting a future daughter-in-law and mother of your grandchildren."

"Yes. That's just it! We don't need Phillip and Miriam having children before their time to finish school. I like her, Agnes, but I am cautious. Four years is nothing for two old birds like us, but it is an eternity to an impetuous 18 year old. She does not appear to be a gold-digger like that Jacob Lawrence was. But time will tell how things turn out for those two."

"What are you going to tell Phillip," she asked.

"What's to tell. He's in love. He has found a good girl who is not only pretty but sharp and intellectually his equal. She has goals and ambitions like he does. I couldn't ask for a potentially better girl for Phillip. He just needs to take it slow so they both reach their goals."

"Mrs. Hammond says that also," Agnes said, nodding her agreement.

"But whoever heard of a four-year engagement?" Dad mused.

"Ha!" Agnes said. "In the Book of Genesis, Jacob was betrothed to Rachel for 14 years."

Dad looked at Agnes and smiled. "Someday I need to probably read the Bible so I have a better appreciation for your illustrations, Agnes."

Later that evening Dad told me he liked Miriam, but wanted us both to wait till we got out of college before we would get serious. Thus, she had the Dr. Robertson's Good Housekeeping Seal of Approval. That was huge in my books.

"Then if you want to get married, then get married. But be patient until then," Dad said. "And don't spoil things by getting her pregnant," he added. "That is your job to reign in your wild horses, not hers." He gave me a serious look.

I nodded in agreement. Dad was right about this. We could end up married with a child before we were ready. Not a good idea! But, damn, that was going to be hard because I found being with Miriam downright intoxicating. It would be easy to get carried away if I didn't exercise self-control.

"Besides, I know you, Phillip. You may press her and one day she might give in. If that happens, I will be a grandfather in nine months. And there goes her plans to be a nurse and yours to be a lawyer. If that happens, I will not bail you out like I did with your Avery Drive prank. Capiche?" he said. He had a stern look I knew all too well. It was a look that if I crossed this line, I might as well change my name. Dad would tolerate pranks to some extent. He would not tolerate my acting like Shanty Irish, as he termed it. So I sort of had his approval and blessing. Yet I also had his stern admonition and warning not to cross certain boundaries and to WAIT for four years! He made me promise not to do anything rash and made me shake hands on it. It was a sobering conversation as such matters often were with Dad. But it meant a lot that Dad approved of Miriam and gave his tacit consent for me to pursue my relationship with her.

CHAPTER 14

GOODBYE TO MOM

The next two months went slow by my standards. We placed second in State in swimming in our league. Mitch and I made plans to be roommates at JBU and work for Uncle Raymond in July and August. Uncle Raymond was going to acquire more land and cattle so he needed an extra ranch hand. I had been going by the hospital to see Mom at least once a week. I made one last trip to the hospital before I left for Oklahoma. I wanted to say goodbye to Nurse O'Connor and tell Mom about going back to Oklahoma. When I arrived at the ICU Nurses' Station, I saw Nurse O'Connor. I had brought two small flower arrangements. One for Nurse O'Connor and one for the ICU Staff.

"Hi, Phillip, what's this?" Nurse O'Connor asked.

"This is a thank you for all you have done for me and my family; and a way of saying goodbye."

"Where are you going, pal?" Nurse O'Connor asked.

"I am returning to work on my great uncle and aunt's ranch and then going to John Brown University in Arkansas. I won't be coming around as much, but I will be back briefly in June, and then again at Christmas."

"Well, we are going to miss you, pal. I always enjoyed your smiling countenance. You sort of lit up the ICU whenever you came up here." The truth was I looked forward to seeing Nurse O'Connor and her staff. She had a tough exterior but that masked a compassionate heart for her patients and staff. Dad had told me that and I had come to experience it. Plus, I enjoyed kidding around with the ICU staff and they also seemed to enjoy the repartee. It had also helped steel me to see Mom. It was never easy to see the frail shell that Mom's body had withered away to. But as I talked to her and held her hand, it enabled me to relax and carry on a monologue conversation about our family and my past week's activities. Sometimes Agnes and I would go together. Agnes always brought some home cooked goodies for the ICU staff, which made her always welcome.

"Nurse O'Connor, I have to tell you that I am really going to miss you too. You really helped me a lot in dealing with Mom's coma."

"You have been a real trooper, Phillip! Not many young men could handle what you have done week by week these past five months. Speaks volumes about you and your family."

"I've grown up a lot these past months. I have been lucky to have had some pretty cool adults in my life. You've been one of those people. Dad said you were the best ICU Charge Nurse in this hospital and I have seen that!"

Nurse O'Connor replied, "Thanks, Phillip. Your father's good opinion is the best kudo you could have given me. He's a pretty wise old bird."

"Yeah, actually my Dad is a pretty cool guy. I have come to see him in a totally different way. I used to be scared of him. Now I see him sort of like you, tough exterior, heart of gold."

Nurse O'Connor's eyes watered at that statement. She put her hand on my shoulder. "I'll walk you into your Mom's room." We went into Mom's room together. Nurse O'Connor gave me a hug and said, "I'll leave you alone now with your Mother."

Mom looked so pitiful, attached to all those machines. In the past five months she had lost more weight. My heart ached for her. I pulled up a chair and took her hand and talked to her. I told her that I was graduating this week and intended to fly out to Tulsa afterwards. I shared with her how I came to realize how deep my southern roots were and had fallen in love with southern culture cuisine and a southern girl. I told her how I realized how much she was like Aunt Louise and this was perhaps why I came to love Aunt Louise and Uncle Raymond so deeply. They reminded me of Mom! I told her that I had come to really appreciate who Dad was and that I could see why Mom was attracted to this dashing young army officer.

I told her that I recognized that she and Dad had grown apart but I could tell Dad still loved her deeply. I knew that Dad came to see her almost every day he was at the hospital. Then I told her again about Miriam. To say she was my touchstone and anchor was an understatement. I read her some of the letters Miriam wrote me. Miss Dressbach had once said that a person's soul was revealed in what they penned on paper. What Miriam wrote me made me desire to pursue her all the more.

She was part of the reason I chose JBU. We would only be three hours apart, but I would see her every holiday this next semester.

"I love this girl, Mom. I want to court her the next four years and truly get to know her. When I graduate from JBU, I want to marry her, Mom. I want the sort of marriage that Aunt Louise and Uncle Raymond have." My eyes began to water. "I won't be coming around much, Mom, but I will pray for you a lot. I love you and miss you, Mom!" I leaned over and kissed Mom. "Goodbye for now." I got up to leave.

As I came out, my eyes were red. Nurse O'Connor looked straight into my eyes. "I am proud of you, Phillip. You have truly loved and honored your mother. We will take good care of her." She patted me on the shoulder.

"Thanks, Nurse O'Connor. You are the best." I gave her a hug goodbye and walked back to the elevator. As I drove home that evening, I had a foreboding that Mom might not linger much longer here on this side of eternity as Abbot Delaurier called it.

CHAPTER 15

RETURN TO OKLAHOMA

Miriam was not able to come to my Prom. Her parents could not afford it and thought one trip to Chicago to see me was enough in a year. I went ahead and attended my Senior Prom to sort of say goodbye to my St. Cyngen's friends, but, I went to the Prom stag.

I had a good time going alone. I got to circulate and talk to all my friends and dance with countless girls whose date did not object to one gig with me. I even got to dance a slow song with Ann. We talked the entire dance. I told her all about Miriam and how I had fallen in love with her.

"I should be jealous of this Haskell, Oklahoma girl, but Phillip, I am pleased for you! I still care deeply for you as a friend, but I see we are moving in different directions, so it is easy to let go of the past."

"Thanks, Ann," I said. "That means a lot because I know you don't say things you don't mean. That is one of the reasons I always admired you."

Ann smiled and said, "Thanks, Phillip." At one point she put her head on my shoulder but she did not stir the passions in me like Miriam did. Ann was going to Northwestern University to study Psychology so we were indeed moving in different paths in life.

"You know, I think I saw how deeply you cared for Miriam last March," Ann said, looking up at me.

"Really? How so?" I asked.

"You never took your eyes off her the entire dinner. You never looked at me once. I knew then that you had found someone who had captured your heart!"

I nodded my agreement. "Yeah, she has, Ann. She was the first person I met in Haskell. We were just friends at first; but as I got to know her better, I developed a crush on her. Now, I know I want to marry her in four years!" That revelation surprised Ann, but she maintained her composure.

"Does she feel the same about you?"

"Yes, she does, Ann."

"Then you both are fortunate to have found each other!" The song was ending and I thanked Ann for the dance and walked her back to her date. It was the final closure in my mind to any lingering doubts I may have had about my choices I had made for college and Miriam! I had a good time at my Prom but I was looking forward to dancing again with Miriam at her Prom.

I was still going to the Haskell Senior Prom with Miriam after my afternoon graduation commencement at St. Cyngen. The plans were for me to fly down to Haskell late that afternoon for her Prom. Joe and Kent would drive me back to Chicago a couple of weeks later and spend part of June with me in Chicago. Miriam was needed at her aunt's flower shop so it would just be us guys. Mitch would return with me to Haskell with Joe and Kent. He would work on Uncle Raymond's ranch and help clear the new land acquired from Hayes Freeman.

My graduation exercise was the same day as my evening flight to Tulsa. I would have my Tuxedo on anyway so I would go straight to Miriam's Prom. Graduation at St. Cyngen was an elaborate ritualistic affair. After the graduation ceremony, I said goodbye to lots of my classmates and their parents. Ann Burns came up to me and gave me a hug.

"I wish you well, Phillip, wherever you go. In some ways you're the same guy I knew, but in other ways you're different, but in a better way. I think your girlfriend in Haskell has a lot to do with this transformation in you. So I think you and Miriam are well suited for each other! I wish you both well." She kissed me on the cheek and said goodbye. I knew she meant what she said kindly. Her father then came up to me and shook my hand and congratulated me on finishing well at St. Cyngen. I thanked him for that compliment. From him, it meant he had forgiven me for the Avery Drive prank. Perhaps I was not so "damaged" any more in the minds of some of the Chicago "Bramens" after all. But that did not matter to me now. I was going back to Oklahoma. Mitch came up and had a smile as big as Chicago!

"We've done it, Robertson; we've graduated." Mitch gave me a hug.

I hugged him back and said, "I'll be back in a couple of weeks and then it is off to Oklahoma, cowboy! I am going to make you an Okie!" Mitch laughed and slapped me on the shoulder but his expression turned from mirth to a serious look and he nodded at me to turn around. I felt a tap on my shoulder. I turned around and saw Stockton Daniels. He extended his right hand to shake my hand. I saw the scars on his wrist from the altercation during Christmas break.

"I would be a piss poor excuse for a man if I didn't thank you for what you did for me that night over Christmas break. It has taken me five months to get the balls to do this. We may not like each other, Phillip, or ever be buddies, but that does not diminish what you did for me. So, thank you again!"

I took Stockton's outstretched hand and shook it. Staring straight into his hazel eyes I realized there was a genuine humility in him. I then did something totally unexpected and drew him into a hug. "You're welcome, Stockton! I would do it for you again. Someone gave me a second chance after a major screw up in my life and it made all the difference. There's a bigger purpose in what occurred at that altercation that night. I think you are one of the most incredibly talented guys in this school, Stockton. I think you have a great future ahead of you."

Stockton's eyes had watered by now and he hugged me back. We released each other and then I added, "I am bringing some buddies back from Oklahoma and I would like you to meet them and help me show them Chicago. I think you would really like these dudes. I will be back in a couple of weeks with them and we will be working at the North Shore Country Club pool in June for Coach DeLagarza. What are you going to do this summer and beyond."

Stockton answered, "I am going to work for my stepdad's landscaping company and then go to the local Community College."

"You want to hang out with us, Stockton, when we come back?"

"When you guys come back, call me. I would be up to spending time with you guys."

"Let's do it, Stockton. Let's make up some lost time for not getting to know each other in high school," I said that, looking straight into his eyes.

"I'd like that Phillip. I want to hear more about why you've changed so much. Good luck, bud." At that Stockton slapped me on the shoulder and went on to talk to other classmates. Mitch looked at me and shook his head.

"Dude, who would have thought that would have ever happened! Why did you invite him to hang out with us?"

"I don't know! I saw a hunger in his eyes and I felt like I needed to include him to be with us."

"Well, one thing for sure, Phillip, life is never going to be dull spending time with you. It is going to be one relational adventure after another," Mitch laughed. Little did I know just how prophetic that statement would become!

"Just wait till you meet some of Miriam's cousins! If you marry one of those girls, one of your son's has to be named for me." Mitch laughed and punched me in the shoulder. A couple of years later, however, I was at the christening ceremony where I was named as the godfather for Phillip Mitchell O'Nalley; Mitch's first born son whose mother was Miriam's cousin. It was to be the beginning of many such christenings and new relational adventures with a younger generation of many a friend's son or daughter!

I was barely able to get out of my graduation reception in time to catch my flight at 4:30 p.m. Dad and Agnes took me to the airport where I said my goodbyes. Agnes gave me a beautiful green jade Jerusalem cross with a gold filigree chain to give to Miriam. "This is my gift to Miss Miriam. Father Tarchelski brought this back for me from a trip to the Holy Land. Somehow, it seems more appropriate for her than me."

I knew this was Agnes' way of blessing my relationship with Miriam. I couldn't think of a sweeter gesture than what Agnes had done and I thanked her for this. I knew how much that cross-meant to Agnes and in time it became one of Miriam's most treasured possessions. I put the cross in my pocket to present to Miriam later. I kissed Agnes and gave her a hug goodbye. My eyes watered a bit as I said goodbye to Dad.

"Thanks for everything, Dad. Thanks for allowing me to return to Haskell." And I hugged him. "And please take care of Mom!"

"I will watch after your Mother! Now, get going, Phillip, or you will miss your plane." What I did not see but Agnes told me later was that Dad had teared up also. She also told me that Dad commented to Agnes that he was truly proud of the way I had weathered the storms in my life and the man I was becoming.

As I looked down as we were approaching Tulsa, I noticed the green of the countryside interspersed with the frequent silver of lakes, rivers and ponds. No, this was no dustbowl as depicted in John Steinbeck's *The Grapes of Wrath*, that was a gross distortion of what

Oklahoma truly was. It looked more like a southern extension of the Land of Lakes, Minnesota from several thousand feet up. I heard the landing gear go down as we made our descent. The sun had a glorious sunset from my window. Uncle Raymond said he had been around the world as a Marine, but never saw such glorious sunsets as in Oklahoma. I believed him. I also noticed that as the sun was setting, a full moon was coming up on the edge of the horizon. It was a stunning sight.

Our plane landed and we disembarked from the jet around 8:00. Only this time it was a beautiful spring night in the middle of May and the temperature was a pleasant 75 degrees with a light wind out of the north. I came into the terminal and immediately saw Aunt Louise and Uncle Raymond at the gate. I rushed up to them and gave Aunt Louise a bear hug. She kissed me on the cheek and said, "Welcome back, Phillip! It is so good to have you back again." My eyes watered somewhat.

"I have been looking forward to coming back all semester. I can't believe I am home in Oklahoma!" I exclaimed.

Uncle Raymond held out his hand to shake mine. I let go of Aunt Louise and said, "Handshake won't do, Coach Hammond! This cowboy wants a hug! I have missed you something fierce and our time together." At that the 60-something tough guy Marine/Coach and I hugged each other.

"Welcome home, son!" was all Uncle Raymond could say and he patted my shoulder as we both hugged each other and silently let tears flow from our eyes. But this time it was tears of joy and reunion. I was home again with this wonderful older couple who had become like a mother and father to me; and in years to come not only me, but to many friends of mine that I brought to their ranch in the Concharty Hills. Aunt Louise said years later my coming back answered prayers of countless friends down in Haskell who had prayed for my return.

The magic of the Concharty Hills had once again played out, only this time in my life. Some people never experience the love of home and family and I was so grateful to have found not one but two homes in the hearts of those who deeply cared for and truly loved me. Abbot Delaurier had once shared the "Prayer of the Confederate Soldier" with me and the words of the closing line of that prayer seemed to fit me. How, after much disappointment and loss of dreams, the soldier discovered a deeper and richer purpose in life by concluding, "I among all men am most richly blessed." So it was with me.

The End

ABOUT THE AUTHOR

Stephen P. Gray is a lifelong Oklahoman who was born and raised in Oklahoma. He has lived all over the state and now makes his home in Broken Arrow, Oklahoma. He attended Oklahoma State University from 1973-1977 where he was a member of the Varsity Swim Team. Upon graduation, he went on to the University of Tulsa College of Law in 1980. He has had a private law practice since 1990 in the Tulsa area. He is married to Shelley Gray and together they have four daughters.